W9-BUC-335

BONNIE

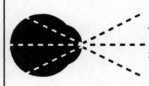

This Large Print Book carries the
Seal of Approval of N.A.V.H.

BONNIE

IRIS JOHANSEN

THORNDIKE PRESS
A part of Gale, Cengage Learning

GALE
CENGAGE Learning™

Detroit • New York • San Francisco • New Haven, Conn • Waterville, Maine • London

GALE
CENGAGE Learning™

Copyright © 2011 by Johansen Publishing, Inc.
An Eve Duncan Forensics Thriller.
Thorndike Press, a part of Gale, Cengage Learning.

Thorndike Press® Large Print Basic.
The text of this Large Print edition is unabridged.
Other aspects of the book may vary from the original edition.
Set in 16 pt. Plantin.

LIBRARY OF CONGRESS CATALOGING-IN-PUBLICATION DATA

Johansen, Iris.
  Bonnie / by Iris Johansen.
    p. cm. — (Thorndike Press large print basic)
    ISBN-13: 978-1-4104-4218-5 (hardcover)
    ISBN-10: 1-4104-4218-7 (hardcover) 1. Duncan, Eve (Fictitious
character)—Fiction. 2. Facial reconstruction (Anthropology)—Fiction. 3.
Women sculptors—Fiction. 4. Children—Crimes against—Fiction. 5.
Domestic fiction. 6. Large type books. I. Title.
PS3560.O275B66 2011b
813'.54—dc23   2011032342

Published in 2011 by arrangement with St. Martin's Press, LLC.

Printed in the United States of America
1 2 3 4 5 6 7 15 14 13 12 11

BONNIE

CHAPTER
1

Atlanta, Georgia
The Past

"What star is that, Mama?" Bonnie lifted her hand to point at a brilliant orb in the night sky. "It's shining so bright."

"That's not a star, it's a planet. It's Venus." She cuddled her daughter closer on her lap. "I've told you about Venus, Bonnie."

"I guess I forgot." She leaned back against Eve's shoulder in the big rattan chair. "Or maybe it's because everything seems so . . . different tonight."

"Different? We sit out here on the porch almost every night, baby." It was a precious time for both of them. After supper, they came out on the front porch and looked at the night sky. Eve had even bought a book on astronomy so that she could point out the constellations to Bonnie. "What's different?"

"I don't know." Bonnie's gaze never left the glittering night sky. "They just seem . . . closer. As if I could reach out and touch them. As if they want me to come and touch them."

Eve chuckled and gave her a hug. "Maybe that's what you should do when you grow up. Would you like to be an astronaut and go from planet to planet?"

Bonnie giggled. "That might be fun. Like *Star Trek.* But I don't have ears like Mr. Spock."

"It could still work." She smiled as she leaned her head back and gazed up at the sky. "But those stars are very far away, and you don't know what you'll find there. Would you be afraid, baby?"

Bonnie was silent, her eyes fixed on the stars.

"Bonnie?"

"I won't be afraid, Mama." She turned her head and looked Eve directly in the eye. "And don't you be afraid either. I'll be fine."

Eve's smile faded. There was something in Bonnie's expression that was making her uneasy. In that instant, she didn't look like her seven-year-old little girl any longer. Bonnie's expression was serene, oddly adult.

Nonsense. It had to be imagination. "I won't." Eve gave Bonnie a kiss on the tip of

8

her nose. "Because I think we'll keep you here on Earth. No skipping from planet to planet. Your grandma and I would miss you too much." She tugged at Bonnie's ear. "And you're right, your ears don't look at all like Spock's." She hugged her again. "And now it's time for your bath. Didn't you tell me that your school picnic is tomorrow? Run in to Grandma and have her start your bath, and you decide what to wear."

"Just one more minute." Bonnie put her head back on Eve's shoulder. "I don't want to leave you yet."

Eve didn't want to leave Bonnie either. That instant of uneasiness was still with her. Why not stay here until it faded away. "One minute. You're not the only one who has school tomorrow. I have to study for my English Lit test when you go in for your bath."

"But tonight is special, tonight is . . . different," she whispered. "Don't you feel it?"

Every day, every minute, was special with Bonnie. From the moment Eve had given birth to her, she had been the center of her world. But maybe there was something strange and beautiful about their closeness tonight. Something that Eve didn't want to give up until she had to do it. The thought brought an odd sense of panic. "I feel it."

9

Her arms tightened around Bonnie's small body. "Yes, I feel it, baby."

Bonnie came running into Eve's bedroom in her yellow pajamas with the orange clowns all over them. Her wild red curls were bouncing, and her face was lit with her luminous smile.

"Mama, Lindsey says her mother is going to let her wear her Goofy T-shirt to the park tomorrow for the school picnic. Can I wear my Bugs Bunny T-shirt?"

Eve looked up from her English Lit book open on the desk in front of her. "It's not can, it's may, baby. And you may wear Bugs tomorrow." She smiled. "We wouldn't want Lindsey to put you in the shade."

"I wouldn't care. She's my friend. You said we always had to want the best for our friends."

"Yes, we do. Now run along to bed."

Bonnie didn't move. "I know you're studying for your test, but could you read me a story?" She added coaxingly, "I thought maybe a very, very short one?"

"Your grandmother loves to read you stories, baby."

Bonnie came closer, and whispered, "I love Grandma. But it's always special when you read it to me. Just a short one . . ."

10

Eve glanced at her Lit book. She'd be up until after midnight as it was, studying for that exam. She looked at Bonnie's pleading face. Oh, to hell with it. Bonnie was the reason Eve was working for her degree anyway. She was the reason for every action Eve took in life. Why cheat either one of them? "Run and choose a storybook." She pushed her textbook aside and stood up. "And it doesn't have to be a short one."

Bonnie's expression could have lit up Times Square. "No. I promise. . . ." She ran out of the room. She was back in seconds with a Dr. Seuss book. "This will be quick, and I like the rhymes."

Eve sat down in the blue-padded rocking chair that she'd used since Bonnie was a newborn. "Climb up. I like Dr. Seuss, too."

"I know you do." Bonnie scrambled up in her lap and cuddled close. "But since it's such a short book, can — may I have my song, too?"

"I think that's a reasonable request," Eve said solemnly. The two of them had their little traditions, and every night since she was a toddler, Bonnie had loved to share a song with Eve. Eve would sing the first line, and Bonnie would sing the next. "What's it to be tonight?"

" 'All the Pretty Little Horses.' " She

11

turned around on Eve's lap and hugged her with all her might. "I love you, Mama."

Eve's arms closed around her. Bonnie's riot of curls was soft and fragrant against her cheek, and her small body was endearingly vital and sturdy against Eve. Lord, she was lucky. "I love you, too, Bonnie."

Bonnie let her go and flopped back around to cuddle in the curve of her arm. "You start, Mama."

"Hushabye, don't you cry," Eve sang softly.

Bonnie's thin little voice chimed. "Go to sleep, little baby."

The moment was so precious, so dear. Eve's arms held Bonnie closer, and she could feel the tightening of her throat as she sang, "When you wake, you shall have cake."

Bonnie's voice was only a wisp of sound. "And all the pretty little horses . . ."

She should get back to her studies, Eve thought.

Not yet. She couldn't pull herself away yet. Bonnie had been so loving tonight. She had seemed to be reaching out for Eve.

She stood looking down at Bonnie curled up asleep in her bed. She looked so small, she thought with aching tenderness. Bonnie was seven, yet she looked younger.

But sometimes she seemed to have a wisdom far beyond her years. She had always been a special child from the moment Eve had given birth to her. Bonnie was illegitimate, born when Eve was only sixteen. Her passionate affair with John Gallo had lasted only four weeks but had given her Bonnie.

And she had thought that she might give her up for adoption, Eve remembered wonderingly. Gazing down at her daughter it seemed impossible to even contemplate. From the moment she had seen her in the hospital, she had known that they had to be together forever.

Forever.

Those teasing words they'd spoken on the porch had only underscored the fact that Bonnie would be growing up and leaving her someday.

Pain.

She didn't have to think of that yet. Bonnie was still her baby, and she would have her for years to come. Until then, she would cherish every moment as she had done tonight.

She bent down and brushed her lips on Bonnie's silky cheek. "Sleep well, baby," she whispered. "May all your dreams be beautiful."

"Dreams . . ." Bonnie's lids lifted drowsily. "Dreams are so wonderful, Mama. You can reach out and touch . . ." She was asleep again.

Eve turned, and the next moment, she was silently closing the door to Bonnie's room behind her.

"She's asleep?" Eve's mother was standing in the hall. "I would have put her to bed, Eve. You told me you had that test tomorrow."

"I'll be okay, Sandra." She'd called her mother Sandra since she was a child. Sandra had been sensitive about appearing older, and so she had never been Mother to Eve, always Sandra. It was just a sign of how much she loved Bonnie that she accepted her calling her Grandma. "I needed a break anyway." She smiled. "And I don't get a chance to put her to bed every night." She headed back down the hall toward her room. "I wish I did."

"You go to school. You work to support her. You can't do everything."

"I know." She stopped at the doorway and looked back at her mother. "But I was just thinking how lucky I am to have her."

"How lucky *we* are," Sandra said.

Eve nodded. "I know how much you love her." And Eve would have had an even rougher time keeping Bonnie if it hadn't been for her mother. She had been with them since Bonnie had been born. "She has a school picnic at the park tomorrow. I told her she could wear her Bugs Bunny T-shirt. I won't be able to be there in the morning. But I should be able to be there by noon after I take my test. You'll be there until I get there?"

Sandra nodded. "Of course I'll be there. I'm intending to stay all day. I wouldn't miss it. Stop worrying, Eve."

"I just want her to have family there. Other kids have fathers, and I'm always afraid she'll feel . . ." She frowned. "But we're enough for her, aren't we, Sandra?"

"I've never seen a happier child." She shook her head. "And this isn't like you, Eve. You never question a decision once it's made. You're not like me, who wobbles back and forth every time the wind blows. Even if John Gallo hadn't been killed in the Army, you wouldn't have wanted him to have anything to do with Bonnie. You told me yourself that it was only sex, not love, between you."

That was true, and Eve didn't know why she was suddenly worrying about Bonnie's

15

not having a conventional family. It was just that she wanted Bonnie to have everything that other children had, every bit of security, everyone to care about her. No, she wanted more. She wanted her to be surrounded by a golden wall of love all the days of her life.

And she was, Eve thought impatiently. No one could love Bonnie more than she did. More than Sandra did. She was being an idiot to start worrying about something that probably didn't bother Bonnie at all. She had never once asked about her father. She seemed perfectly happy with Eve and Sandra.

"Go study," Sandra said. "Stop worrying about tomorrow. Bonnie is going to have a wonderful time." She turned away. "I'm going to bed. Good night."

"Good night." Eve sat back down at her desk. Don't think about Bonnie. Think about English Lit. Getting her degree was a way to protect Bonnie and give her all the things that she should have. This is what she should be doing.

And ignore this nagging feeling that something was wrong. What could be wrong?

Sandra was right. Bonnie was going to have a wonderful time at the park tomorrow.

■ ■ ■ ■

Nightmare.

Nightmare.

Nightmare.

"Let's go over it one more time," Detective Slindak said. "You didn't see anyone approach your daughter?"

"I told you." Eve's voice was shaking. "There was a crowd. She went to the refreshment stand to get an ice cream. One minute she was there, the next she wasn't." She stared blindly at the three police cars parked next to the curb, the people standing around in groups, whispering and gazing at her. "She's been gone for three hours. Why are you asking me questions? *Find* her."

"We're trying. Does your daughter often wander away from you?"

"No, never." She stared at her mother sitting on the park bench with another police officer. Tears were running down Sandra's cheeks, and she was leaning against him. "We were at the swings. My mother gave her money for an ice cream, and she ran to buy it. We could see the refreshment stand, so we thought it would be okay. She said she'd be right back. She wouldn't have just wandered away." But if she didn't, then the

17

other explanation was where the nightmares began. "I talked to the man at the refreshment stand. He remembered her." Everyone always remembered Bonnie. Her smile, the way she lit up everything around her. "He sold her the ice cream, then she ran off into the crowd."

"That's what he told us, too."

"Someone else must have seen her." The panic was rising. "Talk to everyone. Find her."

"We're trying," he said gently. "We're questioning everyone. I've sent men to search the entire park."

"They won't find her here. Do you think I didn't do that?" she asked fiercely. "I ran all over the park, calling her name. She didn't answer." The tears were beginning to fall. "I called and called. She didn't answer. Bonnie would answer me. She would answer —"

"We'll try again," the detective said. "We're exploring every possibility."

"There's a lake. I taught her to swim, but what if —"

"It's an ornamental lake, just a man-made token. It's only a drop of four feet in the deepest spot. And we've interviewed a father and son who have been sitting on the bench by the lake all afternoon. They would have seen her if she'd fallen into the water."

"She has to be somewhere. Find her." That's the only thing she could say. That's the only thing that made sense in a world that was suddenly drowning in madness. Bonnie had to be found. All the radiance and love that was Bonnie couldn't be lost. God wouldn't let that happen. They all just had to search harder, and they'd find her.

"We're sending out another search party," Detective Slindak said quietly as he gestured to the officers starting out toward the trees in the distance. "We've put out an all-points bulletin. You can't do anything more here. Let me have an officer drive you and your mother home. We'll call you as soon as we hear something."

"You want me to go home?" she asked in disbelief. "Without my little girl? I can't do that."

"You can't help more than you have already. It's better that you leave it to us."

"Bonnie is *mine*. I won't leave here." She whirled away from Slindak. "I'll go with the search party. I'll call her name. She'll answer me."

"She didn't before," Slindak said gently. "She may not be there to answer."

He hadn't said "or she might be unable to answer," but Eve knew it was in his mind. Cold fear was causing the muscles of her

19

stomach to clench at the thought. Her heart was beating so hard that she could barely catch her breath. "She'll answer me. She'll find a way to let me know where she is. You don't understand. Bonnie is such a special, loving, little girl . . . She'll find a way."

"I'm sure that you're right," the detective said.

"You're not sure of anything," she said fiercely. "But I am." She started at a run after the search team of officers heading for the trees. "This is all a mistake. No one would hurt my Bonnie. We just have to find her."

She could feel the detective's gaze on her back as she caught up with the search team. She knew he wanted to make her stop. He wanted her to behave sensibly and let them do their job. But it was her job, too. She had brought Bonnie into the world. In the end, that made it only her job.

I'll find you, baby. Don't be afraid. I'll fight off anything that could hurt you. Wait for me. I'll always be there for you.

No matter how long it takes or how far I have to go, I'll bring you home, Bonnie.

CHAPTER
2

Present Day

"The Director is on the phone, Agent Venable." Harley's tone was hesitant. "He sounded a little —"

"Pissed?" Venable said. It didn't surprise him. Dickson was not known for his patience, and Venable hadn't been jumping through his hoops on this assignment. "I don't want to deal with him. Tell him I'm —"

"It's the third call," Harley said.

"And you're afraid he'll shoot the messenger," Venable said.

"I'll give him whatever message you want me to give him," Harley said. "But this time he asked me to give him Agent Ling's cell number."

Shit. "And did you?"

"I said I'd have to look it up." He paused. "But he'll get it."

Venable knew that Hal Dickson, as Director of the CIA, would get any info he wanted if he went to the trouble. But the people who made him go to that trouble would suffer for it.

"Why does he want Agent Ling?" Harley said. "I told him that she was on another assignment."

"And you think he cares? Some of those South American countries are on the verge of revolution, and the situation is getting critical. Catherine Ling spent several years serving in the jungles of Colombia and Venezuela. She has contacts, and people trust her all over South America. She can get information when no one else has a chance. Dickson knows that, and he wants her down there."

"Are you going to order her to go back there?"

Order Catherine Ling? he thought sourly. He could ask her, but he hadn't a snowball's chance in hell of getting her to leave her son, Luke, whom she had just rescued from years of captivity. She'd tell him to go to hell.

Unless he could find a way to stall the director until he found a way to manipulate Catherine into doing what he wanted. At present, he had no hope because Catherine was on a private mission of her own, help-

22

ing Eve Duncan find the body and the killer of her murdered daughter, Bonnie.

Not easy.

Okay, explain, stall, and maybe he'd get through with this without incurring Dickson's anger. The director wasn't a bad guy if you didn't piss him off. Venable had known him before those politicians in Congress had made the Company the bogeyman in everyone's eyes. Hell, let those jokers try to keep to their lily-white rules when every other country played dirty. He knew what pressure Dickson was under. Besides, there were times when he needed the bastard, and he wouldn't have Catherine make him lose that influence if he could help it.

And he wouldn't let Harley take the flak.

"I'll talk to him." He took out his phone and dialed Dickson while he pulled out Catherine Ling's file from his desk. He probably wouldn't need it. He had recruited her when she was seventeen, and if anyone really knew her, he should.

He gazed at her photo as he waited for Dickson to answer. This one was taken on the streets of Hong Kong, where she had grown up. Part Caucasian, part Asian, she was incredibly stunning, with her dark hair, gold skin, and faintly slanted eyes. But it wasn't her looks that made her invaluable. She was one of the finest CIA agents Venable had ever recruited: smart, tough, deadly.

And loyal. Which was going to be the sticking point in getting her to leave Eve Duncan and Joe Quinn at this time.

"Where's Catherine Ling?" Dickson demanded the moment he picked up the call. "I told you a week ago I wanted her in Peru."

"She's on another assignment."

"Screw her assignment. Replace her."

"That's not exactly possible."

"You're refusing me." Dickson was silent. "You're not a fool, Venable. Sometimes I think I'm surrounded by fools, but you're not one of them. Which means you have a reason to take a chance like that. Has Ling gone rogue?"

"No way." He hesitated, then told the truth. "She thinks she has a debt to pay. Eve Duncan and Joe Quinn helped her to save her son, Luke. Now she's trying to give Duncan what she wants most in life. She's trying to find Bonnie Duncan's body and the man who killed her. Nothing is going to budge her until she does it."

Dickson muttered a curse. "Dammit, don't you have any influence on her?"

"Not enough to stop her from doing this."

"There has to be a way. Eve Duncan. Can you appeal to her?"

"No, you don't understand."

"Then make me understand, dammit. Why can't this wait?"

"Because she'd tell me it's waited too long already." He might as well fill him in though it probably wouldn't help. "Eve Duncan had this child when she was sixteen, the father was a Ranger in the Army and was reported dead. She didn't have an abortion or give the kid up for adoption. She kept her. Part of the time, her mother helped take care of her, sometimes Bonnie was in a United Fund nursery while Eve worked. She did correspondence courses at night. She was almost finished when her daughter, Bonnie, disappeared. The police became certain that she was a victim of a serial killer. In fact, they'd thought they'd caught and executed him. Ralph Fraser. He'd killed other children, but he hadn't killed Bonnie. Which meant Eve had no closure. She had to find her daughter's killer. She had to bring her daughter home. It's been the guiding obsession of her life. She has a long-term relationship with Joe Quinn, a police detective, who has helped her search for her daughter. She has an adopted daughter, Jane MacGuire, who is now an artist. But it's the search for

Bonnie that's the center of her universe."

"And she's drawn Catherine Ling into that universe as a satellite," Dickson said harshly. "Let her find her own kid."

"She never asked Catherine to help her." To hell with diplomacy. He'd known Eve Duncan for years, and she'd done favors both for him and the agency. She deserved better than Dickson's condemnation. "Look, Eve Duncan pulls her own weight, and she'd keep Catherine out of it if she could."

Silence. "You like her."

"You're damn right I do. She loved Bonnie more than life itself. Having her kidnapped and murdered could have destroyed her. She didn't let it. She went back to school and earned a degree in Fine Arts at Georgia State. She now has certification as a computer age-progression specialist at the National Center for Missing and Exploited Children in Arlington, Virginia. She also received advanced certification for clay facial reconstruction after training with two of the nation's foremost reconstruction artists. Do I have to tell you how many more degrees she's earned since then? She's world-famous, dammit. She's an icon. Don't you think she deserves to get this one thing she wants in the world?"

Another silence. "Maybe. But if she's been searching all these years, why does Catherine Ling have to be involved? What makes her think that she can help?"

God, he was stubborn. But at least he was listening. That was a start.

"Catherine started investigating Bonnie's kidnapping and came up with a suspect that no one had uncovered. John Gallo, Bonnie's father, had not been killed while in the Army as reported. He'd been captured and thrown into a North Korean prison, where he'd been subjected to seven years of starvation and torture. When he escaped from the prison and landed in a hospital in Tokyo, he was diagnosed with severe mental problems, blackouts, schizophrenia, hallucinations . . ."

"Imagine that," Dickson said sarcastically. "Poor bastard."

"But a prime candidate for a suspect if he bore resentment toward Eve. What better revenge than killing her child?"

"Catherine's reasoning?"

"Yes, sound reasoning. You agree?"

"Yes, so Catherine's after Gallo?"

"She was, but after hunting him down, she decided that she might be wrong. So she decided to go after the two very dirty Army Intelligence officers who sent Gallo to Korea. Nate Queen and Thomas Jacobs.

They were into smuggling artifacts and drugs and sent Gallo to retrieve an incriminating journal held by the North Koreans. He was just a patriotic nineteen-year-old kid at the time, and he thought he was doing his duty to his country. As I said, he was captured and thrown into that prison. It was years after he escaped and fought his way through a hell of a lot of mental problems that he became suspicious of Queen and Jacobs. He went after them."

"I can see why he'd want to put them down for setting him up and letting the Koreans get him. But what the hell did that have to do with the killing of Eve Duncan's little girl?"

Venable could understand Dickson's impatience. The search for Bonnie Duncan's killer had become as complicated as a spiderweb. Keep it as simple as you can. "Queen and Jacobs wanted to get rid of Gallo and remove a possible witness against them. They hired a contract killer, James Black, to go after him. But Gallo is very, very tough, and Black ended up with Gallo's knife in his belly and egg on his face with his employers. Black was furious, and after he recovered, he started planning on hurting Gallo in any way he could."

"So Black killed the kid?"

"That's the way it looked, that's what Gallo and Eve Duncan, Joe Quinn, and Catherine thought. They hunted him down in the Wisconsin woods."

"And put him down? So what's the problem? Catherine should be free now."

"Except that Black swore before he died that he hadn't killed Bonnie Duncan, that John Gallo had done it." He paused. "Evidently he was very convincing. Both Eve Duncan and Gallo believed him."

"Shit. You mean because Gallo had been having mental problems? You said he was experiencing blackouts."

"Yes. Gallo thought he might have had one at that time and killed his daughter. He almost went crazy. He took off into the woods after he killed Black. Catherine went after him, hunted for weeks, and tracked him down."

"But you said she changed her mind about Gallo's killing the kid. Why?"

"How do I know? It was a judgment call. She just said that Eve and Gallo had been stupid to take the word of a murderer even if every instinct told them that he was telling the truth. They should have looked in another direction. The other direction was Queen and Jacobs. Black had been hired as a contract killer many times before by them.

It wasn't logical that they wouldn't have known his intention to kill the little girl. Queen and Jacobs were regarding Gallo as a threat, and he had a history of mental problems. Kill the child and send him over the edge? There was a possibility that they'd been involved or hired someone else to kill Bonnie. So they went after them."

Venable could almost feel Dickson's frustration and impatience at the other end of the line. Well, suck it up, big man. He was almost finished.

"Nate Queen was killed over a week ago, and that left Thomas Jacobs. Catherine and Gallo tracked him to New Orleans, and she's hoping either to force Jacobs to confess or get info from him about who did kill Bonnie Duncan. Gallo has rented a house on the bayou across the Mississippi, where they're going to take Jacobs to interrogate him."

"Then she should be able to tie this up soon," Dickson said. "How soon?"

"I don't know. The last I heard, Catherine had told Eve Duncan and Joe Quinn about Thomas Jacobs, and they were on their way to join Catherine and Gallo in New Orleans."

"You don't know?" Dickson asked. "Give me an estimate."

Screw this. "I don't have a crystal ball, dammit. It will be done as quickly as she can do it. When she gets the information, she'll call me. As you can see, I'm not totally out of the loop."

"That's not good enough. Get into the middle of the loop," Dickson said. "You take as many men as you need and go down to New Orleans and wrap this up. Keep me informed." He hung up.

Venable pressed the disconnect and turned to Harley. "It seems we're going to New Orleans. Now. Get me a pilot and plane. And check the weather. Catherine said the entire Gulf Coast has been fogged in for the last couple days."

Harley reached for his phone. "Are you calling Catherine and telling her you're coming?"

Venable thought about it. Catherine wouldn't appreciate the interference and might react in a way that would make Dickson even angrier. It would be smarter to confront her face-to-face than long-distance. "I'll call her when I get on the ground in New Orleans."

"Which may not be any too soon." Harley looked up from the weather app on his iPhone. "The fog has lifted over Mississippi, but it's still blanketing Louisiana. We may have to take ground transportation out of Mobile."

Venable muttered a curse as he got to his feet. "Then let's get moving."

Jefferson Parish, Louisiana
"They're coming." Catherine turned away from the window where she'd seen what she'd thought were Eve and Joe's headlights. "At least I think they are. I can barely see the headlights in this fog. They should be here in a couple minutes." She leveled a glance at Gallo. "And no matter what Joe says or does, you're not to respond with any antagonism, do you understand?"

"I understand that you're expecting a lot from me." He got up from the chair and crossed to the window. "I believe you're talking about diplomacy. We both know that's not my forte."

No, it wasn't, and she could already see that familiar trace of recklessness in his face. "I'm not having it, Gallo. Joe was caught in the middle before when we were trying to find Bonnie's killer and ended up almost dying. He's just out of the hospital. Joe was the victim, and you can be patient if he's pissed at you."

"And if I'm not, then you'll go after me yourself. I believe you're proving that you're

32

protective of more people than your son," Gallo said. "But I admit I like it better when it's me you're protecting." He watched Joe and Eve get out of the car. "Do you want me to go and greet them?"

And watch Eve have to handle the confrontation between the two men who had shaped her life? Gallo, the father of her child; Joe, the man with whom she'd lived and loved for years. Catherine was already at the front door and throwing it open. "Come in out of this muck. I wish I could offer you a cup of coffee, Eve, but we're limited to bouillon." She made a face. "Not even good bouillon." She turned to Joe. "You look wonderful." She gave him an appraising glance. "Maybe you've lost a little weight. But I knew you'd make it."

"That's more than I did." Eve gave her a quick hug. "And you've lost a pound or two yourself since I saw you."

"I kept her on the run," Gallo said from where he stood by the window. "But no more than she did me. It was quite a hunt." His gaze shifted to Eve's face. "Hello, Eve."

She stiffened. "Hello, John."

Joe stepped quickly forward. "Gallo."

Gallo's expression became wary. "Hello, Quinn. Am I going to have problems with you?"

"I'm not sure," Joe said coolly. "You deserve them. You've been getting in my way since the moment you decided to come back into Eve's life."

"Too bad. I don't give a damn about you, Quinn. It was all about finding out who killed Bonnie. That's still what it's all about."

The two men were like two lions, arching, frozen in place, but ready to attack, Catherine thought. She took a step forward, then stopped. They'd have to work it out for themselves sometime. It might as well be now.

But Gallo had seen that movement from the corner of his eye. "Catherine says I have to be diplomatic since I'm the one who has been causing all the trouble. She's about to step in and take me out."

"I'd be glad to save her the bother." Then Joe glanced at Eve. "But you may not be important enough for me to deal with right now, Gallo."

Oh, shit. Catherine saw the flicker of recklessness appear in Gallo's expression again.

He said, "Perhaps I could up the ante, and that would make you think I'm —"

"Stop it." Eve stepped forward between the two men and faced Gallo. "Catherine said that Jacobs knows who killed Bonnie. That's all I care about. If you love Bonnie as much as you say, then that's all that you should care about, too." She paused. "I thought it was you, John. I'm still not certain it's not. Prove it to me."

"Yes, prove it to her, Gallo," Joe said. "I think we need to talk to Thomas Jacobs."

"Fine," Catherine said. It was time to end this standoff. Joe and Gallo had too many of the same aggressive instincts, and the situation could become explosive. "If you want to ask Jacobs questions, then come upstairs and do it. Maybe you'll have more luck than we did. He wasn't talking."

Gallo hesitated and gestured toward the stairs. "By all means. I was looking forward to questioning the bastard again myself, but I'll forgo the pleasure. Catherine has already pointed out that I need to be kind and diplomatic to guests."

"And you're doing what she wants." Eve was gazing at him searchingly as she started up the stairs. "I find that curious."

"Do you?" He smiled. "But can't you see I'm terrified of your friend Catherine?"

Catherine made a rude sound. "Shut up, Gallo." She turned to Joe. "Jacobs is going to cause us trouble. I hope he'll be more cooperative now that he's had time to think."

"He'll be cooperative," Joe said grimly as he moved past her up the stairs. "Tell me what he's told you so far. No, on second thought, let me start fresh."

"Lord, it's chilly up here." Eve shuddered as they reached the bedroom door. "What are you doing, Catherine? Are you trying to freeze information out of him?"

Catherine frowned. "It wasn't this chilly before." She opened the door. "I don't know why it would —"

"Dear God!" Eve took a step back, her gaze on the bed. "Catherine?"

Catherine's gaze followed Eve's. She went rigid. "No, Eve, no. We didn't — Gallo!"

There was water on the floor around the bed.

Thomas Jacobs was still bound, spread-eagled on the bed, just as they had left him.

And there was a knife sticking upright in his chest.

"Shit!" Gallo pushed by them and ran to the bed. Jacobs's mouth was still taped and his eyes were wide open, staring at the ceiling. Gallo checked the pulse in his throat, but they all knew it wasn't necessary. "Dead. But how the hell —"

"The window." The sheer white drapes

were blowing from the open window, and Catherine was there in a heartbeat. "We were downstairs. He had to come in the window."

Dammit, she could see nothing through the heavy fog.

But she could hear something.

The splash of water being moved, the sound of suction in the mud . . .

"He's in the bayou."

"Heading south." Gallo had already swung his legs over the sill and was climbing hand over hand down the side of the house to the roof of the porch.

Gallo might think he was Spider-Man, but she'd make almost as good time going down to the front door and wouldn't risk falling and breaking her neck, Catherine thought. She turned and was running out the room when Joe grabbed her arm and spun her around.

"One question," he said.

"I don't have *time*, Joe."

"You have time for this one." His glance shifted to Jacobs. "This isn't some con you set up to convince us that Gallo was innocent? You didn't get overenthusiastic with that knife in Jacobs?"

Her eyes widened. "I wouldn't do that, Joe."

His expression didn't lose its hardness. "I wouldn't think that you would. But I wouldn't think you'd be so dedicated to exonerating Gallo either. I don't know what's going on with you, Catherine."

She tore herself away from him, her eyes blazing. "And you think because he once managed to convince Eve that he was the sun and the moon, that he'd dazzle me so that I'd lie for him. No way, Joe. He didn't kill Jacobs, and neither did I. We were both downstairs waiting for you. Whoever did this must have followed us from the casino." She turned on her heel. "And now I'm going to go into that bayou and try to catch the son of a bitch."

"Go on," Joe said quietly. "Eve and I will be right behind you as soon as I figure out which —"

But she didn't hear the rest because she was already down the stairs and throwing open the front door.

Swirling fog.

Dampness.

And the sudden splash of movement in the bayou.

"Gallo!"

"Here."

He was already in the water

She took off her boots and socks, left her

gun on the bank, and made sure her knife was firmly in its holster on her thigh. Then she jumped off the mossy bank and moved in the direction in which she'd thought she'd heard his voice.

The water was only up to her waist that close to the bank, but she couldn't be sure what was in the water with her. Everything from water moccasins to alligators frequented the bayous. Just be careful and look sharp. She couldn't see anything at any distance, but she would be able to tell if one of those predators was within striking distance.

Hell, she hated being blind in this dense mist. And Gallo would also be blind. They'd be lucky if they didn't attack each other. But she didn't want to call out again and draw possible fire.

Or another wicked knife like the one in Jacobs's chest.

Move slowly, as silently as possible in the water.

She listened.

She couldn't hear Gallo moving through the water. Not even a whisper of sound.

Where was —

"Catherine."

She jerked with shock. He was right beside her. His white shirt was plastered to his body, and his sheathed bowie knife was shoved into the waist of his black trousers.

His gaze was fixed on the south. "He's heading in that direction. Every now and then, I can hear him brush against something. Or he'll startle a bird, and I'll hear the wings . . ."

Catherine started forward. "What are we waiting for?"

"He's very good. Damn good. We go too fast and lose his sound, and he could circle and come up behind us. There are times I can't hear him at all. The bayou is deeper once you get a distance from the bank. He's probably swimming." He was silent again. "Do you hear that?"

Birds moving from branch to branch.

"He's going southwest now." He started forward. "You circle and see if you can come at him from the west. I'll track him on the direct route."

"West," she repeated as she started out. "You said Jacobs's killer was so good. Yet we heard him plainly from Jacobs's bedroom."

"He was in a hurry. He'd probably just finished knifing Jacobs when we were coming up the stairs. He needed to get in the water and away from the bank."

"And after those first few minutes, he felt

safe and could take his time."

"As I said, he's really good. Be careful, Catherine . . ." He disappeared into the mist.

But that mist wasn't as thick, she realized suddenly. Gallo had gone at least four yards before she had lost him. Maybe the fog was dispersing.

She went a few more yards, her hopes rising with every step. They had gotten lucky. Yes, the mist was definitely lifting. They'd soon be able to see the bastard who had killed Jacobs.

And the killer would be able to see them.

"The fog's beginning to lift," Joe said, as he and Eve reached the edge of the bayou. "That will help." He grabbed her arm and pulled her toward the car. "We can't help Catherine much in that swamp. Come on, we'll take the car and go along the road bordering the bayou. We didn't see any sign of a car when we drove up to the house, so he must have parked up ahead and around the curve of the bayou. That's where he'll probably be heading."

Eve nodded as she got into the car. "Then why would he jump into —" She answered herself. "A false trail. So that we wouldn't find his car." A bold move, possibly a deadly move. Catherine and Gallo had followed him into the bayou and were trying to find him while lumbering blindly in the thick fog. Joe said it was lifting, but not enough.

Please, let us have a break in this damn fog.

"I'll go slow. Hell, I have to go slow." Joe had already started the car and hit the lights. "You keep an eye out. He could have come back to the bank anywhere along the road."

She nodded, her eyes straining as they tried to pierce the thick layers of fog hovering on the bank. She rolled down the window so that she could better hear anyone moving in the water. Her heart was pounding, and the muscles of her stomach were clenched with fear.

She had a sudden memory of Bonnie's face as she'd seen it earlier as they were driving here, drifting in the fog. Joe had thought that Eve might have imagined seeing the ghost of her daughter because of the stress she was under.

It wasn't imagination. She had seen Bonnie, a spirit so sad that it had broken Eve's heart. Such terrible sadness.

Why? Did Bonnie know what was going to happen and was sad for all of them. For what reason? The death of Jacobs?

Or the death of someone else, someone whose death Bonnie knew would hurt Eve? A chill went through her at the thought. Not Joe. Please God, not Joe. You've just given him a new lease on life. Not Catherine, who had hardly started to know the meaning of joy and had a son who needed her. Not Gallo, who had perhaps suffered more than all of them.

If this is the end, shouldn't it be you and me, baby?

"Eve." His eyes were on the road ahead of him, but Joe's voice was soft but clear. "It's going to be all right. We're going to get through this together."

She nodded jerkily. "I know, Joe."

Together. Yes, they'd be together, but maybe not right away.

Eve could not forget the sadness in her daughter's face.

Let it be me, Bonnie.

Catherine stopped and stood still in the water as she saw the pale, fog-shrouded glow of headlights on the road leaving from the direction of the house.

Joe and Eve.

Smart.

They were betting that the man who had killed Jacobs had a car parked somewhere on that road bordering the bayou. It was reasonable that he'd be heading across the bayou in the direction where he'd left it.

She tried to pull up a mental picture of the curve of the road around the bayou. Gallo had said the terrain was shaped like a hook . . .

And Gallo had told her that they should go southwest.

And sent her west.

But the hook of land surrounding the bayou extended to the east. That would be where that car would be parked. Southeast. And Gallo was heading due south.

And would probably soon veer to the southeast.

Damn him.

Anger was seething through her. The son of a bitch was trying to *protect* her. Who the hell did he think he was? She was every bit as competent a professional as he. She should have slapped that damn macho tendency down as soon as it raised its head. Now it was getting in the way of her job.

And could get them both killed.

But not if she could help it.

She turned and headed southeast.

Jacobs's killer was definitely heading southeast toward the hook of land bordering the bayou, Gallo thought.

He could hear him, and, if he got lucky, soon he might be able to see him.

The fog was lifting for a few seconds, hovering, then closing down again. All he'd need would be those few seconds to draw his knife and hurl it.

If he was close enough.

And he would be close enough.

He could feel the excitement and tension searing through him. Another hunt. But this was nothing like the hunt with Catherine. Even in the darkest hours of those days, he'd known that it was different from anything he'd ever experienced. There might have been lethal danger, but it had been coupled by challenge. This hunt was different. No beautiful, sleek panther who could turn and rend him in the flash of an eye.

This was only prey.

And the sounds of the prey were approaching closer to that far bank.

The fog lifted . . .

Gallo caught a swift glimpse of the shadowy bank, a gnarled cypress tree dipping its roots in the water, Spanish moss hanging from another tree near —

Near a gleam of metal. A car?

He couldn't be sure. The fog had closed

45

in again, dammit.

But that gleam of metal was a little too opportune. The bank had to be the prey's destination.

He began to carefully, silently, swim toward it.

Catherine pulled herself from the water onto the bank. Now that she had a destination, she could move faster over ground. She should be somewhere near the road, and the car would probably not be parked on the road itself but hidden in the shrubbery.

She moved swiftly through the heavy palmettos and shrubbery that bordered the bank. Her sopping-wet clothes were clinging to her body, and the soles of her bare feet were being scratched, cut, and bruised with every step.

Pain.

Her feet were bleeding.

Ignore it. Block everything out. Concentrate on the job.

She had to find Jacobs's killer before he got away.

Find the car. Wait for him to show.

But she had to be careful. She couldn't kill the bastard even though it would be safer.

Eve still needed him. Eve still had to know about her Bonnie. . . .

Eve straightened in her seat. "I saw some-one."

Joe tensed. "Where?"

"He's gone now. I only got a glimpse. This damn fog. Not close. Around that bend. I saw someone climbing out of the water onto the bank."

"Gallo? Catherine?"

She shook her head. "He was thin, wear-ing a dark blue or black wet suit."

"Around that bend?" Joe pulled to the side of the road. "Then we go the rest of the way on foot. We still have to use the lights, and we don't want to scare him off." He got out of the car. "I can do this alone, Eve."

"No, you can't." She jammed her hand into the pocket of her Windbreaker and gripped her .38 revolver. A weapon to protect Joe as Joe had always protected her. Would it do any good? The more time that passed, the greater the cold dread that was icing through her.

She got out of the car and joined him as he strode into the brush bordering the bayou. "You said together, Joe."

He *had* him.

A man in a dark wet suit, tall, thin, moving quickly along the bank toward the gleam of metal that Gallo had identified as a vehicle.

Yes.

Gallo unsheathed his knife as he stood up in the shallow water near the bank.

Dammit.

The prey had disappeared as a fresh billow of fog descended.

No, there he was again. He was moving with a lithe jauntiness as if he had all the time in the world.

You don't have any time at all, bastard.

Bring him down permanently or just wound him? Gallo thought as he raised the knife and lined up the target. It would depend on how long he had before the fog settled down once —

Oh, my God.

No!

His hand holding the knife fell nervelessly to his side as he stared in horror at the man in the wet suit.

No. No. No.

Not prey at all.

But the man had sighted prey of his own, Gallo realized.

His stance had changed and now he was in stalking mode. He'd drawn a knife from

48

the holster at his waist.

Stalking whom?

Catherine.

Catherine, standing at the edge of the trees. Catherine, setting her own trap for the man who had killed Jacobs, the man who had killed Bonnie.

Dammit, what is wrong with me? Gallo thought in agony. Throw the knife.

CHAPTER
3

It wasn't a new vehicle, Catherine noticed as she cautiously approached. It was a beat-up blue Chevy truck and the tires looked worn, almost bald.

No sign of the driver of the truck.

She'd been listening and hadn't heard anyone come out of the bayou.

But she might not have been able to hear him. Gallo had said this creep was good. She trusted Gallo's judgment.

When it didn't concern his damned chauvinistic attitude toward her.

She stopped. She'd been tempted to check out the license plate and the glove box of the truck. Not smart. Better to wait and do all that later. Now she should wait and watch and listen.

Not much watching with this fog, but she could listen.

No sound.

The fog had come in again, and the truck

was only a hazy outline before her. But she'd probably have company soon. Just wait and pounce when he came on the bank.

She stiffened. Something was wrong. She felt it. The hair on the back of her neck was tingling.

"There's someone over there in the trees." Joe grabbed Eve's arm and pulled her to a halt. His eyes narrowed. "I think it's Catherine." He froze. "Oh, shit."

She could see why he was cursing as she saw the tall man in the wet suit directly behind Catherine. Nothing could be clearer than that he was on the attack.

"I can't get a clear shot," Joe said with frustration as he put his gun down. "He's right behind her. I'll shoot *her*, dammit." He moved to the side. "I'll see if I can get him from another angle. Don't call out and startle him. I don't want to have him move on her before I can get my shot."

If there was enough time.

It was going to be Catherine, Eve realized in agony. Catherine was the one who was going to die. And Eve had to stand there and watch it happen. She couldn't even cry out and warn her.

But Catherine had been with Gallo in the bayou. Why wasn't he there?

51

Dammit, where was Gallo?

Throw the knife.

Gallo's hand was frozen on the hilt.

He had to move, but he couldn't do it. Not this time.

It was as if everything were happening in slow motion.

He could see Catherine stiffening and knew those wonderful instincts with which he'd become so familiar were in play.

She *knew.*

Even as he watched, he saw her whirl and start to drop to the ground as she saw her attacker.

Too late.

He was already on Catherine, his knife raised.

It was coming down.

She was going to die.

"No!" The agonized cry tore from Gallo's throat.

He threw the knife.

Dear God, he's fast, Catherine thought as she reached for the knife in the holster on her thigh.

Fall. Roll. Then stab the bastard in the gut.

But he was over her, his dagger coming

down and —

He screamed as a bowie knife pierced the hand holding the knife and came out the other side!

Gallo's bowie knife. She recognized it. And Gallo standing in the water several yards from the bank.

It gave her enough time to roll away and get her knife out of the holster.

"Dammit, get out of the way, Catherine."

She glanced toward the trees. Joe. Trying to get his shot.

She rolled to the side.

The man in the wet suit was cursing as he turned and ran toward the bayou, bent low and zigzagging.

A shot.

Missed.

Then he was in the water. He reached out and jerked out the dagger piercing his hand, and threw it aside as he dove beneath the surface.

Catherine jumped to her feet and was at the bank of the bayou in seconds.

"Gallo, get him!" she called as she jumped off the bank into the water.

Gallo didn't answer, and she couldn't see him. The fog had come down again.

"Catherine, no!" Joe was suddenly standing on the bank beside the cypress tree.

"Come back. Don't take a chance. Don't trust him."

Of course, she wasn't going to trust that murderer. He'd just tried to kill her. "He's okay, Joe. Gallo's somewhere out here, too. We'll get the bastard. He's wounded and losing blood." She was starting to swim away from the bank. "Gallo!"

"Catherine, listen to me." Joe's voice was harsh, his fists clenched at his sides. "It's Gallo I'm talking about. I saw his face. He wasn't going to throw that knife. He wasn't going to save you. Gallo didn't care if you lived or died."

Shock went through her. "No, you're wrong, Joe. He did save me. Look, I can't talk." She began swimming faster. "I'll blow my chance of getting that bastard. You'd better jump in the car and patrol the road. He might try to get out of the water as soon as he can. The blood is going to draw alligators."

"Catherine!"

She couldn't see him any longer. She was surrounded by the thick, heavy mist that felt as if it was going to smother her. She suddenly felt very much alone. But she wasn't alone. There was a murderer out there who had been within an instant of killing her. Was he close? He could be only yards away from her and she wouldn't know it. It would be smart of him to lie in wait and ambush any pursuers. It was probably what she would have done.

Her heart was beating hard, she could feel her pulse jumping in her throat.

She stopped swimming and listened.

She heard . . . something, a displacement of water . . . Where had it come from? Dammit, where was Gallo? She could have used someone to watch her back.

Gallo doesn't care whether you live or die.

She heard the sound again. Closer.

She tensed, her hand reached down and grabbed her knife.

Come and see what's waiting for you, son of a bitch. I've been on my own all my life. What was I thinking? I don't need any help from Gallo or anyone else.

Come and get me.

She listened again. She thought she heard the sound of moving water to the north.

To hell with staying and waiting for him to come after her. Go on the attack. She started swimming toward the sound.

"No!" Gallo was suddenly beside her. "Let him go. Do you want to get killed? He almost had you."

"Let him go? Screw that. Listen. Do you

55

hear him?"

"I don't hear anything."

And she didn't either. He was gone. Or it could have been Gallo that she had heard.

"He's wounded. He's losing blood. He could be getting weaker," she said. "But did you see him tear your knife out of his hand? He acted as if he didn't even feel it."

"Adrenaline. He'll feel it later." He started swimming toward the north. "I'll see if I can zone in on him. You go back to shore and take Quinn and Eve in the car and see if he comes ashore again farther up the road. He'd be crazy to stay in the water with the blood attracting gators."

"That's what I told Joe. He may already be on the road."

"Or he may not. You don't want Quinn to come into the bayou after him. He may have been a SEAL, but I'd think you'd be worried about him having a relapse or getting an infection."

She was worried because that would be Joe's first instinct. He was going to be frustrated as hell because he hadn't been able to pick off Jacobs's killer.

Who had almost been her killer.

She nodded. "I agree he'll probably try to come to shore again. It would be the smartest thing to do since he's wounded."

"Then go back and stop him."

She shot him a glance. "You don't want me here. Why?"

He turned away. "I can do it by myself."

She stiffened. "So can I."

"Then suit yourself. You'll do what you have to do anyway."

He swam off and was lost in the mist.

She was alone again.

He doesn't care whether you live or die.

She hesitated, then started swimming in the same direction that Gallo had vanished.

Every few yards, she'd stop, listen, and swim again. At the end of forty-five minutes she was discouraged and frustrated. She was hearing nothing but the common sounds of the swamp, birds, insects, and occasionally something more heavy and threatening.

Alligator?

"Dammit, give up." Gallo suddenly emerged out of the mist. His lips tight, his eyes glittering with anger. "I just saw a gator up ahead slipping off the bank out of the weeds. It's enough that one of us is out here."

"And why should it be you?" She glared at him. "Alligators follow the blood scent. Maybe we can follow him to the bastard. His wounded hand was —" She stopped and closed her eyes. "Oh, shit."

"What's wrong?"

"Get away from me. My feet have a few cuts from walking barefoot in that palmetto grove, and I was bleeding. I may still be bleeding. That killer isn't the only one who will be attracting alligators. I didn't even think of those damn cuts." She turned and started swimming away from him toward the bank. "Stay away from me, Gallo."

Gallo was swearing, but he was swimming behind her. "You're an idiot, dammit."

"Yes, now shut up and go away."

"The bank should be due west."

"Go away. I won't be responsible for your being an alligator's lunch."

"Be quiet and swim."

She was already swimming as fast as she could. Five minutes later, she saw the hazy outline of the bank looming ahead of her. "There it is." She looked back at him. "Now get away from me and go find him. Be careful. I don't think this damn fog is ever going to lift." She paused, and added deliberately, "It's a wonder that it cleared enough so that you could make a decent throw."

He didn't answer. He turned in the water and once again vanished into the mist.

Eve was standing at the edge of the water when Catherine pulled herself onto the

58

bank. "You lost him?"

"Gallo's still after him in the bayou." She looked down at the soles of her feet. "I had to come back because these torn-up feet are alligator bait."

"I'll say they are." Eve grimaced as she looked down at the cuts. "And I don't have anything to clean them up or bandage them."

"I can wait until I get back to the house. Where's Joe?"

"On the road, checking to make sure that the killer doesn't get away if he comes out of the water again." She added, "Though he wanted to follow you into that bayou this time. He was feeling very frustrated."

"But at least he didn't do it."

"I wouldn't let him. He might have ended right back in the hospital. I'd have knocked him on the head if necessary before I let that happen. I told him I'd stay here and tell you what he was doing, and he could be a hero if and when that bastard came ashore." She looked Catherine up and down critically. "And your feet aren't the only problem. You might end up in the hospital, too, unless you get out of those wet clothes."

"I don't have much choice. This isn't over until we catch him." She was wringing the water out of her hair. "I'm fine."

"You were almost dead," Eve said bluntly. "I was scared to death. Joe couldn't get a bead on him without shooting you. He was swearing a blue streak when he missed that shot at him before the bastard dove into the water."

"He was quick, damn quick." She took off her black shirt and wrung it out. "And he must have a high tolerance for pain the way he tore that knife out of his hand. Gallo said it was adrenaline."

"Maybe." Eve's tone was absent. "You almost died, Catherine. But Gallo came to the rescue." She paused. "I was wondering where he was."

"I was too busy to wonder. And I'm the only one who is responsible for me. Where's that dagger . . ." She was looking on the ground for the dagger her attacker had dropped when Gallo's bowie knife had pierced his hand. "There it is. We don't have to worry about prints. He was wearing the gloves to his wet suit." She picked it up and examined it. "Nothing unusual about it. Commonly used by sportsmen, undersea explorers, and scientists." She smiled at Eve. "I'd bet Joe might have even used one like it when he was a SEAL."

"You'll have to ask him." She was staring at the knife. "The one sticking in Jacobs's chest was much bigger and more vicious-looking."

"This is for utilitarian use. It could be that one was for pleasure."

She shuddered. "Pleasure in murdering a helpless man?"

"Jacobs was afraid of him. At least, I guess it was him that he was raving about. He was afraid of someone. It was what he expected." She frowned. "But it wasn't what we expected. I thought we'd get Jacobs to talk."

"But we might be able to get prints from the truck," Eve said as she turned to the vehicle. "That's more likely." She went around in back of the truck. "Louisiana license plates."

"And I'd bet the truck was stolen." Catherine started forward, then stopped. "I want a forensic team. He was too careful, too good. If he left any evidence, it will be minimal, and I want to have every chance of retrieving it." She turned and dropped on the ground and crossed her legs. "So I suppose we patiently wait until Gallo or Joe brings him back to us."

"Patiently?" Eve dropped down beside her. "That's not like you. Why?"

"It's not like me. And usually it's not like you. But for some reason, you're thinking that's not going to happen. You think that

61

we're not going to get him. I knew it the moment I saw you standing, waiting on the bank."

"Why would you think that?"

"You would have gone with Joe. Why would you have been waiting here for me?"

"I had to make sure you were safe." Eve was looking out at the bayou. "I wanted to know that he wouldn't find and kill you out there. I had to make sure it was over."

"Over? It's not over, Eve. We haven't got him yet."

"But he didn't kill you. I was sure he was going to." She moistened her lips. "I was sure that you were the one. But I was wrong, she must have been sad for Jacobs's death."

"She?" Then she shook her head. She didn't need this right now. She had been shocked when she had learned that Eve believed she was communicating with her deceased daughter. She couldn't understand how a woman as sharp and reasonable as Eve could be delusional. "Bonnie? Eve, I can't handle talking about Bonnie's ghost at the moment. I don't want to insult you by arguing how improbable that is, but I'm too practical not to think that you're fooling yourself."

"I don't want to argue. You have to think

what you have to think. I just answered you. Bonnie knew someone was going to die today, and she was sad about it." She reached out and touched Catherine's arm. "I'm glad it wasn't you."

"And now you think that the threat is over? I suppose she whispered in your ear?"

Eve smiled faintly. "No, did she whisper in yours? I think perhaps she did."

Catherine frowned. "What the hell do you mean?"

"You say I was acting out of character when I didn't go with Joe. But why weren't you chomping at the bit to get back in the water to keep after Jacobs's killer? That's very unusual behavior for you. You're utterly relentless when you have a target in mind."

"You believe I gave up the hunt." Catherine's eyes narrowed on her expression. "I'm interested in why you'd think I'd do that."

"Because you realized that it wasn't the right time, that you weren't going to catch him." She didn't look away from the fog-wreathed bayou. "So why not give in to your concern for Joe and leave Gallo to chase that killer."

"It's not the right time? You're being too weird, Eve."

"Maybe," she said thoughtfully. "But I've

been thinking lately that all of this is like unrolling some kind of ancient scroll. We see a little bit, but not the entire story. And no matter how hard we try, we're not going to be able to finish it until she's ready for it to be finished."

"Well, you'll have to ask her to forgive me, but I intend to unroll the whole shebang according to my schedule and not hers." She got to her feet and crossed to the edge of the bank. "Where the hell is Gallo?"

"But you haven't really been worrying about him since you got back, have you?"

No, she hadn't, Catherine realized. She had been worried about the gators, not the possibility of his encountering Jacobs's killer. "He can take care of himself."

Eve smiled faintly. "And it's over for the time being. Until next time."

"Bonnie's crystal ball again?"

"Call it what you like. I think it's closer to the concept of faith."

"And that scroll you spoke about gets unrolled a little bit more?" She turned to look at Eve. "Well, I've been thinking of a way to jump-start it. Did you and Joe get a good look at that bastard when he was attacking me?"

Eve shook her head. "He was directly behind you until he actually pounced. He was tall, very thin, and his stride was . . . springy."

"His face?"

"No, as I said, he was behind you. And when he attacked, he was bent over you. I couldn't see his features."

"Joe?"

"We can ask him. He had a different angle than I did when he got off the shot. He might have seen his face."

"I hope he did. I had a full view of his features for just an instant or two. It would be good if I had another witness to corroborate my take on him. Gallo was in the bayou, close enough to throw that knife. He probably had a good chance to see him," Catherine said. "You've been trained in police sketching as part of your training, Eve. Can we try to get a recognizable sketch of this guy?"

She nodded. "Since you think that fingerprints aren't very likely, it would be one of our only options. But it had better be soon. Memory fades in an amazingly short time."

"I've been trained in memory retention for debriefing situations," Catherine said. "I'll concentrate and get a picture that will hopefully stay with me."

"Anything remarkable about him?"

A tan face, pulled tight by the hood of the

wet suit. Bushy dark brows flecked with gray. Remarkable? There was something unusual, but it was eluding her at the moment. "I'll have to think about it. Maybe it will come to me . . ."

The fog was growing thicker again, she noticed. Gallo wouldn't be able to see anything. Why didn't he give up? She hadn't been concerned before about Gallo, but now she was beginning to feel uneasy. There was no reason for it. It was probably caused by all of Eve's talk about scrolls and Bonnie, and that other stuff that was pure mysticism.

But she wished Gallo would come back.

He should turn back, Gallo thought as he paused to listen for the hundredth time. He'd been out here for at least ninety minutes, and it had been a futile effort.

How had he gotten away?

He knew the answer.

He was sharp and experienced as he'd always been, and never without an emergency escape plan.

Give it up and go back to shore.

Not yet. He would give it a little longer.

Wait. He heard something.

A motorboat!

He turned in the water and swam in the

direction from which he'd heard the sound of the motor.

The second line of defense for the escape plan.

Get to him before he got away.

If he didn't catch him now, the hunt would go on.

And it would lead Gallo straight to hell.

"Is Catherine okay?" Joe asked, when Eve picked up his call.

"Yes, she came back to the shore not long after you left. But Gallo is still out in the bayou."

"I'm not worried about Gallo. I just wanted to be sure that Catherine hadn't been hurt."

"I take it you didn't see him?"

"I think we've lost him. I've been going up and down this road for hours, with no sign of him. But a while ago, I heard the sound of a motorboat in one of the inlets. He might have had a boat stashed there."

"It's possible." She glanced at the truck. "But it would seem like overkill. If he followed her from the casino, it would take some fast scrambling to set up a backup like that."

"Or someone very practiced in a maneuver like this. I'm on my way back. I should see you in about ten minutes." He hung up.

She turned to Catherine. "He thinks that we've lost him. Maybe a motorboat in the inlet."

"It took Joe long enough to give up searching," Catherine said. "I notice you didn't discuss your theory about the ever-unfurling scroll with him. You could have saved him some time." Then she made a face. "Sorry, I didn't mean to be sarcastic. I just have problems with the idea of fate dictating our lives. I believe we mold our own lives, our own fates, and if we work hard enough, we can make a success of things. I thought you believed that, too."

"I do," Eve said. "But there appear to be some things that are out of our control. I found that out years ago, when I lost Bonnie. After that, I discovered damage control and to work with what I was given."

"A ghost?"

Eve slowly nodded. "I don't expect you to accept the idea. It took me years to come to terms with it."

"Eve . . ." Catherine reached out and took her hand. "I admire you, I trust you, I believe in you. I just can't believe in this particular."

"You didn't believe that Gallo was innocent of Bonnie's death at first. But now you're willing to fight for him." She smiled. "And that's a good sign for an eventual understanding."

"Don't count on it. We'll just agree to disagree. I can't promise that I'll ever —" She broke off and whirled toward the bayou. "I heard something."

Eve did, too. And the next moment, she saw Gallo stand up in the shallow water and wade toward the bank. She felt a rush of relief. He looked tired and discouraged, but he wasn't hurt.

"No sign of him?" she asked as he levered himself out of the water.

"No. He got away."

"Joe said he heard a motorboat in the inlet," Catherine said. "Did you?"

"Yes," he said. "Where's Quinn?"

"He'll be here in a few minutes. He just called."

"Good, I want to get back to the house."

"You said you heard the motorboat. Did you see him?"

"Yes, but he was halfway across the bayou, then he was lost in the fog." He glanced at the truck. "Have you searched it?"

Catherine shook her head. "No, I called Venable, and he's going to arrange to get a forensic detail out here. Though I don't know what our chances are of getting prints."

"Nil," he said flatly. "Maybe trace evidence."

"You seem very certain," Eve said.

"Do I?" He got to his feet. "As certain as I can be under the circumstances. I'd judge he wouldn't leave a trail."

"We may not be able to ID him from prints, but Catherine saw him. I may be able to do a sketch from her description. Could you help? Did you get a good look at his face?"

"No, sorry. You think there's a good possibility that you'll be able to get a close enough resemblance?" He glanced at Catherine. "You'll remember him?"

"I'll remember him," she said quietly.

He looked away from her face, and his gaze traveled up and down her body. "You look almost dry."

She shrugged. "I took my clothes off and wrung them out. You should do the same."

He shook his head. "I'll change when I get back to the house." He turned his head toward the road. "I think I hear Quinn."

Eve nodded as the car came around the bend of the road. "That's Joe." She watched Joe park on the side of the road and called to him as he walked down the slope toward the bank. "Gallo heard the motorboat, too, Joe, but it was moving out of sight when he got to the inlet."

"That's convenient."

Gallo stiffened. "Is that supposed to mean something?"

"He saved Catherine's life, Joe," Eve said quietly. "I think we can do without antagonism and accusations."

"Yes, he saved her life." Joe's gaze met Gallo's. "But why did he wait until he had to target the hand instead of another part of the body? That was an incredibly difficult throw. If he'd missed, it could have been all over for Catherine."

"Perhaps he'd just arrived on the scene," Catherine said. "Gallo wouldn't have deliberately chosen to —"

"Gallo was standing in the water watching his approach," Joe said flatly. "I saw him while I was moving in the brush to take my shot. He was watching, not moving, not lifting his knife. He acted as if he were frozen."

"I took him out," Gallo said.

"Barely," Joe said. "A knife between the shoulder blades would have been a hell of a lot more efficient."

"And would have run the risk of leaving him dead and unable to be questioned. Ask Eve how she would feel about that."

"You're saying that you deliberately risked Catherine on the altar of leaving that killer alive to tell us what we need to know." Joe shook his head. "I don't think so. I think you had another agenda."

"And that would be?"

"I don't know yet." He paused. "Of course, you could have been going to let Catherine be killed, but when you saw me on the bank, you decided you had to make a token effort."

"No way," Catherine said. "You're reaching, Joe."

Joe's gaze never left Gallo's face. "But you still left that bastard alive and able to escape. Then you stayed in the bayou for hours, supposedly searching for him, but came up empty. Even when you were close enough to that inlet to hear the motorboat. A picture seems to be emerging. I'm wondering why you would do all that."

"Keep wondering." Gallo turned away and moved toward the trees. "I'm not defending myself to you, Quinn. I'll see you all back at the house."

"Get in the car, Gallo," Catherine said. "I've been through that brush. It's hell on bare feet."

But Gallo had already disappeared into the palmetto shrubs.

"Okay." Catherine turned to Joe. "You're saying that Gallo didn't want Jacobs's killer caught. Why? Are you still thinking that Gallo had something to do with Bonnie's death? That maybe he didn't kill Jacobs himself but he had an accomplice do it?"

"It's a possibility."

"Bullshit."

"It's not bullshit until I find out why Gallo didn't throw that knife when he had a better chance of taking out his target." He turned away and started up the slope. "And I don't regard any argument you can give me as credible."

She stared at him. "Why the hell not?"

He looked back over his shoulder. "You're being emotional. You're not thinking as clearly as you usually do."

"He made the throw. He saved my life. I was with him in that house, and I know he didn't set Jacobs up to be butchered."

Joe didn't answer as he got into the driver's seat.

Eve could sense the frustration Catherine was feeling. She was feeling a similar frustration, mixed with uneasiness. Yes, Joe's suspicion could be based on his history of distrust of Gallo. But Joe was smart and cool and seldom let anything interfere with his logic. "Come on." She took Catherine's

73

arm and nudged her toward the slope. "Get in the car. I don't want you getting angry and stomping off into the brush like Gallo. After looking at the soles of your feet while we were sitting on the bank, I'm surprised you can walk."

"I'm all right." Catherine started up the slope. "But I won't let Joe make me pissed off enough to hike back." She added through set teeth, "I'm not credible? I'm too emotional? Screw him."

"He used the wrong words," Eve said.

"You bet he did."

"But you wouldn't be this upset if you didn't think that there was some truth in what he said."

Catherine's gaze flew to her face. "Do you believe Gallo was going to let me die?"

"No." She smiled. "But I'm emotional, too. I don't think nearly as logically as Joe. As we've already discussed, sometimes gray seems white to me." Her smile faded. "And there may be a good deal of gray in this scenario. Gallo may not be pitch-black, but he could be bordering on charcoal."

Catherine shook her head. "He saved my life. He wouldn't have let me be murdered." She got into the backseat of the car. "And that's not an emotional judgment."

"No," Eve said as she climbed into the

passenger seat. "It's more like faith."

"How are your feet?" Gallo stood in the doorway of the kitchen, his gaze on Catherine, who was sitting in a chair by the stove, her bare feet soaking in a pan of warm water. "I'm glad you're taking care of them. Salt water?"

"Yes." She met his gaze across the room. "I always take care of myself."

His lips twisted. "Quinn wouldn't agree with you."

"Joe thinks I'm 'emotional.'" She looked at his feet, encased in boots. "You tore your feet up, too, didn't you?"

"Yes."

"You deserve it. You were stupid. I had no choice. But you could have just kept quiet and let yourself be driven back to the house." She sloshed her feet in the water. "Did you bandage your feet before you put on those boots?"

"Yes, I take care of myself, too." He came toward her. "Where are Quinn and Eve?"

"They're calling Jane MacGuire. Eve promised to keep in touch with her."

"And Eve always keeps her promises." He took the towel draped over the chair next to Catherine's. "Did you call Venable again?"

"No, but he called me and said he's on

his way here. He asked a favor of New Orleans Police Department, and the forensic team should be here anytime to check out that truck."

"He's moving fast." He fell to his knees, took her left foot out of the water, and enveloped it in the towel. "It's not that urgent, is it? Not to the CIA."

"No. And Venable has no real reason to come down here. He knows I can take care of it. Which means that he has another reason to move in."

"You're obviously valuable to him." He was gently patting her foot dry. "He wants to make sure nothing happens to you."

His hands were warm through the terry of the towel, and his position at her feet and the action itself were unbearably intimate. She felt a rush of heat go through her.

Not now. The searing sensuality was unexpected, and she felt the tensing that was now familiar. Pull away from him.

She didn't move. She watched him slowly move the terry over her foot. Each stroke was causing her to tense, the blood to rush beneath the skin at his touch. "Venable isn't that protective. He wants something."

"What?" He placed her foot on the floor and lifted her other foot from the water. He began to dry the top, then cradled it in the towel. "You have beautiful feet."

"No feet are beautiful. Some of them are just not ugly."

"You're wrong." His hands tightened around her foot, his eyes focused on the towel. "I never dreamed I had a foot fetish. I keep thinking where I'd like to put —" He drew a deep breath. "That's not where I meant this to go." He began to dry her foot again. "I'm constantly becoming distracted when I'm around you."

"Where did you mean it to go?" she asked unevenly. "I'm curious to know, Gallo."

"I wanted to tell —" He lifted his gaze to meet her eyes. "I never wanted him to kill you, Catherine. No matter what Quinn says, I'd never do that. You trusted me when no one else did, when I didn't even have faith in myself. I was planning on taking him out earlier. I thought I'd have time. But then everything went to hell."

"Why?"

"I wasn't expecting him —" He broke off and threw the towel aside. "Shit." He jumped to his feet. "I never meant it to be that close, Catherine. But I had to target his hand. I tried, but I couldn't do anything —" He was striding to the door. "But I wouldn't have let him hurt you. I couldn't stand that either." He looked at her over his shoulder, and she was shocked at the torment she saw on his face. "That damn Quinn was right about almost everything else, but he was wrong about that. Believe me, Catherine."

Before she could answer, he was gone.

She collapsed back in the chair and drew a shaky breath. She felt vulnerable and hot and bewildered. Those moments with Gallo had been explosive, and she had not come out well. She had responded, not been aggressive. She had not been in control. She should have asked him questions instead of trying to puzzle him out and being swayed by what he was clearly feeling.

What she was feeling.

Dammit, she'd have to go after him and make him —

She heard the sound of a car starting outside.

"No!" She jumped to her feet and ran out of the kitchen, down the hall, and threw open the front door.

Gallo was already driving the car out of the driveway and toward the road.

"Gallo!"

He didn't answer, and, the next moment, the car disappeared around the curve of the road.

"Catherine?" Eve was behind her. "What's

wrong?"

Catherine threw her arm out toward the road. "That's what's wrong. He's gone. He took off."

"Gallo?" Joe said as he came out of the living room.

"Who else? Did he say good-bye? Did he explain more than muttering a lot of disjointed garbage? No." She went back to the kitchen, tossed the water from the pan out the door, and sat down. She glared at Eve and Joe, who had followed her from the front door. "But he's not going to get away with it. I'm going to go after him." She opened the first-aid kit she'd set out in readiness to bandage the cuts on her feet. "But first we're going to find out everything we can put together about the man who killed Jacobs. Dammit, Jacobs was scared because he knew who killed Bonnie. I *know* it. If we'd had just a little more time, we'd have made him tell us everything. It had to be that man we lost in the bayou. We're close, Eve."

"But Gallo may be closer."

"Not for long, dammit," she said through clenched teeth.

79

CHAPTER
4

"Let me help you with those bandages." Eve knelt by Catherine's chair and lifted her foot. "Those cuts look more annoying than serious." She used the antiseptic, then laid it down again. "Though you shouldn't have run after Gallo. We have to cleanse them again."

"I can do this." Catherine ran her fingers through her hair. "Everyone is treating me like an invalid. Gallo was —" She drew a deep breath. "Thanks, Eve. I'm a little upset."

She was more than a little upset, Eve thought. Catherine valued her professional coolness, and she was not displaying that quality at the moment. Who could blame her? Eve was upset as well. Joe's accusations had been very disturbing. "Just what did Gallo say to you?"

"I told you, no explanations." She paused, watching Eve cleanse the cuts. "All he said is that he never meant me to be hurt. I believed him."

"I saw his face," Joe said from where he stood in the doorway. "And he could have thrown that knife before he did. Why are you being so stubborn?"

"Because I saw his face, too," Catherine said. "Five minutes ago, when he told me that you were wrong and that he never meant me to be killed. I've got to go with what I think and feel." She looked down at Eve. "But I believe Joe when he said that he could have thrown that knife before he did. Joe doesn't make mistakes like that. And Gallo's behavior is definitely suspect since he's acting as weird as hell." Her glance shifted to Joe. "We just have to figure out why he's behaving like that."

"Give me a few minutes alone with him, and we won't have to bother figuring out anything."

"We'd have to catch him to let you talk to him," Eve said. "And maybe that's why he took off. He didn't want to cause any conflict."

"Really?" Joe's tone was skeptical. "I've never noticed he's particularly peace-loving." But he was studying Eve's expression. "Are you weighing in with Catherine on this?"

"I'm trying to get to the bottom of what Gallo is up to. You can't both be wrong. Since I trust both of you, there has to be a middle ground." She finished bandaging Catherine's feet and stood up. "And the middle ground has to have something to do with the man who killed Thomas Jacobs. Let's start with him. Appearance. I caught only a fleeting glimpse. You said that you thought that you could give me a good enough description of his face for me to do a sketch, Catherine. We'll leave that for later. He was thin, very thin. That's my sole contribution."

"And tall," Joe said. "I couldn't tell anything about his hair because it was covered by the hood of the wet suit. But he moved like an athlete, smooth, coordinated."

"Age?" Eve asked.

Joe shrugged. "Not close enough."

"Catherine?"

"Fifty, maybe." Catherine frowned. "I'm not sure. There was something . . ."

"It may come back to you when we start the sketch."

"Possible."

"Now, motive?"

"He didn't want Jacobs to talk to us. Jacobs was definitely afraid of someone. He thought he'd be killed if he talked. He told us that he wouldn't have a chance."

"Talked about what?" Eve asked.

"How the hell do I know? Bonnie's death? What else could it be?" Catherine began to put on her socks and boots. "But we'd better start that sketch right away. I want to find that killer before Gallo does, and he has a head start."

"Because you think Joe is right, and Gallo knew Jacobs's killer," she asked quietly.

Catherine nodded. "But that doesn't mean he hired him to kill Jacobs. That didn't happen, Eve."

"It better not," Eve said. "I want to give Gallo a chance, but if he was an accomplice in killing Jacobs, then that means everything he told me about dreaming about Bonnie while he was in that prison in North Korea was a lie. I was so damned touched when he said that dreams of her kept him alive." Her lips tightened. "If it wasn't true, that would mean I was a fool to think that he loved my daughter."

"I can't guarantee that anything he told you about Bonnie was true. Everything to do with Bonnie is strictly between the two of you." Catherine made a face. "I'm limiting my investigating to things that can be proved." She shifted her glance to Joe. "I've been told that I'm in the minority. I found it hard to believe that you were consorting with ghosts, Joe."

"You have no idea." Joe smiled faintly. "Someday, I'll sit down and tell you a few tales that will cause your hair to curl." His smile faded. "Don't be too committed to reality, Catherine. It can trip you up."

"I'm clinging to it with both hands. It's comforting. Now, Eve, where do we get a sketch pad for you?"

"We don't. But I have a loose-leaf notebook in my bag that I can use. It's in the trunk of the car. I can make do with a regular pencil."

"I'll go get it." Joe turned and moved toward the door. "I'll be back in a — I hear a car." He threw open the door. "I think the local sheriff's department is here."

Eve followed him and saw the two white cars with the Jefferson Parish Sheriff's Department on the side drawing up before the house. "Venable got them here fast."

"But I don't want them coming in and finding Jacobs's body," Joe said. "That would prove awkward."

"Awkward?" Catherine joined them at the door. "Yes, I think that would be a little awkward. Venable should be here soon with a CIA crew to do cleanup. Those cops were only told to do the forensic work that we

84

wanted done on the truck."

"Then I'll keep them away from the house." Joe moved toward the two police cars. "I'll take them down the road to the Chevy."

Eve and Catherine watched as he greeted the officers with smooth, friendly authority. A few minutes later he got into one of the patrol cars, and the two sheriff's cars moved down the road.

"That's going to take a while. We might as well get started." Eve pulled out the keys and moved toward the rental car. She paused after she'd unlocked the trunk to look out at the bayou. "The fog is almost gone. Why couldn't this have happened a few hours ago? It would have made every-thing so much easier."

"You mean you don't have a metaphysical reason for the fog, too?" Catherine shook her head. "I'll shut up. I know this was dif-ficult for you to share, and you don't need me giving you a hard time."

"It doesn't matter." She took the notebook out of the trunk and slammed it. "Actually, you took it better than I would have thought." She glanced at Catherine. "And you're under a strain that tends to exagger-ate every emotion."

"And you're not?"

"Oh, yes. But it's buried deep and just waiting to break free. I guarantee that you'll know it when it does." She turned toward the house. "Now let's get this sketch started."

"That's all that we can do before we haul the truck into the pound," Detective Pierre Julian said to Joe. His words were spoken with professional courtesy, but the accent was pure Cajun. "Would you like us to do anything else? My captain said we were to cooperate with you in any way we could."

"No, you've been very thorough." It was true: Julian had gotten down to business as soon as they had reached the truck. His forensic team had swarmed all over it, but the investigation had still been done with great care. "I couldn't have asked for a better team in Atlanta. You seem to have a hell of a lot of experience."

"You think Atlanta's the only place that can deal with crime?" Julian asked. "They may call New Orleans the Big Easy, but if we didn't protect our city, the tourists wouldn't find us that easy to come and visit." He paused. "But we're not used to calls from the CIA. Is this guy supposed to be a terrorist or something?"

"Or something."

Julian shrugged. "Bad news. We've got to stop those creeps. I hear Homeland Security thinks they're just walking over the Mexican border. You want me to take you back to the house?"

Joe started to nod, then shook his head. "Is there somewhere around here that someone could get his hands on scuba equipment or underwater apparatus?"

Julian frowned. "Around here?"

"Maybe on the road from New Orleans to the house I rented. It would have to be fairly close to the house." Catherine and Gallo had been followed to the house, then Jacobs's murderer would have had to backtrack a relatively short distance to pick up that wet suit and equipment and get back in time to commit the murder. "Fifteen or twenty minutes?"

Julian shook his head. "No scuba-rental places. No call for it around here." He grinned. "No one wants to go into the swamps and swim with the alligators. The tourists want to see them, not play with them."

"I can understand that," Joe said. "Okay, no rental places. What about a place that would need that kind of equipment for maintenance of their facility? Is there a fishing sanctuary or a pelican —"

Julian snapped his fingers. "An alligator farm. There's an alligator tourist attraction about fifteen miles back. I guess they'd have to use that kind of scuba stuff every now and then. Is that what you're looking for?"

"It could be," Joe said. "Can we go there and ask some questions?"

"Sure. Should I send the team back to the city?"

"No, have them come with us." He wasn't optimistic about the chance of getting evidence from the truck, but it might be a different matter at the alligator farm. The bastard would have been in a hurry if he was trying to steal equipment and get back to the house. He was beginning to feel a tingle of hope as he turned toward the sheriff's car. "What's the name of this place?"

"Bubba's Alligator Farm."

"Bubba?"

Julian shrugged. "The tourists probably like it. They're always looking for flavor. We give it to them." He got into the driver's seat. "You guys in Atlanta give them plantations and ladies with hoop skirts. We give them Bubba's alligators. But only from a decent distance. . . ."

The sign above the wooden arch of the gates

88

around the huge dirty brown pond was inscribed with bold, red letters.

Bubba's Alligator Farm
Bring the Kids
Come Feed the Prehistoric Monsters

"You can't say that Bubba isn't appealing to the basest instincts," Joe murmured, as they drove under the arch. "And he should be a little clearer. Does he want to bring the kids to feed the alligators?"

"Good point. But you're not being fair," Detective Julian said. "Alligators are throwbacks to prehistoric times. Maybe he's trying to educate the kids."

"Yeah, sure." Joe was glancing around the grounds. All of the alligators appeared to be clustered at the far end of the brown-green pond. Other than a long pier jutting out over the pond, Bubba's farm appeared to consist of three refreshment stands, a gift shop, and a butcher shop sporting the sign with a beefsteak. *Fresh alligator meat.* "And would you let your kids go out on that pier and throw beefsteaks to the alligators?"

"I don't have any kids." He looked at the pier, which had only a slender cord on one side. "Nah, not a good idea. Maybe we'd better have a talk with Bubba."

"After we talk to him about the scuba equipment. Where the hell is he? The place is deserted."

"What are you cops doing here?" A truck had been driven through the gates behind them, and a bald man had stuck his head out the window. "I've got a license. You've got nothing on me. Has the Department of Environmental Quality been complaining? I treat my gators good."

"No one's been complaining," Julian said. "Though I'm beginning to wonder why not. Are you the proprietor of this business?"

"I'm Bubba Grant." The bald man got out of the truck. "Yeah, I own the farm. I'm just trying to make a living like everyone else. A man tries to get ahead, and all of a sudden the cops are down on him."

"I'm Detective Julian. This is Detective Quinn. We have a few questions to ask you."

"I treat my gators good. They're better off than they would be in the swamp."

"Do you use any underwater scuba equipment?" Joe asked.

"Are you crazy? I don't let anyone in the water with the gators. Do you know what that would do to my insurance?"

"Do you have any underwater equipment you use for maintenance? What about when you have an injured alligator or you need to remove harmful debris from your pond?"

"Naturally, I keep my gators safe."

"So you do have underwater equipment."

"A suit, a speargun and some spears." He added quickly, "But I'd never use them on the gators if I could help it. Only self-defense. Maybe to save a kid who fell off the pier in the water or something like that."

"I'm impressed by your humanity," Joe said ironically. "May I see the equipment?"

"Sure. It's in the storeroom behind the gift shop. I've got nothing to hide." He moved toward the shops. "Is this some new rule the DEQ has come up with? Do you want to talk to any of my people? You'll have to wait for a couple hours. We don't open until noon, and no one shows up until the last minute. You can't get good help these days."

"Why noon?" Julian asked.

"The gators have got to be hungry, or they don't put on a good show. They won't come near the pier. People like a little thrill, you know?" They had reached the gift shop, and he pulled out his key, then stopped. "What the hell?"

The jamb of the door was splintered, and the door was slightly ajar.

Bubba was cursing as he pushed the door open. "I've been robbed!" He ran to the cash register and checked it. "The son of a bitches thought I'd leave money in here? I'm no dope." He glanced around the shop and frowned. "I don't see anything missing."

"The underwater equipment," Joe prodded.

"Oh, yeah." Bubba ran to a door and threw it open. "It's gone. Who told you that I'd been robbed? Have you got the stuff? Do I have to identify it?"

"Not until we find it." Joe was kneeling on the floor, examining a stain. "Get the forensic team in here, Julian."

"Blood?" Julian nodded as he checked out the stain. "Our man could have done it on one of the spears."

"If it's his blood." Joe glanced around the room. "Overturned stool a few yards away. Could have been a struggle." He turned to Bubba. "You said no employees were on the premises last night or early this morning?"

"I didn't say that. I said no one was here now. Gil Weber is caretaker and leaves about eight in the morning." He was looking at the blood. "Gil's an ex-Marine. I wouldn't have hired him to guard the place if he couldn't take care of himself." Bubba took out his phone. "I'll call and see if he saw anything." He hung up a few minutes later.

"No answer. But maybe he's asleep. He works all night. That blood can't be his. If he was hurt, there would be a trail of it, wouldn't there? Just a couple drops, then he's gone?"

"Maybe." Joe turned and left the shop. He stood there and stared thoughtfully out at the muddy pond. He glanced at Bubba, who had scurried after him. "Tell me, is it common for your prehistoric friends to cluster all together like that?"

"No, they generally like their own space. They have to have a reason. Why are you —" Bubba's eyes widened in his suddenly pale face. "Oh, shit."

"Joe's back." Eve laid down her pencil and went to the window to watch Joe get out of the sheriff's car and bend forward to talk to the dark-haired young man in the driver's seat. "It's been a couple hours. I thought that he'd be here sooner."

"He might as well have been here," Catherine said ruefully. "We haven't gotten far in this sketch."

"We've determined shape of the face and the nose," Eve said. "That's important. That scuba hood is messing things up. It's very tight and completely hides the hair. Even the hairline would be helpful. Whether it's receding or full. He could even have a widow's peak. You couldn't tell anything about that part of his face."

"I thought I'd be more helpful," Catherine said with frustration.

"You will be," Eve said. "You're distracted. You want it too much."

"Yes, I do. I want it *now.*" Catherine looked at Joe as he came into the house, and she asked, "What's the word? Do they think they're going to get prints?"

"They have prints, but they probably belong to the eighteen-year-old kid he stole the truck from in New Orleans."

"Damn," Eve said.

"But we may still have his fingerprints," Joe said grimly. "He grabbed that motorboat, a wet suit, and a tank from an alligator farm about fifteen miles from here. The equipment was in the equipment room in the back of the gift shop. He broke in and stole a few knives, a speargun, and the suit." He paused. "Evidently the caretaker, Gil Weber, surprised him at it and they struggled, and he apparently knocked him out, then tossed him in the alligator pond."

Eve shuddered. "Dead?"

"He didn't have a chance. I hope he drowned before the gators got to him."

"So he'd already killed before he even

tried to get Jacobs," Catherine said.

"Probably unintentional," Joe said. "But he didn't hesitate when he was discovered." He frowned thoughtfully. "He thinks very fast and follows through. When he found out where his target was going to be, he examined his surroundings and pulled together a plan that would allow him to kill Jacobs and give him his best chance to survive and escape. He must have caught a glimpse of that alligator farm on the way here, and everything clicked in his mind."

"I didn't even notice the alligator farm," Catherine said.

"But you were looking for the house and nothing else. The fog was heavy and drifting in and out." Joe looked at Eve. "Eve and I didn't pay any attention to it when we came here either. We were . . . distracted. The man who killed Jacobs wasn't distracted. He had a purpose and was looking for a way to accomplish it."

"Formidable," Catherine said slowly.

"Yes," Joe said, gazing at Catherine. "And with all the signs of a professional."

"I agree," Catherine said. "But that doesn't mean he was hired by Gallo."

"It doesn't mean he wasn't." Joe glanced at the notebook on the table. "Any luck?"

"Not yet."

"Really?"

"I'm trying, Joe," Catherine said between her teeth. "I'll get there."

"I'm sure you will. But I don't want to wait for it." He turned back to Eve. "Julian is going to take me into New Orleans. I'm going to see if I can push them to get the results from forensics. Do you want to go with me?"

"No, I want to finish the sketch first. I'll follow you when I'm done." She nodded at Catherine. "And Venable is supposed to be here anytime with a crew to take care of Jacobs. Catherine is going to have to see Venable. She said he's been very insistent."

"Whatever you say." Joe brushed a kiss across Eve's forehead. "Call me when you're on your way. I'll let you know if I can accelerate the processing of that forensic report." He headed for the door. "And, if you hear from Gallo, I want to know about it."

Eve waited until the door closed behind him before she turned back to Catherine. "Let's get back to it." She picked up the notebook and dropped down in a chair beside the window. "What about the lips?"

"Wide." Catherine thought about it. "No, a full bottom lip, but his upper lip was thinner. And the left side was a little crooked."

"Crooked?"

"Not really crooked. Just not the same shape as the right. Is that strange?"

"No, few people are born with perfectly balanced features. Some differences are more noticeable than others." She sketched in a mouth and turned the notebook around. "Like this?"

Catherine shook her head. "Fuller lower lip." She sat back and watched Eve make the change. "This is a painstaking business, isn't it? It's a lot different than those computer age progressions you did for me when I was searching for Luke." Memories flooded back to Catherine of sitting beside Eve in front of the computer at her lake house and seeing the photo of her two-year-old son slowly become transformed into the picture of the eleven-year-old he was today. It had been a painful yet poignantly rewarding journey they'd taken together. And the journey to rescue him from his kidnapper had been equally rewarding. She had gotten back her son, and she had found a friendship with Eve that was beyond price. "How accurate is this sketching business?"

"You tell me. You have as much say in it as I do. More."

"Have you done much of this?"

She shook her head. "When I was in college, I did sketching for a photographer, and after I became a forensic sculptor, I occasionally did sketches for the police department. I'm okay at it, but I'm not as good as the usual police artists. You have to know just what questions to ask and take it from A to Z." She smiled at Catherine. "So stop blaming yourself. It's my fault, too, that this isn't going as quickly as it might."

"Joe thought I was stalling."

"Joe doesn't know what to think," Eve said. "It's not that he doesn't trust you."

"Yeah? He doesn't trust Gallo, and he's tossing me into the same camp."

Eve couldn't deny it. "You have to admit that the strength of your support of Gallo is a little strange. He thinks Gallo has managed to exert an influence on you that isn't logical . . . or professional."

Catherine made a face. "He thinks Gallo is some kind of Rasputin?" She stared Eve in the eye. "And what do you think, Eve?"

"I'm the wrong person to ask." She looked back down at the sketch. "I know that some people have a magnetism that is a virtual knockout punch. I believe Gallo is one of them. Why else would I have jumped into bed with him when I was only sixteen? I wasn't stupid or careless, and yet I was both with him. For God's sake, I was in such a fever that I risked getting pregnant."

"And that's one of the reasons Joe has problems with Gallo," Catherine said. "He still sees him as a threat."

"He shouldn't. Gallo was in my past. He doesn't exist in my future." She looked up at Catherine. "Joe is everything to me. You know that."

"But Gallo was the father of your child. There has to be some kind of bond."

Eve nodded. "I can't deny that there is. That's why I wanted desperately for him not to have been Bonnie's killer." How could she explain it? She moistened her lips. "It's as if Bonnie . . . She's part of both of us. I think she loves both of us. Even though Gallo and I will never be together, I don't believe she'd want us to — She'd want that bond to be there." She smiled crookedly. "It's complicated, isn't it?"

"Particularly since you're still not sure that Gallo isn't involved with Bonnie's killing."

"I'm trying to think positive. Gallo isn't making it easy," she said. "Is he a victim or the Rasputin Joe thinks him? I've been going back and forth like a weather vane for the past weeks."

"So have I."

"But now you're defending him. You're in

his camp. You've been willing to fight Joe and me and the whole damn world for him. Why?"

"He didn't do it, Eve."

"Proof?"

"Dammit, he didn't do it."

"I want proof. I need proof, Catherine."

"I'll get it for you."

"You almost died because Gallo didn't throw his knife when he should have. Are you going to risk being put in that position again?"

"He didn't want me to be hurt."

"How can you be sure?" She gazed at Catherine's expression, then slowly nodded. "Poor Catherine. He's got you, hasn't he? Have you slept with him yet?"

Catherine's face flushed. "No, I have *not.* I wouldn't do that."

Eve smiled faintly. "That's what I said when I was sixteen. I had everything to lose and nothing to gain, but it didn't matter. I did it anyway."

"I'm not sixteen. You're my friend, and I got into this to help you. I'm a professional, and I'll do my job."

"I know you will. Look, I'm not angry or resentful because you're feeling the same attraction I felt for Gallo. I don't have the

100

right to be. I've moved on, and so has Gallo."

"I know that," Catherine said. "But you could resent my not doing my job in trying to find your daughter's killer." She paused and then burst out, "Okay, Gallo does — He makes me feel —" She tried again. "He does have an unusual effect on me." She finally said bluntly, "He turns me on. Maybe you're right, and he does have that kind of knockout effect on most women. But I'd never let that interfere. In spite of what Joe said, I wouldn't be emotional about it."

Eve suddenly smiled. "You're being emotional right now. If it wasn't about Gallo, I'd think it was healthy for you. You're usually too tough and cool. A little disturbance isn't that bad. Now let's get this sketch finished. Then I can tell Joe what an unemotional and crystal-clear professional you've been." She turned the notebook around. "Is this his mouth?"

Catherine nodded. "Very close. But his mouth appeared more taut. It was drawn back from his teeth."

"Like an attacking animal?"

"Yes."

"Good. That would change the contour of the face. It would make the cheekbones more prominent. We'll have to take that into account." She was sketching quickly. "Nose, mouth, eyebrows. We're getting there . . ."

"Chin."

"I told you, slightly pointed."

"But when I showed you pointed, you said it wasn't right. Think."

"It looked pointed."

"Then we must have the contour of the face wrong. Since his lips were drawn away from his teeth, maybe it caused the jaw to shift. Why don't we try a modified square?"

"Whatever. We've been at this over an hour, Eve. It's all blurring."

"It won't when we get it right." She showed her the sketch. "Modified square. Yes? No?"

Catherine straightened in the chair. "Yes."

"Chin, mouth, nose, eyebrows." Eve could feel the excitement growing. "Now we go for the eyes. Shape. Round? Oval? Slanted?"

"Not round. Oval, I think."

Eve's pencil was flying over the paper. "Big? Small? Medium?"

"Medium."

"Wide set?"

"No, ordinary."

"Color."

"Light. Gray, I think."

"Skin? Tan? Pale?"

"Sort of tan and weathered-looking."

"Any lines?"

"On either sides of his mouth. The rest of his face was smooth."

"Are you sure?"

"Yes, no. Wait. He was wearing that wet suit, and the rubber headpiece appeared very tight. It was pulling his face taut. I think I remember faint indentations around the corner of his eyes."

Eve quickly added the lines in a sunburst effect. "That looks more natural." She held the sketch up and gazed at it appraisingly. She said absently, "But he's older than —" She stopped, her eyes widening in stunned surprise.

Crazy. It couldn't be. Impossible.

"Eve?"

She shook her head to clear it. Impossible.

But anything was possible in this crazy world that had become her own.

Her hands were shaking as she turned the notebook and showed Catherine the sketch.

"Is this . . . him?"

Catherine's eyes widened. "My God."

CHAPTER
5

"Answer me." Eve tried to steady her voice. "Is this the man who tried to kill you?"

"Yes." Catherine took the notebook and gazed down at the sketch. "Congratulations. I had no idea you could come this close. It's *him*."

"You're absolutely sure?"

"I told you, it's him. That chin is the —" She broke off as she raised her eyes and saw Eve's expression. "What's wrong? You're pale as this notebook paper."

"I just have to make sure you're positive this is the man. I have to know that I didn't make him up out of some subconscious memory."

Catherine stiffened. "Memory?"

Eve took the sketch back and looked at it again. The eyes, the facial features, the brows were all the same. Only the deep wrinkles at the corners of the eyes and the ferocity that was imprinted in every line of that face was different.

"What memory, Eve?" Catherine asked. "You've seen this man before?"

"I think I have. But it doesn't make any sense."

"Who is it? Give me a name."

Eve shook her head. "But he's a dead man. Gallo told me that he was dead."

"Dammit, who is it?"

"His name is Ted Danner."

"And you've seen him before?"

Eve moistened her lips. "A long time ago. And only a couple times. He's John Gallo's uncle."

"What?"

"Ted Danner is Gallo's uncle. He was the reason John Gallo came to Atlanta. I would never have met Gallo, never had Bonnie, if it hadn't been for Ted Danner." She looked down at the sketch. "He was an ex-Ranger who had been injured in the Army. He had been sent down to the Veterans' Hospital in Atlanta from Milwaukee so that he could go to a specialist there. I remember that he could hardly walk."

"Then they must have performed a miracle," Catherine said dryly. "He moved like an Olympic athlete at that bayou this morning. Providing the athlete had all the instincts of a serial killer."

Eve shook her head in bewilderment. "I don't understand it. I liked Ted Danner. I felt sorry for him. Gallo told me that he was the only good thing in his life. Gallo grew up in the slums, as I did, and his parents abused him terribly. His uncle was the only bright spot in a pretty lousy life. He took him away on trips, interceded between him and his parents, taught him everything he knew about being a Ranger. That's why Gallo wanted to go into the service."

"And ended up in that prison in North Korea." She shook her head. "Look, this doesn't seem like it could be the same man. Could you be mistaken? You said you only saw him a couple times."

"That's right, the first time I saw him was when he came to see me months after John Gallo had left me and joined the Army. The other time was after Bonnie was born." Could she be mistaken? She had been only sixteen, and when you were young, you saw everything and everyone differently. A pregnant sixteen-year-old who was just trying to survive those months and get on with her life.

"There's a man downstairs who wants to talk to you," her neighbor, Rosa, said, when Eve opened the door. "I left him on my bench in the yard. Nice man. He said he'd come upstairs, but he has a bad back."

"Who is he? Salesman?"

"I don't think so." Rosa frowned. "He doesn't have that slick look. I didn't get his name. He sort of reminds me of someone."

"That's a help." She came out on the landing and started down the steps. "Look, Rosa, you were supposed to be studying with me this morning and not sitting with your baby on that bench."

"But he needs the sunshine."

"And you need your GED. And you're going to get it. I want you here tomorrow morning."

"Okay." She made a face as she leaned over the railing and called, "You didn't use to be so bossy. Your baby is going to come out of you cracking a whip."

Eve grinned as she opened the front door. "I'll take the chance. That will be two of us to nag you."

She was still smiling as she turned to the man sitting on the bench. "Hello, I'm Eve Duncan. What can —" She inhaled sharply.

He sort of reminds me of someone.

He was a thin man in his late forties or early fifties, with thinning gray-brown hair and olive skin and dark eyes.

John Gallo's eyes.

"How do you do? I'm Ted Danner." The man got to his feet with an effort. "I'm sorry to make

107

you come down. I just couldn't face those flights of stairs. John may have told you that I have back problems."

"You're his uncle Ted." She moistened her lips, trying to recover from the shock. "Yes, he said you injured it while you were in the service."

"I thought he'd tell you about me. We're very close." He smiled gently. "He's like my own son. He's a good boy."

"Why are you here?"

"He asked me to come."

Another shock. "What?"

"Well, actually, he asked me to keep an eye on you when he left for basic training. He said that I shouldn't approach you, that you'd resent it."

"But you're here."

"I tried to keep myself from coming. But I had to talk to you." He looked at the front of her maternity smock. "I saw you on the street three weeks ago, and I was . . . surprised. How far are you along?"

"Eight months."

"And it's John's child?"

"No, it's my child."

"But John fathered him?"

She nodded. "But you don't have to worry. I'm not going to claim him as the father." She paused. "I prefer he not know. You should agree to that. John said you were eager that he have a career in the military. A baby would just get in his way." Her lips tightened. "Don't tell him."

Ted Danner shook his head. "You poor child. You're so alone."

"The hell I am. I'm doing fine. Don't tell him."

"I don't have a choice at the moment. I can't write to him. I don't know where he is."

She stared at him, stunned. "What?"

"Right after basic and Ranger training, he was sent overseas. I heard from him from Tokyo right after he arrived, then nothing."

"That doesn't make sense. You have to be able to trace him. You're military yourself."

"Unless he volunteered for a special mission. John's smart and ambitious, and that would be a way for him to rise through the ranks."

"Just what you'd do," she said dully.

"That's what I've been telling myself." He shook his head. "It's different when it's someone else doing it." His voice was husky. "I love that boy."

She could see that he did. His eyes were moist, and his last words had been unsteady. "But you don't know anything for certain. He could be fine."

Ted nodded. "I've dropped from the radar any number of times, and here I am with nothing but a bad back. I've been doing a lot of praying lately." He stood up. "I thought you should know in case you wanted to do a little praying, too."

She was so stunned that she didn't know how she felt. It was hard for her to believe that the John Gallo she had known could be in any danger. "I'm sure that he'll be all right."

Ted Danner nodded. "I thought you should know. But don't worry too much. It wouldn't be good for you." He started down the walk toward the gate. "If I can do anything for you, let me know. It's the least I can do. John would want me to stand by you."

"You have your own problems. Your nephew would want you to take care of yourself."

"You're a good girl, Eve," he said quietly. "I can see why John cared about you."

She watched him walk stiffly down the street. Poor guy, he was really worried, and John was obviously all he had. But he was jumping the gun. She couldn't believe that John Gallo was dead just because he was temporarily missing. He was so young and strong and tough. Men like him weren't easily killed.

But perhaps, even though she couldn't believe he was truly in danger, she should still pray for the father of her child.

■ ■ ■ ■

Eve gazed in bewilderment at the sketch she'd just created from Catherine's words and description, shaking her head in stunned disbelief. Was she mistaken? It seemed impossible that that gentle, wounded man could be a vicious killer. "He's . . . older. But the age difference would be about right. But that's about all that would be the same except his appearance. The Danner I knew was close to being crippled. He was sensitive, caring. He was no killer."

"That argument doesn't hold water. If he was a Ranger, he was trained to kill," Catherine said.

"Joe was in the SEALs, you're CIA. You were both trained to kill. That doesn't mean you're both murderers."

"It means that we would pull the trigger if we had to do it. Maybe Danner went a step further." She paused. "Some people get to like what they do."

Eve knew that to be true. Joe had told her that the reason he had left the SEALs was that he had started to like it too much. He was afraid he was becoming what he was fighting. "Danner would have had to be

111

twisted out of all semblance of the man I met in Atlanta."

"You said you'd met him twice. The second time after Bonnie was born. Did he seem to have any animosity toward her?"

Eve felt a ripple of shock. She had been thinking of Danner in the context of his possibly killing Jacobs and his attack on Catherine at the bayou. But if he'd had reason to kill Jacobs, then he might be Bonnie's killer. She thought back on that second encounter with Danner when she'd taken Bonnie for a walk in her stroller, going over every nuance, every glance.

"No, he was smiling. He chucked Bonnie under her chin. He said she was going to be pretty as a picture. He said Gallo would have been proud of her." She paused, remembering that incredibly touching moment. "And then he told me that he'd received a notification that his nephew had been killed in Korea and his remains only discovered recently. He was bitter about it. He said that Gallo was only nineteen years old, and his life was hell from the minute he was born. He said the Army shouldn't have let him die before he had a chance to live."

"Bitter? Angry with you, too?"

"No, only sad. He asked if I'd mind if he kept an eye on me and Bonnie. He said he thought that his nephew would want him to do that."

"So he became part of your life?"

She shook her head. "I invited him to come and see us. I felt so sorry for him. I could tell that Gallo had been all the world to him. He said he didn't want to impose. He just wanted to make sure everything was going well for us. If he was looking after us, it was at a distance. I don't remember ever seeing him again after that day."

"I don't get it," Catherine said in frustration. "You're certain that sketch looks like him? There are so many things that don't add up."

"The first is that Ted Danner is supposed to be dead."

"That's not bothering me too much. Deaths can be faked. Hell, the Army obviously faked Gallo's death in Korea. Who told you that Danner was dead?"

"Gallo. When we were at the cabin on the property in Wisconsin, Gallo was telling me how his uncle had brought him up there when he was a kid. He told me that his uncle had died when Gallo was in prison in Korea."

"And you thought he was telling the truth?"

Eve nodded. "I believed Gallo. It didn't

occur to me to interrogate him about his uncle." She added slowly, "Though perhaps I should have questioned everything concerning him. Ted Danner would have done anything in the world for Gallo."

"Questioning might not have done any good," Catherine said curtly. "Gallo could have believed what he told you. Maybe he didn't know that Danner was still alive."

"Why wouldn't he know?"

"How do I know?" She went still, her eyes narrowing. "Though it would explain why Gallo was practically in shock when he saw him on the bank. And, if they were as close as you say, he would have found it nearly impossible to try to take him out."

Eve had been thinking about the reluctance to act that Joe had been so certain he'd seen in Gallo. Joe had assumed that it was deliberate, but Catherine's explanation was also possible. She just didn't know.

How could she know? She was still in shock from the moment she'd finished the sketch and recognized Ted Danner. Except it wasn't the Danner she had known. That expression on the face she'd drawn during these past hours had been pure violence incarnate. "Yes, Gallo was very close to his uncle."

"How close?" Catherine asked.

"I told you about their relationship."

"Give me details."

"I don't know all the details. Gallo rarely talked about his feelings or the past." She made a face. "We didn't talk much at all. An exchange of thought or memories was last on our list of priorities. It was all about the physical."

"Tell me what you do know."

So that Catherine could put together all the pieces and come up with a defense for Gallo. Well, good luck to her. Eve wasn't at the point where she could reason this out. "It's pretty skimpy. John Gallo grew up in a housing development in Milwaukee that was probably a lot like the one where I lived. His family was dirt poor, and evidently his parents were terribly abusive. Gallo once mentioned that his father's favorite form of punishment was putting cigarettes out on his back."

"Son of a bitch."

"That's what I thought. Gallo's only defense was to keep out of his way. It must have been hell on earth except for the times when his uncle came home on leave. When his uncle was medically discharged from the Army when Gallo was in his teens, they lived together, and I guess they took care of each other."

"And they moved down to Atlanta to go to a VA specialist for Ted Danner's back?"

Eve nodded. "And rented a place in a development a couple blocks from where I lived. That's all I know. I've told you everything, Catherine."

"You're right, it's damn skimpy."

"I know." But then everything about those weeks had been fast and volatile as the flicker of a motion-picture film. She had been so caught up in the sexual frenzy with Gallo that everything else had been as ephemeral as the fog outside.

And then there had been Bonnie, and nothing else had seemed important.

"And the only person who can tell us anything else is Gallo," Catherine said. "And where is he, dammit?"

"It depends if Ted Danner is really alive," Eve said. "And whether Gallo knew it. He's either going to join him, or he's going to try to find him." She shrugged. "And what if Jacobs's killer is just a Danner look-alike? It's possible, isn't it?"

Catherine just looked at her.

"Okay, it would be too coincidental." Eve threw the sketch down on the table. "But I wanted to explore every possibility before I made a giant leap."

"You made it," Catherine said. "Now let's

116

go tackle the fact that Ted Danner is probably alive and not the tame pussycat you thought him to be all those years ago. We need to find out why Danner was said to be deceased and where we can find him."

"And where he was when my Bonnie was taken."

"That goes without saying," Catherine said quietly. "Bonnie is always first, Eve. We just have to find the way to her. It will be —" She broke off and raised her head. "I hear a car. That's probably Venable and his cleanup team." She went to the window. "Yeah, that's Venable. I'll go out and meet him. I want to get him in and out as quickly as I can do it. It may not be easy. It just depends on what he wants and how badly he wants it."

"You think he has an agenda?"

"Oh, yes, Venable doesn't interfere with me unless he has reason. He knows me too well." She went to the door and threw it open. "On the bright side, at least, he brought the cleanup crew. We would have had problems disposing of Jacobs's body. After all, he was in the military and supposedly served his country."

"He was a crook, a smuggler, and possibly an accomplice to murder."

"We'd still have problems explaining him

away. Military bureaucracy is almost as bad as congressional bureaucracy. It's better that he just disappear." She strode out of the house and called, "Venable, you took your time. We've been waiting for —"

"Don't go there, Catherine," Venable said sourly as he got out of the car. "I'm a little fed up with this fog and crawling along on these less-than-wonderful highways. Be polite. Be very polite."

Eve watched Catherine and Venable together for a moment before she turned away. They were sparring with the easy familiarity that spoke of a longtime association. Venable was a powerhouse, but Catherine was having no trouble keeping up with him. Catherine had no trouble keeping up with anyone.

She glanced at the Danner sketch again and suddenly shivered. How could kindness become malice? Or had the malice always been there, hidden and waiting to break free? She had a sudden memory of Bonnie in her stroller and Danner bending down to pick up a toy rabbit she had dropped while Eve and he were talking. No, it seemed impossible. She had sought out killers before whom she had thought might have killed Bonnie, but they had been monsters.

Ted Danner was not a monster.

But the expression Eve had drawn of the face of the man who had attacked Catherine had been that of a monster. She pulled her eyes away from the sketch and tossed it on the table before she went out the front door. She needed to get away from the house and Jacobs, who was still lying dead in the bed upstairs. She had to think. The recognition of Ted Danner had come as a tremendous shock, and she was both bewildered and uncertain which path was best. Catherine might know what direction she was going to follow, but she had never met Ted Danner. It was Eve whose life had been the backdrop for this horror of pain and sadness to play out. Catherine had only her own experience and instincts to help her make conclusions.

And that seductive wild card that was John Gallo. Eve knew what confusion he could bring to any woman.

"Eve?" Catherine turned away from Venable as Eve strode past them.

"I needed some air." She nodded at Venable but didn't stop. A moment later, she entered the trees that bordered the bayou.

That was better. She drew a deep breath. Silence, except for the sounds of the bayou. The fog was a mere wisp drifting over the waters. Peace. No pushing and prodding for

119

action from Catherine. She could relax and try to get her thoughts together.

"She only wants what's best. Catherine doesn't know any other way."

Bonnie.

Eve stiffened, gazing out at the bayou, remembering the wisp of a spirit that she'd seen on the waters as she'd approached the house. Sad. Bonnie had been so sad, and it had frightened Eve.

"No, I'm over here." Bonnie was leaning against a tree, dressed in her jeans and Bugs Bunny T-shirt, her curly red hair blazing against the gray bark. "I'm sorry I scared you, Mama. I was scared, too. I didn't know what to do. I didn't want it to happen."

"Jacobs? Then why did you let it happen? Don't you have any influence?"

Bonnie shook her head. "What do you expect? I'm kind of new here." She smiled. "I know it seems a long time since I left you, but it was really only the blink of an eye."

Bonnie always sounded so adult when she came to Eve. It was one of the reasons why Eve had had problems for years believing that she was anything but a dream. In spite of the fact that Bonnie had scoffed at her and told her that she shouldn't expect her to be the same seven-year-old child when she had crossed over. "Blink of an eye. Don't tell me that. It's been an eternity," she said unsteadily. "And I want it over. Catherine almost died. She shouldn't have been caught up in this nightmare. It's not fair. If someone has to die, it should be me."

"Not you, Mama. We can't be together yet." She sighed. "How many times have I told you that everything has its time?"

"I don't care what you told me." She paused. "And you've been saying that we're reaching the end, that's what you told Joe when he was in that coma. He didn't imagine that, did he?"

"No, it's the truth." Her luminous smile lit her face. "And I had to give him some reason to come back. It's very difficult turning anyone around when they've gone that far. But I was betting that if he knew that you'd soon need him, I could do it."

"I thought you meant that you were talking about . . . I was wondering if the end you were talking about was —"

"Dying?" Her smiled faded. "It could be, but I don't know if that's coming. I only know that the path is leading somewhere now, and we all have to walk it."

"And it's making you sad. You scared me when I saw you before."

"I was scared, too. I didn't want it to happen, but I couldn't stop it."

"Jacobs's killing?"

She didn't answer. "I have to leave you now, Mama. I only came because I knew that you were worried about me."

"Don't you dare go away." Her voice was unsteady. "You've told me before that you can't tell me about the person who killed you, that it's lost in darkness. But I think that's changing, isn't it? Tell me who did it."

"It is changing. I don't believe I was meant to know everything before. It's as if I've been moving back and forth on two levels, and neither of them is clear. One has to be with you here and the other one is somewhere else with . . ." She shook her head. "It's gone. Once I leave one level, it's forgotten, yet something lingers, and I know I'll be going back. I've been wondering if the reason there's no recollection is that it's a kind of trade-off for letting me come to you. That I'm not allowed to have everything. But lately I've been getting glimpses, memories, and I think maybe the two levels are coming together."

"That's confusing as hell."

Bonnie smiled. "I'm sorry, Mama. It's confusing for me, too. I just have to trust that it's how it should be. Everything else seems to have a wonderful order."

"Well, it doesn't seem very orderly to me. All I want to know is one thing. Ted Danner. Was it Ted Danner?"

Bonnie didn't speak for a moment. "I don't . . . I've been getting glimpses of him. He has something to do with . . ." She shook her head. "I get a little wisp, but then it goes away." Her face was grave. "But there's so much anger and darkness in him. I think that's part of the reason that he won't come clear. But he's part of that other level, and he's coming closer and closer to you. You have to be careful with him. Watch him."

"Closer and closer. Oh, yes, he was pretty close to Catherine today. He almost killed her."

"Watch him," Bonnie repeated. "The levels are coming together. There's some reason why I have to know now. Some reason why you and my father have to know."

"Gallo?"

"He's my father, Mama. Of course he has to know. And he's not like Joe. I'm having trouble leading him. He's too alone. He's hurting too much. You may have to help me."

"Me? You have more influence on him than I do, Bonnie. You have more influence on all of us. All we want to know is how to find the man who killed you."

"I'll do what I can." She gazed out over the bayou. "The darkness is getting lighter, and soon I'll be able to see everything. Maybe I should have seen it already, maybe I've been hiding away."

"Then don't look," Eve said quickly. "Not if it's going to hurt you, baby. Let it go."

"You never wanted me to hurt. When I scraped my knees or I got a cold, I think you felt it more than I did," she said gently. "And you blame yourself that you weren't able to keep me safe. No matter how many times I tell you that you did everything you could to make my life everything that it should be." Her glance shifted back to Eve. "You gave me such love, Mama. Love doesn't die. It can change, strengthen, become something more than it was in the beginning, but it can't die."

"No, it can't die." Eve's eyes were stinging. "I love you, Bonnie. I'll always love you." She swallowed and tried to smile. "But I think someone made a major mistake in taking you away from me before I could spend a lot more years showing you."

"And I can't stop you from being bitter, no matter how hard I try. I don't know why it hap-pened," Bonnie said soberly. "Maybe we'll find out soon. I think I know when I'm on that other level. I'm going now, Mama. Look out at the bayou. You don't want to see me leave."

"Because it would make me remember those years when I thought I was dreaming or hallucinating when you came to me? I've ac-cepted you for what you are now, Bonnie."

She made a face as she looked out at the bayou. "Though Catherine is going through a major case of skepticism where you're concerned."

"I know. But you're handling it well. Maybe someday . . ."

Bonnie was gone.

Eve didn't have to look back at the tree where Bonnie had stood to know that her daughter had left her. She could tell by the emptiness, the loneliness, that always came when that small figure disappeared.

She drew a deep breath and turned away. This visit from Bonnie had not been like any other she could remember. Yes, in one way it had been the same. Bonnie had come to her because she had sensed that Eve was disturbed and unhappy and had wanted to comfort her. That was how the first visits had started about a year after she had lost Bonnie. She had been spiraling downward and would probably have died before she had begun to dream of Bonnie. At least, she had told herself they were dreams. She had not been able to accept that Bonnie was a spirit at that time. Eve was a realist, and ghosts were not acceptable in her life.

But Bonnie kept visiting her, healing her, and gradually Eve began to believe. Through all the searching that had taken place in the years that had followed Bonnie's kidnapping, Eve had been able to cling to those visits. Because every visit had been filled with love, and there had been nothing frightening or strange about them.

Until Bonnie's appearance when Eve and Joe had been driving up here. It had just been an eerie glimpse, shimmering in the bayou. That had been strange because of the sadness and frightening because in that moment Bonnie had not been the daughter Eve had known.

But surely it was going to be all right. Bonnie had come back to her and been as loving as always. She had known of Eve's disturbance and wanted to soothe her and give her peace.

Soothe her? Not likely. Not when Bonnie's murderer was out there. Not when Bonnie herself had said that the years of searching were coming to an end.

Bonnie's murderer. Bonnie had not really answered her about the possibility of Ted Danner's being that killer. For a moment, Bonnie had seemed to be on the verge of being able to tell Eve something about Danner. But as usual, Eve had backed away from talking about the details of Bonnie's actual killing as she had done in the past.

She couldn't bear to bring that terror back to Bonnie. Her daughter had spoken of the darkness surrounding her death more than once and how could Eve ask her to try to pierce that darkness and remember?

But that darkness was coming closer. Bonnie had said that those two levels, two paths, where she existed were coming together. Eve could *feel* it and so could Bonnie or she would never have said that she might need Eve's help.

That was strange in itself. Bonnie had never asked Eve for help before. She had been the healer, the one who came and gave and drifted away.

Perhaps to that other level where she could not take Eve?

You may have to help me.

Could that request for help be the real reason why Bonnie had come to her?

"Eve!" It was Catherine, waving at Eve to come to where she was still standing and talking to Venable.

Eve shook her head to clear it. The darkness might be coming, but this was the real world intruding and she had to deal with it. She'd talk to Venable, then get Catherine to go with her to New Orleans and take the first step toward finding Ted Danner.

If he was alive. If he was truly the man

who had tried to kill Catherine and murdered Thomas Jacobs. That was still not a certainty.

Is he alive, Bonnie? Is he the one?

But there were no answers from the darkness.

"You were talking to Venable for a long time." Eve turned to Catherine, who had just started the car and was driving away from the house. "Were you right? Did he want something from you?"

Catherine nodded. "A job in South America. The director is pressuring him. Venable doesn't take pressure well. He tends to explode like that BP well that caused all the havoc down here. It surprised me that he even bothered to come. He knows I won't go back there now that I have Luke home. He was just feeling me out to see if there was any way he could manipulate me."

"You don't resent that?"

"Why should I? It's what he does. It's what makes him valuable to the Company. You just have to learn how to ignore it and do your own thing." She shot Eve a glance. "But we may be able to use him. He knows he doesn't have a chance with me until I find Bonnie's killer. He's willing to put manpower on it just to clear my decks."

"I don't know if manpower will do it," Eve said. "We need information first."

"I've already told him I need to know when, where, and if Ted Danner died. That's a start."

She should have known that Catherine would already have been on top of things. "Yes, that's a start."

Catherine's gaze narrowed on Eve's face. "You've been very quiet. Are you okay?"

Eve nodded. "I'm having a few problems with the idea of its being Ted Danner out there this morning." She grimaced. "It doesn't compute. Not with the Danner I met when I was a teenager."

"I don't have that disadvantage," Catherine said. "I only know the bastard who wanted to cut my throat. You say he looked like him, and he had Ranger training. Gallo had trouble putting him down, and there has to be a reason for that. That's enough for me to go on."

It should be enough for Eve, too. Why wasn't it?

Because there was something else bothering her, nagging at her.

The darkness, looming, impenetrable.

I may need your help.

Help with Gallo. It was Gallo whom Bonnie wanted Eve to help.

Why?

He's hurting too much.

What could she do? She thought in frustration. For some reason Bonnie wanted both her and Gallo to be together in this. It wasn't enough that Eve had her own problems with Gallo.

What the hell do you want from me, Bonnie?

"You're scowling," Catherine said. "I'm sorry, I can't feel the same way you do, Eve. I have to go with reason, and Danner is the logical suspect."

Catherine thought Eve was still brooding about Ted Danner, she thought. It was just as well that Eve didn't set her straight. It would only disturb her if she began talking about Bonnie and this frustrating realization that she wanted Eve to help Gallo. Catherine wasn't ready to embrace concepts like that one. Hell, she'd start to close up and edge away from Eve if Eve even gave her a hint. No, she'd keep her own confidence. She didn't need to cope with anything else right now.

Not with the darkness closing in around her.

And the beginning of the realization of the steps she would have to take to find her way through it. . . .

CHAPTER
6

New Orleans

"Pull over here," Eve said suddenly. "Now, Catherine."

Catherine looked at her in bewilderment, but she slowed the car. "Why? This is only Canal Street. We're in the French Quarter. I thought you wanted to go downtown to the police department to meet Joe."

"Pull over." Eve put her hand on the knob. "I have to get out. Now."

Catherine muttered a curse as she pulled to the curb, ignoring the blaring of horns of the cars behind her. "Dammit, what's happening?"

Eve grabbed her suitcase and jumped out of the car. "I have to go after Gallo. You try to work through Venable, but I think Gallo is the key."

"Then we'll both go after him. Don't you leave Joe and me out of this, Eve."

"I won't. I'll be in touch." She moved

toward the alley beside a souvenir shop, ducking past a mime who was performing on the street. "But I have to contact Gallo on my own. He's on the run, and Joe and you aren't going to be able to make him stop and listen. He's on guard. If he knows that you're with me, he may not listen to me either."

"And you're sure he'll stop and listen to you?"

"No, I'm not sure." She looked over her shoulder. "But he may decide to listen to me. I have a weapon that you don't have, a card that I can play. I'll call you." She vanished into the alley and headed for the door of a restaurant with a wrought-iron balcony on the far end of the street.

Would Catherine follow her? She wouldn't have been surprised if Catherine abandoned the car and ran after her. But Catherine was smart and would know that if she did try to intercept Eve, she'd just find another way to handle this on her own.

Eve ducked into the restaurant and moved past a jazz quartet on the small stage to the left of the door. Move fast. Weave in and out of the stores of the Quarter until she was sure Catherine had decided not to search for her. Then stop and make the call.

Fifteen minutes later, she had left the

Quarter and was in the coffee shop of the Marriott Hotel. She dropped down in a booth and took out her phone.

Would Gallo answer her? He would know from the ID that it was her, and he might choose to ignore it. And, for all she knew, he might be on an airplane. He had driven away from the house hours before she and Catherine left.

Stop wondering and make the call.

She quickly dialed the number.

It rang three times before he picked up.

"I don't want to talk to you, Eve."

"Yes you do, or you wouldn't have picked up the call. You might not want to make explanations or answer accusations, but you do want to talk to me. Even if you don't, you'll do it anyway. I've gone to a lot of trouble to lose Catherine and Joe so that you'll feel comfortable about this. I'm not going to let you turn away from me."

"I've already done that. I turned away from you a long time ago, when you were only sixteen."

"But before you did that, I conceived Bonnie. That changed everything between us. You told me once that no matter what happened, there would always be a bond we couldn't break. Bonnie. Neither of us can get away from that, John." She paused. "You

133

ran away, and whatever you're going to do now you want to do it alone. I can't let you do that."

"The hell you can't. You don't have a choice," he said roughly. "Everything has changed. Look, there's been nothing but trouble for you since I came back into your life. I never meant that to happen. I did enough damage to you when I was a nineteen-year-old kid who didn't care about anything but getting you into bed."

"You tried to protect me then."

"Not hard enough."

"I'm not going to argue with you about the past." She added, "But you're wrong: I do have a choice. Because I won't accept it any other way. It has to be you and me, John. Joe and Catherine will try to help, they'll support and do everything they can. But in the end, it goes back to what we did together when we were those kids back in Atlanta. Everything else that happened had to have rippled out from that time like a rock thrown into a lake." She hesitated, then said quietly, "And one of those ripples was Ted Danner."

Silence. "You finished that damn sketch. I thought it would take you longer."

"Or hoped I'd do a lousy job."

"No, that wasn't a possibility. Not you."

"You told me he was dead."

"I thought I was telling you the truth. That's what I was told when I got out of the hospital in Tokyo. I even saw the death certificate signed by the doctor at the VA hospital."

"He looked pretty healthy to me when he was running to jump into that bayou. He's not a young man, and I remembered him to be almost crippled."

"He had a bad back injury that he got in Syria." He added impatiently, "Look, it might not have been him. I have to find out."

"So do I."

"No," he said sharply. "My uncle is my business. I'll take care of it."

"It stopped being your business when he killed Jacobs because he didn't want Jacobs to talk to us. If what he was trying to hide had to do with Bonnie's death, then it's my business." Her voice was steely. "And that means *I'll* take care of it. Did he, John?"

Silence. "Oh, God, I don't know, Eve."

The agony in his voice hurt her, but she had to push it away. "Then we have to find out. Where do we start?"

He was silent, then finally said, "The death certificate. I'm going to Atlanta to see the doctor who signed it."

135

"Then I'm going with you. Where are you now?"

"New Orleans airport."

"If I join you there, I run the chance of Catherine or Joe being there to intercept us. Get a car and pick me up. I'm at the Marriott in the French Quarter. We'll leave from Mobile."

"You're avoiding Catherine and Joe?"

"Only for the time being. I don't know what's coming down with all this business, and I don't want to deal with conflict. How soon can you get here?"

"I didn't say I'd take you with me."

"No, you didn't. But if you think about it, you'll know I'm right. How soon?"

Silence. "Thirty minutes. Be outside the entrance on Canal Street." He hung up.

It was done. She had isolated herself from everyone but Gallo, and she couldn't be sure that his allegiance would ever be as strong toward her as it was to the uncle who had been his savior as a child. Eve slowly pressed the disconnect and leaned back in the seat.

Are you happy, Bonnie? This is going to cause me all kinds of turmoil with Joe and Catherine. Is this what you wanted?

No answer. No feeling either way that Eve had done the right or wrong thing. She

136

would have to rely on herself . . . and John Gallo. But Gallo wasn't Joe, who had never failed her. There had never been trust between her and Gallo. All they had shared was sex.

No, they had also shared Bonnie.

She would just have to trust in Bonnie.

But she would not run away and leave Joe without talking to him.

She braced herself and quickly dialed Joe's number.

"I was waiting for your call," Joe said when he picked up the phone. His voice was tight and she could sense the effort at control. "Catherine just phoned me and filled me in. What the hell are you doing, Eve?"

"Gallo has to be in this. Danner is his uncle, and I have to work with him. And he wouldn't cooperate if you or Catherine were involved right now."

"Then tell him to go screw himself."

She was silent. "I can't do that. It has to be this way."

He didn't speak for a moment. She could almost hear the mental wheels clicking. "Bonnie?"

"He's her father. She wants him to stop hurting," she said wearily. "Do you think I want it to be this way? I want you with me.

I want to hold you. But I told Gallo that the two of us had started all of this, and we had to face the results together. That was the truth, Joe."

"You're shutting me out."

"No, how could I do that? You're always with me. I thought you'd realize that we're way past that now. I'll bring you into this as soon as I can. Help me, Joe."

"I *hate* this."

"I know you do. So do I." She repeated, "Help me. From the moment you came to my house after Bonnie was taken, you've made my life worth living. There hasn't been an hour that I haven't felt that I could get through anything if you were there to help me."

"But I won't be there, dammit." She could sense the struggle that he was going through. For an instant, she thought he was going to lose it. "Okay, I'll give you a little time to work this out with him and try to find out about Danner. But that's not going to stop me from going forward on my own. To hell with Gallo."

She felt a rush of relief. She had not been sure that she could persuade Joe to agree to what she was doing. It was a testament to the way that their relationship had grown in the last weeks that he trusted her to such an extent. When Gallo had first come back into her life, there had been an element of jealousy in his resentment of Bonnie's father. There might still be a little competitive emotion in the way he viewed Gallo. Hell, that was Joe and the way his character worked. If he cared about something or someone, he wanted to be first. But he now knew there was no question about that truth. "I'll let you know where I am and what I'm doing."

"You'd better. Or I'll hunt you down." He paused. "Be careful, Eve. I know that you think Gallo had reason to hesitate when he should have acted at that bayou." His voice was sour. "Catherine says he was in shock. Screw that. Catherine almost died. If he cares so much about Danner, how the hell do you know he won't act the same way if it's your life in the balance?"

"I don't. I won't give you any arguments as Catherine did. I only know I have to do this."

"Then do it, but don't be surprised if I'm right behind you." He hung up.

She wouldn't be surprised, she'd be grateful to have Joe hovering over her. He'd probably be even more concerned if he knew the love that existed between Danner and Gallo. How could you fight an affection a victim had for his savior? It was a tie so strong that it was nearly unbreakable.

Stop sitting here and thinking about all the problems ahead. Be grateful that Joe understood even if he hadn't approved. She wouldn't dwell on it, taking one step at a time. She would just do what she had to do. She checked her watch. It was time to meet Gallo.

She got to her feet, grabbed her suitcase, and headed for the Canal Street entrance.

That was easier than I thought, Bonnie. I wonder . . . did you give me a little help?

"You heard from Eve," Catherine said the moment she pulled up in front of the police station. Her gaze scanned the grimness of Joe's face as he got into the passenger seat. "Where is she? Did you talk her into —"

"I didn't talk her into anything." Joe slammed the door shut. "She'd made up her mind, and there wasn't anything I could have said that would have shifted her even an inch. She thinks that she has to work with Gallo and that we'll cause him to shy away."

"She may be right," Catherine had to admit. "Though it surprised me that she managed to persuade him to let her go with him." Yes, she'd been surprised, and there

140

was a touch of some other emotion she refused to identify. "She said that she had a card he wouldn't refuse. I guess it's that they have a history."

Joe shook his head. "Maybe, in a way." He was looking out the window. "But that's not what she meant."

"Don't tell me." Catherine pulled away from the curb. "Bonnie, again."

"Okay, I won't tell you. But that's what this is all about."

"I know what this is all about. Bonnie's murder, Bonnie's killer. I can accept both of those things as the prime motivators. It's the rest of the other baggage that I have problems with." She held up her hand as Joe started to answer. "And I don't need to accept what you believe or what Eve and Gallo believe. All I have to do is do my job and let the rest of you worry about all that mystic stuff."

Joe smiled faintly. "It's a deal. Do you know, you sound like me a few years ago. I promise I won't try to ram any of this weird bullshit I feel down your throat."

"You'd better not." She smiled back at him. This was the Joe Quinn she knew and respected, her friend, her partner. "So, I take it that we're not going to sit around and wait for Eve to call for help? You can't count on her doing that."

"I think I could. She realizes that we're part of the equation. She's just trying to strike a balance, and right now, Gallo is on the upswing."

"You're being very reasonable." She gazed at him appraisingly. "I'm not sure why."

"Maybe getting so close to the hereafter had a sobering effect on me." He grimaced. "Nah, near-death experiences give you an appreciation for life. And maybe a glimmer of what people are all about. That may be it. I thought I knew Eve before, but it's different now. When I have time, I'll have to analyze what I went through. But I don't believe it made me any more reasonable."

But there was a difference in him, Catherine thought. It was the first time she had been with him for any length of time since he had gotten out of the hospital. He was familiar, yet there were . . . depths. Good God, she was thinking like someone from a soap opera. "I'll take your word for it. But I still don't believe you won't go after Danner."

"Of course I will. That's what I told Eve. Only I'll give her space." He leaned back in the seat. "But not too much."

"What did you find out about the fingerprints?"

142

"What I suspected. No prints on the truck from anyone but the kid he stole it from. But I think we might have gotten a couple from the storeroom at the alligator farm. The minute you told me about the sketch of Ted Danner, I asked Julian to run a match check through the National Database. He'll call me as soon as he gets the report."

"And then we'll know for sure if Danner is alive."

"Presumably," Joe said dryly. "Ghosts don't leave fingerprints. Now let's head for the airport."

"Where are we going?"

"You tell me. You said Venable was supposed to start checking on Ted Danner. Get on the phone and see what he's found out."

Gallo was ten minutes late pulling up before the Marriott in a gray Mercedes.

"You know this isn't a good idea," he said, as she got into the car. "Can I talk you out of it?"

"You know you can't. We've already discussed it. Drive." She leaned back in the seat. "And tell me everything you know about Ted Danner. You can bet that Catherine will have a report from Venable anytime now and will be sharing it with Joe."

"And will he share it with you?"

"If there's anything that might threaten me. Otherwise, he'll probably try to beat me to the punch."

"To protect you."

She nodded. "To protect me. Since Danner almost killed Catherine, I have to assume that he has reason to think it's needed. Tell me about your uncle."

He glanced away from her. "You know he's supposed to be dead. We're not sure that he's not."

"You're sure," she said. "No one knows Danner better than you do."

"I only got a glimpse of his profile."

"And it shocked you so much that you couldn't move." She paused. "I didn't see his face at all. I only saw him moving toward Catherine. That was why I couldn't even make a connection with Danner until I saw the finished sketch. That man at the bayou moved like an athlete, a young man. There was a springiness to his step. The Ted Danner I met was almost crippled. He moved slowly, like an old man."

"Yes, he did."

She was studying his face. "But you still recognized him."

He nodded jerkily. "He wasn't always crippled like that, only after that last mission. All the time I was growing up my uncle was strong as a bull and could beat me in any race. When we were up in the woods, he was so quiet, so good, that he could get within a yard of any forest animal before it knew he was there. I watched him do it any number of times." He paused. "Just as I watched him when he was coming up behind Catherine. It was as if he'd turned back the clock."

"Or had an operation on his spine that turned it back for him. Was that on the books before you left for basic training?"

He shook his head. "He said they had to do all kinds of testing."

"I saw him when Bonnie was six months old, and he still looked crippled. That's a long time to wait for surgery."

"Maybe they weren't sure they could do it." His lips tightened. "He had spells when he was in terrible pain."

"You told me once he was on prescription drugs."

"But he kicked the habit. He wouldn't let himself fall into that hole." He glanced at her. "You're trying to build a case for his being a drug addict, and that would be a reason for his killing Bonnie." He shook his head. "He hated drugs. He told me he'd rather have the pain than mess up his head like that."

"I don't know what I'm trying to do," she said wearily. "Yes, drugs were a possibility. They can turn men into monsters. I thought your uncle was a gentle man, but the man who almost stabbed Catherine wasn't gentle. He was a monster. So I'm trying to make a connection."

"He's *not* a monster. Killing Jacobs doesn't make him a monster. Jacobs was a total son of a bitch. You don't know why he did it."

"Catherine," she reminded him. "Why would he hurt Catherine? He could have just avoided her."

"The truck. She was standing next to it. He needed the truck to escape."

"You're reaching."

"I know," he said jerkily. "I don't know why he would do any of this. Uncle Ted was a good guy. Nobody better. None of this makes sense."

He was in pain. She could see it in the tenseness of his every muscle, the set of his mouth.

Well, she couldn't help him. Not now. She said again, "Tell me about Ted Danner. When did you get to know him? Was he your mother's brother?"

"My father's half brother. They were nothing alike. Ted was younger, and they grew up together in the slums. My father became an alcoholic by the time he was twenty and went straight downhill. Uncle Ted joined the service at seventeen and got out of there. They didn't like each other, and I don't know why Ted visited him when he came back on leave." He shook his head. "Yes, I do know. I think it was me. He wanted to help me. He always tried to step in and keep them from hurting me. He even used to tell me what I should do to keep them from getting angry." He grimaced. "Though that didn't work so well after I got older. I hated them as much as they hated me, and I let them know it. I was lucky I survived."

"Why didn't your uncle persuade them to give you into his custody?"

"He was in the Rangers. He only had his pay. He didn't have a home or a family. He couldn't take on a kid. He tried to be a friend to me. I couldn't expect anything else from him." He added, "He came home on medical leave when I was seventeen, and we got to spend some time together. It was great, like I had real family. My parents were killed in a house fire about four months after he came home. My father fell asleep in bed smoking a cigarette. My uncle and I moved into a flat together. I was planning on going into the Army when I finished high school, but I took off with a couple buddies to see some of the country first. When I came back to Milwaukee, I found out that Uncle Ted was worse and had to go to Atlanta for treatment. I decided to go with him and get him settled before the treatments began." He glanced at her. "You know the rest."

Yes, she knew the rest. She had met John Gallo, and they had gotten caught up in a sexual maelstrom that had altered both their lives and produced Bonnie. "You told me that the death certificate was signed by a doctor at the VA hospital. What was the cause of death?"

"Pneumonia contracted after surgery."

"And what was the name of the doctor who signed the certificate?"

"Lawrence Temple." He paused. "I called the hospital, and he's no longer at the facility. He's now in private practice somewhere in San Antonio. I tried to check on any record of surgery being performed on a Theodore Danner, and they refused to give me any information on the phone."

"So you want to go and question them in person?"

"No, I think we should go find Temple in

San Antonio."

She nodded slowly. "We'd do better to contact that doctor and find out why he falsified the death certificate. Catherine can dig out the information about the surgery. We can count on her."

"Yes, Catherine won't let anything stand in her way. She's relentless."

Her gaze narrowed on his face. There was something in his tone . . . "Do you resent that?"

"God, no. I admire it." He grimaced. "It's just that when her determination is turned on me, it becomes a force to be reckoned with."

"You should be grateful that she's on your side."

"Do you think I'm not?"

"I don't know what you feel about her," she said quietly. "But she's my friend, and for some reason, she believes in you. You'd better be damn grateful."

"Or you'll take me out?" His lips twisted. "You're as fiercely protective of Catherine as she is of you."

"Catherine doesn't trust easily. She's had a rough life. I won't have her hurt." Her gaze was searching his face. She was remembering bits and pieces, phrases, expressions that she'd ignored because of the urgency of the situation. But protecting Catherine had its own urgency. "Just what do you feel about her, John?"

He didn't answer directly. "You don't have to worry about her trusting me. She's too smart for that."

"Dammit, answer me."

"What do you want me to say?" he asked harshly. "That I admire her, that I'm grateful to her for helping me when I didn't deserve it. That I wouldn't have forgiven myself if I'd let her be killed."

"That's quite a bit. Noble sentiments."

"Noble? You know me better than that. There's nothing pure or noble about me." He met her gaze. "All that stuff pales beside the fact that I want to screw her so much that I ache with it. I haven't wanted a woman like this since I met you all those years ago, Eve."

She stiffened. The words were raw and his expression intense, reckless. Yet she shouldn't have been so surprised. She had sensed . . . something when talking to Catherine, but neither Catherine nor Gallo would let down their guard enough to reveal an emotion this intimate.

"Are you satisfied?" Gallo asked. "No, I can see I've upset you. You shouldn't have

150

pushed if you didn't want me to tell you the truth."

"You did upset me." Her gaze was searching his face. "I think you wanted to upset me, or you wouldn't have just come out with it like that. Why, John?"

"Why? Good question." He didn't speak for a moment. "I think I felt guilty. Maybe I wanted absolution."

"Absolution?" She frowned. "What on earth are you talking about? Because Catherine is my friend?"

"No, because I felt . . . unfaithful."

She stared at him, stunned.

"Yeah, I know," he said roughly. "It's crazy. But then, everyone knows that about me."

"Unfaithful to me? That doesn't make sense. Good God, how many women have you had over the years?"

"That's different. They didn't matter. I didn't feel . . . It wasn't anything like what was between us."

"And what you're feeling for Catherine is like what we felt?"

"Yes. No. It's different, but it . . . means something. I don't know what."

"That's clear as mud. And so is your reasoning. There's nothing between us, John. Whatever we were together vanished

151

when you left me. Why the hell should you feel guilty?"

"I shouldn't. You and I tried to keep what we felt from meaning anything but sex." He added hoarsely, "You may have succeeded, but even back then I wasn't so sure that I did. And after I was thrown into that prison, the memory of you stayed with me." He paused. "And then there was Bonnie. I told you once that she'd bind us together forever."

And Eve couldn't argue with him on that score. Why else was she with him?

"You were special to me," he said. "You'll always be special. I know you've moved on. Hell, I'm beginning to think I've moved on, too. God knows, it took me long enough. So maybe next time I want to screw Catherine, I won't feel as if I —" He drew a deep breath. "Sorry. I didn't mean to let all this loose on you. Forget it."

"I can't forget it." She stared at him in frustration. "And I can't ignore it. This is nuts. You were not unfaithful to me because you want to go to bed with Catherine. We both know that." Her lips thinned. "Absolution? John Gallo, that's the height of absurdity."

"Yes." He smiled. "And I'm beginning to feel better with every word you're hurling at me. What's between us is so damn compli-cated that it's good to get it out in the open. Now I can try to seduce Catherine and not worry about anything but having a good time."

"I didn't say that," she said, exasperated. "You don't have any responsibility to me, but you'd better act responsibly with Cath-erine."

"You know I don't have a history in that direction." His smile faded. "But I'll try to change my ways if it will please you, Eve. I guess I could try this pure, noble crap."

"Bullshit," she said bluntly. "You like your way too much, and I never remember you not trying to take it."

"Not if you said no."

But she had never said no to him. She had been too dizzy and hot and completely involved with her first sexual experience. And she doubted if Catherine would say no to him either. Not for long. He still pos-sessed the sensual magnetism that had drawn Eve to him, but now it had matured and become even more potent. Eve could see it, feel it, but it didn't touch her. As he'd said, she had moved on.

But to Catherine, Gallo's charisma would be fresh and stormy and strike sparks.

"Don't hurt her, John."

"You flatter me." He moved into the lane that led to the Mobile airport. "Catherine is probably tougher than either one of us. She wouldn't let me hurt her."

Eve hoped that was true. It was true that there was no one more wary than Catherine. But her friend had never met a man like John Gallo.

He glanced at her when she didn't speak. "I'm trying to be good, Eve," he said quietly. "I know I'd be rotten for her. That's one of the reasons that I took off and put some distance between us. Catherine has the misfortune to believe in me." His lips twisted. "Even after I came within a heartbeat of letting her be killed." He shrugged. "So instead, I let you come along for the ride. Here we are together again, Eve."

"Only until we find Ted Danner. It's all about —" Her phone rang, and she glanced at the ID. "It's Catherine." She pressed the button and turned up the volume. "What's happening?"

"I could ask the same of you," Catherine said. "I didn't like the way you left me, Eve. It wasn't fair."

"I know. I didn't want an argument, and you would have given me one."

"You're damn right I would have." She paused. "Is Gallo listening?"

154

"Yes."

"You take care of her, Gallo. If you don't, I'll cut your heart out."

"Always to the point," Gallo said. "I have no intention of letting anything happen to Eve."

"Intentions don't always translate to the final product. Joe wants to talk to you, Eve. But I wanted to make sure you heard about the fingerprint tests that Joe had New Orleans PD run on the prints found in the gift shop at the alligator farm. The results just came in."

"Danner?"

"Absolutely positive."

Gallo muttered a curse as his grip tightened on the steering wheel.

"I heard that," Catherine said. "It's too bad you don't like it, Gallo. Face it. He's a murderer."

"There could have been reasons."

"And what reason did he have for tossing that night security guard to the alligators?"

"Self-defense. Quinn said there were signs of a struggle. He could have been surprised and acted instinctively."

"Maybe. I'm not counting on it. I'm handing the phone to Joe, Eve."

"Right." She braced herself. "Where are you, Joe?"

"At the gate in New Orleans waiting for a flight to Atlanta. We're going to go check out Danner's records at the Atlanta VA Medical Center."

"Gallo tried to do that. The administrative office wouldn't give him any info. I knew you and Catherine would be able to find out about him." She paused. "Gallo and I are going to San Antonio to check out the doctor who signed the death certificate for Ted Danner. I'll let you know what we find out."

There was a silence. "You will?"

"Joe, for Pete's sake, I told you I wasn't trying to close you out. It's just not possible for me to work with you right now."

"Because of Gallo," Joe said harshly.

"No, because of Bonnie." She added quickly, "I've got to go, Joe. I'll call you when I have an update." She hung up and turned to Gallo. "You heard it. There's no doubt any longer. It's Danner."

"But how?" he asked through set teeth. "Why?"

"That's what we have to find out."

"You told Joe we were going to San Antonio," Gallo said. "How do you know that they won't be there before us?"

"I don't. But it wouldn't be smart of them now that I've explained my position. And

Joe and Catherine are both very smart. They don't like it, but they trust me." She added quietly, "And I won't violate that trust, John. They've gone through hell, and they deserve to see the end of this. You set the rules, and I had to go by them." She shook her head. "No, I wanted to go by them. You scared me. I know how you feel about your uncle. I'm not sure how you'd respond if it came to a choice."

"I didn't let him hurt Catherine."

"But Joe said you took a chance on a risky throw. Why?"

"I wasn't thinking, dammit. I couldn't believe it was happening. I meant to aim for his back."

"But you aimed for his hand."

"It was too late to —" He drew a deep shaky breath. "I could have killed him with that bowie if I'd struck his back. I couldn't kill him, Eve."

"I know. And that's why I don't want to expose Joe and Catherine if you're faced with that choice again."

"But you're willing to risk yourself," he added mockingly. "It appears you're not as smart as Joe and Catherine. Where's your sense of self-preservation?"

"You'll do what you have to do. I'm not afraid no matter what choice you make."

"How fatalistic," he said. "I'm not sure I like your attitude. You were always a fighter, Eve."

"Who says I'm not now?" She shrugged. "But I guess I am a fatalist in this. I'll do everything I can to survive, but this time I may not have any say in it." She stared him in the eye. "And you might not either. It could be that's why we're supposed to be together."

"Don't be melodramatic. We're not going to die," he said. "I won't accept any of that bull." He was silent a moment. "I don't want to die. There was a time, when I thought I might be the bastard who had killed Bonnie, that I didn't want to live. I thought I should burn in hell. Then Catherine came along and told me in her less-than-gentle way that I was an idiot to take Black's word, anyone's word, without positive proof and kicked me into high gear. She said she'd learned a hell of a lot about me when we were playing cat and mouse while she was stalking me in those woods in Wisconsin. If she didn't believe I was capable of killing Bonnie, why should I? She convinced me. I'd fight to live now." He frowned. "If I'm not to blame for it after all. I've just remembered something Jacobs said when I was questioning him. He was blaming everyone but himself for Bonnie's death. Including me. He said it was my fault."

"I'm surprised you didn't latch on to the blame before this," she said in exasperation. "Dammit, you said he was blaming everyone. Why should it be your fault if you didn't kill Bonnie?"

"But it was my uncle who killed Jacobs. Who might have killed Bonnie."

"Then it was his crime."

"Maybe." He pulled onto the entrance ramp for Mobile airport. "We'll have to see, won't we?"

CHAPTER
7

"Forgive me, Father, for I have sinned. It's been six weeks since my last confession." Ted Danner closed his eyes as he bowed his head in the confessional. "It wasn't my fault, Father. I did what I should have done when a demon tries to do evil. You've always told me I have to fight the demons." He added bitterly, "I know you meant the demons inside me, but I can't win those battles. But even if you don't believe me, there are other demons, and I can sometimes win over them." He could feel the tears well to his eyes. "What else could I do? It was a wicked demon, and I had to strike out before it devoured John, Father Barnabas. It had teeth that were sharp as knives. . . ." He swallowed as he remembered the blood gushing from Jacobs as his knife went into his chest. "I've tried so hard to hide from them. But I'd warned this demon that he mustn't do evil. I did warn him, Father."

"I know how you've fought them, Ted." Father Barnabas paused before asking, "Just how did you strike out?"

"I don't remember." It was not the truth, and he'd have to confess that the next time he came to confession. Lying was only a small sin. But he couldn't tell the priest what the demon had forced him to do. Father Barnabas was the only one who could save him, and this sin was too great to forgive. He might not intercede for him and he'd be left to burn in hell. That couldn't happen, God listened to priests. "Forgive me, Father. It wasn't my fault. I left him alone for years, but I couldn't do it any longer. It would have destroyed me."

"Only God can destroy you, Ted." Another pause. "I haven't seen you for weeks. I've told you before that the confessional is important for you. You need it."

"I know. But I've been good, Father. My thoughts have been pure. I've done good deeds. I've tried to make amends for my sins. I know I shouldn't have missed confession." He whispered, "Nor have fought the demon. Give me a penance. Make me clean again."

"If you don't remember what you did, how can I know what penance to give you?

Think. Tell me, Ted."

He could feel himself being swayed by the priest's persuasiveness as he always was whenever he was near him. All Father Barnabas had to do was stare into his eyes with that look that seemed to have almost hypnotic power, and Ted wanted to do anything, give anything. "I told you, I can't do that. Why do you keep asking me?" He could feel the rage rising in him, and he had to control it. He had to remember that Father Barnabas wasn't one of the demons, he was Danner's salvation. The priest told him so all the time. "And God cast out Lucifer. He knew how evil demons can be. He would forgive me. You have to forgive me, too."

"Ted, it's not up to me. It's in God's hands. Let's pray and ask Him for forgiveness."

"He doesn't listen to me." His voice was tense with anger. "Why should He? You're the one who has to get Him to forgive me. I couldn't help it. It was like a giant wave of flame that was drowning me. I couldn't see, couldn't feel anything but the searing of the — He should have stopped me. I didn't want to hurt them."

"Them?" Father Barnabas asked slowly. "More than one demon?"

Alligators swarming in the dirty brown pond.

A dark-haired woman, beautiful as a Delilah from Hades, staring fiercely up at him as he had brought the knife down.

Not really demons. But he couldn't accept that rage, not vengeance could make him do anything so horrible. If he did, then he'd be beyond all forgiveness. "I don't remember."

"I think you do, Ted."

"No." He wouldn't remember. Why did the priest keep telling him to remember when it hurt him to do it? Was Father Barnabas his enemy, too? No, that couldn't be true. Control those thoughts. Change the subject to the reason he was here. He forced a smile. "I'll try to come here more often, Father. I promise. But I need you to help me now. Did you do what I asked?"

"Of course I did."

He tensed. "Then tell me what I need to know."

The priest shook his head.

Danner's hands clenched.

"I prayed," Father Barnabas said gently. "I don't always get an immediate answer. Sometimes, I don't get the answer you want."

Danner could feel the rage rising within him. "But you're a priest, dammit. God won't listen to me, but He'll listen to you. I have to *know.* What does she want? What does the little girl want from me?"

"Perhaps if you told me a little more, we could work through this. Who is this little girl?"

"I don't want to work through anything. Just tell me what she wants, so that I can give it to her. She won't leave me alone until I do."

"I'll pray again, but I can't promise. Perhaps you could talk to her yourself. Or perhaps her parents."

Talk to her? Panic was causing his heart to pound. "No, I can't talk to her. You have to do it." He jumped to his feet. "I'll give you more time, but you have to help me. Don't tell me you can't do it. You can do anything. You always say you want to help me. This is the only way you can do it. I trust you, Father. Try again. Help me."

"Ted, talk to me. Not about this little girl if you don't want me to ask questions about her. Tell me what else you've been doing."

If he talked to the priest, he would be at his mercy as he had been all through the years. Danner could feel his frustration begin to turn to rage. Calm. Don't turn on the only man who could help him. Don't let loose the rage. Resist the temptation to

164

step into the cubicle that had heard a million sins and kill the priest. That would truly make him one of the demons that were his enemies.

"Ted?"

"Just pray and find out what I need," Danner said hoarsely. "And give me forgiveness."

"If you were in the right, why would you need forgiveness?"

Why did the priest keep asking him questions? *Kill* him.

No, that was the demon whispering. He couldn't listen.

He jumped to his feet. "I have to go. Good-bye, Father."

"Don't go. Come back to my office. You need me, Ted."

Dear God, he did need him. But he was past the help the priest could give him except for this last request. "I have to go," he said jerkily as he left the confessional. "Don't fail me again."

"Ted!"

Danner ignored Father Barnabas's shout as he ran out of the church and down the stone steps.

He shouldn't have come. He was hurting, and Father Barnabas had not been able to heal him. No, that was not true. The priest could do anything, his powers were without limit. He had not wanted to heal him. He had only wanted to tear aside the scabs of Danner's wounds and watch him bleed.

As his hand had bled when John's knife entered it.

He looked down at his bandaged hand, and the tears stung his eyes once more. Pain. Broken bones. Not John's fault. John would never hurt him.

He must have demons whispering in his ear, too.

Catherine Ling. The Delilah.

He had recognized that quality in her when he'd first seen her earlier that night at the casino, when she and John had taken Jacobs captive. Beautiful, exotic, a sorceress weaving her spell. As John and the woman had hunted down Jacobs, so had Danner followed and stalked them, waiting for his chance. He had watched, listened, finding out what he could about her. He had thought that perhaps she could be spared, that she was only a temptress that John was using for pleasure. Then later, when she'd been stalking him at the bayou, he'd known that she had to be destroyed.

He cradled his torn, broken hand. He'd have to change bandages soon. He had taught John how to throw that knife with deadly accuracy at the cabin in Wisconsin, when John was only a boy. They had laughed and made bets, and for a little while, Ted had felt whole again.

Not John's fault. It was the demon.

It was Delilah.

He was gone.

Father Barnabas stood on the top step and gazed out in frustration at the empty street.

He should have been quicker. He should have sensed how close Ted Danner was to breaking and running. He had been concentrating on how to tear through the wall around Danner and reaching him and had not realized how tightly the man was balanced.

And he knew how dangerous Danner could be when he was upset like this. Before he had been able to control him and he had thought that when Danner had come to him pleading for help with the child, he could lure him back to him. What had set him off this time?

Well, he wasn't about to find out anytime soon unless he was able to give him what he wanted. He had become the enemy to Danner. He had felt the vibrations, the guilt, the searing rage that was fueling the man. He had been bracing himself for possible attack.

Danner was changing, becoming dangerous. Could he control him? Control was of the utmost importance with Danner.

He could do it. He had done it before through the years. All it took was perseverance and subtle manipulation. Danner regarded him as the only light to overcome the darkness that was trying to take over his soul.

As long as he kept thinking that was true, the control would be rock solid.

"This is a far cry from a VA hospital," Eve said as Gallo pulled into the parking lot of the San Antonio Medical Center. It was a small brick-and-glass building that appeared sleek, modern, and affluent. The lot was occupied by a BMW, a gray Lexus, and a small red sports car. The neighborhood in which the medical center was located had the same air of prosperity as those luxury vehicles. "It seems Dr. Temple has moved up in the world."

"Or down," Gallo said grimly. "It depends on who you ask. I've met a couple of doctors who take care of servicemen and there are none better."

"Everyone has a right to improve their lot

in life," she said as she got out of the car. "It's the capitalist system."

"You defend it, but how much do you charge for your forensic reconstructions?"

"Enough to make a living." She waited for him at the plate-glass door. "I'm no martyr, John. I can't be —"

"Excuse me." A tall, tanned man in his early fifties had come out of the door. He was dressed in white shorts and T-shirt and gave Eve a dazzling smile. "Beautiful day, isn't it?" He jumped into the red sports car and the next minute had roared out of the parking lot.

"Dr. Temple. I couldn't reach —" A blond woman in a nurse's uniform had run out of the building and was staring in exasperation at the sports car disappearing down the block. "Dammit to hell."

"That was Dr. Temple?" Gallo asked. "We need to see him." He glanced at the badge on her uniform. "Ms. Dawbler."

"Stand in line," the nurse said sourly. "He's booked solid for the rest of the day." Then she forced a smile. "He had an emergency, and I've had to cancel everything for the afternoon. I couldn't reach his noon appointment, and I was trying to tell him before he left. If you'll come inside, I'll try to set you up for tomorrow."

169

"Emergency?" Eve repeated. "He didn't look as if he were rushing off to the hospital."

"I can't help how it looked," she said shortly. "Dr. Temple told me it was an emergency. Would you like to make an appointment or not?"

"He had a golf bag in that sports car," Gallo said. "Does he play at a local country club?"

She started to nod, then repeated, "It was an emergency. Excuse me, I have to go back inside and phone him." She turned and went back into the medical center.

"What a charming man," Eve murmured ironically. "It's a beautiful day, and he ditches all his patients and takes off." She headed back to the car. "But I have no intention of waiting around to see him tomorrow. I'll check out all the country clubs in this general area on the computer, then start calling. I'd bet it's not too far from the medical center. He impressed me as a man who wouldn't want business to interfere with pleasure."

Twenty minutes later, she turned to Gallo and handed him the number she'd scrawled on a notepad. "Diaz Country Club. It's near the river. About a fifteen-minute drive."

"Right." Gallo started the car. "You did

the search. Now I'll do the interrogation. Okay?"

"I'll see when we get there." She was thinking of what Gallo had told her. "When did Temple leave his job at the VA hospital?"

"Three months after he signed the death certificate for my uncle."

"What a coincidence. How convenient. And then he came here and settled down in the lap of luxury."

"A payoff? Look, my uncle had no money. He couldn't have even had treatment if it weren't paid for by the government."

"But Nate Queen and Thomas Jacobs had money to burn with all the drugs and smuggling they were doing. And Ted Danner had some connection to them, or he wouldn't have killed Jacobs." She glanced at him. "So we have to look for that connection, John."

He shook his head. "Uncle Ted wouldn't have —" He stopped. "Okay, I'm in denial. But it doesn't make sense."

It didn't make sense to Eve either. But that didn't mean it wasn't true. "Then prove me wrong. Heaven knows that I feel like I'm walking through a maze. I'm just trying to follow the trail and hope I get a break."

"Dr. Temple?" Eve asked. "Could we have a moment?"

"No, can't you see I'm busy?" Lawrence Temple frowned as he glanced up at Gallo and Eve, who had pulled up in a golf cart next to where he was teeing off. He looked down at his ball again. "Who told you where to find me?" Then he glanced back at Eve. "Didn't I see you at my office?"

"Barely. You were in a hurry."

"Make an appointment."

"I don't think so," Gallo said. "We're in a hurry. Answer our questions and we won't bother you again. I want to know about a patient, Ted Danner, you had at the Atlanta VA Medical Center shortly before you came here."

Temple stiffened warily. "I don't have time for past history. Please leave, or I'll call security."

"That might not be a good idea. Falsifying a death certificate is a criminal offense. Your new patients might not appreciate being treated by a doctor who might be picked up by the police at any time."

Bingo, Eve thought. Temple had turned a little pale beneath that golden tan.

But he recovered quickly. "I don't know what you're talking about. I'd caution you not to risk a lawsuit by this nonsense. I know how to protect myself."

"I imagine you do," Gallo said softly. "But

172

I have no intention of bothering with bringing you up on charges. I don't have the time. I think we'll just go to my car and have a discussion. Then, if I like your answers, I'll let you walk away."

Temple moistened his lips. "I'm not going anywhere with you. Who are you anyway?"

"John Gallo. Theodore Danner is my uncle."

"Was," Temple said. "He died of pneumonia. I regret your loss, Mr. Gallo."

"My uncle was seen in Louisiana only yesterday. We've verified his fingerprints. Which means that you're in trouble, Temple."

"That's not possible," Temple was no longer pale but flushed with anger. "It's some sort of a mistake. You can't pin anything on me."

"I'm not going to argue with you," Gallo said softly as he crossed to stand before Temple. "I'm only going to listen to you. I'm very angry, you know. I loved my uncle, and I have an idea he was victimized. You can either prove you weren't the one who did it or face the consequences." He stared him in the eye. "You're a doctor. You know how easy it is to cause a massive hemorrhage if you know what you're doing. I do know what I'm doing. It would take me less than fifteen seconds."

"It's broad daylight." Temple said hoarsely. "There are people all over the green. You wouldn't do it."

"Fifteen seconds. And no one is noticing anything but their own games. I'd put you in that golf cart and just walk away." He took a step closer. "Look at me. Then tell me I wouldn't do it."

Eve inhaled sharply as she looked at his expression. She had only seen that raw ferocity once before in Gallo, and it was truly intimidating.

Temple jerked his gaze away. "You asshole. I think you'd do anything."

"Get in the cart, Eve," Gallo said. "You drive us to the parking lot, and I'll sit in back with Dr. Temple."

"You're going to let him do this?" Temple asked Eve. "It's kidnapping, you know."

"No, it's an invitation to join us in our car for a drive and have a discussion," Eve said as she got in the cart. "Anything else is entirely in your court."

Temple hesitated, then moved jerkily toward the cart. "It's all a mistake. I'm innocent of any wrongdoing."

"Pat phrase. You sound like you're in a court of law already," Gallo said.

"You can't prove anything." Temple got

into the cart. "And Danner would be a fool to testify that I was guilty of anything. He'd be convicting himself. They came to me. He was supposed to just disappear, dammit."

"You may be right." Gallo got into the cart. "You may not be worth our while. We'll take a little drive along the river, and you can convince us. . . ."

"Let me out here, and I'll forget this ever happened," Temple said, as they cruised by the river thirty minutes later. He turned to Gallo, who was sitting next to him in the backseat. "I have a decent amount of money. We can make a deal."

"I believe you've already made a deal," Eve said over her shoulder from the driver's seat. "Who approached you? Danner himself?"

He hesitated. "Look, I can't talk about this. I was warned that it could mean —" He broke off. "I didn't do anything to harm anyone. I just signed the damn death certificate. Nobody cared whether Danner lived or died."

"I cared," Gallo said. "Who paid you off?"

Temple was silent. "You wouldn't really cause a stir and tell everyone that I committed a crime? That would be . . . awkward for me. I have a reputation here."

175

Eve couldn't believe it. Temple was sitting next to Gallo, who was angry and probably the most dangerous man he had ever met, and he was worried about his reputation? Either his vision or his priorities were seriously awry. "We don't care about your reputation, Temple. Give us answers, and you just might survive to play another golf game."

He frowned. "Golf is important. It's not only a game, it's a way to cement my status in the community. I realized as soon as I got here that an affluent practice could be just a stepping-stone to get me where I want to be. I have a chance to run for lieutenant governor next year." He gazed warily at Gallo. "You can see that I can't let you libel me."

"Talk to me," Gallo said. "Who gave you the money to declare my uncle dead?"

He hesitated. "You'll protect me? It's not as if I did anything really wrong."

Gallo put his hand on Temple's throat and squeezed. "Talk."

Temple gasped, and Eve could tell that the lethal danger of the situation had finally become real to him. "You're crazy. Jacobs told me that this wouldn't happen. He said nobody cared about Danner."

"Then you should have asked him why he

was trying to cover his tracks." Gallo's grasp loosened. "It was Thomas Jacobs? How? Why?"

"I don't know why. It didn't matter to me." He added bitterly, "Just because I was near the bottom of my class at med school, I was stuck in that hospital treating a bunch of vets. Do you know how much I made there? Guys I went to school with had jobs on easy street. I deserved better."

"Those vets deserved better," Eve said. "I'm beginning to be glad Jacobs bribed you out of there."

"Jacobs didn't mention why he wanted Danner declared dead?" Gallo asked.

Temple shook his head. "He just said he wasn't important, and no one would follow up if there was a certificate that stated Danner was dead."

"He was a patient at the hospital? You were his doctor?"

"No, he had been discharged after he'd been treated for pneumonia. I'd never met him." His hands clenched. "At first I thought maybe Jacobs had helped Danner to cross to the other side because of insurance or something. I was scared I'd be an accomplice. But I checked the hospital records, and Danner didn't have insurance. So I thought it was safe to take Jacobs's money."

"Pretty flimsy," Gallo said. "There are other reasons than money to kill a man."

"I *wanted* that money. I had to have the money. It was my chance."

"So you scrawled your name and took the cash."

"I didn't hurt Danner. I didn't hurt anyone. Jacobs promised me that Danner was safe, and he just wanted to disappear. He said it was sort of like the witness protection program. After all, Danner was an ex-Ranger. It could have been true."

"And you didn't give a damn if it was or not."

"No." His lips curled. "But if Danner's still alive, as you said, then maybe Jacobs was being up-front about it after all. Go find Jacobs and ask him."

"I found him. So did Danner. Jacobs ended up with a knife in his chest."

"Oh, shit." Temple moistened his lips. "That's not good."

"Yes, it might interfere with your political plans."

Temple recovered immediately. "You can't prove I had anything to do with it. Jacobs paid me in cash and told me that it wouldn't be smart for me to mention his name again. I never saw him after that. Why would I? I had what I wanted."

"But maybe you wanted to eliminate a possible roadblock in your political plans?" Eve suggested. "The police might be interested in your —"

"No!" His chest was rising and falling. "You can't do this to me. I never saw Jacobs after the night he gave me the money."

Eve was not sure that they hadn't plumbed the extent of Temple's knowledge. "You said you checked the hospital records. Was there anything in them that —"

"I was only checking for insurance. I didn't care about anything else. I've told you everything I know." His teeth bit into his lower lip. "Jacobs is really dead?"

"Very. Did Jacobs tell you where this witness protection program was going to send Danner?"

"I didn't ask."

"Of course you didn't. You wanted to erase him from your mind. Just a signature, then off you went. No forwarding address in Danner's records?"

"No."

It was like pulling teeth. "Who were his doctors at the hospital?"

"That was years ago. You expect me to remember? I didn't care who was treating him. Probably some loser. What difference does it make to you? He'd been released."

"But he might have kept in contact with his doctor or nurse if they had developed a relationship."

"With our caseloads, we didn't have time to develop relationships. We had to get them in and out."

At least, that had been Temple's philosophy, Eve thought. "Nothing struck you as unusual in his records?"

He shook his head. "I keep telling you. It didn't matter. He was just another vet. None of them mattered."

And it didn't matter that those vets had given their bodies and lives to keep parasites like this walking the earth, she thought bitterly. She didn't know how Gallo was keeping his temper. He had spent seven years in that prison in Korea because he'd thought it was his duty as a soldier to protect his country.

"Pull over, Eve," Gallo said softly. "Temple and I need to take a walk together."

Her gaze flew to his reflection in the rearview mirror.

He was not keeping his temper as she had thought, she realized. His dark eyes were glittering in his taut face.

Shit.

"I'll pull over," she said. "But Temple is

180

the only one who takes a walk. We're through with him, and I won't let him interfere with what we have to do."

Gallo's gaze never left Temple's face. "He wouldn't interfere. I'd be very quick."

"No, John. He's scum, but I'm not letting you leave a trail of bodies behind us. He's not worth it."

"I agree. That's exactly why we should take a walk."

"Body?" Temple's eyes had widened in alarm. "You're talking about killing me? Why? I only told you the truth. Everyone knows that you —"

"Shut up." Eve pulled to the side of the road. "Get out and get moving."

Temple scrambled out of the car. "I'm going. Keep him away from me." He took off at a trot. "Think about it. No one has to know about that past history. Name your price." He saw Gallo get out of the car. "Anything you want," he said panicked as he started to run. "Money is what it's all about. Everyone knows that."

Eve saw that Gallo's muscles were tensed, and his gaze was fixed on the fleeing Temple. He was very close to having that tension explode into action.

"Don't go after him," she said quietly. "Get in the car, John."

"He's a weasel," Gallo said tightly. "But sometimes weasels can be dangerous when they're in the right position. How careful do you think he was when he was a resident at that hospital? Those guys were helpless, and they deserved someone to tend to them who would at least give them adequate care. Hell, they should have let those patients keep their guns before they turned doctors like Temple loose on them."

"He's not in that position any longer. I'm sure there are good doctors at that hospital, too." Distract him quickly. "We have to find out who treated your uncle and see if we can get a lead. Is there anyone else you can think of who might know anything about him? You once mentioned to me he was engaged at one time."

"She married someone else when he was overseas, and he never saw her again."

"You're sure?"

He shook his head. "I would have said yes if you'd asked me that a few days ago. I'm not sure of anything about him any longer."

"Did he have any close friends?"

"No, he was pretty much of a loner. Occasionally, one of his Army buddies would come to town, and he'd go out for a drink."

"One of them might still know something. Get in the car and make a list of the ones who you remember."

His glance shifted back to Temple, who was still running and was almost out of sight. "You're trying to throw a red herring in front of me."

"Yes, but it's a necessary red herring."

He glanced back at her. "Catherine would have let me take him down."

"Would she? I don't believe you know her well enough to assume that." But Catherine might have understood that black-and-white philosophy where evil was instantly punished. She had lived in the same deadly world as Gallo. "At any rate, Catherine and I are different in that respect. Get in the car, John."

He gave one last glance at Temple and turned away. "We didn't find out as much as I hoped from him." He got into the car. "Other than it was Jacobs who was the payoff man. Jacobs often did the dirty work when he and Queen needed a job done. But how the hell did Uncle Ted become involved with Jacobs?"

Eve shrugged. "I have no idea. And we may not know until we catch up with Ted Danner. So why don't you start making a list of possible people your uncle might have contacted?"

"I don't think it will do much good." He

took her computer, opened a document, and started to type. "But I'll try to remember."

She reached for her phone. "And I'll try to get in touch with Catherine and see if she's managed to tap into the hospital records."

"I'm at the Records Office now," Catherine said when she picked up Eve's call. "Joe and I just got here. Venable was having trouble accessing records because the confidential aspect is sometimes doubled at a VA hospital. Some of these guys were special ops, and it's best that no one gives al Qaeda a chance to ID who they are. They always have bull's-eyes painted on them."

"But you think you'll be able to get them?"

"I'll get them. Give me another twenty minutes. The records clerk isn't a bad guy, he's just careful. What do you want to know?"

"Temple was a bust. The only information he could give us was that Jacobs was the one who paid him for falsifying the records. He doesn't know why. He also has no idea where Danner is now. We're looking for any contacts we can find who will give us a lead. Nurses, doctors, therapists."

"I'll see what I can do." Catherine paused.

"What did Gallo say when you told him that Danner was definitely alive and raising general hell?"

"What would you say if the only person you'd loved from the time you were a kid was turning out like this? Denial. Bewilderment. Even guilt toward you because he couldn't force himself to kill Danner when he threw that knife."

"Idiot. He stopped him, didn't he? That's all that's important. I'll call you when I get through these records." Catherine hung up and turned to Joe. "Temple told them that Jacobs was the payoff man for the bogus death certificate. No other information. They want to see if we can find a possible contact with someone in the hospital who could tell us where Danner is now."

"Then let's get going," Joe said as he gestured to the clerk sitting at his desk across the room. "Work some magic, Catherine."

"No magic needed," Catherine said. "Sincerity is the key word here. You could do it as well as I could."

"I beg to differ," Joe said dryly. "He might give in and give me what we want eventually, but not in twenty minutes as you promised Eve. Unless I got rough with him. But persuasion is always better, and you garnish persuasion with a certain glamour that makes it more palatable."

She suddenly whirled on him. " 'Glamour'?" she repeated. "Bullshit. I *hate* it when you or anyone else assumes that I try to use seduction as the answer to every problem. I'm not a whore. I use my brains, not my body, to do my job."

"Whew, I didn't mean to cause an explosion." Joe's smile faded. "I know you're not a whore, Catherine. I never meant to suggest anything like that. But I also know that you're not too stupid to know what your effect is on the male population. It's all one package. I've known that from the beginning. Eve thinks that it would offend your independence to ever use the fact that you're a gorgeous woman to shift the balance in a fight. I told her I didn't agree. It's just another weapon that you have in your arsenal. You prefer not to use it, but you wouldn't discount it if it came to life or death. You're a survivor, like me. And you're a very practical woman."

She shouldn't have lost her temper. That outburst had come out of nowhere. It had been a rough few weeks, and she was feeling ragged and frustrated. "Yes, I am." She met his gaze. "I have to live. I have a son, Luke, to support and try to give a decent life. Would I do anything in the world to keep him safe? You bet I would. I'd steal or whore or kill. But you have to choose what's important enough to you to blow all the barriers. So far I've only found one, Luke." She smiled faintly. "And you've found Eve. Yeah, I'm like you, Joe." She moved toward the clerk. "And you're right, if necessary I'll use the fact that men can be persuaded to give me what I want just on the chance they might get a chance to jump me. So let's get that information and call Eve back."

Providence, Georgia
The sun was going down over the great canyon in a burst of glory. Light and beauty were all around Danner, but he could see only blackness.

Despair was washing over him in a great wave. He had come rushing back from seeing Father Barnabas to assure himself that he could still be saved; but even in this place, there was no solace. The darkness was creeping toward him, over hills, through the trees, blocking out the light.

"You're wrong, Ted. The light is still here. You're just not seeing it."

He stiffened and whirled toward the hillside.

The little girl in the Bugs Bunny T-shirt,

her red hair blazing in the failing light, stood there staring at him.

"No!" He whirled and ran away from her, stumbling, falling, picking himself up, and running again. His heart was beating so hard it was hurting him. He had to get away from her.

Why had she come? To torment him? To tell him that there were more demons for him to fight?

"Ted."

She was following him.

He wouldn't look at her. "Go away." His voice cracked as he tried to control it. "I'll do what you want. Give you anything. Just go *away*."

He knew she was speaking, but he closed her out as he ran through the hills.

Get away from her. Get away from the darkness.

Go back to the world and do her bidding.

Go back to the priest and force him to find out what he needed to know.

Go back and kill the demons.

CHAPTER
8

"Here it is, Joe." Catherine pulled up the file on the hospital computer. "Theodore Danner." She checked the date of entry and date of last treatment. "He was a patient here for a number of years. First, for his spinal injury, then follow-up rehabilitation. Eve said he was almost crippled when she met him. His surgery must have been very successful."

"Apparently," Joe said. "He was moving like a young man when we saw him at the bayou. Who was his surgeon?"

Catherine back-clicked. "Dr. Kevin Donnelly." Then she frowned. "No, that's not right." She clicked back another page. "Dr. Michael Worzak did the spinal surgery. It was a brilliant success, total recovery. But it was the last mention of Worzak. All of these other pages are appointments with Kevin Donnelly."

"Rehab?"

"No, there are notations of appointments with Donnelly even before the spinal surgery. They sent him to Donnelly on the recommendation of his doctor at the VA hospital in Milwaukee." She frowned in puzzlement. "Maybe Donnelly wasn't a surgeon and only did the preliminary. I'll try to go back to the letter of recommendation and see why Donnelly was assigned as Danner's physician. Danner must have been in tremendous pain. There's a list of medications here administered to Danner that would choke a horse." Her gaze traveled down the list. She stiffened. "Shit."

"What is it?"

"Thorazine. I remember that drug. Hu Chang used it occasionally as a base for some of his potions."

"Your resident Hong Kong witch doctor?"

"That's not funny. Hu Chang is brilliant."

"And lethal."

"Sometimes." More often than not. She and Hu Chang had worked together when she was a teenager in Hong Kong on less-than-legal endeavors. He was amazingly creative when a poison or drug was needed. "But he's my friend, so keep quiet, Joe. Thorazine, dammit." She was checking the other medications. She recognized a few, and they were all leading in one direction.

She flipped back to the beginning of Danner's file. It was the letter of recommendation from a Dr. Herbert Nils from the VA hospital in Milwaukee. She started to read.

She inhaled sharply. "My God . . ."

"I want to talk to Gallo," Catherine said when she called Eve ten minutes later. "You listen, too, Eve. Put me on speaker."

"You found out something?"

"Yeah, something I should have suspected. Are you there, Gallo?"

"He's here." Eve turned to Gallo and handed him her phone. "Talk to her."

"Yes, talk to me, Gallo," Catherine said. "I'm a bit pissed about your trying to avoid me. I didn't deserve it, and you're an ass for doing it. Though I don't know why I should care."

"Neither do I, Catherine." He paused. "What do you want to say to me?"

"I don't want to say anything to you. I want to ask you a question. What do you know about a Dr. Herbert Nils?"

"Nothing." He frowned. "What should I know?"

"He was your uncle's doctor at the VA hospital in Milwaukee. You were with him when he was undergoing treatment up there, right? You and your uncle shared an

191

apartment?"

"That's right. But for the last year before we moved down here, I was traveling the country with a couple buddies. When I came back, he told me that his doctor had recommended he go to a specialist in Atlanta."

"Dr. Nils suggested it?"

Gallo frowned. "I think that was the name."

"And did you ever meet him? Did he ask you to come in to discuss your uncle's condition?"

"No. My uncle was always intensely private. Particularly when he came back after his discharge. He'd always been so strong, and I think it embarrassed him that he wasn't the man he once was."

"And did you meet his doctor in Atlanta?"

"I was only in Atlanta about six weeks before I went to basic training."

"And you were obviously suffering a pretty intense distraction when you got down there."

Gallo glanced at Eve. "You could say that."

"Why are you asking these questions, Catherine?" Eve asked impatiently. "What difference does it make whether Gallo knew his doctor?"

"It makes a difference to me," Catherine

said. "I had to know if Gallo knew about Danner. Gallo's not stupid. I couldn't see why he would be so damned shocked, and I didn't want to think he was a liar and pretending."

"What the hell are you talking about?" Gallo asked roughly. "I don't lie, Catherine."

"I couldn't be sure. You've been behaving pretty weird since your uncle showed up on the scene."

"Why would I lie about knowing Nils?"

"Thorazine."

"What?"

"It's one of the meds your uncle was taking. You told me once that he was once addicted to prescription drugs. It doesn't surprise me. The amount of drugs he was given at the hospital in Atlanta was staggering. I imagine they kept him pretty well out of it in that VA hospital in Milwaukee, too."

"He was in pain."

"Maybe. But that wasn't the main reason he was given drugs."

"What is this Thorazine? And why would that have made you think I was lying to you?"

"Thorazine is a very powerful drug, and it was prescribed by both Nils and your uncle's doctor in Atlanta. I recognized it because Hu Chang used it as one of the ingredients when he concocted a knockout potion that could also cause severe disorientation."

"I imagine most pain medication can be used to do that."

"Yes, but Thorazine was better than the majority of drugs." She paused. "Because it was used in psychiatric treatments for schizophrenia. It was also useful in cases of split or multipersonality when combined with other drugs."

"What?"

"Dr. Nils was a psychiatrist. The honorable discharge Ted Danner received from the Army was on the condition that he seek help and have regular therapy from an accredited psychiatrist."

"No, he had a back injury."

"Yes, but that was minor. He would have been able to return to active duty after his operation except for his mental problems."

"It's not true," Gallo said harshly. "He was as sane as you are. And he wouldn't have lied to me."

"He did lie to you. It was all in that letter from Dr. Nils." She paused. "Something happened on that last tour of duty in the Middle East. According to Nils's letter, Danner's superiors said that he was behav-

194

ing irrationally and had fits of violence. They had noticed it before, but it became more pronounced, and they couldn't overlook it. Then there was an incident."

"What kind of an incident?"

"Nils didn't know. Perhaps the military didn't want to crucify Danner after his years of valiant and loyal service to the Army. Or maybe they just didn't want to cause a situation that might be awkward for them. Anyway, the doctor who recommended the discharge merely said that Danner had done something that made it impossible to keep him with his unit, and they discharged him. Nils tried to treat your uncle, but he wasn't having any luck. Danner wouldn't talk to him, so he referred him to a specialist in Atlanta who was supposed to be the best psychiatrist in the Veterans Administration. Dr. Kevin Donnelly."

"He would have told me. He wouldn't have lied."

"He loved you. You had a case of king-size hero worship. Do you think that wasn't important to him? Mental problems carry a certain stigma in our society."

"I wouldn't have cared. I would have helped him."

"But he'd always been your savior. He couldn't stand to have the situation reversed."

Gallo was silent, and Eve could see the conflicting emotions struggling in his expression. He finally said, "And you think he was so sick in the head that he could have killed Bonnie?"

"I'm not saying that. It's a possibility. But maybe he only knew about her death and the people who killed her. Why would he kill Jacobs? All I'm saying is that the ugliness we saw in Danner in that bayou may have been growing in him for years. We have to find out the rest."

"How, dammit? You said he wasn't talking to Nils, and Temple hadn't even seen him before he signed that death certificate."

"The psychiatrist who treated him in Atlanta may be the key. Dr. Donnelly's records show that he was treating him at least twice a week for years. There were a couple periods when he saw him every day for weeks. I'd judge by that that Danner was cooperating with Donnelly. He must have thought he was making progress, or he would have recommended alternate treatment."

"You mean put him in an asylum. He's not crazy. No one can tell me he is."

"She's not trying to tell you he's crazy, John," Eve said quietly. "Start thinking with

196

your head instead of your emotions. He had a problem, and it might have caused him to do something that he wouldn't have done if he'd been well. We have to find out if that happened."

"So that you can kill him?" Gallo's eyes were glittering in his taut face. "That's where this is leading, isn't it? You told me once that you'd kill the monster who murdered Bonnie without a second thought."

"And I would." She met his gaze. "I won't lie to you. If I find out that Ted Danner killed my little girl, I'm not going to care about his mental problems. I'm only going to care that he robbed Bonnie of her life. You may be torn, and I can understand it. But there's no way I could pity him. It's not possible for me. You see him as wounded, and I see him as a monster." She paused. "And I *will* kill him if he's guilty. I won't wait for a court to declare him incompetent and let him free or put him in some plush booby hatch."

"I can't let —" He broke off and drew a deep breath. "What are we talking about? He didn't do it. I know he didn't do it."

"Well, I don't know that, John," she said grimly. "And if you get in the way of my finding out, I'll take you down."

"Cool it," Catherine said quickly. "We'll

find out, Eve. I think Donnelly is the key. There must have been some kind of bond between them since they were together all those years. The relationship between patient and therapist is usually very intimate. The psychiatrist often is looked upon as almost a father figure."

"Not my uncle," Gallo said grimly. "He wouldn't have chosen to look upon anyone as a father figure. He told me my grandfather was an addict and abused both him and my father. That's why he was so horrified when he became addicted to prescription drugs."

"Regardless, there could have been an element of emotional dependence on Donnelly," Eve said. "What did Donnelly's case files on Danner say?"

"No case files. Which doesn't surprise me. A psychiatrist's records are usually ultra-confidential. Donnelly wouldn't have turned them over to the hospital for anyone to riffle through."

"Then how do we get in touch with him to ask him questions? Do you have an address or telephone number? Can you contact him through the hospital?"

"He's no longer with this hospital. He resigned a number of years ago. He left no forwarding address. He placed all of his former patients with other psychiatrists and left his position."

"Someone has to know where he's at," Gallo said. "He must have had contact with other doctors and patients and their families. Particularly if he went to the trouble of placing his other patients with competent professionals. He can't just have disappeared."

"Maybe he could," Catherine said. "If he was paid enough."

"You're thinking that Temple's payoff and Donnelly's resignation might not be a coincidence?"

"Donnelly had his last appointment with Danner two weeks before Temple signed that death certificate. Something big was going down about that time."

"You believe that my uncle may have told Donnelly something in a therapy session that Donnelly used as a bargaining tool?" Gallo asked. "That his confidentiality only went as far as his wallet?"

"I don't believe anything right now. I'm just throwing ideas out there to see if they stick." She paused. "But I located something else in Donnelly's records. I had to dig because it was buried deep. Donnelly was involved in a court case about that time, a patient's mother accused him of experimentation, of implanting false memories into her son's mind."

"What was the verdict?"

"I don't know, the court records were sealed. He didn't lose his license, but it might have spurred him to leave the hospital. Joe is talking to the head nurse in the psychiatric ward right now. The records clerk said she'd been here at the hospital for the last twenty years, so she'd have to have been familiar with Donnelly. I'll let you know as soon as he comes back." She hung up.

Eve pressed the disconnect and gazed at Gallo. "Well?"

"What do you expect me to say?" He turned away. "Am I scared and sick to my stomach about all this? Hell, yes. But all we know for sure is that my uncle lied to me, and he had a problem. We'll have to see what Quinn finds out."

"Yes. That hospital doesn't appear to have a great staff, does it? First Temple, and now this Dr. Donnelly. Memory implant? That would be truly criminal to experiment on a sick man." She dropped down in the chair. She felt scared and sick, too. She couldn't forget the image of the gentle, kind man who had looked at Bonnie and told Eve what a pretty little girl she was. "But I don't see how you could have been fooled. I was a stranger to him, but you must have suspected he wasn't quite . . ."

"Sane? He was more normal than anyone I knew. Almost everyone I grew up with was a little twisted and lived in dysfunctional homes. It went with the territory." His lips twisted. "When you live with poverty, vice, and drugs, you don't expect normalcy. You know that yourself, Eve."

Yes, she did. That's why she had fought so desperately to get away from that life so it wouldn't taint Bonnie. "You didn't notice anything different about him when he came back from overseas when he was discharged?"

"No." He thought about it. "It's hard to remember. No, maybe he seemed a little quieter. But I was a teenager, and I was self-centered like most kids and might not have noticed. There wasn't anything weird about him. He was a good guy, Eve."

She didn't answer.

His lips thinned. "It's true. He was the best —"

Eve's phone rang and she glanced at the ID. "Joe." She punched the button. "What did you find out, Joe?"

"I found out that the people here who know Donnelly aren't willing to talk about him. I talked to a nurse and two doctors on staff. The head nurse was wary about giving out any information at all. She said he was an exceptional doctor and had a great rapport with his patients. She knew nothing about any court case."

"Good, then there's a chance that Danner bonded with him," Eve said. "Did you get an address?"

"No, she hasn't heard from him in several years." He paused. "According to her, the reason he quit was that he was suffering severe burnout. He was going to take a rest before he opened his own practice."

"Where did he go? Can we trace him?"

"We can try. He was going to visit a cousin, James O'Leary, who lived in Ireland."

"Ireland? What city?"

"Dublin. The cousin might know something. I've already placed a few calls, and Catherine is having Venable do some checking. We should know soon." He paused. "Are you okay, Eve?"

"Fine. Confused, a little scared. But I'll get through it."

"You always do." He didn't speak again for a moment. "I don't like the way this is playing out. I want to come to you."

"Not yet." She wanted to see him, too. It

didn't seem right that she wasn't working beside him toward finding Bonnie. Yet it had been her choice, and she had to stick with it. But it was damn difficult.

"There's no reason," Joe said roughly. "Tell Gallo that we're going to find his uncle no matter what he does. I'm not going to let him find him first, so that he can decide whether or not he wants to keep him away from us. Danner is a prime suspect, and there's not going to be a cover-up."

"You know I wouldn't let that happen." She was watching Gallo's face. All the torment and uncertainty had faded, and his face was hard and without expression. What was he thinking? Whatever it was, she had to find out. "I have to go, Joe. Let me know what you learn from Donnelly's cousin."

"Eve, I mean it. I don't trust Gallo, and you shouldn't either. I need to be there with you."

"You will be. I love you." She hung up the phone. She studied Gallo for a moment. He had closed himself away from her, and she wasn't sure how to reach him. "Joe seems to have hopes of a breakthrough if he finds out where Donnelly is right now. Do you think that your uncle would have confided in this psychiatrist?"

"How can I be sure?" Gallo shrugged.

"The man you tell me he's become isn't the Ted Danner I know. You're looking at this with an objectivity that I don't possess."

"Objectivity?" She shook her head. "What the hell do you mean? This is about Bonnie. There's no way I could ever be objective about Bonnie's murderer."

"Listen to you, you've already convicted him," he said fiercely. "You're wrong. He wouldn't have killed a child."

"I hope not, for your sake." She glanced away from him. "But we have to figure out a few things before we can even delve into what he'd do or not do. How did he make a connection with Jacobs and Queen? Did you write to him and tell him that you'd been contacted by them to go into North Korea on a special mission?"

"No. As you know, Jacobs and Queen were in Army Intelligence, and they told me it was top secret." His lips twisted. "I had no idea what a dirty secret it was going to turn out to be. Drugs and smuggling instead of saving the world from nuclear proliferation. I was a fool."

"How could you know Jacobs and Queen were criminals? They deceived the Army for years." She went back to the main subject. "If you didn't tell him about Jacobs, how did he find out about them?"

"I don't know. My uncle was sharp. He'd been a Ranger for years, and he had contacts with all kinds of brass in different departments of the Army. People liked him, trusted him. Maybe he found out that Jacobs and Queen sent me on that mission."

"And that would make him angry. He was very protective of you, wasn't he?"

"Of course he was," Gallo said curtly. "He got used to trying to keep me safe from my dad. But that doesn't mean he'd go after a superior officer just for sending me on a dangerous mission. Why would he? He knew being a Ranger was risky. When I told him I wanted to join the service, he tried to talk me out of it."

"But you wanted to follow in his footsteps. He must have felt terribly responsible when he thought you'd been killed on your first mission."

"And you're saying that sent him off his rocker?"

"I'm not sure. Maybe not. I remember when Danner told me that you'd been killed, he was very bitter against the Army and anyone else who might have been guilty of contributing to sending you to your death. So he might not have been as philosophical as you think about accepting the risks of your being a Ranger."

Gallo was shaking his head.

Lord, he was stubborn. But how could she blame him when she was forcing him to look at his uncle in a completely different way than he ever had before. Tough. "It's true. He loved you, and he was bitter. That's all I know. I thought it was perfectly natural. I had no idea he had a mental problem." She had a sudden chilling memory of Danner smiling down at Bonnie and telling Eve that her daughter looked like Gallo. She had not looked any deeper than the obvious in any of Danner's actions. She had felt sorry for him. But had there been something ugly and twisted of which she hadn't been aware in that contact with Bonnie? "All we're doing is guessing. We have to get Donnelly's records of his therapy sessions with Danner."

"And we have to find Donnelly before we can do that." He turned away. "And I'm not going to wait around for Quinn or Venable to locate this cousin in Dublin. I'm going to start making phone calls myself."

"Because you want to be two steps ahead of them?"

He gave her a cool glance. "Does that surprise you?"

"No, right now for you it's all about getting to Ted Danner before any of the rest of us do. But it's not going to happen. I'm sticking with you all the way. I'm not letting you out of my sight, John."

"Really?" He tilted his head. "You're still so sure that Bonnie wants us to be together?"

"Yes." She met his eyes. "I thought it was because she knew you were in pain and needed to be here when we found out what happened to her."

His smile was twisted. "And you don't feel like that any longer?"

"Another reason occurred to me. Perhaps she wanted me to be with you to make sure that everything went as it was supposed to go. That you didn't try to stop me from finding Bonnie and the man who killed her."

"You believe I'd do that?"

She couldn't read his expression. There was hardness in the curve of his lips, and his dark eyes were glittering with a hint of recklessness. Yet she was still aware of the underlying pain that lay beneath that hardness. In which direction was he headed? Eve knew that he loved Bonnie. But he also loved his uncle and was very grateful to him for years of protection and affection in a barren world. "I don't know what I believe right now. But I'm not going to take a chance. We're joined at the hip until we find your uncle." She smiled wearily. "So you can call information in Dublin and see if we can locate Donnelly's cousin if you like. Do you know how many O'Learys there will be in that city? I'm going to call Catherine back and see if Venable or Joe can narrow down the odds. We'll see which method will get us what we need the quickest."

It took over an hour for Catherine to get back to Eve about O'Leary's phone and address.

"I found him," Catherine said. "O'Leary owns a pub outside Dublin."

"What's his phone number?"

Catherine rattled off the number. "But you don't need it. I talked to him. He was belligerent as hell and drunk as a skunk, but he did finally answer a few questions. He hasn't seen Donnelly since he visited him after he left the hospital. He stayed with O'Leary for about three months, then went back to the U.S."

"Does he have an address?"

"Not a current one. He hasn't heard from him since about a year after he left Dublin. It appears they didn't get along too well. O'Leary likes his pints a bit too much, and his cousin was always trying to make him cut down his drinking. Actually, from what

208

Venable tells me, O'Leary is an alcoholic. I can see a psychiatrist trying to help him with his problem, but O'Leary didn't appreciate Donnelly's interfering in his life."

"Where was Donnelly's last address?"

"A university town near Valdosta, Georgia."

"What? He's not practicing any longer? He's teaching?"

"He wasn't on the staff as far as we can tell. Joe and I are going down there to ask some questions. Do you want to meet us there?"

Gallo was shaking his head.

"Maybe not," Eve said. "We're in the car on our way to the airport to catch a flight for Atlanta. And I imagine Gallo wants to talk to O'Leary himself. Let us know what you find out." She hung up, and said to Gallo, "Though I don't know what you think that you can find out from O'Leary that Catherine didn't."

"Probably nothing. But there's no use all of us converging on that university town. I'm my uncle's next of kin, and maybe the hospital would tell me something they wouldn't tell Catherine and Quinn."

"And you don't want to get too close to Joe or Catherine," Eve said shrewdly. "They might get in your way."

"Very perceptive. I don't deny that could be part of it." He gazed at Eve. "When we get to the airport, I'm going to try to call O'Leary and see if I can catch something that Catherine didn't find out. She said he was drunk. But after I make that call, I'm boarding the first flight to Atlanta." He paused. "But you might prefer to catch a flight to Valdosta to meet Catherine and Quinn. You might find it more profitable."

"Forget it," Eve said grimly. "I'm not leaving you, John."

"I was afraid that would be your answer." He looked back at the highway, and said soberly, "I hope you won't regret it, Eve."

She hoped she wouldn't either, she thought. She didn't know whether staying with Gallo would translate into protecting him or battling with him. She didn't want to do either. She wanted to be with Joe at this crucial time.

Stay the course. Every instinct was still telling her that she had to travel this path.

But why, Bonnie?

"Why, Bonnie?"

Bonnie lifted her head as Eve's words swept to her like a wind through autumn leaves.

So much pain. So much bewilderment.

She couldn't always hear her mother when

210

she spoke to her when Bonnie was here on this plane. As she'd told Eve, it was like being in two different worlds with different rules and memories. She was not allowed to take this world with her. The balance was difficult, and letting her go back from here to Eve's world was a trade-off. It was usually only when Eve needed her most that she could break through the barrier and be there for her.

Why?

I wish I could tell you, Mama. I don't know myself. I'm feeling my way and hoping that everything will come together. I have to have faith that it will. I don't even know why it couldn't have happened before. I wanted all the hurt to go away for you, and it hurt me that it didn't. But there's that wonderful order here that I have to trust.

As Bonnie was doing this moment in the middle of this forest that teemed with life . . . and death.

She fell to her knees beside the injured doe that was soon going to pass to the other side.

She could see the deer's heart beating frantically with fear. Fear was always the most terrible part of the passing.

Don't be afraid. I'm here with you. She gently put her hand on the deer's head. I'll show you. See? You'll be safe soon, and there will be nothing but the joy. Do you see it?

The doe was quieting and looking up at her with eyes that no longer held the fear, only the wonder.

Trust. Love. It's all there waiting for you. It's only the beginning. Do you see it?

Wonder was being replaced by the joy in the deer's eyes.

And Bonnie knew she was beginning to see it.

"Why are you phoning me? Why the hell are you bothering me?" James O'Leary's voice was rough with irritation and slightly thick from the alcohol he'd obviously been imbibing. "I've already talked to that nosy Ling woman. She wouldn't leave me alone. I told her I didn't have time to talk to her. I have a business to run. Now you come asking me the same questions."

"Because I'm not satisfied that she got the right answers," Gallo said.

O'Leary muttered a curse. "I'm hanging up now."

"And I'll call you back. If you don't answer, then I'll get on a plane and be knocking on the door of your pub within a matter of hours. I won't give up, O'Leary. And I'm much more difficult to deal with in person. It would be much smarter if you give me a few moments right now."

Silence. "What the hell did Kevin do to you all?"

"Nothing that would get him in trouble with the authorities. We just need some information from him that he may have obtained from one of his patients."

"Then he won't tell you anything. I used to ask him to tell me if those nuts he talked to had any weird stories that would give us a chuckle. He'd never say a word. Asshole."

"You didn't get along with him?"

"He was always trying to get me off the booze. It's not his business. Just because he doesn't want to have a good time, why try to keep me from doing what I want to do? He was lousy company, always sitting around brooding or taking walks. He said that he had some heavy thinking to do. That was okay, but when he tried to tell me what to do, I blew up. I told him I didn't want him around here any longer."

"You kicked him out?"

"I had a right. We got along real good when we were in school together, but then he got all serious and telling everybody what to do. He wouldn't leave me alone. He even offered to hypnotize me to get me to quit drinking. He said that it would reinforce my will. I've got plenty of will if I want to use it. I know what's good for me." His tone was surly. "I told him to go and lecture someone else and leave me to go my own way. Do you know what he said? The bastard said if I needed him, to call, and he'd be there and work with me."

"Terrible. And you only received one card from him after he left Dublin? The one from Valdosta, Georgia."

"I got a couple more from him, but I tore them up. I didn't need him whining at me."

"From Valdosta, Georgia?"

"Yeah, I told the Ling woman that was the only address I had from him." He suddenly burst out, "It's not as if I'm some kind of criminal, dammit. So I like to drink a little. I don't hurt anyone. He acts as if I'm going straight to hell. I threw that rosary down the toilet."

"Rosary? He gave you a rosary?"

"No, some priest stopped by the pub about a year ago."

"You didn't mention that to Catherine Ling."

"Why should I? I just wanted to get rid of her. And all she wanted was to know if I had an address for Kevin."

"I think she would have been interested. What was the name of this priest?"

"Father Dominic from some church in Atlanta. He said he'd just come from Rome,

214

and he'd promised my cousin he'd get a rosary blessed by the Pope and give it to me."

"What church in Atlanta?"

"I don't know. I didn't ask. I told him to tell Kevin to go to hell. I don't need his rosary."

"The name was Father Dominic?"

"I think so. I didn't pay much attention. I just wanted him out of my pub."

"And that's the last contact you had with Kevin Donnelly?"

"That was no contact. I told you, I threw the rosary down the toilet and told the priest to get out." He was silent. "When you get hold of Kevin, you tell him that I'm doing just fine. I don't need him or anyone else telling me what to do."

"I'll be sure to let him know." Gallo hung up and turned to Eve. "Father Dominic. He had contact with Donnelly no longer than two years ago." He paused. "And Donnelly offered to use hypnosis to help O'Leary stop drinking."

"It could be an innocent offer. Hypnosis is often used by psychiatrists. It doesn't have to mean that he's endangering anyone."

"He was brought up on charges for implanting false memories. What better way than using hypnosis? I'll slit his throat if he was doing his experiments on my uncle." He checked his wristwatch. "We have forty minutes before our flight. Let's get to the gate and see if we can start making some phone calls to see if we can find a church in Atlanta that has a Father Dominic."

"There may be more than one."

"Then we'll start interviewing all the Father Dominics and try to find the right one." He took her elbow and strode toward the security gates. "And hope to hell he'll lead us to Kevin Donnelly."

CHAPTER
9

"Only two Father Dominics in the greater Atlanta area," Eve said as she hung up her phone thirty minutes later as she went down the jetway to the plane. "One in Marietta, the other in Buckhead. I'm opting for the one in Buckhead. O'Leary said the priest who visited his pub was a young man, and the priest in Marietta is in his sixties. The priest who is at St. Cecelia's is no kid any longer, but he's much younger. I tried to call him at the church, but he's not going to be there for the next six weeks. He's helping out at a church in Rome, Georgia."

Gallo frowned. "That's north of Atlanta, isn't it?"

"Yes, northwest. It's closer to Chattanooga than Atlanta, but we can make it an hour or so. I got the address from the secretary. Suppose we rent a car when we arrive and drive straight up there?"

"That sounds like a plan," Gallo said.

"We're more likely to get answers if we question him face-to-face."

"I doubt he's going to give us any problem. After all, he's a priest. We explain what we want, and he tells us where to find Kevin Donnelly." She sat down and fastened her seat belt. "Priests are definitely not any kind of threat."

Danner's hands clenched with frustration at his sides as he watched Father Barnabas from where he stood inside the garden shed. The priest was on the outdoor basketball court with the two young boys. He was laughing, his T-shirt wet with sweat as he ran down the court and made the basket. The two teenage boys groaned and ran to retrieve the ball.

The priest was happy. Once, Danner would have been glad that Father Barnabas was able to take such joy in life but not now.

He *needed* him. He had been trying to see him since early morning, and the priest had always been surrounded. First, with those sober people who had come to arrange a funeral, then with these kids from the boys' club. None of them were important. Couldn't Father Barnabas feel the torment that was tearing at him? His need was greater than theirs. The child was getting closer and would not leave him alone.

But if the priest was able to sense his torment and anger, perhaps he was afraid. Father Barnabas had great powers, and perhaps he'd been able to sense Ted's anger the last time he was here. Maybe he was trying to avoid him.

He could feel the rage growing within him.

No, control it. That was the demons again. Father Barnabas was never afraid. Even when he suspected that Danner was not . . . normal, he would only become more quiet, stronger. He would talk to him, soothe him . . . cleanse him.

Get rid of those boys, Father. Send them home.

I need to talk to you.

The little girl came to me again.

Help me. I have to do what she wants me to do.

I think she wants me to kill the Delilah demon, but I can't be sure. I can't make a mistake. That would be another sin, and I have committed so many.

Maybe it's something else that I have to give her . . .

"Very impressive," Eve said as she gazed at the huge gray stone church looming on the corner of the street in the long rays of the afternoon sun. "And unexpected in such a small Southern town. Atlanta is heavily Baptist, not Catholic."

"Well, evidently, they must have enough people to fill this cathedral." Gallo parked the rental car. "It looks very Gothic."

"Yes." Eve jumped out of the car and started up the stairs. "But I'm not very interested in architecture at the moment. We need to find this Father Dominic. I just hope —"

"Just a minute." Gallo's phone was ringing, and he glanced at the ID. "Catherine. Go on. I'll catch up."

"Right." She swung open the heavy oak door of the sanctuary. "I'll be here. Though we may have to go to the residence if there's no Mass scheduled for —"

"May I help you?" A tall, thin man in clerical garb was coming down the aisle toward them. "I'm afraid Mass isn't until seven tonight. We had to change the schedules because of the services we had to add." A crooked smile lit his thin, angular face with warmth. "Are you a member of our parish? I don't believe I've met you yet. I'm a little new here."

Pay dirt, Eve thought. "Father Dominic?"

"That's right." He shook her hand. "And you are?"

"Eve Duncan. No, I'm not a member of your church. I have a few questions we'd like to ask. I wonder if I could speak with you."

"You're thinking about joining? I'd be glad to accommodate you, but if you need any information about St. Michael's, you really need to talk to Father Barnabas. This is his church. I'm just visiting and helping out. Father Barnabas has had an unusually heavy surge of people who have joined the church lately." He shrugged. "Though that's not unusual. Times have been hard lately, and people have a tendency to turn to God when they're in need."

"Even in your church in Buckhead? Not many people are in financial need in that area, Father Dominic."

His smile faded. "How did you know that my church is in Buckhead?"

"Because you're the one I came to see. Not this Father Barnabas. May I sit down?"

"Of course." He gestured to the pew next to them. "This is God's house, not mine." He smiled again. "Well, maybe it's a little Father Barnabas's. He seems to put his stamp on everything around him."

"That's interesting," she said absently as she sat down. Get down to the reason that she was here. She just hoped he was the right Father Dominic. She hadn't even established that fact yet. "Several years ago, you visited a James O'Leary at his pub in Dublin. Is that right?"

"O'Leary?" He made a face. "Oh, yes. Not one of my most pleasant memories. He threw me out."

She gave a relieved sigh. First bridge crossed. "After you gave him a rosary blessed by the Pope."

He nodded. "And I prayed for his soul after I left him. I'm not even sure the Holy Father could —" He broke off, gazing at her curiously. "Why are you asking me this?"

"Because you told O'Leary that his cousin, Kevin Donnelly, had asked you to give O'Leary the rosary. I need to know how to find Kevin Donnelly."

He tilted his head. "You don't know?"

"If I knew, would I be asking you?" she asked impatiently. "The hospital where he worked isn't being very cooperative. We'll track him down, but there's no reason why you can't tell us where he is. It will save us time."

He chuckled. "You sound like a bill collector. Though I know Kevin would never be a deadbeat."

"You know him well?"

"Very well."

"When was the last time you saw him?"

He didn't answer directly. "Why do you want to find him? Are you one of the patients he worked with at the hospital?"

"No, but I have questions about one of this patients." She said. "You're trying to protect him? I don't want to cause him any trouble. I just want to locate one of his ex-patients and ask Donnelly a few questions."

He shook his head. "Kevin won't disclose any confidences."

"Isn't that up to him? There's a very good reason for him to tell me what I need to know." She added deliberately, "Life or death, Father Dominic. So why don't you tell me when you saw him last and where I can find him now."

"Life or death?" He was silent a moment. "Truly, Ms. Duncan?"

She looked him in the eye. "I don't lie, Father."

He nodded slowly. "No, I don't believe you would." He thought for a moment. "I don't know why I'm trying to guard him. He can take care of himself. He'd laugh at me." He grimaced. "He does that quite a bit actually."

Present tense. She stiffened. He was going to give her the information. "Tell me."

"When did I last see him?" His lips turned

up at the corners. "About forty-five minutes ago."

"What?"

"And where can you find him?" He nodded at the door to the left of altar. "Out in the garden. He's trying to repair the fountain."

She stared at him blankly. "He's a handyman?"

"Kevin is many things, a regular jack-of-all-trades." He stood up and helped her to her feet. "And actually I offered to try to fix the fountain, but he said it was his responsibility." He paused. "Since it was his church."

Her gaze narrowed on his face. "Are you saying what I think you're saying?"

"That Kevin is the priest who requested I come here and help him for a few weeks?" He nodded. "Father Barnabas."

She had suspected it was coming, but she was still stunned. "Why?"

"I assure you that he wasn't trying to go undercover or some such nonsense. He took the name when he graduated from the seminary."

"In Valdosta, Georgia." She was putting the pieces together. "That's where he went to seminary."

He nodded. "That's where I met him. We were students together. We became friends.

We're still good friends. Kevin is a remarkable man. It's not often a man gives up a lucrative medical practice and years of training to devote himself to God."

"Why did he do it? You're saying he had some kind of calling?"

"I'm saying that he's a fine man," he said quietly. "And that if you want to know anything else about him, you should ask him yourself." He gestured to the door. "And tell him if he wants to go to the office and talk to you, I'll take over repairing that fountain." He smiled. "Kevin gets fixated on a project once he starts it. He won't stop until he finishes. He's always sure that nobody else can do it as well as he can. I always tell him that God doesn't approve of the sin of vanity."

"And what does he reply?"

"He says that God wouldn't have given him a mind and a skill if He hadn't meant him to use them." He started to turn away. "Kevin always has an answer."

"I hope he has a few for me," Eve said grimly as she headed for the door he'd indicated. "I have a friend, John Gallo, who should be here soon. He stopped outside to take a phone call. Would you tell him what you told me and where I am?" She saw him hesitate, and added, "He's no threat to

Kevin Donnelly either. I promise you, Father Dominic. All he has to do is answer a few questions."

He nodded. "I believe you. As I said, Kevin can take care of himself." He headed down the aisle. "If he couldn't, he wouldn't be capable of caring for hundreds of parishioners." He glanced over his shoulder, his eyes twinkling. "With the help of God . . . and his friends, of which I count myself one of the more intelligent. I'm afraid I have a bit of vanity myself."

She could feel the excitement tingle through her. Close. She was so close. She had never dreamed that she'd be lucky enough to be heading straight to Kevin Donnelly when they'd driven up to this cathedral. "A little vanity never hurt anyone." She was moving quickly toward the door. "Thank you, Father." She opened the door, and her gaze quickly searched the spacious rose garden. It was a lovely, formal garden with a two-tiered stone fountain in the center of it. The fountain was encircled by three stone benches.

But there was only a dark-haired teenage boy in a Bon Jovi T-shirt near that fountain. He was squatting down and peering at —

"Give me the screwdriver, Billy."

"Did you find it, Father?" He moved, and

Eve could see that the side of the fountain had been jacked up, and a man was on his back and half under the fountain.

"I think so. It's calcium deposits blocking the filter. If I can clean them out, the water should run fine until I can get a new filter."

"Do you want me to do it?"

"No, not this time. I'm getting it. But the next time I expect you to be able to recognize the problem and be able to take care of it. You're studying to be a gardener, and taking care of the hardscape is as important as the planting."

It had to be Kevin Donnelly, Eve thought, as she walked toward them. Though all she could see was two black-clad legs protruding from beneath the fountain.

But when she was within a few yards of the fountain, he suddenly scooted out into the path with a quick, lithe, undulating motion. "Done." He grinned at the boy and handed him the screwdriver. "Go turn the water back on. It should flow like the Red Sea rushing back to drown the Egyptians."

"You shouldn't be so bloodthirsty, Father." The boy chuckled. "You're always telling me that I need to —" He broke off as he saw Eve. His smile faded, and he quickly whirled on his heel. "I'll go turn on the water." He hurried down the path toward

227

the church.

Eve's gaze followed him. "I didn't mean to scare him off." She turned back to the man who'd emerged from beneath the fountain. If this was Kevin Donnelly, he was a man in his fifties, with a strong, tall, muscular body, a shock of gray-flecked hair, and blue eyes surrounded by laugh lines. "You'd think I had a contagious disease."

"You're a woman," Kevin Donnelly said as he wiped his wet hands on a towel he'd picked up from the ground. "Billy has problems with women."

"He's shy?"

"No, just wary." He got to his feet. "Forgive my appearance. I've been training Billy on the basics of becoming a gardener. He has a real talent for it. I'm Father Barnabas. Is there something that I can do for you?"

"Father Dominic thought you might." She paused. "I've been looking for Kevin Donnelly."

He grinned. "You've found him."

"Also Father Barnabas?"

He nodded. "One name I was given, the other I took. These days, sometimes it's hard to remember that other life."

"Well, your cousin, James O'Leary, remembers you very well." She paused. "But he didn't know you had become a priest."

"He wouldn't have understood. He didn't accept my advice as a psychiatrist, he certainly wouldn't have let me help him as a priest." He shrugged. "I know a few people in the city, and they keep an eye on him for me. When he reaches the point of no return, I'll be there for him."

" 'Point of no return,' " she repeated. "And what is that?"

"Everyone comes to a meeting in the road with God when they've reached the final pit. They either follow Him away from it or leap into the abyss." He took out his handkerchief and wiped his brow. "But sometimes if there's someone there to explain the rules, it can make a difference."

"Yes, it can."

"Why did you phone my cousin James?"

"It was the only lead I had. The people you worked with at the VA hospital are very close-mouthed about you. Why is that?"

"Because they're good friends, and they knew I wanted to make a final break with my patients there. I set them up with fine, competent doctors who could help them, but many patients develop a dependence on their psychiatrists that's difficult to break if they find they can maintain contact. The best way is to make a clean break. When I started at the seminary, I made it impossible for me to be found." He tilted his head. "Yet you found me. I'm very curious why you bothered." He stiffened. "Unless you're a relation to one of my ex-patients?"

"Not a relation. Definitely connected." She paused. "Ted Danner. I need to know everything you know about Ted Danner."

His wariness became even more obvious. "Indeed?" He murmured, his gaze searching her face. "And why is that?"

She was silent. How much to tell him? She was suddenly aware that this man exuded a power that was very formidable. All of that casual, almost boyish charisma had vanished. "He recently murdered a man. He may murder others. Who should know better than you that he's unbalanced? You treated him for a number of years, didn't you?"

"Murder." His lips tightened. "You're sure? Not self-defense, not an accident?"

"A dagger in the chest isn't usually an accident."

His eyes closed for a moment. "Dear God in Heaven. Lost. Truly lost." His eyes were glittering with moisture when he opened them. "And mad . . ."

"You're surprised? Yet you must have known that was a possibility. You were his psychiatrist. Didn't he ever give you a glim-

mer that he was capable of killing someone?"

"Of course he did. He was a Ranger. He
was trained to kill." His lips twisted. "He
was praised when he did it right. The Army
made him what he was, then threw him to
us to heal when he became . . . unstable."

"You're blaming the military?"

He wearily shook his head. "I blame no
one but the world we live in and what it
does to us." He added bitterly, "And the
demons it causes to rise within our souls.
Ted Danner knows all about those demons.
He's obsessed with them. He probably
thought he was killing one when he stabbed
that man."

She stiffened. "You say that with some
authority. You know Danner very well?"

"As you said, I treated him for years."

"But you cut your ties to him as you did
your other patients?"

He was silent. "I cut all ties."

She had seen something in his expression.
"But did he accept it? Danner was a Ranger,
he was smart. He would know how to track
you down. Did he have some kind of pater-
nal fixation on you? Have you seen him
since you left the hospital?"

He didn't answer the question. "Who are
you? And what are you to Ted Danner? You

said you weren't a relation. Are you with the police?"

"No, my name is Eve Duncan."

He slowly nodded. "I thought I recognized you. You're the forensic sculptor. I've seen your photo in the newspaper. What do you have to do with Ted Danner?"

"You tell me." She took step closer to him. "What did he say to you?" she asked fiercely. "No one was closer to him. First, as his psychiatrist, then his priest. He did search you out, didn't he? Did he mention my daughter?"

"Your daughter?" He shook his head. "Why would he —" He stopped, as the realization hit him. "You daughter was killed years ago. You believe Danner did it?"

"I don't know. She was taken about the time you left the hospital and stopped treating Danner. Did he ever talk about her?"

He shook his head in bewilderment. "Why would he?"

He was telling the truth. "She was also the daughter of John Gallo. You must know about John."

"Ted Danner's nephew." The priest nodded. "He loves him very much. He probably doesn't love anyone else on this Earth."

"You know that, and you didn't know about Gallo's daughter?"

"Perhaps Danner didn't know." Then he muttered, "Or perhaps he did. It would explain so much. The little girl . . ."

"He knew," she said jerkily. "He knew about my Bonnie. And what would it explain?"

He didn't answer directly, "And you think he killed her?"

"It's possible. I'm going to find out. I'm going to find him. You have to help me."

He shook his head.

"Don't tell me no," she said fiercely. "You're a priest, a man of God. I've told you that Danner has already killed and might kill again. You can't let him go free. You know where he is, don't you?"

"No."

"But you've been in recent contact with him. You could find him. He must have told you something. You've got to help me."

"God will help you."

"It's your duty, dammit."

"My duty is to God and my vows."

"So pure. But how pure are you, Father? You appear to have gotten off scot-free on that charge that was leveled at you several years ago. But it just occurred to me that if you were afraid that Danner might bring new evidence and testify against you, it might ruin your bright new life. You might not want him to be found. Were you experimenting on Ted Danner, too?"

His gaze was narrowed on her face. "You've done some in-depth research, haven't you?"

"Answer me."

"But I don't have to answer you. You obviously wouldn't believe me if I did."

"Does Danner come to you in the confessional?"

"Yes. But very infrequently."

"Then you must know — you have to know something."

"And you know I can't violate the confessional."

She didn't know anything but that she didn't trust anything that he was telling her. "Not even to catch a murderer, to prevent another murder?"

He was silent. "I couldn't violate my vow. I'd have to do it in another way. I can only try to find Danner myself and prevent him from striking at another of his demons."

"Demons? You mentioned that before. What are you talking about?" She added bitterly, "Or is that something else that you have to keep confidential?" She took a step closer to him. "You listen to me, Father Barnabas. My daughter is dead and may have been killed by Ted Danner. I have to find him. I have to know everything about him. I won't stop until I do. I'll follow you everywhere you go." She paused. "And I don't care about your vows. You have to tell me what he told you."

"I can't do that," he said quietly. "You must see that I can't betray a trust. As a psychiatrist, I was bound by one oath, and when I became a priest, I became bound by an even stronger one. Either way, I mustn't break my vows."

"Or you could be protecting yourself and using your vows to keep me from finding Danner." She added deliberately. "Implanted false memories, Father Barnabas? What a horrible crime."

He looked her straight in the eye. "Yes, it is."

"Did you do it? What was the verdict of that court?"

He smiled faintly. "Another vow that I can't break. I agreed to a sealed testimony. You wouldn't want me to get in trouble with the law."

He wasn't going to help her, she realized in frustration. The priest was staring at her with an expression that was firmly determined. "Danner is a criminal. The authorities are looking for him. They won't understand about your vows, Father Barnabas."

He smiled faintly. "God will understand. I can't please everyone, Ms. Duncan. I have to choose. I realized that a long time ago." He glanced away from her. "Who is Danner supposed to have killed?"

"Thomas Jacobs." Her gaze was studying his face, but she could see no change of expression. "You don't recognize the name?"

His smile deepened. "I understand you deal with faces all the time in your profession. Can't you read me?"

"Maybe." She was silent a moment. "I don't believe he told you anything about Jacobs. But that's a guess. I don't know you, and you're obviously smart and have a good deal of self-control."

"And you're desperate to learn something you can sink your teeth into. I'm a great disappointment to you."

"You're damn right."

"And you're in pain. Such pain." He nodded thoughtfully. "I'll tell you what I can, Ms. Duncan. You won't be satisfied, but it may help you get through this." He gazed at the water now flowing from the fountain. "First, you have to know that I have no real idea where you can find Ted Danner. For the first few years after he found me and started coming to confession, he worked

236

here at the church. But then he slipped away and only came back every several months. I tried to get him to return, but he said that he was too comfortable here and that he wasn't meant to stay with me."

"That sounds amazingly self-sacrificial. I'm finding that fairly unbelievable in the context of what I know about Danner now."

"Why? Every man has to fight the sin within him. Danner's battle was more extreme than most." His lips tightened. "And as long as he stayed on his medicine, he was able to manage it. But he stopped taking it when he said it weakened him, and he was afraid he couldn't fight the demons."

"What demons?"

"He would have to identify them for you. He wanted help with them, but he would only talk about them vaguely. I couldn't pin him down."

"And you have no idea where he went when he left you or what he was doing?"

"I know he was working as a volunteer for the Salvation Army for a while in Birmingham. But then he left them, too, and started to go from job to job."

"He wasn't a young man, and he'd been injured. How could he get work?"

"The spinal operation was a complete success, and he worked out for hours every day.

He said he had to keep strong. He was almost fanatical about it. He had a tent, and there were times he lived off the land for months at a time."

He was telling her more than she had hoped. Not enough, but maybe she could push him. "Danner didn't tell you he had killed?"

He didn't answer for a moment. "Of course he did, and it tormented him. But it was always about his time in the service." He hesitated. "I cannot tell you any personal details, but perhaps it would be better if I give you an idea how my sessions with Danner proceeded. That would not be a violation. After a dozen or so appointments, he began to start loosening up. He told me about his nephew. He was completely devastated when he heard Gallo had been killed in Korea."

"But he didn't tell you about my daughter, Bonnie?"

He shook his head. "You have to understand. Danner is a very secretive man, and he's always surprisingly insecure in his relationships. I had to pull stories and feelings out of him." His lips twisted. "After we crossed the bridge in the doctor-patient relationship, I always had the feeling he didn't want to disappoint me. It's not unusual to have a patient like Danner develop a certain dependence on my good opinion. But that was a real hindrance in getting anything of any significance done. He didn't want to tell me anything that he thought would turn me against him. I've never been able to overcome that reluctance."

"And he never told you anything about Bonnie?"

"I wouldn't lie to you."

"Wouldn't you? But you said 'the little girl.' What little girl? Danner must have told you something about Bonnie."

He shook his head. "Nothing clear or concise. He never referred to her by name." He paused. "Though he did mention a little girl."

She stiffened. "Did he tell you what he did to her?"

"You don't understand. He never spoke of this little girl as a victim. He refers to her as if she's alive. It may be another child."

"Then you have to tell me where I can find her. He's a murderer. We have to get her away from him."

"I don't think that she's in danger. If I were to describe his feeling for her, I'd say he was intimidated."

"What?"

"That's my impression." He shrugged. "And that's all I can discuss with you. You had a right to know that I have no definitive information concerning your daughter." He turned away. "Rules are rules, but I don't believe God would want you tormented like that."

"Wait."

"I have to go and change, and I have an appointment with a young couple who are being married. I've told you all I can."

"Wait. You said he was lost . . . and mad. And what's all this talk of demons?"

He paused, then said, "During his bad times, he believes that he's surrounded by demons and that it's his duty to destroy them."

"Bad times? Does he have good times?"

"Oh, yes, he can be kind and generous, and he wants desperately to be good. But those times have become less frequent lately." He added soberly, "Which makes for a very dangerous condition. One moment he's fairly stable, and the next he's . . . volatile."

"You mean dangerous."

"Considering what you've told me, I have to assume that's true."

"I don't know about his good times, but I've witnessed one of his bad episodes," Eve said grimly. "He almost killed my friend Catherine. You said that you'd go after him yourself. How can you do that if you don't know where he is? Was that the truth?"

He smiled. "I don't lie. Good afternoon, Ms. Duncan."

She couldn't let him go. "John Gallo is probably inside with Father Dominic now. Will you talk to him?"

"Of course." He was walking down the path. "He's Danner's nephew. There must be great love between them. He's probably suffering right now. It's my job to alleviate suffering." He glanced over his shoulder. "But, no, my answer to him will be the same as to you. I've told you all I can reveal about Ted."

Her hands clenched as she watched him walk away from her. Questioning the priest had been like battering against an invisible wall. He had been courteous, cool, and tough as nails. There was no way to reach him and get past the barrier of his damn code. What could they do? It wasn't as if they could use force against him. How did you manage to overcome a code that had led Kevin Donnelly from the secular to the pulpit? He had given up everything because of his beliefs.

Maybe. Unless that pious front hid an inner corruption. She should have pinned him harder on that court case.

But she had to do something. There had to be a way, and she wasn't going to find it staring after the priest like this.

She started after him.

"Don't do it, Mama. You'll only get upset, and he won't change his mind."

Bonnie.

She turned to see her daughter sitting on the edge of the fountain. The sun was shining on her red curls, and the spray surrounded her in a misty aureole.

"He's got to change his mind. I have to find Danner."

"I think you'll find him, but it can't be through Father Barnabas. He's not going to give in."

"He might if I keep after him."

Bonnie shook her head. "That won't happen, Mama. He and Ted Danner have been together for a long time."

"So he's going to let Danner have a chance to kill again?"

Bonnie didn't answer.

She gazed at her in despair. "I don't understand how this works, Bonnie. I believe Danner may have killed you, dammit. Why won't you help me?"

"It has to play out the way it's meant to do. I

don't understand either, Mama. I'm trying to help, but I told you that it's only gradually becoming clear to me." She shook her head. "But I can feel your pain, and it hurts me. I want it to be over, Mama."

Lord, so did she. "Then go and make that priest help me. What good is being a ghost if you can't pull a few strings?"

Bonnie chuckled. "It doesn't work that way. Though I'm learning things all the time." She added softly, "Beautiful things, Mama. You can't imagine. I can't wait to show them to you."

"Neither can I, baby." Eve felt the tears sting her eyes. "But it was pretty beautiful when I had you with me, too."

Bonnie nodded. "But that was only the start. There's so much more." She got up from the fountain. "But we have to work our way toward it. We'll be together. But you're still on the path, and you have wonderful companions to travel with you."

Joe, Jane, Gallo, Catherine . . .

"I'm going now. Now forget about going after Father Barnabas. I don't want you to get in trouble."

"What? Do you think I'd mug a priest?"

"No, but there's no telling what else you might do to make him give you what you want." Bonnie grinned at her. "And you can be

243

very determined about getting what you want, Mama."

"I don't promise not to try with Donnelly. I don't trust him. Even if he's not as bad as I suspect, he has no right to put roadblocks in our path just because he's worried about Danner's soul. Your soul is the only one I care about."

"That's not true. You care about the souls of a lot of people. You just don't think about souls very much. People on the path are usually too busy to do that." Her smile faded as she met Eve's eyes. "You have a wonderful soul. It's deep and strong, like a clear, powerful river. It sweeps everyone along and makes them feel safe, as if they know they're headed in the right direction."

Dammit, her eyes were stinging again. She smiled unsteadily. "It sounds . . . wet."

Bonnie didn't return her smile. "You made me feel safe."

"I didn't keep you safe."

"You've told me that before. I didn't know what to answer you then. I do now. It was one of the things I learned. It was time for me to go."

Eve shook her head. "Seven years old?"

"Years don't make a difference. I was ready." She said gently, "You kept me safe, you gave me love, you made my stay beautiful."

Bonnie was the one who had made their time together beautiful. As she stood looking at her, Eve could feel the golden haze of those seven years enveloping her. She could remember every moment, every word, every touch. "I love you, baby."

Bonnie nodded. "I know. In the end, that's all there is, Mama. No regrets, just the love."

"Is that why you came to see me today?" Eve asked unevenly.

"I felt I had to be here. I wanted to come before. I knew there wasn't a threat yet, but I could feel your pain. But there are things I can do on that other level that I can't do for you yet. Wonderful things . . . It took me a little while to break away. Here, everything is confusing, and I can't see what's going on. I just have to work my way through it. But I had to do something to help you."

"You did help me." She cleared her throat. "Though I can't see things as you do." She made a face. "And don't tell me that I will someday. I have to do what I have to do. So unless you can offer me a little nudge toward getting that priest to give us a little assistance, I'd better go and see what I can do." She had to leave before she lost her resolve. This time with Bonnie was too precious, the love too strong. She turned and moved toward the church. "And I won't cause Father Barnabas any distress about — well, maybe a little distress. But not enough to worry you."

Bonnie didn't answer.
Eve didn't have to look back to know she had left her again.

CHAPTER
10

It was the child again.

Danner's heart was pounding with fear as he stared at the little girl standing by the fountain. He had been hovering in the garden house, waiting impatiently for the chance to approach Father Barnabas, when Eve Duncan had appeared. It had shocked and disturbed him, but he had not been terrified.

Until the child had appeared when the priest had left.

Danner staggered back and leaned against the wall of the garden house, trying to fade into the plaster. He was sweating, his palms cold and wet.

It was the child again. What was the little girl doing here?

Had she known he would be going to Father Barnabas and meant to stop him?

Hide.

Hide.

Don't let her see you.

He had to keep hidden until he was sure she had vanished, then go find the priest. Talk to him, and perhaps the priest would be able to tell him what he needed to know.

What do you want from me? he thought in agony as he stared at the child. I'll do anything. Just leave me alone.

The sweat was causing his palms to slide down the wall behind him.

He drew a shaky breath as he realized that the child had now vanished. When her mother had followed Father Barnabas into the church, she had faded away. The threat was gone . . . for now.

Why had she followed him here? How had she known he was going to see the priest?

But she had not seemed to be aware he was here. She had not turned to him, called his name. She had spoken to Eve Duncan, then gone away.

Perhaps he had not been the child's target. She had seemed to only want to be with her mother. When they had been speaking, the two had been totally absorbed, and even he could see the intense love that radiated between them.

He felt a jolt of pain as he remembered the way they had looked as they gazed at each other. Loneliness.

Sorry. Sorry. Sorry.

But it did no good to have regrets. The child would not accept it. She would keep coming until she got what she wanted. She would torment him until the day he died.

I'll give it to you, he thought in agony. *Anything you want. I just have to go to Father Barnabas and have him help me find out what it is that you want. Stop following me and let me alone.*

He suddenly stiffened as a thought occurred to him.

Follow?

He inhaled sharply as the thought began to grow and formulate.

Yes, that was it!

That had to be it.

He had been wrong. It wasn't the Delilah demon he had to kill at all.

The great load was being lifted from him.

He pushed away from the wall and opened the door of the garden house. He didn't have to wait to see Father Barnabas. He had the answer now.

The little red-haired girl had not been in pursuit, following him to this garden.

She had led him here.

Father Barnabas was no longer with Gallo when Eve came into the sanctuary.

Gallo whirled to face her as she came toward him. He was clearly not pleased. "What the hell? I couldn't do anything with Donnelly. He's hard as nails."

She nodded. "Frustrating. And I'm sure I didn't find out anything more than you did. I was hoping that he might lean a little toward confiding in you since he has a relationship with your uncle." She grimaced. "And it's not as if we can physically 'persuade' him to tell us anything. He's presumably doing what he believes is right. It's his duty to keep his silence."

"Presumably. Providing he's not more of a criminal than my uncle. And if he is doing what he thinks is right, hell, someone may get killed while he does his damn duty."

She tilted her head as she gazed at him. "You've been fighting desperately against believing that your uncle is guilty. Now you're suddenly worried that he may go on a killing spree?"

"I'm still fighting," Gallo said. "Father Barnabas said that he'd had years when he'd lived a good, productive life. Jacobs was a son of a bitch. My uncle may have had reason to kill him."

"And the man at the alligator farm?"

"It was a struggle. Maybe it was self-defense."

"And he was close to murdering Catherine."

"What do you want me to say?" Gallo said tersely. "So it looks like he's not sane. I can't give up on him until I find him and know for sure."

"He spoke to the priest about a child."

"He wouldn't kill an innocent child. He wouldn't kill Bonnie."

"You're sure. I can't be certain of anything connected to him. I was hoping that we'd be able to persuade Donnelly to break a rule of confidentiality when we found him." She added dryly, "But that rule of confidentiality has suddenly become almost impossible to breach for more reasons than one."

"We'll get beyond it."

"Maybe we should call Catherine back." Her lips twisted. "She could probably get a very sophisticated truth drug from her friend, Hu Chang. It's a thought."

He suddenly went still. "Not a bad one."

She quickly shook her head. "I was joking."

"I'm not. We get what we want. If Father Barnabas is telling the truth about his devotion to his vows, then his soul and conscience would be clear. He couldn't blame himself."

"How do you know? He might feel as if

he should be able to resist the drug."

"He's a priest, not a saint." He paused. "And he might not be doing a good job at being either one."

"No, Gallo," she said firmly.

"Catherine would agree with me."

Eve knew he was probably right. "Then you won't ask her, will you?"

He was silent. "It would be the most efficient way to handle it."

"Gallo."

"I'll think about it." He looked at her. "If you can suggest another way that we can get what we need from him."

"He seemed confident he could reach Danner. We keep close to him and follow him."

"But he said he didn't know for certain where my uncle was."

"Then he might be expecting Danner to come to confession. We just have to be patient for a little while."

"With the emphasis on little," he said. "I'll play it your way for now, but if it appears to be going nowhere, I'll call Catherine and ask if Hu Chang has given her anything that would be —"

"No."

He smiled faintly. "I may not have to call her or do anything at all. When I talked to her on the phone, she said she and Quinn would be on their way here. She'll analyze the situation and make her own decision."

Eve should have expected that to happen. "You told her that we had a lead on Donnelly."

He nodded. "They had already found out that Donnelly had become a priest at that college in Valdosta and taken the name of Father Barnabas. We just combined info and came up with this church as a reasonable meeting place. Quinn is going to be very suspicious. He isn't going to be any more inclined to understanding the priest's reluctance than I am."

No, three warriors with a practical mentality about getting what they want. She might be fighting this battle alone. There was a certain logic to their argument, and she was tempted to go along with their reasoning.

But she had promised Bonnie that she would be careful with Father Barnabas. In her daughter's eyes, that would include the possible disturbance of the priest's conscience.

"Then I'll have to explain my point of view." She met Gallo's eyes. "We have to find another way. There has been enough hurt to the innocents. I'm just as eager as you to find Danner, and we will." She added crisply, "Now what's the most efficient way for surveillance of Father Barnabas?"

He frowned. "I don't like —" He broke off. "The most practical method is observation and maybe to bug his car."

"And how can we do that? Where can we get the equipment?"

"We can call Quinn and get him to contact the local police and get them to help." He shook his head. "But that would probably mean dealing with red tape. It would be quicker to get the equipment ourselves from one of those local spy-and-surveillance stores you see in some of the malls."

"They can't be that popular. Do you think they'd have a store here in Rome?"

He shook his head. "I'll check on the Internet, but a small town would probably not be worrying too much about spying on nannies or checking to see if their kids are on drugs. But they'd have them in Chattanooga, and that's right next door."

"Then go get what we need."

"You think our good priest is lying about knowing where my uncle is right now?"

"No. It's hard to judge, but I don't think he lied to me. But I don't want to take a chance that he might make a good guess. Do you?"

He slowly shook his head. "We're getting

too close. Let's go."

She shook her head. "No, you go. I'll stay here." She held up her hand to stop him as he opened his lips to protest. "Observation, remember? One of us has to keep an eye on Father Barnabas."

"And who would keep an eye on you?"

"Do you actually think Father Barnabas is going to attack me in this church?" She gave him a steady glance. "It's not likely. He told me he had an appointment with a young couple who are going to be married. You'll probably be back before he's even finished with them."

He didn't move. "And you won't try to follow him if he takes off?"

"I won't do it without calling you."

"And what if my uncle decides to show up for confession?"

"Then I'll have to play it by ear." She smiled faintly. "So stop borrowing trouble and get back here so that you don't have anything to worry about."

He hesitated, then turned on his heel and strode toward the door. "It shouldn't take me more than a couple hours. Stay here."

She didn't answer.

He glanced back over his shoulder at her. "I don't like this," he muttered.

Then he was gone.

She was relieved that he had actually left her. The suggestion she had made was reasonable, but Gallo was very protective.

It must be because her argument about the safety of the sanctuary was reasonable and the time involved so little.

She did feel safe here.

She gazed around the sanctuary.

Peace. Beauty. Stained-glass windows depicting St. Francis and the animals. The crucifix over the altar.

She was not a Catholic, but there were many things she liked about the religion. The confessionals. Releasing guilt and pain by voicing them could only be healthy, both physically and mentally.

The idea that worshippers had followed the same rituals for centuries.

And the soothing silence of this sanctuary that closed out the present and brought back the past.

She sank down in the pew to the left of the aisle and closed her eyes.

Memories were flooding back to her.

Not bitter but gentle, precious memories.

Bonnie that moment in the hospital when Eve had first seen her.

Bonnie singing her special songs with Eve before she went to bed.

Joe holding Eve, smiling at her, tilting his

head thoughtfully as he listened to something she said.

"Are you waiting for Father Barnabas? You did find him, didn't you?" She looked around to see Father Dominic coming down the aisle. "You and Mr. Gallo seemed to be very intent on talking to him."

"I found him."

The priest's brows rose. "Not a satisfactory meeting? It doesn't surprise me. He's pretty well rejected the life he led before he entered the seminary, but he's very protective about his former patients. He can be very stubborn."

"Yes, he can. But so can I. Where is he? He told me he had an appointment with a young couple."

Father Dominic nodded. "He should be done now. I saw their car leaving about ten minutes ago. He's probably still in the office."

"And where is that?"

He nodded at a door to the right of the altar. He shook his head. "I know you must be in distress, but you'd be wise to accept Father Barnabas's decision," he said gently. "He won't change his mind."

"Thank you, I know you only want to be kind." She headed for the door. She smiled over her shoulder. "And maybe also to protect a fellow priest from having to deal with an annoying person from his past. I'm not going to cause him any trouble . . . at the moment."

The priest chuckled. "Father Barnabas can handle trouble. It's what we're taught to do in the seminary."

"And what I was taught growing up on the streets. So we have that in common."

"Though I doubt you'd handle it in the same way. You won't talk to me instead? I can't help you with information, but I'm a good listener."

"And you'd like to defuse any situation for him." She shook her head. "You're a good friend to him. But you can call him and warn him I'm coming if you like. He might be able to escape out the back door."

He shook his head. "He wouldn't thank me for that." He turned away. "If you change your mind, I'll be in the confessional."

"Waiting?"

He smiled. "Not for you particularly. We always hold confession at this time."

He was a nice man, she thought as she moved toward the arched opening, and very loyal to Father Barnabas. It was interesting to know that Father Barnabas could inspire that kind of loyalty. But it also pointed out what an enigma was this man who had been Kevin Donnelly.

The oak door of the office was closed, and she hesitated before knocking.

She didn't really think that questioning him again would do much good. She had principally wanted to make sure where he was in the church so that she could keep an eye on him as she'd told Gallo.

But she wasn't sure that he was still in the office as Father Dominic had guessed.

She knocked on the door.

No answer.

"Father Barnabas."

No answer.

Check to make sure.

She had been joking about him slipping out the back door, but he might have done that. She started to open the door.

"No! Get out!"

"Don't be rude, Father. Let her come in."

That last was not Father Barnabas's voice.

Yet she recognized it.

She pushed the door open.

Father Barnabas was sitting on a green-padded office chair at a desk across the room.

Ted Danner was standing behind him, a knife to the priest's throat.

"Run!" the priest said. "Out! Now!"

"But she won't do that," Ted Danner said. "Because she knows that it might save her but not you, Father. I knew the moment I met her years ago that she was one of the givers, not the takers."

Eve had been frozen, but now she took a deep breath. "Perhaps I've changed, Danner. It was a long time ago that you came to see me when I was pregnant with Bonnie. People do change." She continued meaningfully. "Events change them. Murderers take away everything that makes life worth living. That can twist their lives and what they are."

He flinched but quickly recovered. "You haven't changed. Not really. You're not going to go anywhere as long as you think that I may hurt the priest."

And Eve couldn't deceive him that she would be that hard. She could only try to go around the situation from another direction. "But you don't want to hurt him, Danner. Why would you? He's been your friend. He's been trying to help you for years. Why are you here anyway?"

"Because you're here. You're the one who is causing the problems for the priest." He said jerkily, "Do you think I want to hurt him? I thought he could save me, but now I know that's not going to happen. I only want to do what's right, but you're against me. You came here to turn him against me. If you hadn't shown up here hunting for me, he would have been safe. But I know now that's the way it should be, how it's meant to be. I should have guessed it."

"I did come to ask his help, but he refused me."

"But you wouldn't stop, you'd keep after him. You're determined, and you'd have convinced him to trap me."

"Put the knife down, Ted," the priest said quietly. "It's you who will be hurt if you keep this up."

"I can't put it down. It's all up to me now," Danner said hoarsely. "You wouldn't help me, you wouldn't tell me what I needed to know. I asked you and asked you. You were probably protecting her and hoping I wouldn't know. Now I have to do it all myself." He stepped back and gestured with the knife. "Come in and close the door, Eve. Throw your handbag on that couch and come forward with your hands raised."

"When you let Father Barnabas leave."

"I can't do that. He's not my friend any longer. He would run and tell everyone where I am."

"Do you mean tell your nephew, John? He's not here."

"I know. I watched him drive away. I would have waited if he'd still been here. He would have tried to stop me, and I might have hurt him. I mustn't hurt John."

"Because you love him," Father Barnabas said gently. "Can't you see that's going to happen sooner or later unless you give yourself up to the authorities? How many times have you told me how much alike the two of you are? It will be either you or him, Ted."

"It will be later, and, by that time, I won't care if he kills me. It won't matter." He grabbed the priest's arm and pulled him up from the chair. "Eve, go out ahead of us through the back door to the garden. Then we're all going to go out the garden gate and up the street to where my car is parked. When we reach it, I'll let the priest go." He met Eve's gaze. "Don't try to run, don't make any attempt to attract attention, or I'll put this knife in his back."

"No!" She quickly came into the study and closed the door. She threw her handbag on the couch. "You want me to come with you? Why?"

"You have to come with me. You're the reason I came here."

"She's not a demon, Ted," the priest said. "Tie her up and let's get out of here. I'll go with you somewhere, and we'll talk."

"I know she's not a demon. I was wrong. I understand now. It's not a question of demons." He pushed Father Barnabas toward the door. "I know how to keep them under control now. Coming, Eve? She's waiting for you. I'll take you to her."

Eve stiffened as if he'd struck her. "What are you talking about, Danner?" But she had a chilling idea that she knew what he was talking about.

"The little girl."

Eve's breath left her body.

"You're not taking her anywhere, Ted," Father Barnabas said. "This isn't smart."

"You can't expect a madman to be smart," Danner's lips twisted. "Do you think I don't know you've always thought I was crazy? You were always so gentle, so patronizing. But you weren't there. You didn't see them."

"You are smart. And you can choose to fight madness or let it destroy you. We've talked about that before. Come with me, let me talk to you." He paused. "I can't let you do this."

Oh, Lord. Danner couldn't see the priest's expression, but Eve could. He was going to make a move on Danner.

And Danner's knife was within six inches of Danner's back.

She moved swiftly toward the desk. "Stay out of this, Father. This is between Danner and me."

But Father Barnabas's muscles were bunching, tensing.

And she couldn't let him attack Danner to save her.

She was too far from Danner to attack him. But there was a granite paperweight on the desk.

The priest was going to make his move. He started to turn on Danner.

"No!" She leaped forward and snatched up the paperweight on the desk. She brought it down on the priest's head, then moved to get between him and Danner's knife.

The priest staggered and fell against the desk.

The edge of Danner's hand sliced down on the side of the priest's neck in a karate chop.

Danner stepped back as he watched Father Barnabas crumple and fall unconscious to the floor. "Fool," he muttered. "I didn't want to hurt him. I like him."

"But you threatened him," she said. "What did you expect? He's a man who would try to guard and protect. It's his vocation."

"I know, I know. But he should take care

of himself. He made me do it." He glanced at the granite paperweight still in her hand. "Drop that and come along. Or you might force me to reconsider my feelings about Father Barnabas."

She hesitated. It was her only weapon.

But it had only been effective because she'd had the advantage of surprise. She released the paperweight, and it fell to the floor. "You said something before." She moistened her lips. "You said 'she's waiting. The little girl.' What did you mean? Why do you want me to go with you?"

"Because she wants you to go." He gestured with the knife. "We have to leave now. Someone might come."

She didn't move. "She?"

He opened the door to the garden. "I keep telling you, the little girl."

She inhaled sharply. "What do you —"

He shook his head. "No more talk. It can't happen here. It's not the right place. Come on."

She stared at him, her heart pounding. What was the right place?

Because she wants you to go.

The words of a madman?

Or a message from Bonnie? The opportunity to bring her daughter home.

"Why are you being stubborn?" He was

frowning. "You have no choice."

She had a choice, but if she made the wrong one, he might kill her right now, and Bonnie might be lost forever.

And wasn't this what she had wanted? To find Ted Danner, to make contact and make sure that he was Bonnie's killer? To find Bonnie? It might not be the way she wanted it to happen, to be helpless and at his mercy. Of course it wasn't the way she wanted it to happen. But she might still be able to work the situation to her advantage. She had no weapons, but Joe had trained her in hand-to-hand martial arts and Danner might not expect her to be versed in any deadly skills.

She moved toward him. "I'm coming."

"I thought you would once I got rid of the priest." He stepped aside to let her precede him. "I knew everything was going to come out all right for me. I should have relied on myself in the beginning. But I was so afraid. . . ."

There was a police car parked in front of the cathedral, its lights blinking.

"Oh, shit." Gallo pulled up behind the police car and jumped out of the car. A TV news truck pulled in right behind him, and techs and reporters were right behind Gallo as he took the steps two at a time and burst

266

through the front entrance of the cathedral. Father Barnabas and Father Dominic were sitting in a pew talking to two men dressed in dark suits, and there was a uniformed officer beside the altar.

Gallo stopped short as the media crews poured down the aisle on either side of him and ran toward the priests and police.

Not good.

No Eve.

Father Barnabas looked up and saw him and fought his way through the ring of reporters and strode toward him down the aisle. "I'm sorry," he said gently. "I tried to stop him."

"My uncle?" Gallo said jerkily. "Eve? What the hell happened? I thought she was safe. I was gone less than two hours. Did he hurt her?"

The priest shook his head. "I don't think so. He wanted her to go with him. He threatened me to make her do it." He smiled ruefully as he rubbed his temple. "As I said, I tried to stop him. Eve Duncan hit me on the head to keep me from rushing him. I wasn't expecting that. She was evidently trying to protect me."

"Yes, Eve can be unpredictable," Gallo said absently. Unpredictable and brave and strong. Dammit, he should never have left her. "Did he give you any idea where he was going to take her?"

Father Barnabas shook his head. "When I woke up, they were gone, and Father Dominic was standing over me."

"He didn't say anything?"

"He said that he knew Eve wasn't a demon."

Gallo muttered a curse. "Is that supposed to be good?"

"Yes, Danner thought he was surrounded by demons, particularly of late. The last time I saw him, I even wondered if he included me in that group." He paused. "And he believed he had to destroy demons. It's a good thing that he doesn't think Eve Duncan is one of them."

Gallo felt a chill. But what if his uncle changed his mind? "Then why did he want her to go with him?"

Father Barnabas hesitated, then said, "He said the little girl was waiting for her."

The little girl.

Shit. The chill he was feeling became pure ice.

"You believe he was speaking of Bonnie Duncan?" the priest asked quietly. "And the little girl who is waiting is dead?"

"Yes."

"And that would mean he's going to —"

"It doesn't mean anything. Maybe he knows who killed Bonnie. There might be some other explanation." No, he wouldn't believe it. But it still scared the hell out of him. "Listen, you've got to tell me where you think I can find him."

"I don't know. If I did, I'd tell you." He met Gallo's eyes. "I'm not a fool. I know that she's in danger. Danner has gone over the edge. He wouldn't listen to me." He paused. "But I may be able to help you find him. I don't want to be left out of this. I know him very well." He paused. "Better than you, Mr. Gallo."

"You know him as some kind of sicko. That wasn't the man I knew while I was growing up."

"Then we'll have a complete picture, won't we? But I never considered Danner a sicko. All I knew was a man in torment, trying to find solace for his pain." He glanced over his shoulder. "Those detectives will be getting restless. I was planning on asking them to allow me a few moments alone with you to break the news about Eve Duncan's kidnapping. But you were lucky that you came in with that horde of reporters, and the police were too busy to pay any attention to you. But I'd better get back to them."

"Did you tell the police who I was?"

"Of course, I wouldn't lie to them. I skimmed over your connection with Eve, but as next of kin of her abductor, they'll be very interested in talking to you."

The last thing he needed was to have the police interested in him, Gallo thought in frustration. He was still wanted in Wisconsin for questioning, and there was no way he could waste time being grilled by the local police when he had to find Eve.

"I have to get out of here."

The priest nodded. "I thought you would. Go on. You'd better be very quick. As I said, I won't lie to them." His lips tightened. "But I believe that the people who know Danner best have the best chance of catching him before he does something . . ." He trailed off as he turned. "Go. I'll be very slow getting back down that aisle to them. Call me if you run across anything that I can help you with. I'll be trying to remember any details about him that could make sense about where he might take her."

"Or what he wanted with her. I can't believe he wants to kill her."

The priest didn't answer as he moved slowly down the aisle.

Gallo whirled and ran out of the church and down the steps. In seconds, he was behind the wheel of his car and tearing away from the curb and down the street. Get away. Put some distance between him and the police.

Think.

He could do little else but think in those minutes of flight. Father Barnabas's words were pounding in his mind like a drum. Why? His uncle would have no reason to target Eve.

But if they were right about him, his uncle was without reason.

He felt sick. So many memories were flooding back to him of those days of his childhood. Ted Danner had been hero and savior to him.

And in a world in which Gallo could trust no one, his uncle had never once let him down. The man who killed Bonnie was a monster. How could that friend of his childhood be a monster?

It didn't matter. Stop thinking of anything but the fact that Eve had been taken and could die. No matter what rejection he felt about the possibility, he had to admit that it existed. What to do next?

He didn't pull into a rest stop off the main road until thirty minutes later.

He knew the first thing to do. Gather all the help he could around him to find Eve.

He pulled out his phone and called Catherine. "How close are you to Rome?"

"About an hour. Are you still at the cathedral?"

"No, but you'll run into half the Rome police department there." He paused. "I screwed up. I left Eve alone for less than two hours at the church. I thought she'd be safe there."

She was silent. "What are you saying, Gallo?"

Lord, this was hard. "She wasn't safe," he said haltingly. "My uncle showed up and took her. I don't know where she is."

He heard Quinn cursing in the background, then suddenly Quinn was on the line. "I may kill you, Gallo."

"I wouldn't put up a fight. Except that it may take all of us to get Eve out of this alive."

"You're sure she's still alive?"

"Father Barnabas said that he believes that she is. He said that my uncle said that she had to come with him." He paused and then forced it out. "He said that the little girl was waiting for her."

Quinn was cursing. "That sounds weird as hell. Tell me everything that's happened since you arrived in Rome."

Gallo quickly filled him in, and then ended with, "Now we have Father Barna-

272

bas's cooperation. At least, that's what he told me. He's not going to attempt to reach out to my uncle on his own. He said he'd try to recall details of what he'd been told by him through the years so that we can make a pattern."

"Try? He'll recall every single detail, or he'll wish he had."

"The third degree? I thought that was no longer politically correct. Particularly when applied to a man of the cloth."

"It's Eve, dammit."

And that meant every method was on the table as far as Quinn was concerned. And Gallo was feeling the same way. Father Barnabas could be totally sincere or the prime demon who had tormented his uncle over the years. "Then nudge his memory. Can you contact the local police and see what their investigation manages to un-earth?"

"That goes without saying," Quinn said curtly.

Then Catherine was back on the line. "What did Eve have with her when she was taken? Any weapon?"

"No, the priest said that she was forced to put down her purse when she entered the study."

"What about her phone?"

"Maybe. She was carrying it in the pocket of her slacks."

"Good. We can start there. I'll call Venable and see if he can get a GPS trace."

"My uncle is no fool. He'll find that phone."

"But we may have a little time before he does. We can determine a direction. For the rest, we may have to rely on Eve."

"For God's sake, how can she help?" he asked bitterly. "My uncle was a top-notch special services officer. If you're right about him, he's now also a maniac who would —" He stopped and drew a deep breath. "Sorry. I'm not thinking, only feeling right now. I should have been there to help her."

"Yes, you should have been there," Catherine said coolly. "But now we have to forget that and find her. Eve is very clever, and I've never met anyone more determined. A sharp mind can be more lethal than any weapon. Now where are you?"

"About forty miles west of Rome. I couldn't stick around the cathedral. The police would have checked me out and gotten that warrant on me from Wisconsin."

"No, that would have been a nightmare waiting to happen. We'll meet you, and — No, Joe is shaking his head. He wants to go to the cathedral and talk to that priest. He

274

said if the priest knows anything about where to find Danner, he'll choke it out of him if he has to. He can drop me off somewhere to rendezvous with you and go on there without me. The minute we find out anything about Eve from Venable or the priest, we'll take off on the trail. I'll call you when we get closer, and you can give me exact directions." She hung up.

Gallo pressed the disconnect.

As usual, after talking to Catherine, he felt as if he'd had a shot of adrenaline. She always cut through every emotion that got in the way of accomplishing what needed to be done.

He needed that shot of pure, clear energy right now.

He needed Catherine Ling.

CHAPTER
11

"Are you okay, Joe?" Catherine shot a glance at Joe's face after she hung up the phone. His expression was grimmer than she'd ever seen it. Who could blame him? She was feeling pretty damn grim herself. "We've got a start. The priest may remember something."

"And he may not. If he does, he's going to tell me. No, I'm not okay. I want to kill Gallo."

"Yet either one of us might have done the same thing. There didn't seem a very big risk."

"That doesn't help."

"Because you're feeling and not thinking. Like Gallo."

"And you're defending him."

"It was clear he didn't want anyone to defend him. He's piling enough guilt on himself to sink the *Titanic*." She looked out the window. "Yes, I'm defending him.

Someone has to do it. This isn't the time to fight among ourselves."

"I know that." His grip tightened on the steering wheel. "But it's easier to imagine taking Gallo apart limb by limb than it is to imagine what could be happening to Eve."

Catherine knew what he meant. She was blocking out all thought of the threat aimed at Eve. "As I said, we have the priest. And if Gallo can contact Danner, we have a chance he'll have enough influence to shift the scales. Father Barnabas said Danner loves Gallo."

"If we can contact the bastard." His lips tightened. "And if Gallo can stop worrying about him instead of Eve."

"Gallo will do everything he can to find Eve."

"So you're going to join him and shepherd him in the right direction?"

She shook her head. "There's no shepherding Gallo. I'm going to join him for two reasons. There's no use both of us hovering over Father Barnabas and trying to prod him. I'd just be spinning my wheels. Gallo and I are both trained hunters. I'm CIA, and he was a Ranger. If Venable or you can give us a lead, then we can get on the trail."

"And leave me out?"

She smiled faintly. "Are you kidding? A

two-prong attack is always more effective. You know that, too, or you wouldn't be heading for the cathedral when you want to go directly after Danner and grab Eve from him." Her smile faded. "But I'll have Danner's affection for Gallo to use against him, and I'd do it, Joe."

"If Gallo will let you."

She shook her head. "I'd do it. That bastard had no right to take Eve. We have to get her back." She met Joe's eyes. "Alive. We'll get her back alive, Joe."

He didn't answer.

"Joe?"

"I'm not sure, Catherine," he said thickly. "I'm not sure how this is going to end. I just know I'm scared shitless."

And so was Catherine, but she couldn't admit it right now. Keep busy. She reached for her phone. "I'll call Venable and get him working on that GPS. If that doesn't work, I know Eve will find a way to let us know where she's located or where she's going."

"You have a lot of faith in her."

"Of course, and so do you. Eve can do anything she wants to do."

He didn't speak for a moment. "You're right, and that's what's scaring me." He added somberly, "Anything she wants to do."

■ ■ ■ ■

"We've been driving in circles." Eve broke the tense silence that had stretched between her and Danner for the past two hours. She was gazing out of the window of the truck. "Just where are we going, Danner?"

"I have to be sure we're not followed. A diversionary tactic," Danner said. "I'm not afraid of the police. I can handle them. But you came to the church with John. He mustn't be part of this."

"Because you don't want him to know what you are?"

He looked at her. "Are you trying to make me angry? You can't do it by throwing John in my face. He's always been the best part of my life."

"I know you loved him."

"Not past tense. I do love him."

"He loved you, too." She paused and then said deliberately, "Of course, he didn't know you were a murderer."

"Yes, he did. I killed in the military, and I never tried to hide it from him. I served my country, and he was proud of me."

"But were you proud?"

"I served my country."

"You didn't answer me."

"I don't have to answer you. Why should I? I won't make excuses. I don't have to talk to you at all."

She ignored the reply, and went on, "You might have felt like a patriot for a while but that changed, didn't it? Your psychiatrist who first examined you after you came back from Syria said that something happened that tipped the scales and sent you off the track. What was it?"

"Why are you asking me all these questions? What do you care? That has nothing to do with what's happening now. Do you think that we're going to form some kind of bond? You'll be disappointed. I can't afford to do that."

She nodded. "I could have formed a bond with the man who came to see me and Bonnie when she was just a baby. I felt sorry for you. I wanted to help you. All I saw in you was sorrow, not rage. What happened, Danner?"

"Shut up. I don't need your help. I didn't then, I don't now. You're the one who needs help."

Her gaze searched his face. "Why, Danner?"

"Can't you see? Are you stupid? You're sitting there, with your hands tied, and you know what I am." His gaze searched her face. "And you keep asking me questions. Why aren't you afraid?"

"Do you want me to be afraid?"

"I want you to stop asking me questions."

"You don't have to answer them." She looked down at the ropes binding her wrists in front of her. "No, I'm not afraid. But being tied does make me feel helpless. I suppose that increases your sense of power."

"Yeah, it does."

She smiled faintly. "I think you're lying. I believe it makes you uneasy to see me like this."

"Believe what you like." He was silent a moment. "Why aren't you afraid? I did kill Jacobs, you know."

"I know. And you would have killed my friend, Catherine. Why?"

"Demon. The moment I saw her, I knew she was a Delilah."

"I don't know about Jacobs, but Catherine is no demon. I'm not sure there are demons."

"Then you're a fool," he said harshly. "They're all around us. Look away from them, and they'll have you." He tore his gaze away from her. "You have to fight them all the time."

"And what would they do if they caught you?"

281

"They'd devour my soul," he said simply.

"And is my Bonnie a demon?"

He stiffened. "I don't want to talk about the little girl."

"Father Barnabas said you've never spoken of her by name, that you only talk about a little girl. That little girl is Bonnie, isn't she?"

"I won't talk about the little girl."

"Why not?"

"Be quiet."

She was disturbing him. His hands were clenched on the steering wheel, and there was a flush burnishing his cheeks. The mere mention of "the little girl" had done this to him.

"I'll be quiet for now." She looked away from him. "But you'll have to answer me sometime, Danner."

"No, I won't. I'll shut you up."

"By killing me?"

"I don't want to talk about it."

Change the subject. "Where are you taking me, Danner?"

"To the place."

"What place?"

"Her place."

She inhaled sharply. Dear God, was he speaking of the place where he'd hidden Bonnie's body? Her heart was starting to pound. After all the years of searching, was she this close? "I don't understand. Explain. Please."

He shook his head. "You'll know later. She'll tell you."

She was so frustrated she wanted to shout at him. So damn close.

Control. Patience. She drew a steadying breath. "Okay, I'll let it go. But I have to come back to it. I have to know everything, Danner. If I make it easy for you. If I go with you, if I don't fight you, will you tell me what I need to know?"

He didn't speak for a moment. "You won't fight me?"

"No."

"I don't want you to fight me. I'd hurt you, and John wouldn't like it."

Danner's reasoning was complex and bewildering. She was almost sure he intended to end her life. Evidently, killing her was all right, but not inflicting pain. "No, John does care about me. He would be angry if you hurt me."

"I don't know why it should matter to me," he said jerkily. "It's just a drop in the ocean. He'll never feel the way he did about me before. But I have to do the best I can. I know it would matter to me. I've never wanted to cause anyone pain." His eyes were glittering with moisture. "You make it easy for me and I'll tell you anything you want to know." He added hoarsely, "And I'll promise to make . . . it easy for you."

He meant her death, she realized. She had been almost sure that was to be the final act, but it still gave her a tiny shock.

"Now you're afraid?" His gaze was narrowed on her face.

"No." Shock, not fear. He was taking her to Bonnie. What was there to fear? One way or the other they'd be together. "I'm . . . eager."

"You think you're going to get out of it, that you'll be able to get what you want, then get away from me."

She didn't answer.

"You won't be able to do it." He suddenly turned the wheel, and the truck was bouncing along a rutted dirt road into the forest that bordered the highway. "But I still think you'll keep your promise. From the moment I met you I knew you were a straight shooter. I thought that John was lucky to have met you, before he went into basic training. I never had much luck with women. I got so I couldn't trust them. But you were different. Honest . . ."

She was being jounced from side to side on the seat, and tree branches were striking the windshield. "Does this road lead some-where?"

"Yes." They suddenly came out of the trees into a small clearing. "Here." He braked and stopped the truck. "Time to ditch the truck and start out on foot." He jumped out of the truck and came around to the passenger seat. He jerked her out and quickly ran his hands over her body. He pulled her phone out of the pocket of her slacks. He muttered a curse. "Dammit, I should have searched you before you got in the truck." He threw the phone on the ground and smashed it under his foot. "That damn GPS signal."

And there went her only way of being tracked. "The curse of modern technology." She added sarcastically, "You mustn't blame yourself. You were in a bit of a hurry kidnap-ping me at the time. You were so concerned about roping me like a calf to be branded."

"Shut up." He turned toward a tarp canvas structure stretched between two pine trees. He grabbed a backpack and slipped it on. "We have to get out of here. They'll be able to trace that phone."

"Probably." She was looking at the tarp. "This is a surprise. A home away from home. Maybe I should have expected it. Father Barnabas mentioned that you lived off the land on occasion. Why, Danner?"

"It keeps me away from the demons. There are animals here, but the demons don't take over their souls. I'm safe here." He picked up a Magnum pistol and gestured to her to go ahead of him. "Stop asking questions and start out. We've got a long way to go."

"But you said you'd answer my questions." She moved forward in the direction he'd indicated. "How far, Danner?"

"It should take us maybe two days if you don't hold me up. We have to travel through the woods and avoid the roads. It's rough country."

"I won't hold you up, Danner."

"I'm not so sure. You're not the tough sixteen-year-old kid you were when we met all those years ago. I would have bet on her. These days, I hear you spend your life messing around with clay and stuff."

"You evidently have kept track of me." She glanced at him over her shoulder. "Then you must know my purpose in 'messing around' with that clay."

"Yeah." His glance shifted away from her. "Skulls. But I don't like to think about it. You shouldn't mess with the dead."

"I don't agree." And Danner's statement had put her on edge. It didn't bode well for

286

his telling the truth about taking her to Bonnie. "And neither would the parents of those children I managed to identify."

"I don't like to think about it," he repeated.

Don't argue. She had to balance very precariously on this fragile thread that bound them together. The priest had said that Danner could shift from sanity to madness in the space of moments. Right now, he appeared to be almost normal, but she didn't want to throw him into that other sphere. She had to analyze every word, every thought that he expressed, sift it for truth or fantasy, and perhaps go back to it later. She had to keep herself from going on the attack so that the words would flow and tell her what she needed to know.

Not an easy task.

There were moments when the possibility that this man had killed her Bonnie stabbed into her, and she wanted to turn and rend him.

But she had to be sure.

And nothing must stop him from leading her to Bonnie.

"No, I'm not sixteen any longer." She turned and started down the path. "But you'll find those years haven't made me less tough. Strength comes from inside. I don't quit, Danner. I won't hold you up."

Gallo was standing by his car in the parking
lot of the Shoney's Restaurant in Calhoun,
where they'd agreed to meet, when Joe
pulled into the space beside him.

Gallo straightened, his gaze fixed warily
on Joe.

He should be wary, Catherine thought, as
she got out of the car and pulled out her
duffel. Joe was scared and feeling helpless,
and that made him ready to explode. The
best thing to do was get Gallo away as soon
as possible.

"Let's get out of here. Joe wants to get to
that church and question Father Barnabas."
She threw her duffel in Gallo's car. "I called
Venable, and he said he'd get cracking on
the GPS fix. I also told him to find a way to
get a look at those sealed court records of
Kevin Donnelly's trial. That will take some
time, but we've got to see who we're dealing with in our Father Barnabas. He should
be calling me back anytime now on the GPS
fix." She turned back to Joe. "I'll let you
know as soon as I hear anything. It's going
to be okay, Joe. We'll get her back. Come
on, Gallo."

"Wait a minute." Gallo was still braced
and wasn't moving, his gaze on Joe. "It

shouldn't have happened. You want to say anything? Do anything? I'll take it."

Joe looked at him without speaking. Catherine could almost feel the explosive anger vibrating from him. She instinctively stepped forward, readying.

Joe didn't even glance at her. "Yeah, I want to say something, Gallo. I'd take you out in a heartbeat if I didn't think that I might need you. Do you know why you let it happen? You've been a professional, you're sharp, and you're not careless. So why make that mistake? Because even now you can't believe that son of a bitch, Danner, is a killer. Subconsciously, you didn't believe he was a threat to Eve. Well, you're wrong, and I'm going to tell you how you're going to make it right. The next time you have to choose, it's going to be for Eve. If someone is going to die, it's going to be Danner . . . or you. At the moment, I don't give a damn which one."

Gallo's lips were tight, and his eyes were glittering. "It will be for Eve." He whirled and got in his car. "I promise, Quinn."

Close. Very close.

Catherine quickly slipped into the passenger seat. "I'll be in touch, Joe."

But Joe was already pulling out of the parking space and didn't reply.

Gallo didn't move. He was gazing straight before him. "He's right, you know. I made a choice, and I didn't even realize it. I decided not to believe what everyone said about him. And Eve is the one who is paying for it." His lips twisted. "And I can't even say that I believe it now. It hurts too much. All I can say is that I have to be sure that whoever gets hurt, it won't be Eve."

He *was* hurting. She wanted to reach out and touch him, comfort him. It was hard for him to admit that pain to anyone.

"It would kill me if anything happened to Eve." He glanced at Catherine and forced a smile. "I love her, you know. Oh, not in the usual romantic way, we're past that. But we've shared too much not to feel something for each other, and that will go on. Can you understand that?"

"Yes. I'm not blind, Gallo. You should love her. She's worth loving. I love her, too. Now let's stop talking about how we'd feel if anything happened to her and set about keeping that from happening."

"Rebuke accepted." His smile was no longer forced as he started the car. "I can always count on you to blow away any sentiment that's clouding the clarity of perception. I apologize."

"You have a right to be a little less than

clearheaded. But only a little, Gallo. We have to —" Her phone rang, and she glanced down. "Venable. I'll put it on speaker." She spoke into the phone. "What have you got, Venable?"

"The GPS signal led to a location about forty miles outside the town of Caryville, Georgia. Not in the town itself, but somewhere in the woods surrounding it." Venable paused. "Then it disappeared entirely. We lost it. Do you want me to send a man from Atlanta to check it out?"

"No, we'll cover it. Give me the exact coordinates." She scrawled down the directions as he gave them to her. "Thanks, Venable."

"No problem." Silence. "I like Eve Duncan. If you need me, I'll come."

"If we need you, I'll call. Danner isn't stable. We have to be careful about spooking him with too much manpower." She hung up. "Caryville, Gallo."

He nodded. "I checked the GPS while you were talking. It's about an hour south of here." His foot pressed hard on the accelerator. "Or less."

They arrived at the Caryville city limits in forty-five minutes.

Catherine glanced at the coordinates. "There!" She pointed at the lay-by with a strip of road leading off it. "He must have entered the woods there." She braced herself against the impact as he drove down the rough road. "What the hell . . ."

"The trees are thinning up ahead." He drove into the glade and screeched to a stop as he saw the truck parked by a tarp. "Down!" He drew his gun as he dove out of the car.

Catherine was already on the ground on the other side of the car.

No sound but the soft whir of birds and insects.

No shots.

"Danner!" she called.

No answer.

Gallo was on his knees on the ground behind the rear wheels of the truck. "I'll check under the tarp. You look in the cab of the truck."

"I think it's okay. I don't think he's here." But she was still tense as she pulled herself up to glance inside the truck. Danner might not be here, but that didn't mean he might not have left Eve dead in the vehicle. She expelled a sigh of relief as she saw that neither Danner nor Eve were in the cab. "Empty." She turned toward the tarp. "Anything?"

"No." He was standing under the tarp and

gazing at the neat stack of canned goods piled in one corner. "Supplies enough for a few days' stay. He wouldn't need more. He's woods savvy." He opened a metal box set against the tree. "Ammunition."

"Weapons?"

"No, he must have taken them with him." He was examining the cartridges. "A Magnum and an M16. The rifle is still here."

"Taken them with him where?" Catherine asked. "And why take Eve? If he was going to get rid of her, this would be the place to do it." She was examining the tire tracks. "He didn't change cars and double back. He left the truck here and must have set out on foot." She glanced at the woods surrounding the glade. "We just have to find his prints and track him."

Gallo nodded as he moved toward the north. "And hope that he's not waiting to pick us off."

"It's promising that you admit that's a possibility, but I don't believe there's any danger. That's why I wasn't too worried that he'd still be in this glade. No matter what he feels about anyone else, it appears he still cares for you." She turned and rounded the hood of the truck to head for the south border of the glade. "And if I'm lucky, I'll bask in that warm, fuzzy circle that surrounds you. Though from what I remember of him standing over me at that bayou, I may not be —" She broke off as she knelt on the ground. "I think I found the missing GPS." Her finger touched the wreckage of the iPhone. "Eve's phone. We definitely won't be able to track her by that." She got to her feet and moved across the glade. "So we rely on ourselves and not technology."

He smiled slightly. "It's not as if we don't have experience."

His words brought back a flood of memories of those weeks she had stalked Gallo in the wilds of Wisconsin before she had become convinced he had not killed Bonnie. That time had become a fascinating and challenging game when the prey had turned hunter, and they had gradually begun to know each other in ways that neither had dreamed. For the briefest instant, she felt a stirring of the sensual heat that had become a part of the chase before she blocked it. "Yes." She met his gaze. "And this time we'll be working toward the same goal. We'll be doing this together."

He nodded and turned away. "It may take two of us. My uncle is sharp and experienced. He'll try to cover his prints. . . ."

When Joe was twenty minutes from the

cathedral, he placed a call to Father Barnabas. He didn't expect it to be picked up, but he took the chance. It rang four times before it was answered.

"Father Barnabas, my name is Joe Quinn. I need to talk to you. I know you've undergone a terrible experience but —"

"Where are you, Detective Quinn?"

"About twenty minutes from you. Detective? Eve told you about me?"

"No, we didn't discuss anything but Ted Danner. But the detective who questioned me seemed to have tapped a good deal of information regarding you and Eve Duncan. He asked me if I knew you, and he told me that he had to question you. I told him that you had nothing to do with the taking of Ms. Duncan, but he said that it was always necessary to question the husband or significant other in a relationship."

"That's true. Is the detective still there?"

"No, he just left. But there's a policeman on duty. I reminded him about the adage about locking the barn door after the livestock was stolen, but he insisted anyway. If you wish to see me privately, it would be better if we met in the rose garden in the back. You can go to the cross street beyond the church and double back and go in the garden gate."

"You'll meet with me?"

"Certainly. I've been expecting you. Eve Duncan is a strong woman, and her disappearance would cause ripples that go far and deep. I'll see you by the fountain in the garden."

There was a uniformed policeman on guard outside the cathedral when Joe drove past it and up to the cross street. That meant that the back entrance would likely be unguarded.

Ten minutes later, he was walking down the garden path toward the fountain. It was dark, but the fountain area and the man sitting on the bench beside it were illuminated by a gas lamppost on the rosebushes on either side.

"Father Barnabas?"

"Sit down, Detective Quinn. I'd stand to greet you, but I'm still a little woozy." The priest smiled. "I'm sure that Eve Duncan didn't mean to hurt me by that blow to the head, but it was immediately followed by one by Ted Danner. He definitely meant to put me out of action for a while."

"Yet the two of you have had a close relationship that's spanned years." He sat down on the bench. "He was willing to give that up just to make sure he got his hands on Eve? Why?"

"Lately, our relationship has not been as close as it once was. He won't listen if I don't say what he wants to hear." The priest's smile faded. "Danner has changed. He claimed that his medication is keeping him from being alert enough to guard himself from the demons and refused to go back on it. His illness has become uncontrollable. There are times when he believes everyone is his enemy."

"But you refused to help Eve when she asked you to help her find him."

"I've been trying to bring him back to some kind of normalcy since the moment I started treating him at the VA hospital. There have been times when I thought I was coming close. I thought it was my responsibility to find him before he did any more harm." He met Joe's eyes. "*My* responsibility, Detective. There is so much good in Ted Danner. I've watched him work with the children of the parish here. He wants to do what's right. I don't want him hunted and shot down like a rabid dog. I want to get him under treatment again."

Joe shook his head. "It's not going to happen. Not if he killed Bonnie Duncan. Not if he hurts Eve."

"But what if he didn't do either? He has a chance."

297

"All I care about is Eve's chances." Joe's lips tightened. "And I'll be the one who shoots Danner if he even touches a strand of her hair. You turned Eve down, but you're not going to refuse me, Father."

His brows lifted. "Are you threatening me?"

"If you don't show me a way to find Danner, I'll regard you as an accomplice. I don't care if you're a priest or the Dalai Lama."

"And you love Eve Duncan very much." His gaze shifted back to the shimmering spray of the fountain. "Love is a wonderful thing. Through all his torment, Danner still feels love. That's why I think he can still be saved."

"Then you should have saved him when you had a chance instead of shunting him off to another psychiatrist and joining the priesthood."

Father Barnabas flinched. "Do you think I haven't thought about that? I wasn't vain enough to think that I was the only competent psychiatrist in the country. I thought I was doing the right thing. I'd come to a point with some of my patients that I'd tried every skill I'd learned to bring them back to the human race. I couldn't do any more. I couldn't perform miracles. But God can do what I can't. I decided to quit claiming I was brilliant and all-knowing and give Him a chance."

"And you're not sorry?"

The priest shook his head. "Why? Occasionally I get to even be present for one of his miracles. Sometimes they're small, sometimes they fill me with wonder. No, I'm not sorry."

Dammit, I like this man, Joe thought with frustration. He might be conning him and hiding his real agenda but, if that was what he was doing, he was a superb actor. Ignore that warm charisma and force him to do what he needed him to do. "Then you can get God to keep Eve safe and deliver Danner to me, Father. Either that, or it's up to you."

The priest chuckled. "It doesn't work that way. I'm permitted to observe, not orchestrate. But you're right, it is up to me. You're not going to have to damage your conscience by harassing a priest."

"My conscience isn't in danger. Not if it concerns Eve." He met his gaze. "And I regard you as damaged goods in the clergy department. You may be very dirty."

"And I may not. You're not sure."

"Evidently, the court wasn't either. I can see you'd be a very believable witness. But your obsession with finding Danner could be —"

"Not what it seems," the priest said. "But you'll have to accept that if you want to find Danner yourself."

He tensed. "You're going to tell me where I can find Danner?"

"I'm going to tell you where we can start."

"We?"

"I told you, I'm going with you," Father Barnabas said quietly. "I'm not going to give up my chance of saving Danner. But I can't run the risk of having him hurt Eve Duncan if I can prevent it, so I'll permit you to accompany me. You have that right. But I have the right to try to keep Danner alive if I can and try to end his torment."

Joe frowned. "It's a lousy idea. You could get hurt. You'd get in my way."

"Your concern is truly touching. It's a possibility, but just because I wear a white collar is no sign that I haven't lived in the real world. I was in the army myself when I was a kid fresh out of high school. I know how to survive."

"But not how to attack. Or if you did know, you chose to forget it. I don't believe in turning the other cheek, and I don't like the idea of having to protect you when you do."

"Get used to it. I'm going to be with you until we find Danner."

Joe stared at him in exasperation. The priest's expression was calm but completely resolute. "We'll talk about it. What's your starting point?"

"You mean you'll try to talk me out of it."

"What's the starting point?"

"The little girl."

"What? Bonnie?"

"He never mentioned her name. When I asked who he was referring to when he spoke about a little girl, he never answered. He just continued talking about her." He frowned thoughtfully. "For a little while, I thought that she was a fantasy in one of his delusions. Then I believed I caught a hint of pain, and I wondered if he couldn't bear to recognize her, put a name to her. That could be more likely if he killed her as Eve thinks." He shook his head. "I can't believe it. He loves children." Then he said soberly. "Or perhaps I can. A sin like that could turn a man to madness. But I can't promise that the child Danner talked about is Bonnie. He spoke about her as if she were alive."

"He's crazy. It's got to be Bonnie," Joe said impatiently. "It can't be a coincidence. His nephew is Bonnie's father. And Danner took Eve, dammit."

"It seems likely. As I said, I believe we have to look to the child. We have to find her, and we may find him."

"So simple," Joe said bitterly. "We've been trying to find Bonnie for years, Father."

The priest nodded. "Danner has been talking to me about the child for the last four years."

Joe shook his head. "Bonnie was taken long, long before that."

"Maybe God didn't want her to be found. He does things in His own time."

"I can't be that philosophic. Why do you think that we'll find Danner when we find her? It could be a hallucination. And what makes you think you can find her anyway?"

"If it's a hallucination then it has a home, a place where Danner thinks he interacts with the child. I have a general idea where that is."

"A home? What do you mean?"

"Four years ago, Danner left his job with me to go to work for a charity in south Georgia. The Rainbow Connection. It's a camp for disadvantaged kids. I tried to persuade him to stay so that I could keep an eye on him. But he said he couldn't do it, that he was too far away from the child. She might need him. He kept his job with that charity for almost two years, then gave it up. But Max Daltrop, the head of the organization, told me he remained in the area. And I know it for a fact because Danner mentioned it whenever he came to confession. He said he couldn't leave there although the demons were always surrounding him. He had to protect the child."

"How?"

The priest shook his head. "He was usually irrational by the time he started to speak of the child. And his attitude changed as time went on. She was suddenly no longer a child to protect but to fear. Toward the last, he was frightened, agitated. He wanted her to go away. But he said that she wouldn't go until he gave her what she wanted. He seemed to think that I should be able to know what that was. He'd ask me several times in the periods that we came together."

"And you believe whenever he left you, he'd go back to the child?"

"I can't be positive. As I said, he was irrational. But I thought at the time that was what he was doing."

"And you believe that would be where he would take Eve? How certain are you?"

"Enough so that's where I was going to go to find Danner when Eve Duncan told me that he was wanted for murder."

Joe began to feel a flare of hope. It was a slim chance, but it was something to go on. "And where is this charity camp? South, you said?"

He nodded. "Near Jasper, Georgia."

"Will you give me the telephone number of this administrator . . . Daltrop?"

"I'll call him myself . . . on the drive down to see him. I've already phoned him and asked him if he could give me an address for Danner, and he didn't have one. But he'll make his staff available for questioning, and they may know something."

"I didn't say I was going to go down to the camp. As you said, it's definitely not a sure thing. I don't have time for mistakes. I'll talk to —" His phone rang, and he glanced at the ID. Catherine.

"I have to take this, Father." He punched the button. "Have you zeroed in on him?"

"Yes, Danner abandoned his truck, and he and Eve are on foot. Not surprising since Gallo said Danner was used to living off the land. He taught Gallo everything he knew about that. Since Danner knew that there would be pursuit, he'd feel more comfortable in the woods than on the roads. It took a while, but we found the footprints. He tried to mask them at first but he gave up about a quarter mile into the woods. He was probably losing too much time. Now he's just trying to move as fast as possible and ignoring pursuit. He'll probably make a few diversions to throw us off the trail, but I believe they'll be minor."

"Which direction is he heading now?"

"Due south."

"Keep me informed." He hung up and looked at the priest. "South."

Father Barnabas nodded. "Give me ten minutes to change clothes and grab an overnight bag. I've already spoken to Father Dominic about taking over for me." He got to his feet and smiled. "Don't be so troubled. I'm not your responsibility. I either go with you or by myself."

"You know you're not giving me any choice."

"There has to be a balance, Detective. Just as there is in a court of law. I'm for the defense."

"Maybe. But it's Eve who needs the defense."

"She has you and all the people who care about her." He moved down the path toward the sanctuary. "I won't be long, Detective."

"Joe." It was a surrender. "Evidently we're going to be on fairly informal terms."

"Kevin. If it will make you more comfortable to think of me in a more secular way."

305

"It won't. You are what you are. And I'm not sure what that is at the moment. Besides, I thought you were supposed to have abandoned that other life entirely."

He shook his head. "I just tried to add to it and let it enrich me. In most cases, I succeeded." He disappeared into the sanctuary.

CHAPTER
12

How far had they gone? Eve wondered wearily. She had lost track after the first seven or eight miles. It had been dark for some hours now, and that distance must have increased accordingly. The paths that Danner was following were only narrow rutted trails, and the overhanging thorny bushes tore at her clothes and face. She'd had to stop innumerable times to disentangle her hair or shirt.

The path they were on now was particularly bad because it was following a shallow creek bed and her feet were wet and the mud was sucking at her shoes.

She muttered a curse as one shoe was pulled off her right foot. She balanced on the other foot as she reached down to retrieve the shoe.

"You should have worn sensible shoes. Why are women so impractical?" Danner had turned and was standing beside her with a scowl on his face.

"They are sensible. They're just not mountain boots." She added dryly, "I wasn't expecting to go hiking." She was trying to brush the mud from the sole of the shoe. "I'll be ready to go again in a minute."

He stood watching her for a few seconds, and then grabbed her wrists by the ropes binding them and pulled her off the path into the shrubbery.

"What are you doing? Dammit, don't be so impatient. I have to get the mud off so that —"

"You looked like a stork standing there on one foot," he growled. "Or maybe a scarecrow. But you're so torn-up that I wouldn't put you in a field. The crows would laugh at you." They had reached a small clearing, and he pushed her down on the ground beneath a giant oak tree. "We can afford to take a short rest. It will take time for John to find the trail again after the last two red herrings I threw at him."

"You think Gallo is after us?"

He nodded as he threw some branches in a pile and lit them. "He's behind us somewhere. I can feel him."

"Imagination?"

His lips twisted. "You mean the crazy old fool is having hallucinations?"

308

She met his gaze. "Maybe."

He shook his head. "Father Barnabas thinks that I'm crazy. Sometimes I am. But some things I know better than he does. He thinks demons don't walk the earth."

"And you do?"

"I know they do. They're always right behind me." He took her shoes and put them before the fire to dry. "And I can't let them catch me."

"How long have you been seeing demons?" She paused. "Does the child see the demons, too?"

"No," he said sharply. "I'd never let her see the demons." He whispered. "But sometimes I wonder if they've already got her. She won't leave me alone."

Move carefully. Don't disturb the mood that was opening the gates. "Why do you think that is?"

"I'm not sure, but I have an idea now. I have to try it anyway." He sat back on his heels and looked at her. "You've done well. No complaints. No whining."

"Whining?" She made a face. "Terrible. No wonder you don't think well of women if you've run into that quality."

"I've always wanted to think well of them. I've always wanted to think well of everyone." His face clouded. "But there are so many demons in the world. John's parents were demons, you know."

"I know he said they were abusive."

"They were demons. I just didn't recognize it at the time. They were family, and I tried to work with them to save him. If I had known, I would have destroyed them."

"When did you start recognizing demons when you saw them?"

"Syria. One night in Syria."

"They just appeared to you?"

"You're trying to make me say I'm seeing things."

"I'm trying to get you to talk to me. You promised you'd talk to me, Danner."

"Not now."

"Why not?"

He gazed at her. "Why not?" he repeated. "You won't believe me." His gaze shifted to the blazing fire. "I'd been sent into the mountains of Syria to destroy a munitions stronghold held by the militants. I planted the explosives at the building and climbed up into the rocks above the village to set them off. My captain was waiting there for me in the helicopter. I'd done a good job setting that charge. I always did a good job. I was proud of myself. I gave it another five minutes after I reached the helicopter before I pressed the button. It blew." He swallowed. "But something was wrong. The munitions should have blown, but they didn't. There were no explosions. Except the one I'd set off when I pressed the button. The entire building was on fire, but there were no ammo explosions." His hand slowly clenched. "And then I saw the children. Dozens of children running out of the burning building. They were burning, too. They looked like torches in the darkness."

"What? I don't understand."

"It was an orphanage. We'd been fed the wrong information by our informants. They wanted to claim a U.S. atrocity. The children were burning . . . I could smell their charred flesh. And the ones that weren't on fire were being picked off by snipers from the edge of the village. I went crazy. I tried to get back down to help them, but it was too late. No one else was coming out of the building. Dead. All dead. And I could see those sons of bitches coming into the village to check to make sure no child had survived."

"My God."

"God wasn't there that night. Only the demons. I could see them outlined by the fire, in their dirty robes. They were dressed like Arabs, but I knew who they were, moving among those small bodies. Demons. I screamed and grabbed my rifle. I jumped out of the helicopter, but I was tackled before I got more than a few yards. My commanding officer said I couldn't be seen there. I was going to make things worse. They had to do damage control."

"Damage control?" she whispered. "Children."

"They were dead, and an international situation was still to be saved. And they saved it. They bribed and coerced and made it go away." He added, "And they wouldn't let me go back and destroy the demons. I told them I had to do it, but they said that there were no demons that night. I couldn't get anyone to believe me. Will you believe me, Eve?"

The story had shocked and sickened her and given her an insight into Danner that had an element of pity. Understanding was acceptable, but she could not feel sympathy. This was a man who might have killed her Bonnie. "You could convince me. Searching for Bonnie, I've encountered many individuals who could be demons." She leaned forward and picked up her shoe. "Including you, Danner." She was struggling to put on the shoe. "But I'm tired of talking about demons. I want to talk about the child."

"No." He pulled out his knife and cut the ropes binding her wrists. "This will make it easier for you to walk. You're slowing me down."

"You're not afraid I'll manage to escape?"

"I'd catch up with you before you went a quarter mile." He turned away. "But you're not going to run away. You're willing to take any punishment that comes along. You want to go with me."

"How could you know that?"

"I saw your face at the priest's study. You were . . . eager."

And he was very perceptive. "You could be mistaken."

He shook his head. "And I saw you earlier in the garden with her."

She lost her breath. "Her?"

He turned away. "The child. Let's go."

"Oh, no." She took two steps and her hand closed on his arm. "You don't leave me like that. You *saw* Bonnie."

"I told you I saw the child."

"No, stop that crap. Why won't you say her name? You saw Bonnie."

"It hurts me."

"Then let it hurt you. My daughter is dead, and you saw her. You just told me so. Why would you see a dead child, Danner? This dead child. Did you kill her?"

"Stop talking about her. It hurts me."

"I won't stop talking about her. I can see

her spirit because she's my daughter, and she wants me to do it. But why you, Danner?"

He tore his arm away from her grasp. "Why do you think? She wants me to see her, too. She wants to torment me. She doesn't understand . . . I have to make her understand."

"Understand what?"

"That I'm not fighting her, that I'll give her what she wants. But I had to find out what that was first. Even Father Barnabas couldn't tell me. I asked him, and he said to pray about it. I had to *know*."

"And now you do?"

"She wants you," he said simply.

"What?"

"In that garden I could see that there was so much love between you. She wants her mother. All little girls want their mothers. That's what she wants me to do. Not to kill any demons. She wants me to give you to her."

She stared at him, stunned. Then she realized the words had stunned her but not the basic thought behind them. The hints had been there to be read.

And, he was right, she had been eager to read them.

"It won't be bad," he said softly. "I won't

hurt you. She wouldn't like that."

"Stop that. Say her name. She's not an anonymous 'child.' She's Bonnie. Say it."

He didn't speak for a moment. "Bonnie."

It was hurting him. She could tell. Then she realized why. "It's because you don't want to recognize her as a person, you want to keep her at a distance. Well, she is a person, a wonderful, wonderful person. From the moment she was born, she was special. I could tell you stories."

He shook his head. "Don't do it."

"Then don't ever let me hear you call her anything but her name."

"Okay. It doesn't matter. I can stand it. It's all going to be ending anyway." He turned away. "It's time to go."

Ending. Bonnie had spoken about the ending, and now Danner was doing it, too. But it might not mean the same thing to him. "What do you mean?"

"If I give you to her" — he paused, then said with an effort — "to Bonnie, then it's over for me. I can stop running from them."

"Them?"

He turned away. "Enough talk."

"Not nearly enough. One question. Did you murder my daughter?"

He ignored the question and was heading back toward the path. "Come on, you've had enough rest. I'll let you sleep a couple hours later."

He wasn't even looking back at her over his shoulder. He was sure that she would come with him. How could he be that sure she wouldn't run for her life?

In that garden there was so much love between you.

Had he been able to see more than the love that bound Bonnie and her together? Had he seen a guideline that Bonnie had drawn for him? Eve had been totally shocked that he had been able to see Bonnie. Bonnie had come to her and to Gallo and to Joe and no one else. Not even Jane. It was reasonable to guess that it was the love that had drawn her to them. The love was always there and clearly visible when she was with Bonnie.

But Danner felt no love. He was afraid of Bonnie. He only wanted to get rid of her.

And offering Eve up as a sacrificial offering was the way he planned on doing it. He thought that was what Bonnie wanted. Yet Bonnie had always told Eve that she had to wait, that they couldn't be together because it wasn't her time.

But had Eve's time come now? Was that why Danner was seeing Bonnie?

Too many questions. Perhaps she was

reaching too deep. Outside of scientific medical knowledge of hallucinations, there were also stories that the insane sometimes saw visions and spirits not visible to normal people. At any rate, Danner was not going to answer any more of her probes right now. She was lucky she had managed to get as much information as she had from him.

Or maybe not so lucky. He was becoming too human to her. Yes, there was no doubt he had moments of sanity as well as madness. Yes, there had been reasons that had caused him to slip into that half-world. But you could not forgive evil as great as the killing of Bonnie because of what had happened to him. It was better that she only thought of him as the monster who could have murdered her Bonnie.

She could call him mad, but she could not call him a monster until she knew for certain that he had killed her daughter. He had refused to say the words, dammit.

But it had to be him, and she would know everything before she was through.

She started to push after him through the heavy brush.

"They built a fire here," Gallo said as he knelt beside the huge oak tree.

"How long ago?" Catherine asked.

He studied the grass and the drying mud beside the ashes. "Six, maybe seven hours ago."

Catherine frowned. "That's a big lead."

He nodded. "But at least he's stopping to rest on occasion. That will lose him time." He looked up at Catherine. "And he's still got Eve with him."

And that was a circumstance beyond price, Catherine thought. Every time she caught sight of Eve's tracks after a period of losing the trail, she felt a surge of profound relief. This terrain was rough as hell and hard to get through. Who the hell knew if Danner would get impatient with dragging Eve with him and decide to dispose of her.

She stood up. "Let's get going. We've lost too much time on that last —" Her phone rang. "It's Joe." She punched the button. "We haven't caught up with them yet, Joe. But Danner still has Eve with him. Are you still at the church?"

"No, I'm at the Rainbow Connection. A youth rescue camp at Bradburg near the Alabama border. Father Barnabas said that Danner went to work for the organization because of its location. He said he had to be near 'the child.' "

She stiffened. "What?" She pressed up the volume. "Why didn't you tell us?"

"This is only a slim lead. If you can track him, then that was our best bet."

"But it was a lead to where he might be heading. Where is this Bradburg?"

"A couple hours' drive from Atlanta, near Columbus, Georgia."

Gallo was already pushing buttons on the apps on his iPhone. He glanced up at her. "We're heading in the general direction. If he doesn't change course, it could be his destination."

She shook her head. "Joe said the camp was close, not his destination." She spoke into the phone. "Doesn't anyone know anything about Danner down there?"

"His job was to take kids hiking and canoeing. He did what he was supposed to do and didn't cause any trouble. He was a loner. Every week or so, he would take off and go camping for a few days."

"Where?"

"No one seems to know. Like I said, he was a loner."

"Wasn't anyone curious, dammit?"

"No one I've found so far. I've talked to several of the employees and counselors and not come up with anything. I still have a few to question."

And if they knew anything, Joe would get the information, she knew. He would be relentless. "Then we'll keep on the trail. At least we know what may be his general direction. It would help if we could tighten a noose around him from both directions. Let us know." She hung up and turned to Gallo. "How long will it take to get to this Bradford?"

"In this kind of heavy brush? At least another day. Providing that's where he's headed." He glanced at the app again. "And providing that he doesn't veer off course and head for Florida. It's only guesswork by Father Barnabas that he'd head in that direction."

Catherine agreed with him, but at least they had another possibility if they lost Danner in these woods.

No, they wouldn't lose him. That wasn't an option. She moved toward the trail. "We'll check his movements every few hours and compare it to the destination on the map in the apps. Maybe it will give us some indication."

"You know he could cut back to the road and hijack a car?"

"But that would be hard with Eve in tow. And he evidently intends to keep her with him."

"Thank God."

She glanced back at him. "That sounded

pretty profound. You're losing your faith in Danner's innocence?"

"I didn't say that." He was silent, then said, "I want to believe he's still the man who was my friend as a boy. I just can't afford to let anyone else be hurt because I want it to be true. I wasn't lying to Quinn." He met her gaze. "Every act I do from now on will be based on the idea that my uncle wants to kill Eve. If I have to do it, I'll take him out."

And it was tearing him apart, Catherine could see. But there was no doubt in her mind that he meant every word he said. He was tough and hard-edged and he'd smother any hint of softness now that he'd made his decision.

But that didn't mean that decision would necessarily have to become reality.

She glanced away from him. "You never can tell, but I don't think that's going to happen."

He must have caught something in her tone. His gaze was suddenly narrowed on her face. "And that means?"

"Nothing."

"I think it does." His lips were suddenly indented with the faintest smile. "My God, Catherine, I believe you're planning on offering me a bizarre gift . . . of sorts. Incredible."

"I'm not planning anything. Sometimes, things happen."

"And that happening might include your taking out my uncle so that I don't have to do it. You'd do that for me?"

"It has nothing to do with you," she said crisply. "All of this is about Eve and for Eve. It's probably in the cards for Danner to be eliminated, so that Eve can live. I'd be more efficient in doing that since I don't have any emotional baggage. Why should you do something that could scar you for the rest of your life? It would be easier for me. Do you know how many kills I have?"

"I imagine the number is formidable."

"It can be an ugly world, and I'm an agent. I do what my job calls for me to do. Do I like it? No, but I believe it's worthwhile."

"And do you believe I'm worthwhile, Catherine?"

"The truth? Worthwhile to me? I'm not sure. But I want you to live, so that I can find out. And I don't want you to make stupid mistakes and get yourself killed because you hesitate when you should move."

"I won't hesitate. That's over, Catherine.

I'll handle this. Back off."

She shrugged. "We'll see how it plays out." She turned away. "But don't flatter yourself that I'd do it for you. It would be for Eve . . . and for me."

He chuckled. "And that flatters me enormously. I can do without your making this huge sacrifice to keep me from undergoing all this mental and emotional suffering. I like the idea much more of your selfishly trying to keep me balanced in case you can make use of me."

She had thought he'd feel that way. It was much better that she kept the situation on that level. She could be as honest as she could with him as long as it did not make her vulnerable.

Or show him that she was already vulnerable.

"Then we understand each other."

"Yes." He was suddenly turning her to face him. "Sometimes, I understand you, Catherine." His fingers gently traced the line of her cheekbone. "It's not easy. You're as complicated as Chinese cybercode. But when we keep it basic, I get a glimmer . . ." He was touching her lips with his forefinger. "And it makes me want to go deeper."

She should break away. This wasn't the time or the place. Neither of them wanted this to happen. The emotion had whirled into being like a tornado touching down out of a still sky.

She didn't break away.

His fingers were warm, smooth, but she could sense the strength he was restraining. The knowledge of what lay behind that gentleness was erotic. Light and dark. Velvet and knife-edge. Lord, he was a fascinating man. The faint dent in his chin, his dark eyes fixed intently on her face, his well-shaped mouth, full and sensual. Stunning, perfectly stunning. Good looks rarely impressed Catherine, but Gallo was . . . unusual. He radiated a male sensuality so strong that it almost obscured the other, more conventional, elements. It made her want to reach out and touch him, get closer, absorb the scent of him, rub against him like an animal in heat. She could feel the pulse in the hollow of her throat begin to pound. Her cheek where he'd touched it was tingling with heat.

"I'd like to understand more," he said softly. "I'd like to explore . . ." Then he shook his head, and his hand dropped to his side. "Stay out of it, Catherine. Stay away from me. You'll be better off on both counts."

The abruptness of his withdrawal jarred

her. It was right, but it should have been she who made that move. It only emphasized the vulnerability that she was always on guard against. "Yeah, that's not a bad idea either." She took a step back. "But I choose what's good for me, Gallo." Dammit, her body still felt flushed, tingling, ready. And it had only taken a touch. The realization annoyed and bewildered her. What the hell was this yen that she had for Gallo?

She turned her back on him. "And I may choose to let you stumble around and get your throat cut. I'll have to take it under consideration."

"He's heading in this general direction." Joe turned to the priest as he hung up the phone. "But Catherine says he's smart, and it's going to be difficult. She'll let us know if he veers off in another direction as he approaches this area." He looked out the window of the office at the grounds that contained neat rows of tents and project areas that were teeming with teenage boys and girls. "But I may have to take off and join them if we don't get a lead here. This has proved a zero so far."

"We have a few more counselors to question," Father Barnabas said. "I told you that we wouldn't get much more help from the administrator."

And he had been correct. Max Daltrop had been pleasant, busy, and noncommittal, with the emphasis on busy. He had said that he had barely known Ted Danner but that he'd had good reports on him from the supervisors. Then he'd hesitated before requesting that they be careful about leaking any information about an alleged criminal who had acted as a counselor here. Joe couldn't blame him. As far as he could tell, this camp did good work, and all it would take would be a hint of scandal to have a rush of bureaucrats pouring in to investigate closing it.

The priest's gaze was on Joe's face. "Max is a good man. He's trying to cooperate."

"I know. I won't cause him any trouble unless I have to do it." He looked down at his list. "We have three names left. Two supervisors, Bob Kimble, Dory Selznik, and a counselor, Ben Hudson."

"Suppose you take Kimble and Selznik, and I'll take the counselor, Ben Hudson. I believe that might be the most efficient path."

"Why? Any reason?"

"Ben Hudson is twenty but has the mental capacity of a child of ten. I have the back-

326

ground to deal with him."

"Ten? And he's a counselor here?"

"Why not? A job makes any man feel worthwhile. Max put him in charge of teaching weaving and leather crafts. He's almost an expert at it, and he does a good job of showing the kids how to do it."

"And why does Daltrop think that we could get any information out of him? It doesn't seem likely."

"You never know. Danner spent a lot of time with him while he was working here. The kid trailed around the camp behind him like a puppy dog."

Joe stiffened. "He did? Then that might mean he trailed him outside the camp."

"And it might not. Max thought that it could be possible. But he asked me to do the questioning."

Joe's lips twisted. "Because he didn't want me to be rough on one of his protégés? I'm not that much of a hard-ass. I don't target problem kids."

"No, but you could be impatient. According to Max, Ben is kind of special. He doesn't want him hurt. Ben's had a rough enough life. His father is a thief and a drug runner who is in jail right now for hitting his landlady and knocking her down a flight of stairs. Ben tried to stop him and ended up at the bottom of the stairs, too. The father has a record a mile long and evidently only kept Ben with him to get welfare payments. The state took Ben away from him twice, citing abuse, but let him go back. Our wonderful DEFACS wanting to give a parent every break. Even when it breaks the kid." He turned and headed for the door. "I'll talk to you after you finish with Kimble and Selznik. I believe they're in the mess tent." The next moment, he'd left the office and was striding toward the tents.

Joe didn't move from the window, watching him as he reached a large tent on the perimeter and squatted beside a slim, sandy-haired young man sitting on a camp stool. The boy's fingers were flying over a leather belt, and he looked up with a smile as Father Barnabas began to speak to him.

Special, the priest had called him. Perhaps in more ways than one. That smile was joyously luminous and touched his face with a radiant gentleness. There was something vaguely familiar about that smile. . . .

Then it came to him. It was reminiscent of the sketch of Bonnie that Eve had drawn and hung in the hallway of the house on Brookside. Strange that this boy would remind him of Bonnie.

Perhaps not so strange. This boy, too, had

been captured in forever childhood.

He tore his gaze away and headed for the door. He was wasting time standing here staring at the kid, but there was something about him that had riveted him. Forget it. Ben Hudson seemed to be talking to the priest, and Joe should be heading toward the mess tent. He'd probably make much more progress questioning the two supervisors about Ted Danner.

And perhaps a few questions about Ben Hudson. . . .

He called Father Barnabas over an hour later. "I'm coming up with nothing. Neither of the supervisors had much to do with Danner. They both said that he was a loner and didn't encourage company. They remembered he would go away almost every weekend, but they assumed he just liked camping. What about you? Did Hudson know anything?"

He hesitated. "Maybe. I'm not sure. The kid is willing to talk about Ted Danner. He said that Ted is his best friend. It's clear he cares for him."

"Then if he'll talk, what's the problem?"

"He talks about how Danner taught him to make leather vests as well as the belts. He tells me how Danner played cards with him every night. Not what we want."

"What about Danner's weekend trips?"

"He says he doesn't remember. He freezes up."

"Then he knows something."

"Maybe he doesn't remember."

"And maybe he does. I'll be over there in five minutes to question him."

"I'm staying while you do it," the priest said quietly.

"I'm not arguing." His tone became mocking. "Maybe we can play good cop, bad cop."

"No bad cop. Not with this kid."

"That would be your answer regardless. I'll see you." He hung up. He could feel a tingle of excitement as he headed for the door of the mess. It might be a mistake to feel any stirring of hope. This was a special kid, and he might only be confused.

But his every instinct was humming.

Ben Hudson was indeed a special kid, and he was not confused.

Joe knew from the moment that the boy looked at him after the priest's introduction that there was not confusion but a simple, almost pure, clarity about Ben Hudson. The impression was largely due to Ben's wide-set blue eyes and that smile, which seemed to hold a kind of joyous wonder.

"I'm very glad to meet you, Ben," Joe said quietly. "I won't take very much of your time, but I have to have some questions answered. You know I'm a detective?"

Ben nodded tentatively. "Father Barnabas told me. That means you're with the police. Are you going to put me in jail?"

"Why would I do that? Have you done something wrong?"

"I don't think so. But my father used to say that he never did anything wrong but that the police were always after him."

"Why did they arrest him? What were the charges?"

He shook his head vaguely. "Lots of things. Selling drugs, stealing stuff, hitting the woman who rented us the apartment. But he told the police he didn't do any of it. That it was all lies."

"And you think he was telling the truth?"

He looked away. "I wanted to believe it. Our landlady was a nice woman. She hurt herself bad when she fell down the stairs. I went to the hospital to see her."

"Was she angry?"

"No. She cried. She told me to run away."

"And did you do it?"

He shook his head. "I couldn't leave my father. He needed me. He said it was a son's

331

duty to take care of his father. He wasn't well and couldn't work. But I was strong."

And the leech had fastened onto the kid and hadn't let go.

"Then how did you end up here?"

"They took him away and put him in jail. I didn't have anywhere to go, so my landlady found this place. Mr. Daltrop said I could stay for a little while." He smiled. "That was eight months ago."

"Evidently, you earned a place for yourself if you managed to stay this long."

"They think I'm smart, that I do a good job. They like me here. Everyone likes me."

An entry.

"Did Ted Danner like you?"

His smile faded. "Yes."

Back off a little. "Why do you think that?"

"He would come to my tent and talk to me. He taught me how to play checkers. He had a big knife, and he'd take me into the woods and show me how good he could throw it. Sometimes, he'd let me go with him when he camped out."

Yes.

"Where was that? Where did he go?"

Ben moistened his lips but didn't reply.

It would have been too great a piece of luck if Ben had answered that question, Joe thought. "What did he talk about?"

He frowned. "Just stuff."

"Not people?"

"He talked about John. He liked him a lot. I think he was a relation." He stopped, troubled. "I don't want to talk about Ted. Do I have to do it? Will you arrest me if I don't?"

Say the words, and he'd get what he wanted. The boy would probably believe him.

"No, I won't arrest you. But why don't you want to talk about him? He seems to have been very nice to you."

He didn't answer.

"Why, Ben?"

"He told me not to talk about him," he said in a low voice. "Before he left, he told me that I mustn't tell anyone anything about — He told me not to say anything. So I can't do it even if you put me in jail."

Don't tense. Don't show any sign of the excitement that was beginning to grip him, or the boy would sense it. "I've told you that I won't put you in jail. I just wonder why he wouldn't want you to talk about him when you said he was such a good man. Did he do something wrong?"

"No." He jumped to his feet. "I don't want to talk anymore. I want you to go away."

"Joe," Father Barnabas said.

He was afraid Joe was going to browbeat the kid. He had to admit that he was tempted. The stakes were too high and the time too short.

He couldn't do it, not if there was any other way.

"I can't go away," he told Ben. "I have to stay until you decide to answer my questions. If I don't, then someone I love very much could get hurt. Your friend might hurt her."

"Ted? Ted wouldn't hurt her. He wouldn't hurt anyone who didn't try to hurt him."

Joe jumped on that last sentence. "And did you see him hurt someone who did try to hurt him? Is that what you can't tell anyone?"

"I didn't say that." His hands clenched into fists at his sides. "You're trying to trick me."

Joe drew a deep breath. "Listen carefully, Ben. You don't believe your friend, Ted, could hurt anyone. You may be right, but sometimes people can be kind to some people and unkind to others. Particularly if they're sick inside. One minute they seem okay, then the anger comes."

Ben nodded. "Like my dad."

The boy had completely leapfrogged the explanation Joe had been trying to make.

Try to bring him back around. "Was your father like that, too? Like Ted?"

"No, not like Ted. Ted never hurt me. Ted said my dad didn't have a right to hurt me. He said he wouldn't let him do it again."

He stiffened. "Wait a minute. Danner knew your father?"

"No, he only said that when I told him my dad was on his way here to take me away from the camp. He'd gotten out of jail and wanted me to go back and help him."

"But how would Danner stop him?"

Ben shook his head. "He said he'd tell him to go away."

"And that would do it? I don't think so."

"You're wrong. My dad never came to see me here. Ted met him before he got here and made him change his mind. He made him go away."

Joe and Father Barnabas exchanged glances.

"Have you heard from your father since then?" Joe asked.

He shook his head. "But he might come back now that Ted has gone away."

"I wouldn't worry about that happening," Joe said. He would leave it at that. The kid's father was obviously a bastard who would use and abuse a boy like Ben, but the kid didn't need to be made to feel any guilt about what had probably happened to him. "I think Danner probably frightened him away. That's what I was trying to tell you about your friend, Ted. Sometimes, he can frighten people. If he frightened my Eve, she might try to run away and hurt herself. Some people deserve to be frightened, but not Eve. We have to find her and make sure that Danner doesn't do anything to cause anything bad to happen to her."

Ben shook his head. "He told me not to talk about him." He turned and went into the tent.

"Very deftly handled. You were more diplomatic than I thought you'd be," Father Barnabas said. "I'm impressed."

"I'm not, I didn't get what I needed. You thought I'd tear him up just to get what I want? Fate and life have done enough to that kid. For an instant, I was actually in full sympathy with Danner. I would have wanted to take down that bastard of a father, too."

Father Barnabas shook his head.

"I didn't expect you to agree," Joe said. "But you'll admit that Ted Danner could have been tempted to rid the boy of his father?"

"I'll admit that Ted Danner has many temptations, and it's difficult for him to know how to handle them." His gaze went to the tent. "But it appears that the boy could be a help to us. He's more familiar with Danner than anyone here. I was surprised that he said Danner took him when he went camping. All those people we interviewed were right. Danner was always a loner."

"That's what I've been hearing from everyone," Joe said. "But maybe Ben didn't represent a threat to him." He remembered the boy's luminous smile, which had reminded him of Bonnie's in Eve's sketch. It would have been hard for anyone to believe that smile hid anything threatening. "And Danner did have a relationship with Gallo when he was a boy. Perhaps he made some kind of connection."

The priest smiled. "You're analyzing. Would it be too difficult for you to accept that God might have brought them together for a reason?"

"But then that would mean that God wanted Danner to take out Ben's father. Not exactly a merciful plan. How do you explain that?"

"I don't. God has many faces, and I wouldn't presume. I just believe that it's easier to look at the big picture than try to take it apart. Though I've noticed you have a mind that tries to decipher at every turn. Since God gave you that brain, it would follow that He wants you to use it." He glanced back at Ben's tent. "So what's your next step?"

"I go after him, I keep after him. There's not much time. I have to find out where Danner is taking Eve."

"You'll be careful?" His gaze never left the tent. "I have a . . . feeling about him."

And Joe knew what he meant. He'd been fighting that same protective instinct that Father Barnabas was experiencing. It was weird as hell. Ben was . . . unusual, like a light shining in the darkness. You wanted to make sure that light was never dimmed. In a way, that instinct was incomprehensible. The rough life the boy had evidently lived had never managed to extinguish that inner glowing. Why did Joe feel as if he had the responsibility of taking care of Ben? Was that what Danner had felt when he decided to guard the boy in his own lethal way?

Dammit, he didn't want to worry about this kid. He had to find a way to use him to find Eve.

"I'll be as careful as I can be." He followed Ben into the tent.

The boy was cutting lengths of suede and didn't look up when Joe stopped before

338

him. "Go away."

"I can't do that. But I won't try to persuade you to do what's right. I'll let Eve do that." He reached in his pocket and drew out his wallet. "It's hard to think of people if you only have a name. I thought you should have a face, too. This is one of my favorite photos of Eve." He thrust the photo in front of Ben's face. "It was taken at our home on the lake. She looks a little dreamy but there's nothing really dreamy about her. She's always thinking, always feeling. She had the dreams blown away a long time ago. I guess that's why I like this picture. I want to give her back those dreams."

"Dreams? I have dreams." His gaze was on the photo. "They used to be bad. But now it's different."

"Is it? Because your father went away?"

"No, I don't think so." He put down the strip of leather and took the photo and stared at her. "She looks . . . nice. I think I know her."

"You've probably just seen a photo of Eve. She's in the papers a lot. She helps find lost kids."

He shook his head, his brow knitted with a puzzled frown. "No, that's not right. I know her." He gave Joe back the photo. "I'll remember. Sometimes I forget things, but I always remember."

"You said she looked nice. She is nice, Ben. You don't want anything to happen to her."

"Ted wouldn't hurt her."

"But he won't let her go. What if she fights him? What if she can't persuade him that she —"

"You said that you wouldn't talk about it." He reached down and turned on his portable radio, and music suddenly blared. "I'm not listening to you."

"Then I'll wait until you decide to do the right thing for Eve." Joe set the photo on the bench beside the boy. He dropped down on the floor and crossed his legs. "But there's not much time, Ben. Accidents can happen very quickly."

"I want you to go away."

"I can't do that. She needs me. You have to help the people who need you. You have to do what's right."

"Then stay. I don't care."

"I believe you do, Ben," Joe said gently.

Ben lowered his eyes and began to work on his weaving.

Would the photo of Eve do it?

It was possible that it would. That photo moved Joe every time he looked at it. But Joe loved Eve, and she was a stranger to this boy.

Yet he had said she was not a stranger. Who knew what went on in the mind of a boy like Ben? Joe could only hope and risk a little time. Far better than using force and brutalizing the boy as his father had done.

But, as he'd told Ben, time was running out.

CHAPTER
13

"Take the photo away," Ben said.

It was the first time Ben had spoken in the last two hours. He had worked steadily, not looking at Joe, but Joe had seen his eyes wander several times toward the photo beside him on the bench.

"Does it bother you?"

"It mixes me up. You mix me up."

"Then talk to me. Ask me questions. Maybe I can straighten it out."

The boy didn't speak, but his expression held a kind of helpless anguish.

"Okay," Joe said. "I'll ask the questions and try to work it out. You want to keep your word to Ted Danner. But you know that Danner's taking Eve was the wrong thing to do. It was the kind of thing your father would do. Isn't that right?"

"He won't hurt her."

"But you're afraid of the accidents, aren't you?"

"I don't like accidents. They scare me."

"Then the best thing to do is get her away from him. Then there won't be an accident. But he won't let her go, we'll have to take her. To do that, we have to know where he's going with her."

"I don't know that."

"But you know where he went when he left the camp on weekends. I think he's probably taking her there. Don't you, Ben?"

"He . . . likes it there sometimes. Some-times it scares him."

"Why would it do that?"

No answer. Skip the questions before they caused him to skitter away. "We agree that it's best that Eve doesn't stay with him. Now we have to find a way to find her."

He shook his head. "I promised him."

Blank wall.

"You're afraid I'll hurt him."

Ben raised his eyes and met his gaze. Joe was once again aware of the gentle clarity that seemed to see beyond and through him. Piercing vision. Knowing vision. "You want to do it," he said. "No matter what you say, you want to hurt him. Because of the woman. Because you're afraid for that woman in the photo."

Joe couldn't lie. If he did, the boy would see right through him, and he would lose any hope of cooperation. "You're right, I want to stop anyone who would hurt her. And I would hurt Ted Danner if I thought he was going to do it." He paused. "If it came to that moment, I believe you would find a way of stopping him, too. If you thought there would be an . . . accident."

"I wouldn't like it. I couldn't do it."

"No one is making you do it." Ben was close, but Joe had an overwhelming barrier to overcome. "Suppose I do everything I can not to hurt Ted Danner. If I can take Eve away from him without hurting him, I'll do it."

"You will?" Ben's gaze searched his face. "You promise?"

"I'll promise that if he doesn't hurt Eve, I won't hurt him."

"Ever?"

All he had to do was say yes. He slowly shook his head. "I'll probably have to go after him, but I would do it anyway. It won't be because you broke your promise. The only result of that will be that Eve will be safe."

Ben's gaze was on his face. "You didn't want to tell me that."

"Sometimes it's hard to do the right thing, particularly if it might hurt someone else."

"Yes." He looked down at the photo of

Eve. "And it's hard to know what's right or wrong. What's right for you may be wrong for me. It's confusing. I don't always understand."

"None of us do, Ben."

Ben lifted his gaze from the photo. "But lately things are becoming clearer. It's like lifting a curtain, isn't it?"

"Is it? And what's causing that curtain to lift, Ben?"

"I'm not sure. I think it's the dreams. . . ."

"Will you help me, Ben?"

He didn't speak for a long time, then he slowly nodded. "I'll take you to the place."

"You don't have to do that. Just tell me where it is."

"No." Ben got to his feet. "I have to go with you. I have to make sure nothing happens to Ted. That's how it has to be." He headed for the door of the tent. "I'll go tell my supervisor that he needs to replace me for today." He smiled. "Though it will be hard for him. I'm real good at my job. Everyone says so."

"I don't doubt it," Joe said gently. "While you're gone, I'll let Father Barnabas know that you've changed my mind."

He watched the boy wend his way through the tents on the way to the office. It had been difficult as hell to persuade the boy to

345

go along with him. Even now, he wasn't sure if he'd succeeded or if the kid's troubled conscience had been the guiding influence. Whatever it was, he'd take it. He hadn't expected to run into a boy like Ben here.

Like Ben? He had an idea Ben was unique. He might be slow and have to work his way through the complexity of the human condition and the world around him, but that was not really a handicap in Joe's eyes. The world ran too fast, judgments were too quickly made, treasures too often lost.

And Ben would hold on to a treasure with all his strength as he was doing with his friendship for Danner. Even when his conscience was being tormented about the danger to Eve, he was still going to make sure no harm came to Ted Danner.

And could Joe keep his promise to Ben about not hurting Danner? He had hedged it, made conditions, but the promise had still been made. He had tied his own hands until he could get Eve free. A fine balance.

All right, accept it. Who knew what would go down when he caught up with Danner? The only thing certain was that Eve would live, Eve would be free.

"You found out what you wanted to know?" Father Barnabas had come to stand beside him at the entry of the tent.

Joe nodded. "I will soon. Ben's going to take me to the place where Danner used to camp." He gave the priest a sardonic look. "And I didn't even have to use a rubber hose on him."

"I'm a better judge of character than that," Father Barnabas said quietly. "Under certain circumstances, I'm sure you could be brutal, but not to a boy like Ben." He turned away. "I'm coming with you. Don't argue."

"The hell I won't argue. This is the end of the line for you. I don't trust you. If we're getting close to Danner, I'm not going to have to risk looking over my shoulder every minute."

"That's your problem. I'm either going with you or following behind. Make up your mind."

"I could put you out and there wouldn't be a decision."

"But you'd hesitate to do that. Because there's a part of you that believes that I'm what I seem on the surface and not one of Danner's demons."

The priest was right, Joe realized in frustration. His time with Father Barnabas had allowed a strange, complex relationship to develop between them. He alternated between liking and believing him and a distrust that was probably what he should be feeling.

Father Barnabas's gaze was on Joe's face. He nodded. "I'll get my sleeping bag from the car."

"Sleeping bag? You came prepared."

He smiled. "I'm the urban type. I don't like sleeping on the cold ground. I might even let you and Ben take a turn using it."

"I'm sure you'd consider that your duty," Joe said dryly.

"Not necessarily. It might be my duty to strengthen your physical stamina or to strip you of all creature comforts to give you both time to contemplate your sins." He grinned. "I have choices."

Stop. Rest. Sleep

Those words had been repeating in Gallo's mind for the last two hours. He had to ignore them. He had to keep going.

Stop. Rest. Sleep.

Crazy.

Perhaps it was just his body telling him that it was best to take a break.

"We can stop for a while and get our breath." Gallo looked up at Catherine from where he was kneeling by the side of the path. "Danner stopped here and took another break. That's the third in the last seven hours. He's letting Eve rest."

"Maybe he's letting himself rest," Catherine said. "He's not a young man any longer, Gallo."

"He hasn't changed that much. You saw him at the bayou. He's still very tough." He leaned back against a pine tree. "We're making good time, and he's losing it with every stop. I figure we'll be almost on top of him in about five hours."

"Then we should keep on going. I don't need to rest."

No, Catherine would never admit to a lack of strength and endurance, he thought. Hell, maybe it wasn't a matter of pride. She did have amazing staying power. Everything about her was amazing.

Stop. Rest. Sleep.

"It's been over twenty-four hours. We have to be at the top of our game when we overtake them. Rest," he said. "Forty-five minutes. If you can nap, do it."

She shook her head. "I can't sleep. I'm wired." She sank down beside him before taking out her iPhone and checking the apps. "These last hours we've traveled right in line with the coordinates Joe gave us for that camp. That's got to be where he's heading." She frowned. "No, not exactly in line. We're a little east. But he might veer back."

"Or he might not. Stop worrying. We'll find out when we reach him."

She was silent. "No, I can see you're not worrying."

He opened his eyes. "I'm not stalling so that we'll lose him, Catherine. We can afford this rest."

She studied his expression, then settled back against the tree beside him. "I know we can. I know all the rules about conserving strength and all that bull. It's not a code-red situation. Danner has a destination, and he's not mistreating Eve yet." She added through her teeth, "But we're not there, dammit. And this is Eve." She drew a deep breath. "Okay, forty-five minutes. Though I'd be a hell of a lot more relaxed going full tilt after Danner. I don't understand why you don't feel the same way."

"I do. I can't tell you how much I need this to be over." He closed his eyes again. "But this is the right thing to do, Catherine. I *feel* it." And that feeling was tugging, nagging at him with increasing intensity.

Stop. Rest. Sleep.

"Well, I don't feel it."

"And you're so damn tense that you're about to break apart."

"I'm not. I wouldn't —" She suddenly broke off as he pulled her into his arms so that her cheek lay against his shoulder. "What are you doing, Gallo?"

He wasn't sure. It had been an impulse. "Nothing carnal . . . I don't think." Though his body had responded the minute he had touched her. Block it. This wasn't the moment.

Something else was coming that was far more important.

And where the hell had that last thought come from?

Stop. Rest. Sleep.

"Relax. I just want to hold you."

She was still taut and resisting. Then she was suddenly relaxing, her body flowing into his.

That heat and hardening again.

Block it. Not now.

"Why, Gallo?" she muttered.

"I don't know. I just want to hold you. I want you to be calm and . . . with me." His hand was gently stroking her hair. "Your hair smells good."

"You're a little crazy, Gallo," she muttered.

"So I've been told."

"I can't remember anyone ever wanting to just . . . hold me."

"And considering the fact that you're one totally desirable lady, you may never experience it again."

She was silent a moment. "This is important to you, isn't it?"

"It's important."

She shrugged. "I don't understand it, but I guess it's okay."

"Even though you believe I'm a bit wacko."

"People need different things at different times."

"Close your eyes, Catherine."

"They are closed."

And he could feel the muscles of her body relaxing. "Forty-five minutes, Catherine."

"You already said that."

But she was quiet now, and his own body was still and no longer needing her. He could feel her strength but no disturbance. That was how it should be. That was how he knew instinctively that it had to be.

He could go on now. . . .

It was hot in the darkness and he could smell his own sweat.

He opened his eyes and saw the manacles fastened to the wall and the dirty straw on the stone floor.

His heart jerked in panic.

He knew this place, this cell. Prison. North Korea.

The pain.

"I'm sorry. It will go away. I've never tried to do this kind of dream, and I'm not very good at it. I brought you in at the wrong time."

Bonnie. Red curls shining under the light flowing into the darkness from the barred window, wearing jeans and a Bugs Bunny T-shirt. Sitting beside him in the darkness. As she had visited him all those other times during the seven years he was in prison.

And the pain was suddenly gone.

She smiled. "I told you so. The stink of this place is bothering you. I can take that away, too."

"I thought . . . Oh God, I thought I was out of here."

"And you are. I'm sorry. It won't be for long." Her smile faded. "I didn't want to bring you back here, but it was the only way that I could be sure of reaching you. It was the only strong familiar time we shared. I had to be sure that I was here with you quickly. But this is only a dream. That time is all over. It's only a dream."

He drew a deep breath as the panic almost faded. "Or was that other time a dream, and is this reality?"

She smiled. "I promise you."

Peace. Love. Bonnie.

A dream, just a dream of that nightmare place, and even the nightmare was gradually being shaded with strands of light. He could almost hear the sound of the songs she used to sing to him in this hellhole. "I thought I'd killed you, Bonnie. It wasn't true, was it?"

"No, I tried to tell you. But you wouldn't listen. I couldn't get through to you." She smiled. "All you wanted to do was jump off that cliff."

"And you wouldn't let me."

"No, that's never the way. It messes up everything." She leaned back against the wall and looked around the cell. She whispered, "This is a terrible place. When I found you here, it made me so sad. You were so brave and strong, and they were hurting you. I wanted so to help you. I wanted you to know you weren't alone. I wanted you to believe that someone cared about you."

He remembered the dreams of Bonnie that had kept away the pain and made him fight to live. "You did help me."

A brilliant smile lit her face. "I'm glad. I thought I did." The next moment, the smile had vanished. "I'm slipping away. I have to talk quickly."

"Slipping away?"

"I'm usually pretty good at this dream stuff, but I'm having to divide up my concentration now. I can probably only hold on for another few minutes."

"Then why did you come?"

"I had to tell you something." She added gently, "And you're hurting. I had to let you know that I'll try to help you."

"Eve. Forget about me. Can you help Eve?"

"I'm trying to get near her. That's why I had to use a dream to reach you. I have to use most of my effort trying to reach her. He keeps pushing me away. He's so strong right now."

Fear iced through him. "Will he hurt her?"

"I hope not," she said soberly.

"Dammit, don't you know?"

"I keep seeing Mama, then in his hand a knife."

Gallo muttered a curse.

"That's why I had to come to you now," she said quietly. "I think he'll use the knife. I think the decision to use it is what's giving him his strength."

"But you're not certain."

"And you don't want to believe he'd do it. Neither do I. I'm scared for Mama. But Ted Danner's not always the same. He changes. I think she's safe now, but I don't know for how long. When you get to Mama, you have to believe you may not be able to talk to him." She paused. "You have to believe he'll do it. In your heart and in your head."

He could feel the tears sting his eyes. "Sometimes I have trouble with both. It's . . .

355

hard, Bonnie." He tried to smile. "Hell, you're a ghost. Isn't there some great master plan that you can tap into and help keep her safe?"

"Oh, yes, there's a plan. And sometimes I get glimpses of it. Sometimes I can help, and that's wonderful." She smiled radiantly. "But I'm only learning now. It's not in my hands. There are so many things I don't know yet. But I think that there are different ways that the plan can end if the soul has not crossed over. It's possible we can change it. That's why you have to help. You have to get to Mama. You have to help her. And I'll help her, too. . . ."

She was gone.

He felt a wrenching regret and a piercing loneliness. And then the darkness of the prison and the memories it contained were gone, too.

Swirling. Vanishing.

"Gallo!"

He opened his eyes.

Catherine was looking up at him with a frown. "Your heart was going triple time. I shook you, but you didn't stir." She sat back on her heels. "Are you okay?"

He nodded and straightened. "I must have drifted off."

"It was more like a tidal wave than any gentle drifting. Nightmare?"

"Sort of." He stood up and reached down and pulled her to her feet. "It's over now."

"What's over?"

The return to that ugliness of the past that had been transformed into salvation by the visits of one small girl. He wasn't about to explain what had transpired to Catherine. She was having enough problems coming to terms with the stories and beliefs about Bonnie that were coming at her from all sides. "We have to get going."

"I'm not arguing. But aren't you being a bit erratic? It's not as if you've been slacking. It's been less than fifteen minutes."

He'd thought it had been much longer. Or as if time itself had stopped.

I keep seeing Mama, then a knife in his hand.

He felt the same panic he had when Bonnie had first said those words.

"It doesn't matter if I'm a little erratic. Live with it." He strode into the brush. "We've got to get moving."

A knife in his hand . . .

"How much farther?" Eve asked as she glanced behind her. "Are you ready to tell me where we're —"

The metal of his knife was gleaming in Danner's hand.

357

Eve stopped short, her breath catching in her throat. She watched him touch the edge of the blade with an almost caressing forefinger. He was looking down at the knife in total fascination, then his thumb was stroking the hilt as if it were alive. "Danner?"

He lifted his head and looked at her. His eyes were clouded, and she wasn't sure that he recognized her.

This was not good.

What Father Barnabas had said about Danner shifting from sanity to madness in the space of a moment flew back to her. This could well be one of those moments. She had to be extremely wary.

"Why do you have the knife out?" She moistened her lips. "Do you need to cut this brush? It doesn't seem any worse than —" He wasn't listening to her. She had to break through the dark fog that seemed to surround him. It had caught her off guard. He had been silent for the last few hours, but he hadn't said much since their journey had begun. She'd had no idea that such danger had been brewing. She had been focused on just getting to their destination, getting to Bonnie.

And she would never find Bonnie if she couldn't control the actions of this man who seemed to teeter back and forth on a lethal tightrope.

Think.

If she ran, then he'd be after her in a heartbeat.

Danner had Ranger training. She had been taught to defend herself, but she was not Catherine and did not have her skills.

Okay, then it had to be verbal attack.

"You don't want to cut brush with that knife," she said quietly. "You want to use it on me. Why, Danner? I've done what I promised. I thought you wanted to take me to Bonnie. Why give it up now?"

"The demons," he whispered. "They're trying to get to me. I can feel them push and pull at me. But I won't let them do it."

Demons. Use the demons that obsessed him to control him. "That's right, keep them away. But you're not thinking straight. You said you wanted to give me to Bonnie. What good would it do to kill me now? You had a reason to take me to Bonnie, or you would have killed me when we were with Father Barnabas back at the church." She wasn't getting through to him. Try another path. "Or do you think I'm a demon too, Danner?"

"I'm not sure. I didn't . . . think so. The little girl didn't think you were a demon. She wanted you." He was frowning. "But sometimes the demons take over, and I can't tell the difference until they're ready to pounce. They don't always look like demons."

"I'm not a demon." She turned and moved slowly back toward where he stood. Not too fast. No threat. She could already see him tensing. She stopped before him. "As you said, Bonnie doesn't think I'm a demon."

"But maybe she's one now, too," he whispered. "Maybe they caught her when I wasn't around to keep them away." His eyes were suddenly glittering with tears. "I hope they didn't. God, I hope they didn't. I have to stop them. I have to stop all of you."

His hand was tightening on the knife. Eve could see the muscles of his body tightening, readying to spring forward toward her.

She instinctively braced herself. No, stop it before she had to defend herself. "Bonnie isn't a demon either. I'd know it if she had changed." She stared him in the eye. "Remember, you said you saw us together and you could see how much we loved each other. Do demons love? I don't think so."

"No, hate," he said hoarsely. "Only hate."

"Then you wouldn't have chosen to take me to her if you hadn't been sure that she had love for me. Isn't that right?"

"Maybe. I'm confused right now."

But his hand had never loosened on the knife.

"That's because the demons want you to be confused. They don't want you to take me to Bonnie. They know that if I'm with her, I'll protect her, that I'll never let them have her." She took a step closer so that she was only inches from him. "I'd keep all the forces of darkness away from my Bonnie. There isn't an angel or demon who could stop me from doing that. Look at me, Danner. You'll see it." She reached down and lifted his hand grasping the knife until the blade was pressing against her throat. She held his gaze with all the passion and strength of will that was her love for Bonnie. "See it," she repeated fiercely. "And if you don't, then use that knife that's at my throat."

It was a gamble. His hand was shaking, and she could feel the blade prick her skin.

Believe me, she willed the thought with every bit of her mind and soul. I have to bring my Bonnie home. It can't end like this.

His eyes were flickering, shifting, changing.

Help me, Bonnie. Help me, baby.

He stepped back, and the hand with the knife fell to his side.

Eve let out the breath she hadn't known she was holding.

The moment of danger had passed . . . for now.

Had she convinced him? Or had Danner's madness, which always seemed to be hovering in the shadows, just retreated?

Or had Eve been given the help for which she'd prayed?

It didn't matter. Danner's eyes were clear, his expression as close to normal as she'd experienced since he'd taken her. She moistened her lips again. "You do believe me. That's good. I'm glad that you've gotten over that particular misconception. I don't usually have to defend myself against the charge of being a demon, and I have to really reach to do it."

He was gazing at her in bewilderment. "You're joking with me."

"Purely involuntary. I admit to being a little shaken, and that's how I generally handle it."

"You're frightened," he said slowly.

"You caught me off guard. A knife usually has that effect on me."

He was staring at her with an expression that had an odd element of regret. "I do have to kill you. I can't do anything else. You didn't seem afraid before. I was . . .

surprised."

"Get over it. As I said, you caught me off guard. This time self-preservation kicked in." Her lips tightened. "You're worrying that I'll break my word about making it easy for you? You're wondering if it's worth it to you to wait and take me to where you want to . . . do it."

"Yes."

"I won't lie to you. I'm not afraid to die. Sometimes there seems to be more waiting for me there than here. But that's only sometimes. Self-preservation, Danner. If I can live, I'll do it. But you won't have to worry about my being difficult for you until after you've taken me to where I can find my daughter." She met his eyes. "I'm not as sure as you are that she wants what you want. I'll have to see."

He didn't speak for a moment. "You're . . . honest. I knew that from the moment I met you when you were just a kid. You were pregnant and alone, and you were still fighting and telling the world to get out of your way."

"I wasn't entirely alone. There are good people in this world, Danner. I thought you were one of them. You would have helped me if I'd asked, wouldn't you?"

"You didn't ask. You didn't want me. You

363

didn't want John."

"Is that why you killed my daughter?" Her hands clenched. "You did kill her, didn't you? Tell me."

He didn't answer. "I thought you were right, that John would want to be free if he came back from Korea. I was glad you didn't want him to marry you just because you were having his kid. I would have helped you, but I didn't want you hanging on John, keeping him back."

Memories of that time were bombarding her. Nights of passion with John Gallo. The first moment she'd seen Bonnie at the hospital. This was becoming incredibly hard.

"I never wanted to hurt John," she said unevenly. "But I did hurt him by keeping my daughter to myself. I never realized that until later. I was given a special gift, and I wouldn't share it. Did you realize that I'd hurt him and wanted to strike back? I just don't understand."

"I'd never let you hurt John," Danner said roughly. "I'd never let anyone hurt him."

She'd struck a nerve. "Yet you're doing it now. Don't you know how John feels about what you're doing? He loves you, and he can't understand what you've become."

"I know." Danner's voice was low and threaded with pain. "But I have to do it. I have to give the child what she wants so that she'll go away and stop the torment."

"Bonnie," Eve said between set teeth. "I've told you —" It didn't matter what he called her. Why argue with him? "You've told me yourself that John is probably right behind us. What will you do when he catches up? You may have to kill him to keep the demons away."

"No, I won't do that. He won't catch up. We're almost there."

She jumped at the sentence. "Where?"

"Providence." His lips twisted. "Did you think you were tricking me? It doesn't matter if you know. Not now." He turned and started up the trail. "Come along, Eve. By this time tomorrow it will be over."

Providence. The only Providence she knew was in Rhode Island. Was it a real place they were going or a figment of Danner's imagination? Or was it a term he was using to describe the situation? The last few minutes should have taught her how unstable he could be. Providence. Truth or fantasy, it was the only clue, the only weapon she had.

If she could find a way of using it.

"Where on earth is he taking us?" Father Barnabas gazed at Ben, who was climbing the hill several yards ahead of them. "It seems as if we've been going around in circles for the last few hours."

"We have," Joe said. "We passed that triangular rock twice."

The priest shook his head. "Then the boy doesn't really know where he's going. Why didn't you give up and stop him?"

"Because there's a chance he does know. There was no uncertainty about what he was doing. He took every turn with perfect confidence. I believe there's a possibility that Danner took this route when he led Ben to his place." His gaze was fastened on Ben's back. "He liked the boy, but he wouldn't entirely trust him. He'd be afraid he could be fooled or manipulated. So he took him on a route that would make anyone with him think he didn't know where he was going and give up on him."

"Interesting theory. But how long do we consider it a valid premise?"

"As long as we can. Look at him. He thinks that he knows where he's going. I'd bet he subconsciously counted every twist and turn that Danner made and is repeating them." His lips twisted. "Have a little faith, Father."

"That was unfair. I have faith. But perhaps I'm like Danner and not sure how the boy's mind works. You seem to be a step ahead of us."

"I'm guessing." He only hoped that he was guessing right. Why was he so certain that Ben was the key to finding Eve? Just because that smile reminded him of the sketch of Bonnie? Because he seemed to shine when everything around Joe was in darkness? He should be thinking analytically, not relying on instinct.

Screw it. Instinct was all he had right now.

"It's just ahead." Ben was looking over his shoulder at him. "I'm glad we got here before dark. The ground is rough for the last stretch. I fell twice when Ted was leading me up here." He didn't wait for an answer, but lengthened his stride and disappeared around the curve.

Yes.

The way to the top of the hill was as treacherous as Ben had said. Slippery shale alternating with sandy ground that gave away from beneath their feet. Joe had to stop twice to pull Father Barnabas back on the trail when the shale had thrown him into a skid. The last yards, which should have taken a few minutes, stretched into almost twenty.

The sun was going down in a blaze of scarlet when they reached the top of the summit.

Ben was looking out at the hills and ridges surrounding them. "Beautiful." The sun was bathing his face with a soft glow. "Isn't it beautiful? Ted couldn't see it. I don't know why. I tried to tell him how it made me feel. But Ted said it was a trap, and demons lurked everywhere."

"Did you believe him?" Joe asked quietly.

"The first night he brought me here. It scared me. But then I found out that he was wrong."

"How did you do that?"

He shrugged. "I don't know. I just woke up in the morning and looked out at the ridge and knew there was nothing bad out there."

"The ridge?"

Ben pointed to the ridge to the far north. "I think that's where Ted went when he left me. He said I had to stay here and not follow him, or the demons would get me."

A surge of excitement electrified Joe. He went to the edge of the cliff and looked out at the ridge. Screw the demons. I've got you, Danner. "He was only gone one night?"

"The first night. After that, sometimes only four or five hours."

What the hell was Danner doing beyond that ridge?

He'd find out.

"Wait until dawn." Father Barnabas was standing beside him. "You'll break your neck on this hill in the dark. You have time. Ted Danner isn't there yet."

"And he won't come up this way. I'd bet he only brought Ben up here so that he could put a barrier to keep him from following him." His gaze went back to the ridge, which appeared to ramble for miles. "It's damn long. What the hell is on the other side?"

"The place," Ben said. "But no demons. I promise you, no demons."

"I'm not sure about that."

"I am."

"I'll check my GPS and try to see what's beyond that ridge. It'll give me an idea of the topography." He smiled faintly. "But I doubt if it has the capacity to identify demons."

"You're teasing me. That's okay. I don't mind." Ben was gathering branches from the trees on the slopes leading to the hill. "I'll build a fire. It gets cold at night in the hills."

Joe smiled. "But Father Barnabas has his sleeping bag."

"We can flip for it," the priest offered.

Ben shook his head. "I like to sleep on the

ground. It helps me be closer."

"Closer to what?" Joe asked.

Ben didn't answer directly. "Just closer." He was kneeling and making the fire. "I like it here. It's kind of peaceful."

Joe wasn't feeling at all peaceful. He could feel the blood zinging through his body, and his heart was pounding. At last he was on the way to getting a handle on this nightmare. Should he try to go explore that ridge? He didn't have any doubt he could make it, but Father Barnabas was right about the smart course being to wait for daylight. He'd be going at it blind, and he didn't know what the hell he was looking for. He might do it anyway. He didn't know if he could be patient enough to wait.

"No, Joe." The priest was gazing at him. "Think about it first."

Joe nodded curtly. "I'll call Catherine and Gallo and tell them where we are and see if we can get any idea about where Danner is now. If he's anywhere near, then I'm going." He turned and went toward the fire. "I need some light to get our position on the GPS and Google that damn ridge. I think Ben brought a pan, instant coffee, and some bottled water if you want to fix a hot drink. It's already getting cool."

"Later." Father Barnabas was looking out

at the ridge, which was only a purple-shaded blur in the falling darkness. "Ben is right, there is peace here. I think I'll go over there in the trees by myself. I'll see you soon."

Maybe he was going to meditate or pray or whatever priests did in cases like this, Joe thought. Though a case like this wasn't that common. Or perhaps he was planning what his next move would be in order to find Danner before Joe did.

"You watch him." Ben was sitting back on his heels, his head tilted as he stared at Joe. "He makes you worry. Why?"

Joe shrugged. "He's a puzzle. He may not be what he seems to be."

Ben's gaze went to the priest. "But why should that worry you? It's all good."

"Is it? How do you know?"

"Can't you see? He kind of shines inside. Like you, Joe."

"Me?" He shook his head. "Not likely, Ben."

"Not exactly the same. He's deeper, softer. But he does shine, Joe." He smiled brilliantly. "And he only wants to help. You don't have to worry."

What would Ben know? He thought even Danner was good. How could Joe believe him?

Yet he did believe him. Looking at the boy's face, he believed every word he'd spoken. Crazy.

No, it wasn't crazy. That beautiful clear simplicity wasn't to be denied. Dammit, he suddenly knew he didn't want to deny it. Maybe the kid could sense or see something that Joe couldn't. "Well, I can't see the shine from this distance, so I guess I'll have to go and get a little closer look at him. I'll be right back." He turned and strode toward the trees where the priest was sitting.

"A problem?" Father Barnabas asked as he looked up and saw Joe's frown. "May I help?"

"Yes." Joe stopped in front of him. "You can stop being a damn martyr and shrug off all those good intentions and vows of confidentiality that you took as a priest and as your alter ego the great psychiatrist. I'm tired of wondering if you're going to try to push me under a bus. I want to go after Danner with a clear head."

The priest's brows rose. "What brought this on?"

"Ben says you shine. I don't have his vision. I'm just a cop who's grounded in reality. I want to see if you're the real thing or fool's gold."

"I have my fool's-gold moments. Don't we all?"

"Yeah, but I think that Ben would be able to weigh that in and come up with the right answer."

"You seem to have a good deal of faith in Ben."

"I have to have faith in something or someone right now. I *need* it."

Father Barnabas smiled. "So do I. That's why I took a moment to myself."

"Talk to me. Why are you going after Danner? Does he know too much about you, maybe too much about what the Ezra Bonafel court case was all about?"

"I'm not supposed to discuss the court case."

"To hell with that. I'm going to find out anyway. One of Catherine's CIA buddies is investigating it. Sealed or not, he'll know everything about it soon."

Barnabas's smile faded. "I'm sure he will. The CIA can be very efficient . . . and ruthless. But he's got to be very careful."

"Why?"

"Tell the CIA to drop it, Joe."

"Talk to me. What was so bad in those transcripts that they sealed the records? Why did the judge do that?"

Father Barnabas was silent.

"Why?" Joe asked again. "Why did the judge do it?"

The priest finally shrugged. "Because I asked him to do it."

"You did it? Why?"

"Because it would have hurt people who were vulnerable." He shook his head. "You're not going to give up, are you? If I tell you, will you call off those CIA bloodhounds?"

"Maybe. If I think you're telling the truth. But you can be sure that I'll let them dig until eternity if you don't tell me anything."

The priest smiled faintly. "You're tough, Joe." He looked away from him at the horizon over the ridge. "The Ezra Bonafel charge was brought by Ezra's mother, Dorothy. She claimed I had imprinted false memories through hypnosis on Ezra. The memories were of sexual abuse inflicted on Ezra as a child by his father. She refused to believe that the abuse had happened . . . although Ezra believed she knew about it."

"What made her think that the charge would stick?"

"I'd done a few papers in medical journals on the possibility of being able to imprint or erase memories. Ezra had blocked out what had happened to him as a child, but the memories began to come back to him during therapy. His mother went berserk. Actually, she was probably more unstable than Ezra. She loved Ezra and couldn't admit even to herself that she would permit him to be hurt. She had to have someone to blame."

"And that was you?"

"Oh, yes. She had to make Ezra believe that I was the enemy and not she. I knew she didn't stand a chance of winning and that it was going to hurt her and Ezra far more than it did me. I tried to talk her out of pressing charges, but she wouldn't agree. The best I could get was a trial with the least possible publicity in a small town south of Atlanta."

"She lost the case?"

"Yes. And she suffered a nervous breakdown two weeks after the judge handed down his decision. Ezra stood by her. I believe the responsibility of taking care of her helped them both to heal."

"And what helped you to heal?"

"The knowledge that I'd tried to do the right thing." He grimaced. "But it brought me to the point that I realized that my patients sometimes needed more help than I was able to give. I had to do some serious thinking." He looked back at Joe. "Don't let those court records surface. It would hurt

Ezra and his mother too much. Maybe God's helped them to forget all that pain they went through."

"No bitterness?"

"Why would I be bitter?"

Joe studied him in surprise for a moment. Because a woman had done her best to destroy him? No, he could tell that Father Barnabas was sincere. "No reason."

"You believe me?"

"I believe you." He turned away. "I can't do anything else. Who am I to argue with a man Ben thinks is golden?"

Father Barnabas chuckled. "Not only do I 'shine,' but now I'm golden? I must be truly blessed."

Joe glanced at him over his shoulder. "Do you know, I think you just might be at that."

A few moments later, Joe sank down across from Ben at the fire. The boy was sitting with his chin resting on his raised knees, his gaze fixed on the fire.

Joe was silent for a moment. "Weren't you even curious about where Ted Danner was going beyond that ridge?"

"No. I could tell he didn't want to tell me. There are things I don't like anyone else to know, too." He smiled. "But he liked me to be here when he came back from the place.

At first I thought he was just being nice to me, but I think maybe he was lonely like I was."

"Past tense. You're not lonely any longer?"

He shook his head. "I'm . . . full now."

"What?"

"There were so many things I didn't understand. Everyone around me seemed to see everything so clearly, and I couldn't. And the things I could see, they couldn't. I was different."

Yes, he was, and Joe didn't know what to answer. "Different isn't always bad."

"But I'm not different. I was wrong." Ben smiled. "None of us are different on the inside. Or if we are, it's only good."

"And because of that, you're not lonely any longer?"

"I think that's it." He was silent a moment. "I get confused. There's so much that comes when she touches me."

Joe stiffened. "She?"

"I didn't tell you the truth." Ben stared into the fire. "I told you that I didn't know how I knew that when I woke up that first morning that everything was all right."

"That was a lie?"

"That was the first night the dream came. She told me. She said, 'Don't be afraid, Ben. Not of anything. There are no demons unless you let them into your heart. Some things might hurt you, but they don't matter. Look beyond them, and all you'll see is all the beauty inside you.' " He smiled. "Fancy words, but somehow I knew what she meant. That was nice. It made me feel . . . safe."

"Who is she, Ben?"

Ben looked at him. "Why do you ask me? You know her name. I knew when you were talking to me in the tent that she'd talked to you, too. I could feel it. It was almost as if I could see her beside you."

"Did you?" Joe said, through the tightening in his throat. "Is that why you decided to bring us here?"

"I trust you," he said simply. "You dream about her, too. You wouldn't lie to me or do anything bad."

"Listen, Ben, I'll try to keep my promise to you. But I don't know what's going to happen."

"Neither do I. But she told me not to be afraid of anything. But you're afraid, aren't you, Joe?"

He wished he wasn't afraid. He wished he could embrace the same glowing simplicity and faith as this boy who seemed to have reached out into the mist and touched Bonnie because of that same simplicity. But he didn't have the right to sit and wait and hope. He was the one who had to take responsibility and not wait for help. It was Eve who was in danger.

And nothing must happen to her.

Joe nodded. "I'm afraid. But I'm glad you aren't."

Ben was studying him. "It's the woman in the photo, it's Eve."

"Always." He paused. "She's Bonnie's mother, Ben."

His eyes widened. "Why didn't you tell me?"

"I didn't think it would mean anything to you. I didn't know about the dream."

He nodded slowly. "Ted mustn't hurt her. It would be bad." Then his expression cleared. "But we can help her. And we mustn't be afraid."

Because Bonnie had told Ben that he shouldn't fear anything.

"I'm going to sleep now." Ben was curling up on the ground, facing the fire. "I like it here. Do you hear the wind through the trees? It's kind of like a song . . ."

"Would you like some coffee?"

"No, I want to sleep. The times I've come here with Ted, the dreams have come. I think it's easier for her here. . . ."

"You've had more than that one dream?"

He nodded, his eyes closing. "She talks to me. She tells me things. She teaches me. She makes me understand, and every time she leaves me I'm . . . bigger, fuller."

"Do the dreams come even when you're not here?"

"Yes, but not as often." He cradled his cheek beneath one hand. "She likes it here. The animals . . . the deer . . ."

"Eve would like to know that."

"Tell her . . ."

He was asleep.

Joe gazed at the firelight playing over Ben's face. Are you dreaming of Bonnie now? Is she with you? What is she teaching you?

But that was between Ben and Bonnie, and no one should interfere.

Dream, my friend . . .

He got to his feet and moved several yards away from the fire before he pulled out his phone. No dreams for him. He had work to do.

First, to find out was beyond that ridge. He checked the coordinates on his GPS and punched them into Google.

It took a minute for the overview to come on the screen.

"What the hell!"

CHAPTER
14

"It's Joe." Catherine punched the access on her phone and turned up the volume for Gallo. "What's happening? Did you find out anything at the camp?"

"Enough. How close are you to Danner?"

"The signs are getting fresher. We're moving fast. I'd say a few hours."

"That's too long. You have to get closer to him. There's too much territory, and you could lose him."

"What?" Gallo said. "We're doing the best we can. What do you mean? You have an idea where he's headed?"

"Almost certainly. I'll give you the coordinates I know." Joe rattled off the coordinates. "But this is where I am. He won't come directly here. There's a lot of wild country around here, acres and acres. Low hills, flatlands, and a giant ridge."

"What ridge?"

"Something weird. I'll send you a photo

of the area I Googled that's beyond the ridge I'm facing now."

"Those coordinates put Danner and Eve about six hours away from you," Catherine said. "And Gallo and I are about eight hours."

"You'd better be right on top of him when he gets here. We could miss him, dammit."

"Why? If we know the approximate —" Her phone pinged, and she cut over to look at the topographical photo Joe had sent her. "Holy shit." She showed the photo to Gallo, then cut back to the call from Joe. "It looks like the Grand Canyon."

"Not nearly as grand, much smaller, but it's wild enough to cause us a problem. If that's where he's taking Eve, we could wander around there and not find them until it's too late."

"If?"

"Like I told you, that area is only one part of the area he could be headed for. There's too wide a choice. Check Danner's exact projected destination from where you are now. He should have to commit very soon."

"A Grand Canyon in Georgia?" Catherine asked. "Have you ever heard of it, Joe?"

"I have a vague memory," Joe said. "I've never seen it. It's one of the natural oddities that appeal to some tourists."

"And how much territory are we going to have to worry about?"

"Surrounding hills, flatlands. Too much. It's enough to be fatal to Eve if we're not close enough. We have to narrow it down."

"We'll be right behind him."

"Call me," Joe said curtly. He hung up.

Catherine flipped back to the Google overview. "This isn't good enough for anything. I'll call Venable and see if he can get a satellite image of the canyon and surrounding area so we'll have an accurate map." She started to dial. "After that, we've got to get moving." She could feel the blood pumping through her veins as the adrenaline surged. At last, they had a chance to get ahead of the bastard. "We made up a lot of the distance between us in the last few hours. We can —" Gallo was shaking his head. "What's wrong? We can do it."

"I don't doubt you for a minute. You can move mountains. Or at least a minor Grand Canyon," he said. "But we might catch up with him just a little too late. We can't afford to do that."

Her gaze was narrowed on his face. "What are you suggesting, Gallo?"

"I'm suggesting you go after Danner alone. I'll cut back straight east until I get to a farm or ranch and borrow a vehicle and take off on the nearest highway or road that will take me to this canyon. I'll be much faster than you on foot. As soon as he gets close enough to the canyon area so that you can see where he's heading, you call me, and I'll be there to meet him." He tilted his head. "Much more practical?"

She thought about it from all angles. "Yes," she said slowly.

"Then I'll take off." He started to turn, then whirled back to her. "Don't try to get him by yourself, Catherine. Wait until we get to the canyon."

"It would be questionable whether I'd even be able to reach him by the time he gets to the canyon area. I doubt if I'd be able to get ahead and ambush him."

"But you'd do it if you got the chance." He shook his head. "Call me. Let me help you, dammit."

She gazed at him for a moment. "I'll call you . . . and Joe."

His lips twisted. "Because you still don't trust me."

"No, I don't," she said bluntly. "No one knows how you're going to react until the moment you see Ted Danner. Not even you, Gallo." She turned her back on him. "I'll see you at the canyon."

She could feel his gaze on her back until

she turned the curve in the path. What did he expect? She would not tell him that she trusted him. She had eyes and a brain and the experience to know that nostalgia from the past could twist motives and emotions in the present. She would not be anything but honest with him.

But for that brief instant, she had wanted to tell him what he wanted to hear.

Forget it. That impulse might have been okay coming from another woman. Not her. Her entire life had been based on being totally herself and not giving one bit of that self away to anyone to buy affection or respect or a haven from fear. It didn't matter that Gallo had an effect on her that was both powerful and unusual. She would fight to give him a chance. She would stand beside him and fight the enemy.

If he realized who that enemy was.

She had been trying hard not to think how she would feel if someone she loved suddenly became the enemy. That would be strange. She loved so few people in this world. Her son, Luke, Hu Chang, who had been friend and teacher, Eve . . .

Why was she thinking about this? She had a job to do.

If Gallo held any resentment that she

could not lie to him, then he could deal with it.

She had another problem to deal with.

How fast could she get to Danner and Eve?

And how could she take Danner out when she got there?

Danner was growing tenser, edgier with every mile that passed.

And Eve could see that the tension was having an effect on his finely balanced stability. He had not reached for his knife again, but she had seen him staring at her with frustration and impatience. He wanted this over.

Well, so did she. But she could not chance Danner's ending it without her finding Bonnie. What if he changed his mind and decided that Eve's death didn't necessarily have to take place at the site he had chosen? He had been close to that decision only a short time ago. She had been able to distract him then, but she couldn't be sure of doing it again by confronting him. She had to change tactics . . . and try to get help on board.

Focus. She had to get Danner to focus on his original plan and reinforce it.

She turned to face him. "You said we were

close. Were you lying to me?"

"We're close." He raised his head, staring at the top of the trees. "I can feel the chill."

"Chill. You're afraid?" She grimaced. "Oh yes, your demons. You take me to my daughter, and I'll protect you, Danner."

"You won't be able to do that."

He meant because she'd be dead. She felt a chill herself. Ignore it. Get him to focus. "How close are we?"

"An hour, maybe two."

She moistened her lips. "And then you'll kill me."

He didn't answer.

"Why are you waiting? Why drag me all the way down the state when you could have killed me at the church in Rome?"

"It's . . . her place. I have to make sure that she knows I'm giving her what she wants."

She was silent. "Yes, that would be important. You're going through all this trouble, and you don't even know if it's what she wants."

"I don't know whether it makes a difference if I wait."

She had thought that was the direction in which he was leaning. "It would make a difference."

"How do you know?"

"She's my daughter. You said that you saw us together and that you knew we were close. Wouldn't I know her better than anyone?" She paused. "Don't you think she's the one who needs to make the decision?"

He shook his head. "She's already made it. She led me to the church. It's what she wants. I *know* it."

Cross that argument out. His tone had been absolutely positive.

He thought that Bonnie wanted her to leave this life and cross over to the next.

Oh, Bonnie, it's an argument that I've had with you all through the years, and I could never convince you. He has it all wrong.

Unless you've changed your mind.

"I'll accept what you say," she said quietly. "Perhaps you're right. Because I do know that Bonnie wouldn't want me to be murdered and thrown into a ditch somewhere like you did her."

He flinched as if she'd struck him. "No. No. No. I didn't."

"You're protesting too much. Why else would you be afraid of her?"

"She won't leave me alone."

"But she'll leave you alone if you kill me?" Move carefully now. His eyes were glaring at her, and his hands were opening and closing at his sides. "So you take me to this 'place' and kill me to please my daughter. Am I going to be allowed to have some clergyman to bless my soul? What about calling your friend, Father Barnabas?"

"No," he said hoarsely.

"No help to send my soul to heaven? Bonnie wouldn't like that. Then what about letting me call the man I love to say good-bye? Joe and Bonnie have grown very close through the years. She wouldn't be pleased that you'd deny me that final solace."

"You're trying to trick me."

"You could listen to the conversation. I deserve to say good-bye. A short conversation, then I won't ask anything else of you. What harm would it do? You're taking everything else from me. Let me say good-bye." She stared into his eyes. "If you do, I'll tell Bonnie that you were kind to me, that you let me go with gentleness."

His expression was tormented. Then he spun her around and gave her a push up the trail. "No, I won't do it."

Okay, no chance of communicating with Joe. But evidently she'd changed the focus, and Danner wasn't going to kill her on the trail. She'd take what she could get.

"Wait."

She stopped and turned to face him.

He thrust his phone into her hand. "Call him. I'm listening to every word. If you try to trick me, then it's all over."

Which is what he wanted anyway.

She looked down at the phone. What was she going to say?

Providence?

It was the only clue she had to give him, and she wasn't even sure that it was a valid one. And how could she —

"Call him," Danner said curtly. "It's what you wanted. It's what you say she'd want."

Why was she hesitating? She knew that Joe was searching for her though she had no idea how close or far he was to her. She'd try to get him what information she could. If it wasn't enough to help, then she'd still get to fulfill the purpose she'd given Danner. She had no idea if she was going to survive, and to be able to say good-bye to Joe was a gift that was without price. "That's right." She cleared her throat. "I'm just surprised." She quickly dialed Joe's number.

It rang three times before he picked up. "Quinn."

Lord, it was good to hear his voice. "Joe."

There was a silence. "Eve. My God, where are you?"

"I can't talk about that, or he'll make me

hang up. Don't ask questions. I don't want to waste our time together." She paused. "We don't have much time left."

"What do you mean? I'll kill him."

"Hush. Listen to me. I have to make every word count. We've been together so long that sometimes I'm afraid that I haven't said the things that I should. There's always been Bonnie with us or between us. I didn't tell you that if you hadn't come into my life that there would have been no life. You've been my friend, my lover, my salvation." She had to stop as her voice broke. "Pay attention to what I'm saying, Joe, this is important. Fate brought us together that day when you came to my house to try to find my Bonnie. And it's fate that's tearing us apart right now. We've got to accept it."

"The hell we do."

"I'm not going to argue with you. You always do what you want anyway. But I just don't want you to go through anything more for me. I love you, Joe. Thank you for being in my life."

She hung up the phone. The tears were running down her cheeks, and she wiped them away on the sleeve of her shirt. She handed the phone back to Danner. Had he caught the word she had slid into the conversation? It had been subtle. Maybe too subtle for Joe, too.

Danner was studying her face. "You do love him. You didn't love John like that." His expression was thoughtful, almost sad, and completely without that hint of vague disorientation that seemed to come and go. In that moment, he reminded Eve of the man she'd met when Bonnie had first been born.

"No, and he didn't love me. You have to be a grown-up to know what love's about. We were just kids." She drew a deep breath. "Thank you for letting me talk to him. I'm ready to go to Bonnie now."

He didn't move. "I have to do it. I can't let you go."

"I know you can't." She met his gaze. "But we made a bargain, and I've kept my end of it. I think you've been having second thoughts, and you can't do that. It's your demons that are making you think those thoughts. You take me to Bonnie, and when we get there, you tell me everything. That's how it has to be. Do you understand, Danner?"

He reached out and gently touched her tear-wet cheek. "I have to do it, Eve." Then he turned and moved through the brush.

Joe drew a deep breath as he savagely

punched the button to disconnect the call. He felt angry and helpless, and he wanted to tear the phone apart.

"Joe?" Father Barnabas was gazing at him across the campfire. "Eve?"

"Yes." He had to think. But he was so torn up inside that he was having to try to calm down and try to be objective. Objective? Hell, no. "Danner let her make the call. It was a good-bye, have-a-nice-life call. I'm going to kill him. And there's no way you're going to stop me, Father."

"No, that has to come from you." He glanced at Ben, sleeping a few yards away. "You made him a promise."

"I said I'd try. I didn't say —" He closed his eyes. "I'm ready to explode. I can't let him do this to me. I have to go over what she said. Eve's smart and wouldn't have wasted time just to tell me good-bye."

"Was it a waste?" the priest said gently.

Eve's voice telling him she loved him, telling him that their life together had given meaning to hers.

"God, no." He opened his eyes. "But she would still have concentrated on finding a way to beat Danner if there was a way. She'd try to tell me where she was or where she was going." He grabbed his notebook from his pocket. "Give me a minute. I want to put down everything she said word for word and see if I can see anything."

You've been my friend, my lover, my salvation.

His hand was shaking as he wrote. Steady it. Don't think of those words that meant so much, Eve who meant more than life. Search for something else.

"Anything?" Father Barnabas asked.

"Nothing. But there has to be —" He stopped. "Maybe . . . Here she said for me to pay attention, that it was important."

Fate brought us together that day when you came to my house to try to find my Bonnie. And it's fate that's tearing us apart now. We've got to accept it.

"Accept what? Accept fate. That may be the key word." Lord, he was reaching. But he was desperate, dammit.

"But to unlock what door?" the priest asked.

"I don't know." Okay, clear his mind of emotion and think coolly and analytically. Probe deeper. Investigate.

He grabbed his iPhone and pulled up the dictionary app. Meaning of fate. Destiny. Fortune. Chance. Providence. Luck.

He called Catherine. "Did you get Venable to zero in closer on that entire ridge area?"

"Yes, it just came in."

394

"Give me the names of towns or tourist sites anywhere near it."

"Narrow it down. What are you looking for?"

"Fate."

She was silent. "No Fate. Americas, Lumpkin, Providence, Eufaula."

"Providence?" His heart was pounding as he glanced down at his thesaurus list. "I think that's it."

"What?"

"I'd bet that Danner will be taking her to Providence."

"Why? On what authority?"

"Eve."

She inhaled sharply. "You talked to her?"

"She got Danner to let her call and say good-bye."

"Shit."

"Yes, but she's still alive. And we know where she's going."

"Maybe."

"I don't need skepticism, Catherine. I've got to believe that's what she was trying to tell me."

"And I hope you're right. I just pulled up the info on Providence. It's your Grand Canyon area. Providence National Park. That's a sizable acreage, and it can be entered from any number of directions. If we don't get to him before he gets to it, we're going to have a hell of a time. I'll keep after Danner and hope to get a visual on him before or when he enters the canyon so I can call you and let you know an approximate location." She paused. "And I'll call Gallo and tell him that they're probably heading for Providence."

"Call? He's not with you?"

"No, we split up. He was going to find a car and truck and drive to the area you told us about. He called me an hour ago and told me that he'd run across a farmer at an apple farm who sold him a dilapidated old Buick. It runs anyway, and he's on the highway. I'll let him know that you've zeroed in on an approximate location."

"No."

"Yes. We may need his help if we have to try to intercede with Danner to get Eve away from him. Danner still has affection for him."

"I don't need —" He muttered a curse. He was being stubborn. He should take any help he could get. "Do what you like."

"I will." She hung up.

"She helped you," Father Barnabas's gaze was on his face. "But you're not pleased."

"I'll be pleased." He sat back on his heels. "When I get in a position where I can

396

control her. Catherine is used to running the show."

The priest's lips curved in a faint smile. "And you're not?"

"But it's my show. Eve is mine." He got to his feet, went to the edge of the hill, and gazed out at the ridge. The moon was high and casting a glow over the trees and rocks. The area beyond the ridge still appeared dark and mysterious, but he finally knew what lay beyond it. Wildness and steep rocks and a canyon that shouldn't have been there. A terrain Joe knew nothing about, across which he'd have to follow or ambush Danner, who was probably familiar with every inch of the canyon. "Six hours. That will make it about dawn when Danner gets here."

"What are you planning?"

"Going down this hill." He made a face. "I should say sliding down this hill and making my way to Providence. I'll recon-noiter the area, then camp out with my binoculars and wait until he shows up."

"I'll go with you." Joe turned to where Ben had raised himself on one elbow. He did not know when the boy had awakened, but he was staring gravely at Joe. "I have to go."

"No, you don't," Joe said roughly. "The

397

last thing I want is to have to take care of you, Ben. You stay here with Father Barnabas."

Ben was shaking his head. "There's something for me to do. I have to go." He sat up and began to put out the fire. "I have to be with you when you find them."

And Joe might have to kill Danner in front of the kid. What kind of guilt trip would that lay on Ben for bringing Joe here?

"It's okay." Ben was looking at Joe with a gentle smile. "Stop worrying about me, Joe. It's going to work out as it should for me."

Joe felt a sudden chill. The kid was comforting him, yet he felt —

"Let him go," Father Barnabas said quietly. "You can't stop Ben, and I'll take responsibility for him."

"I suppose that means you're going, too," Joe said jerkily. "Well, you're right, I can't stop you. But stay out of my way." He turned and strode toward the path leading down the hill. He suddenly whirled back to where Ben was putting out the last of the embers. "Did you . . . sleep well?"

The radiant smile that Joe found so like Bonnie's lit the boy's face. "Yes, Joe."

But that was all he was going to say, Joe realized with frustration and that same flicker of fear. He turned and started down the hill. "That's good, Ben."

"Providence," Gallo repeated, his grasp tightening on the phone. "It's possible but not a sure thing, Catherine."

"Joe doesn't care that it's not carved in stone," Catherine said. "It's all we have, and he intends to go for it. You make up your mind what you're going to do. I'm close to Danner, but I may not be able to verify his precise destination until the last hour or so. By that time, you may not have time to position yourself." She added without expression, "It might all be over by the time you get there."

"You think I want that?"

"I didn't say that. Call me from wherever you decide to enter the canyon." She hung up.

Gallo pressed the disconnect. He wasn't angry with Catherine's suspicions. She had every right to doubt him. He had been fighting with everything within him to find a way to absolve his uncle of blame. But he couldn't sacrifice Eve on the altar of his love for Ted Danner. He couldn't forgive Ted if he'd killed Bonnie. And he could only prove himself by acts, not words.

Providence.

The old Buick didn't have a GPS, so he

had to access his phone. He dialed it into the apps.

Do something, anything. Ever since he'd gotten on the highway, he'd been bombarded by thoughts and memories of his uncle Ted.

His friend, his family, the first person who taught him to trust in a world that was devoid of it.

Eve. Bonnie. How had the three people he loved become entangled in this nightmare that was tearing him apart?

It had happened, and now he must deal with it.

His eyes were stinging as he checked the directions for Providence.

"Any sign?" Father Barnabas asked.

Joe lowered the infrared binoculars. "Nothing." It was not dawn yet, but that shouldn't have prevented him from seeing signs of life. They were inside the canyon area, and he could scan the area immediately outside. But it wasn't as if there was a fence to seal off the canyon. The surrounding area was as porous as Catherine had said, and there were thickets of trees that could shelter any interloper, dammit. All he could do was keep a constant vigil and hope that Catherine could notify him when Danner approached.

If she had even been able to get close enough to Danner to give him that information. She would have had to escalate her speed, then make constant observations once she was within sight of Danner and Eve.

He lifted his binoculars again.

Nothing.

Come on, Catherine.

He glanced at Ben, who was sitting on the ground beside him. The boy was calm and hadn't said a word since they'd left the hill.

"Okay?"

Ben nodded but didn't look at him. "She's near, Joe."

He stiffened. "Who's near? Eve?"

Ben shook his head.

And Joe wasn't going to delve any deeper. Eve was the only one he had to worry about at the moment. He scanned the thickets.

His phone rang.

Thank God. Catherine.

"Do you have a visual on them?" she asked.

"No, what the hell are you talking about?"

"They're in the canyon. They have to be. I finally caught sight of them fifteen minutes ago. They were on the trail outside the park, and a few minutes later, they disappeared."

He muttered a curse. "We're watching the area. I haven't caught a glimpse of them. What were their coordinates when you lost them?" As she read them off, he checked them on the GPS. "That's twenty minutes north of here, toward the ridge. He didn't come all the way down to the main Providence area. It's high country." He jumped to his feet. "I'm on my way."

"I'm following his trail from where he entered the canyon," Catherine said. "I'll call you if I spot him."

Shit, Joe thought. "Twenty minutes."

Too long.

Panic.

"Joe!"

He didn't pay attention to the priest's shout as he started to run.

Twenty minutes. Who knew what could happen in that time?

Eve . . .

CHAPTER
15

Something was different, Eve thought.

The ground was sandy, and the trees were thinning on either side of them since they'd made that last turn. The sky was still a cold gray, the trail misty, and she could make out very little in the dimness.

But something was different.

"You said we were going to Providence," Eve said. "When do we get there?"

"We don't." Danner didn't look at her. "It's Providence National Park, and it's four miles from here. We don't have to go through the main part of the park. We just have to border the edge. I found this path years ago, and it saves me time when I just have to check."

"Check?"

"Hurry." His pace increased as the ground beneath their feet began to climb. "You said you wanted to be here, didn't you? I wanted it, too," he asked roughly. "Well, you're here."

And Danner's voice was jerky and his face pale and taut in the dimness.

She was here.

Eve felt an excitement that was part eagerness and part dread.

Bonnie?

"Look at you," Danner's gaze was fixed on her face. "They say I'm crazy, but you know what I'm going to do, and it doesn't matter to you."

"It matters. But I can deal with it." She wanted him to stop talking. The excitement was building, and she had to control it. Why wasn't it just sick horror? This had to be her daughter's murderer. He had not said the words, but it had to be true. "I've tried to find answers since the day Bonnie disappeared. I've been searching for my daughter for a long time." Her stride unconsciously quickened.

I'm coming, Bonnie. I'm going to bring you home. You've always said it didn't matter to you. But it matters to me.

"You shouldn't have wasted your time looking for her," Danner said.

"Waste? It wasn't wasted."

"It did you no good. And it didn't help her. You couldn't keep them away from her."

He was talking about his demons again, Eve realized, and she was sick to death of it. And she didn't have to put up with it now. The end was near. Either he was taking her to Bonnie, or it would all be revealed as a big lie spoken by this madman. "I've told you before. I can take care of my little girl. There are no demons who could touch her. They're all in your mind. I'm sure your doctors have told —" She stopped. They had suddenly come out of the pine trees and were standing on a summit overlooking the canyon. She inhaled sharply. "Dear God. Where are we?"

The sun had not risen, but the dawn sky was shaded with pink and violet, and streams of golden light were falling on the canyon and the trees below. A silver ribbon that must have been a creek wound around the land at the bottom of the canyon. Beautiful. Lord, it was beautiful. It took her breath away. "I . . . didn't expect this."

"It's the place, the canyon. I searched for a long time before I found it." Danner had already turned away from the canyon and was starting to climb again. "It's the only place I could find where the demons couldn't come. But I think they're here now, too. I . . . have a bad feeling."

It was happening again. She could see the

tension beginning to grip him. She'd been aware that it was growing for the last ten minutes. The violence was beginning to fester within him as it had once before. She had been able to deter that violence, but could she do it now? How much time did she have before that tension broke, and he turned on her? She'd have to fight him, and whether she lived or died, the knowledge of what happened to Bonnie could be lost.

Make him talk now. Make him tell her. Be bold. It seemed to work with him. Don't let him think of her as a victim. "Stop hiding behind those tall tales, Danner. You're a coward. You couldn't even say her name. You made up a fantasy about those so-called demons because you didn't want to face your own guilt."

He whirled on her. "It's not true." His eyes were blazing in his taut face. "They're here, they're everywhere. I had to stop them."

"Stop them from what? Killing my Bonnie? But you couldn't do that. No demon murdered her. It was you, Danner."

His hands reached out and clutched her shoulders. "It was a demon. A demon killed the child."

"Bonnie. And it was you. No one else."

His hands slid to her throat. "I wouldn't

have done it. Why would I do it? She belonged to John."

"She belonged to me. I told you that I didn't want John to have her. So you were angry and decided to punish me by killing my daughter."

His hands tightened on her throat. "I didn't kill her. I wanted to save her."

His grasp was bruising, cutting off her air.

"You're hurting me. You didn't want to do this, remember? You wanted to take me to her first. And we're so close now."

"Close enough," he muttered. His eyes were glittering. "I can take you to her later."

"But then you'd break your promise to me. John always said you'd never break your word. Is he wrong?"

His grip was loosening but not releasing her. "I never lied to John."

"Except about your mental illness."

"That wasn't really a lie. I wasn't sick. They wouldn't believe me. They weren't there. They didn't see the demons kill those children in the mountains."

"No one is seeing the demons but you. Why should I believe you?"

"Because it's true."

"I don't know that. You're afraid of Bonnie, aren't you? You're willing to do anything to make her leave you alone. Why would

407

you be afraid if you didn't think there was a reason for her to come after you?"

"Because she doesn't understand. She thinks I did it. She doesn't know."

"Neither do I." She held his gaze. "*Tell* me."

His eyes were glittering. "It was the demon."

"And what was the name of the demon? Does he have a name? Is it Ted Danner?"

"No. It's Black. Paul Black."

A ripple of shock surged through her. Black, the assassin that Gallo had killed weeks ago, the man who had been hired by Queen and Jacobs to take the blame for killing Bonnie. But Black had told Eve before his death that he had not done that killing.

And she had believed him.

She still believed him.

"You're lying, Danner."

He shook his head. "No, he was a monster. I saw him watching the little girl, and I knew what he was. He was standing outside your house on Morningside Drive, and I could see the shadow he was casting against the flames."

"Flames?"

"No, that's not right." He moistened his lips. "That was the house in the village. That other time. No flames. Just the little girl getting off the bus and running up the street toward home. The sun was shining, and she was laughing."

How many times had Eve stood on the porch and watched Bonnie run toward her, laughing and telling her something that had happened at school? "You saw Black standing there watching my Bonnie? Why were you there?"

"I had to stop him. I knew that he hated John and wanted to hurt him. John had made him look like a fool in front of Queen and Jacobs. They'd hired him to take John out, and he'd failed."

"How did you know about Queen and Jacobs and how they'd victimized John?"

"When they told me that John was dead, I had to find out what had happened to him. John was smart. John was good. And those bastards used him and threw him away. I went after them. I searched for years until I found out what they were. I was going to take Queen and Jacobs out, but then I heard that John had escaped from that prison. I went to Jacobs and Queen and told them I was going to tell John everything and that I was going to blow the whistle on their drug dealing."

"Wait. John was told that you were dead when he was in the hospital in Japan."

"I might as well have been dead. Everyone thought I was crazy. I was having trouble getting off the medication. I didn't want John to come back and see me like that." His lips twisted bitterly. "I made a deal with Queen. He promised me that he and Jacobs would make it up to John. They said they'd make him a rich man. He'd have a good life. All I had to do was keep my mouth shut and disappear."

"And you agreed?"

"They told me what the Koreans had done to him. I knew what John had gone through. I couldn't help him. He deserved to have a new start."

After being tortured and starved and cheated of all hope in that darkness in his cell. "Yes, he did. So you made the deal and disappeared."

"I made the deal." His lips tightened. "But I told them I'd be watching them, and if I saw any sign that they were trying to hurt John, I'd come back. And I did watch them. They got him well, then started to send him off on missions. I didn't like that, but they said that they had to allow some time to pass before they could gather a fund together to give to John."

"They were playing you."

"And I would have stepped in, but then

410

Black came back to Atlanta. He was one of Jacobs and Queen's private hit men."

"And he was angry because John had humiliated him." She said slowly, "I suppose it could be true."

"It's all true."

But there was more to the story than he had said.

"What else?"

"He killed the little girl to punish John." But Danner was looking away from her.

"No. That's not all." She took a step back, and he let his hands drop from her shoulders. She braced herself. She didn't want to hear the answer to this question, but she had to ask it. "How . . . did he kill her?"

"That's enough." He pushed her forward up the hill. "It's time now."

She jerked away and whirled to face him. "No, it's not enough. How do you know he killed her? My daughter was taken at the park. Were you there? Did you see him do it?"

"I saw him."

"You were there?"

He moistened his lips. "I was there."

"Then you saw Bonnie?"

"I saw her. It was crowded, but I saw you with her on the swings. Then she ran away across the park toward the ice-cream truck."

Eve could see Bonnie darting in and out of the crowds as she ran to get her ice cream. "And you saw Black there."

"I told you I did."

"Where was he?"

"Close," he whispered. "So close. I knew it was going to be that day. It was so crowded. It would be so easy for him. I had to stop him."

"But you didn't stop him, did you?"

"I did. I did. I talked to her. I told her she had to go with me. I told her that there was a bad man who might hurt her or her mother. She believed me. She wasn't afraid. She looked up at me, and she smiled. She said, 'It's all right, Ted. Don't be scared.' "

"She knew your name?"

"I guess so. I don't know how. Maybe I told her. I whisked her out to my car, which was parked in the street. I saw Black, but I didn't know if he'd seen her with me. I had to hide her from him. I told her to jump in the trunk, and I'd let her out when it was safe. She didn't argue. She did what I told her." He swallowed. "She did what I told her."

"He followed you?"

"I wasn't sure, but I had to get her away. What if he'd seen her? I kept driving. I caught sight of a car that might have been

Black's a dozen times. I got caught in a traffic jam, and I was scared that he'd catch up with me. But then I finally broke free and got off the freeway. I drove out of the city until I came to the lake. Then I jumped out of the car and ran around to let her out." Tears were running down his cheeks. "But he'd killed her. She was curled up as if she were asleep, but Black had killed her. The demon had taken her away."

Eve stared at him in shock. "Oh, my God," she whispered. "It was hot that day. She wouldn't have lasted any time at all in that trunk."

"No, he killed her. It wasn't my fault. I'd never have killed John's little girl. She was a pretty little girl and so brave . . . I wouldn't have done that."

Eve closed her eyes. "Heat. You thought you were saving her from Black but that trunk must have been hot as an oven. The heat killed her."

"No! Stop saying that. I told you what happened." His voice was harsh as he pushed her forward up the trail. "I kept my promise. Now it has to be over. She has to leave me alone. I have to give her what she wants."

Her eyes opened, but she could barely see through the tears. "She's here?" After all the years, the uncertainty. "You brought her here?"

"Of course I did. She's John's little girl. I had to find a special place for her. But she wouldn't leave me alone. I tried to tell her that Black had killed her, but she wouldn't believe me. Wherever I turned, she was beside me. Lately, it got worse. I tried to run away, but she was always there." His hands clenched. "But I didn't know what she wanted."

And Danner couldn't let himself believe that it had been his fault that Bonnie had died. A horrible accident that had become a guilt that had dominated his life and destroyed whatever sanity he still possessed.

"Listen. I can tell you what she wants."

He shook his head. "I know now. A little girl needs her mother, and I took her away from you."

And Danner wasn't going to be dissuaded. She was so shaken that she didn't even know if she could make the attempt. She would have to go along with it until she could either say something that would strike the right note or make a break.

Or find a way to kill Danner? He had killed her Bonnie. Accident or not, he had taken the daughter who had made her life worth living. Could she forgive him? She wasn't sure that was possible.

She would think about that later, when she was able to reason and not just feel. At that moment, she couldn't think of anything but Bonnie. An eagerness was beginning to spark within her.

He was taking her to Bonnie.

"She's on that cliff!" Joe stopped skidding across the sandy ground and shaded his eyes with his hand. "And that's got to be Danner."

"Yes, that's Ted," Father Barnabas said. "But how do we get to them?"

Good question, Joe thought. The cliff on which Danner and Eve were standing was several hundred feet above the valley floor, and it appeared as if they were going still higher.

Not by standing here wondering, he thought impatiently. "We go south, pick up that trail, and start climbing."

And hope they were in time.

"There's another trail that I ran across five minutes ago that would be quicker."

Joe turned at John Gallo's voice to see him coming toward them. "How much quicker?"

"Maybe only a few minutes." Gallo added grimly, "But a few minutes can be enough." He turned. "I'm heading back and taking the trail up to that cliff. Come if you like."

Joe hesitated for only an instant. Gallo was an expert woodsman and tracker, and it didn't matter how Joe felt about him personally. He was right, a few minutes could be enough to make a difference. He strode quickly after him. Ben and Father Barnabas were only steps behind.

Gallo glanced back at them as he moved swiftly through the trees. "This isn't your job, Father. You shouldn't be here. And who's the kid?"

"Ben. He's a friend of your uncle's."

"You're John Gallo." Ben was gazing at Gallo. "Ted told me about you."

Gallo was frowning. "What?"

"Ben came along to protect Danner," Joe said. "He doesn't trust me."

"He shouldn't trust any of us," Gallo said, his lips tightening. "And I don't know if he's going to get the chance to help him. We have to worry about Eve." He turned back and increased his pace to a trot.

Joe caught up with him. "Where's this trail? Time is —"

"There." Gallo was now on the trail curving toward the cliff and running hard. "And I know all about time. When did you catch sight of my uncle and Eve, Quinn?"

"Just before they started up the hill again."

"Well, I saw them a moment or so before that," he said jerkily. "And he had his hands on her throat."

Shit.

"Get rid of the priest and the kid, Quinn," Gallo said. "They're going to get in the way."

"Maybe not." His head was lifted, his gaze on the trail on the summit where Eve and Danner had disappeared. God, he prayed not. "I'd think you'd be grateful to have them. They're both on Danner's side."

"It only means I may have to fight my way through them," Gallo said hoarsely. "I promised myself that Eve has to come first. I'll keep that promise."

He meant it, Joe realized. Good. At least, he didn't have to worry about Gallo's turning traitor at the last minute. It was one small light in a nightmare scenario.

"At least get rid of the kid," Gallo said. "He makes me . . . He shouldn't be here."

But he was invited, Joe wanted to tell him. He may belong here more than any of us. But that would require explanations, and he wasn't about to make them. He increased his speed and passed Gallo as they reached the hill. "It's too late. Deal with it."

I'm coming, Bonnie. I'll be there with you soon.

Do you feel me? Do you hear me?

But there was no answer. If Danner was truly taking her to Bonnie's final resting place, wouldn't Eve have sensed her near? Not necessarily. Bonnie had never been predictable.

The higher they'd climbed, the pine trees had become thinner, sparser, then disappeared entirely. They were replaced by huge boulders and canyon walls that jutted in and out like a giant maze. A dozen cracks seamed the rose red of the stone that led off the trail and disappeared into dark crevices.

"We're almost at the top of this canyon," she called to Danner. "And it's all rock. Where's Bonnie? Have you been lying to me? Has it all been one of your hallucinations?"

"Be quiet." His voice was rough. "I don't lie. You said that before. You said there was no demon. But it was a demon who killed the little girl."

He was referring to Bonnie as the little girl again. Was it because he could not bear to acknowledge her identity now that they were close to her? Eve was beginning to understand his reluctance to acknowledge that it was Bonnie who had appeared to him. If he rejected the thought that he had been to blame for Bonnie's death, it was

418

natural that he would not want to admit that it was her spirit that was haunting him. The little girl had to be anonymous. He rejected Bonnie's spirit as he had rejected the thought that he had killed her.

"We're almost at the top of this canyon, and there's nothing but rock. I don't —" She stopped on the trail, her heart leaping to her throat, her gaze on the huge dark crack between two canyons to the left of the trail.

"Bonnie?"

"You've found me, Mama. I kept telling you that it didn't matter, but you wouldn't believe me."

"It mattered to me."

"And I guess that's why you finally found me."

"Where are you? I don't see you."

"You will. Not right now. He's suffering so much that I can't get near you."

"Damn him."

"No. Don't be angry. Can't you see? I know everything now. The two planes have come together, and I remember what happened. There mustn't be anger."

"I don't see. He took you away from me. I am angry. I won't let —"

"She's here, isn't she?" Danner was staring at Eve, his face pasty white. "But I don't

419

see her."

She could no longer sense Bonnie, and the sudden loneliness sparked even more anger. "You're keeping her away." She looked at the looming dark crevice. "You bastard. You stuffed her in that black hole? What did you do? Just pile a bunch of rocks on her body?" She was striding into the narrow space between the rock walls. It was dark and so close it was claustrophobic. She could see the shadow of a large boulder blocking the path ahead.

"Get out of my way." Danner was pushing her aside and going ahead. He rolled aside the boulder and pushed her through the opening out of the darkness. "If she's here, it must be because she wants you here, too. Can't you see? I was right. I have to do it."

After the darkness, the daylight almost blinded Eve.

She stopped, stunned.

"Shit, where's he taking her?" Joe said between set teeth, as his gaze flew down the path and the dark crevices on either side. "This part of the canyon looks like a rabbit warren. It will be a nightmare trying to follow him into any of those crevices."

"And no footprints," Gallo said. The trail had become rock and stone once they left the lower part of the trail. "If we had shale, I could at least tell if it had been disturbed." He stopped and gazed down one of the twisting passageways between the walls. "I'll check out this one. You take the next path over there."

Joe nodded. Taking the openings one by one was the only thing they could do, but it was a waste of time. Dammit, they had no time to do an extensive search.

"No." Ben was suddenly beside Joe. "Not there. Not this one. Straight ahead."

"We have to eliminate every possibility, kid," Gallo said.

"No, straight ahead." He put his hand on Joe's arm. "She's not there."

Joe looked at him.

"I have to be with you. But not here." He added urgently, "Tell him. We have to hurry, Joe."

Joe hesitated, gazing at the boy's pleading expression. Then he said slowly, "We'll split up, Gallo, we can cover more area. You search here, and I'll go straight ahead." He whirled and started running up the path. He could hear Gallo cursing behind him, but when he glanced behind him, Gallo had disappeared down one of the crevices.

Ben caught up with Joe and passed him.

Follow him. He seems to know where he is going.

And God knows Joe had no idea.

Eve was frozen with shock. She couldn't believe her eyes.

Greenery where there had been only rocks, grass so well tended it looked like velvet. A flowering magnolia tree, shiny-leafed shrubs, plum leaf azaleas, small, exquisite pink roses, delicate lantana, and golden sunflowers . . . She was on the edge of the rose-hued canyon wall on a cliff that was perhaps thirty feet in diameter. It was sheltered by a network of vines on all sides that made it into a secret garden.

Secret Garden. Yes, that was what it reminded her of, that classic children's tale about a garden of magic beauty that had the power to heal because of the love that gone into bringing it to life.

"What is this, Danner?"

"It's the place." He gazed at the garden. "It took me years to make it for her. I had to bring in lots of soil, and the vines to shelter it from the weather. And the flowers had to be hardy and not take much care. I couldn't bear to come here too often after I gave it to her. She frightened me."

Her gaze was wandering around the garden and stopped at a twisting path that led upward along the edge of the canyon. "What is that?"

"It's a path that goes to the top of the canyon. It took me a year to hack it out of the wall."

"Why?"

"I couldn't be sure that the demons wouldn't find her. I had to have a route to take her out of here."

"An escape hatch?" she asked softly. "Good heavens, you thought of everything."

"Are you laughing at me?"

"No, there's nothing funny about this."

It was sad, tragic.

"No." His gaze went to the far west corner of the garden, then glanced quickly away. "There she is."

Bonnie.

It was a raised plot of earth that was surrounded by the same gorgeous blossoms that were everywhere in the garden. A simple carved cross marked the grave.

Eve slowly moved to stand before it.

Here I am, baby.

No special sense of presence. She had not believed Bonnie when she had told her that it would not matter whether she found her body. That she was always with her, that it was memories and love that made the difference. She could almost see Bonnie standing in front of her with an impish I-told-you-so smile.

Okay, so you were right. But I'm glad to be here anyway.

And maybe she would have felt something more special if Danner had not been here.

Danner, who was standing looking at her from a few yards away.

He was getting ready. She could see the tension in the set of his shoulders . . . and his eyes . . .

"It's a beautiful place," Eve told him quietly. "I'm glad that you gave Bonnie such a wonderful garden. She loved flowers."

"She was John's daughter. I had to take care of her after the demon killed her. I had to find a place to hide her so that the demons wouldn't steal her soul as well as her body."

"And you brought her here."

"I thought she'd be safe. I took care of her. I made a beautiful place for her. I kept the demons from finding her." His expression clouded. "At least, I thought I had. But they started coming at me. I heard that Queen and Jacobs had lied to me and were trying to destroy John. I had to stop them. But even after they were dead, it didn't stop. There are so many demons. . . . Everywhere

I turned, I saw them there in the shadows, waiting."

"But not here, not in this place."

"No, the little girl was safe here." His lips were twisted. "But she wouldn't stay. I'd see her in the canyon. Sometimes I'd even see her in the camp or in the city. She'd look at me with those big eyes, and I knew she wanted something from me, but I didn't know what it was."

"And you were too afraid of her to stick around and ask." She was putting together the pieces of the tragic puzzle that had haunted all their lives. "Because you thought she'd want revenge because you'd killed her."

"She didn't understand. It wasn't me. I saved her."

"I think she understood more than you could believe." Eve was gazing at the cross. "You should have tried to listen to her."

"You don't know what you're talking about." His voice was rough. "I tried to hear her, but all I could see were her eyes looking up at me that day at the car. 'I'm not afraid, Ted,' she said. Did I tell you that?"

"Yes."

"And then I let the demon kill her." His hands clenched at his sides. "But she's safe here, the demons can't reach her. But she has to stay. You see that, don't you?" He took a step closer. "She won't leave if you're here with her."

"Another lovely cross for me, Danner?" Eve asked, her gaze on the grave.

"You love her. You want to be together. Don't you want to keep her safe?"

"With all my heart."

He was only a few feet away, and his hand was grasping the hilt of his dagger. "It will be quick. I know how to do it. No pain, Eve. Don't fight me. I know you want it."

She did want it. The thought of being with Bonnie was almost irresistibly alluring.

"No, Mama, it's not your time."

"Well, that stirred you to action. You always say that it's not my time, but you promised us that this was the finish. It wouldn't be a bad ending, baby."

"Mama."

Eve was suddenly bombarded with a kaleidoscope of pictures of her life with Joe, her life with Jane, of her work, intense, satisfying, worthwhile. Rich life, sweet life, a life full of love, a life worth living.

"I know. I know. I won't let it happen."

How to do it? She had no weapon.

He was blocking the way that led to the passage that had brought her here.

No choice. She'd have to take the path that led to the top of the canyon. Perhaps she could find a rock or branch up there to use to defend herself.

"Come here," Danner said. "Don't make me come to you. Show me that you understand. It will only be a second, and it will be over."

Get past him, feint to the left, then run for the passage leading to the top of the canyon.

"I'm coming." She held his gaze as she took a step forward. "You won't hurt me? You promise?"

He smiled. "I promise. I'm like you. I only want to make her happy."

And she believed him, she realized with a wrench of pure pain. Through all his torment and fear, he only wanted Bonnie to be safe in body and spirit. "That's all I've ever wanted, too. To bring her home."

He looked at her in wondering surprise. "But she is home. Who could ever want a more beautiful home? Don't you see the flowers? You said she — No!" She had ducked under his left arm, bringing her heel up to kick his left kneecap. His leg buckled, and he staggered.

She heard him cursing as she ran toward the path leading up the cliff.

427

"You're not supposed to do this. I don't want you to fight me. Can't you see I'm doing what's best for her?"

"No, all I can see is that you're the demon trying to rob my daughter of what she wants to happen. You're *wrong,* dammit." She had reached the cliff and was tearing up the path.

He was right behind her.

Faster.

She had to go faster.

The wind was tearing at her hair.

The top of the canyon. How far was it, dammit?

She could hear his steps pounding on the stones.

Faster.

Then she had reached the summit.

Weapon. Find a weapon.

A loose rock?

No, there was a branch underneath a scrawny pine tree that was balanced precariously at the top of the summit.

She could hear Danner's strained breathing behind her.

She grabbed up the branch and whirled to face him.

"Eve!"

Joe was at the top of the trail, running toward Danner, a gun in his hand. A sandy-haired boy was close behind him. "Get away from him, Eve. You're in the way of my shot."

But Danner was turning, drawing his own gun, pointing.

"No!" She threw herself forward to grab his gun.

Too late.

"Joe!" she screamed.

Everything seemed to occur in slow motion.

Joe running toward them.

Danner's finger squeezing the trigger.

And the boy who had been following Joe was suddenly even with him.

"Get away, Ben," Joe shouted.

But the boy dove in front of Joe, knocking him to the ground.

A bright blossom of blood appeared on the boy's white shirt.

Dead?

"Ben!" Danner's voice was hoarse with agony, his gaze on the boy. "Stupid kid. I never meant — Why did you —"

"But you did," Eve said fiercely. "You probably killed him, Danner."

"No. No." He was staggering backward, dropping the gun, his gaze on the boy. Then he whirled and was running toward the trail.

Let him go.

Eve ran toward Joe. "Are you all right?"

"Yes." Joe was rolling over and lifting the boy off him. "But Ben's not. Why the hell did he —" He carefully laid the kid on the ground, his gaze on the blood on the boy's shirt. "Shit."

"Who is he?" Eve whispered as she fell to her knees beside them. The boy was pale, and that horrible wound . . .

"Ben Hudson. He told me where to find you." He was opening the boy's shirt and examining the wound. "Dammit, I shouldn't have brought him."

"Is he going to die?"

"I don't know." He took out his handkerchief and folded it. "I don't have any idea about his internal injuries. All I can do is try to stop the blood."

"I'll do it." She took the handkerchief and pressed it above the wound. "You call 911 for medical help, then go after Danner."

"I should —"

"No." She didn't lift her eyes from the wound. "Stop Danner. It has to end, Joe. He's like a wounded animal who will keep striking out and killing until he's put away. He can't do anything else."

"No." The boy had opened his eyes and was staring up at her. "He didn't mean to —"

"I know," she said quietly. "But it happened, and it will keep on happening. There's no telling when he'll decide that one of us is one of his demons. He's not sane, Ben. He almost killed me two times before today. And Joe almost died just now."

"Don't kill . . . Ted. He has to know — Fresh start."

"What?"

The boy's eyes were closing. "Beginning. He has to know that it can begin . . ."

He was unconscious.

Joe was rising to his feet. "If I'm going to catch up with Danner, I have to go. You're sure you want me to leave you?"

No, she desperately wanted to go with him, but she couldn't leave this young boy who had saved him. She nodded. "Go."

"Father Barnabas was just behind me. I'll send him to —"

She stiffened. "The priest? No."

"He's okay, Eve. Trust him." He was running toward the trail. "I'll explain later."

She stopped him as he started down the trail. "Bonnie's death was an accident, Joe. Danner didn't mean to do it."

"And what does that mean? How do you feel? What am I supposed to do? Kill him? Have him thrown into prison?"

She shook her head. "I don't know how I

feel. I'm still angry. I'm still cheated. I want revenge for her death. And it's all mixed up with the horrible feeling that everything went terribly wrong, and anything I do will just make it more terrible." She met his gaze. "It's your call, Joe. I won't tell you to hold your hand when it might put you in danger. I just had to tell you."

He nodded curtly, then vanished down the path.

She moved the pad on Ben's chest. The pad was soaked with blood. Was the flow easing? It was hard to tell.

"You . . . want to go with him." Ben's eyes were open again. "You're afraid for him."

"Yes, shouldn't I be? Your friend, Danner, tried to kill him."

"I . . . think he'll be all right."

"I don't want to think. I want to know."

"I can't tell . . . you that."

"Stop talking, it's not good for you. Worry about yourself, not Joe."

He was silent a moment. "You think I . . . may die."

Yes, she did. He seemed very close. "You'll be fine. Don't be afraid. Just hold on."

"I'm not afraid. I was once. But she showed me that it would only be a new start with nothing to hold me back . . . and beautiful."

Her grasp tightened on his hand. " 'She'?"

His gaze was on her face. "She looks like you. Sometimes I can't see her, only hear her. But when I see her, she looks like you."

"Does she?" she asked unevenly. "Well, I think she would want you to hold on, just as I do."

He nodded and closed his eyes. "I just wanted to tell you so that you wouldn't feel bad. You looked so sad. . . ."

"Eve!"

Her gaze flew to the trail to see Father Barnabas coming up the path.

"How is he?" The priest was frowning as he came toward her. "Joe passed me on the trail and told me what had happened and asked me to come and help you." He knelt beside Ben. "He said he'd called 911, and they'll contact the ranger station." He put his hand on the boy's shoulder. "Help's on the way, Ben."

Ben nodded but didn't answer.

It's a new start . . . and beautiful.

But she didn't want any new starts happening for this boy who had saved Joe's life. And she'd be damned if she'd let Joe wander off into the great beyond either.

"Hold the compress," she told the priest as she got to her feet. "I'm going after Joe." She looked down at Ben. "And you hold on and don't go anywhere. She may think it's okay, but I don't. And I'm sure Bonnie didn't mean it like that. We all have to stick together around here." Her glance shifted to the priest. "You take care of him. Don't you let him die. I want prayers and rosaries and anything else you may think will help." She turned and strode toward the trail. "Do your job."

CHAPTER
16

Danner!

Catherine had only caught a brief glimpse of the man streaking down the twisting path toward the bottom of the canyon, but she'd recognized him. She had not seen that shock of silver hair at the bayou, but he moved with that same lithe alacrity that had so surprised her.

She tensed. It would take her five to ten minutes to intercept him, and there was a possibility she might lose him. Call Gallo.

She dialed quickly. "I've spotted Danner. He's alone. Where the hell is Eve?"

"I don't know. We lost them after he started climbing the west wall of the canyon. Joe and I split up to search."

Catherine muttered a curse. "That's not good. I have to find out where he left her." She didn't want to think of the question of how he'd left Eve.

Dead. Alive. Wounded.

435

"Where are you, Gallo?"

"Still on a path on the canyon wall."

"Then you're no help. Danner's headed for the bottom of the canyon."

"Wait for me. I'll be there."

"No time. I'm not letting him leave the canyon without telling me where he left Eve. If she's unconscious, it could take us days to find her."

"Wait for me." The phone crashed in her ear as he hung up.

Screw it. The time was over for waiting and also for working as a team with Gallo. If she could lever herself from that overhanging oak tree down to the next level of the path, she would make up a good deal of the distance. She slipped her phone in her jacket pocket and started down the trail toward the oak tree.

Run.

Don't slip on this damn sandy shale, Danner told himself.

One false step would throw him off the path and into the canyon over a hundred feet below.

But he couldn't see for the tears running down his cheeks.

He had killed Ben. Why had the boy come after him? He hadn't wanted to harm him.

He had been closer to Ben than he had been to anyone since the time he'd spent with John when he was growing up. He had wanted to protect him and take care of him. To keep all the demons away from him.

Dead. Dead like the little girl. He had killed him as he had Bonnie.

No!

It was the demon, Black, who had killed Bonnie.

He wouldn't have killed the little girl.

But he had done it. If he could kill Ben, then he could kill Bonnie.

"Stop where you are, Danner."

A woman had come out of the brush at the side of the trail, a gun in her hand. Long, straight, dark hair, slightly tilted dark eyes, framed in long lashes. He knew that face. Catherine Ling, who had been with John at the bayou.

"Where is Eve, you bastard?" she asked grimly. "Give me an answer in ten seconds, and you'll live for a little while longer."

Eve. He should not have run away even if he'd been sick about killing the boy. Eve was still alive. He had failed Bonnie. It would be okay. He could make it right. But he had to get away from here first. Then he could concentrate on finding Bonnie's mother again.

"Is she dead?" Catherine asked.

He shook his head. "She fought me and ran away. She shouldn't have done that. It's not what the little girl wanted."

"Where is she?"

"With the boy." He was sobbing. "I killed the boy." Too much pain. Get away. Get rid of her.

He dove sideways and kicked out and struck her gun with the toe of his boot.

It fired and the bullet ricocheted off the wall of the canyon. Then he was running into the brush, the thorns and branches whipping at him.

She was running after him.

Pull to the side and ambush her.

Not now.

Keep running.

Keep running.

Keep running.

Run away from those children in the flaming house in the mountains of Syria.

Run away from Ben, with blood blossoming on his shirt.

Run away from Bonnie, lying so still in the trunk of his car.

Bonnie.

"You have to stop." It was John calling from behind him. "Don't make me come after you."

John was hurting. He could always tell when the boy was hurting. How many times had Ted chased after John when Ted's brother had beaten him? John had always tried to hide it from him, but he always knew.

"You have to make it right," John's voice was hoarse with pain. "I'll try to help you through it, but you have to give yourself up. And you have to tell me where you left Eve."

He kept on running.

"Stop," John said. "For God's sake, stop. Or I'll have to shoot you. Don't make me do that."

He looked over his shoulder and saw John aiming his gun.

He kept on running.

He didn't hear the shot until the bullet entered his kneecap. Pain. He fell to the ground. Then, as he was levering himself up against a tree, he saw Catherine Ling come out of the shrubs ahead with a gun in her hand.

She was staring at him with no expression. "You should have stopped, Danner."

John was beside them now. "I would have done it, Catherine."

"I believe you. But you would have given him every chance to surrender, and I was tired of pampering him." She bent over

Danner and plucked his gun from his jacket. "Is Eve still alive? I want an answer, and I'll know if you're lying."

Yes, she would know. He had thought when he had first seen her that she was a demon, a Delilah, who was as lethal as she was beautiful. "Yes, but you can't have her. It wouldn't be right. I'll fight you. She belongs to the child."

"Wacko." She turned to John. "I'm going to call Joe and see if he knows anything about Eve. If you can persuade Danner to talk, do it. Or I will."

John pushed past her, closer to Danner. "Why?" His voice was ragged. "Why didn't you tell me that you were sick? It wouldn't have mattered to me. I would have helped you. I loved you, dammit."

Danner shook his head. John's words were hurting, scalding him with shame. "I couldn't do it."

Catherine hung up the phone and turned back to them. "Eve is safe. She and Joe are together. I told him where we are."

John breathed a sigh of relief. "Thank God." He turned back to Danner. "You didn't hurt her. Maybe we can still make this —"

"Go away, John."

"I can't go away," he said harshly. "You

didn't kill my daughter. I know you didn't. Say the words."

Of course, he could say the words, Danner thought. It was the demon, Black, who had killed Bonnie.

But what if it wasn't?

Bonnie.

His head was exploding, he could feel the veins of his neck swell and distend.

Bonnie.

"No!" He lunged forward and got to his feet.

He was running, trying to get away from that hideous truth.

"Don't move," Catherine said.

He paid no attention, he was hobbling, his leg buckling with every step.

Catherine took a step forward. "Stop, Danner."

Bonnie!

He slipped, fell, and was tumbling from the path down the sandy incline toward the bottom of the canyon.

"What the hell," Eve breathed. She and Joe had stopped on the cliff above the trail where Catherine and Gallo stood. She watched Danner skidding down the side of the incline. "He'll be killed!"

"Maybe not. The ground is very sandy,

that means soft." Joe took her elbow and was running toward the trail. He added grimly, "But I may take care of that when I get down there."

He meant it, Eve thought, as she tore down toward the canyon floor. She was angry, too, but she was also filled with dread and wrenching sadness. It wasn't what she had expected to feel toward Danner. He was a murderer. He had tried to shoot Joe. He had killed Bonnie, and he might have killed that boy, Ben. Why couldn't she just feel the anger and the thirst for revenge? Why did she keep seeing Danner as he had been when he'd smiled down at six-month-old Bonnie in her stroller and handed her the rabbit she had dropped?

Tragic.

But all tragedies had to end.

She stumbled, almost fell, but Joe caught her.

Joe was always there to catch her, to protect her, to stand by her.

As Danner had been there to protect Gallo. If things had been different, if Eve had let Danner into their lives when Bonnie was a toddler, would he have been there to love and protect her, too? Would everything have been changed?

Stop trying to second-guess every action

she had taken. She was human. All she could do was play the cards she'd been given.

"Just below," Joe said as he took her hand and started skidding down the incline. "I see Catherine, but not Gallo."

"And Danner," Eve said. "I don't see Danner. Maybe he —"

And then she saw Danner.

Blood.

Danner was lying on his back near the bottom of the canyon. He had fallen on a large branch and the force of the fall had broken the branch and caused the jagged point to pierce his body and exit from his chest.

She stopped beside Catherine, who was standing a few yards away from Danner. Gallo was kneeling beside him, examining the wound.

"Is he dead?" she whispered to Catherine.

"I don't think so." Catherine was short of breath, her chest rising and falling. "Not yet. We just got down here, and Gallo has been trying to see if he has a chance."

Eve's gaze flew to Gallo's face. He was pale, his eyes haunted, and there was a long scratch on his right cheek. He was going through hell, and he looked it. "It doesn't look good."

Catherine shook her head. "I'll try to get some help for him." She glanced at Eve. "If that's what you want. He's probably not going to last anyway. Tell me what you want me to do. I know how long you've been searching for your daughter's killer. If you want him dead, I'll let him go."

And cause Catherine to shoulder the blame for killing Danner?

Eve shook her head. "I don't think he's going to make it either." She looked at Gallo. "Make the call. If he lives, then we'll deal with him."

Catherine took out her phone. "We're surrounded by this rock canyon right here. The best I can do is get out from under these trees and hope I can pick up a signal." She moved toward an opening in the trees several yards away. "Joe, you've got a satellite phone; come with me, and you try if I don't get through."

Joe frowned. "Dammit, I don't give a damn if he —" He looked at Eve. "Okay, but it's a waste." He strode after Catherine.

He was probably right, Eve thought. But who the hell knew what was right or wrong? In this moment, she did not. There was too much history, too much pain. And the pain was still here. She could see it in Gallo's face, feel it in all the memories of the years. She moved closer to where Gallo was kneeling beside Danner and put her hand on his shoulder. "How bad? What do you think?"

Gallo jerkily shook his head. "I can't even stop the blood. I don't know how many organs that branch damaged."

"Catherine and Joe are trying to get him help."

"That's more than I expected." He reached out a hand and gently touched Danner's hair. "He was so damn good to me, Eve."

"I know."

"It's crazy. How could he do it? He killed my daughter." He reached out blindly and covered her hand on his shoulder. "Our daughter."

"Our daughter," she repeated. Yes, in this moment they were bound together as they had never been during Bonnie's life. "And it *was* crazy. He wasn't sane. He told me . . . it was an accident. That he was trying to save her."

"Do you believe him?"

"Yes."

"But it doesn't take the pain away."

"No, but it takes away some of the horror. I've always been afraid that Bonnie was helpless, terrified. It was one of my worst

445

nightmares."

"He was trying to save her?" Gallo's eyes were moist. "Like he tried to save me. He *did* save me, Eve."

"But he didn't save —"

"Hurts . . ." Danner's eyes were suddenly opening, staring up at Gallo. "I . . . fell."

"Yes." Gallo took his hand. "But I'll take care of you."

"How could you do that? You're just a kid. Give me a minute, and I'll get up and get us back to the cabin."

Did he think he was back at that cabin in Wisconsin where he'd taken Gallo so many times? Eve wondered.

But Danner's gaze was now on Eve. "I know you. You have a little girl. . . ."

"Yes, I do."

He suddenly tensed. "The demons. You have to keep the demons from finding her."

"I have her safe. Forever."

"But I have to help. I have to —" He began to cough, and a rivulet of blood flowed out of the corner of his mouth.

He was dying, Eve realized. There was no doubt in her mind. "I don't need you. My Bonnie is safe. I'll watch over her."

"No, it's my job." His head was thrashing back and forth. "I have to do it. It doesn't matter if I'm afraid. I have to do it."

446

"I'll do it for you," Gallo said thickly. "Just rest."

Danner's eyes were clinging to his. "I tried to save her for you, John."

"I know you did."

"I failed you. I failed her." His eyes closed. "Go away."

"No."

"Go away." He jerked his hand away from Gallo's. "I don't want you. You make me feel — Go away."

Eve couldn't stand it any longer. She turned and moved a few yards from Danner and Gallo. She crossed her arms across her chest to still their trembling.

"Take him away, Mama."

"Bonnie?"

"Take my father away. They're both hurting too much. I can't help him."

Eve hesitated, then strode back to Gallo. "Come on," she said unevenly. "Leave him."

"No."

"Leave him." She stared him in the eye with all the force of her entire will. "He won't need you. I promise."

Gallo gazed at her in bewilderment, then slowly got to his feet. "He's dying, Eve."

She nodded. "But he's hurting because you're here with him. He's full of regret and guilt and pain. Let him go, John." She took

447

his hand and drew him a few yards from
Danner. "It will be —"

Gallo stiffened. "Bonnie?"

Did he sense her, too? Eve wondered.

No, he could *see* her. She was here.

Bonnie was standing over Ted Danner,
looking down at him.

Her expression . . .

Compassion, tenderness, sadness.

"What are you doing, Bonnie?"

But Bonnie was not paying any attention to
anyone but the man at her feet.

"Ted."

Danner opened his eyes. He saw her. His
body stiffened. "Go away. It's not my fault. I
tried to do what you wanted. Why do you keep
following me?"

"Because you won't listen to me." Bonnie
fell to her knees beside him. "You've never
listened, Ted. But now you will, won't you?"

"No. I want you to go away."

"Because you're afraid of me?" Bonnie
smiled. "Why should you be afraid? I'm no
stranger to you. We've been together a long
time."

"You don't understand."

"I understand that you're afraid that I'm
angry with you, that I want to hurt you."

"Yes, because you think that I'm the one

who hurt you. You don't believe it was the demon."

"No, because I don't believe in demons." She took Danner's hand.

He shuddered and tried to pull away.

"No, hold my hand, and the fear will go. You're not afraid of me, you're afraid of the darkness. You've been in darkness for a long time and haven't been able to break free of it. Sometimes it got lighter, then when you weren't expecting, it came back. Isn't that right?"

"And then the demons came."

"But it's light now, and you can see in every corner. Everything is bright and clear and beautiful. And there are no demons. There will never be demons again."

He was gazing into her eyes. "You promise."

"I promise."

Silence. "You're not angry with me."

"I've never been angry with you. Why should I? I always knew that you meant no harm, that it was love that made you take me that day. Love for my father, even love for me. I tried so hard to tell you."

"I . . . hurt you. Forgive . . . me. I wanted to say that to you, but it was too late. Everything was too late."

"It's never too late. You'll see. I'll help you."

"Will you?"

"Shall I show you?"

Silence.

Then a brilliant smile lit his face. "It starts again? It's a long road, a hard road, but I can make the ending different. I can begin again."

"Is that what you saw? It's different all the time. Beautiful but different." She leaned closer, and whispered, "Now go to sleep. It's time. Don't be afraid. I'll be there for you. I won't let you get lost." She smiled luminously. "I've learned so many things, Ted. You'll learn them, too. Just hold my hand. Don't let me go."

"Bonnie . . ." He was smiling back at her, his face alight with sudden eagerness. "No, I won't let go."

He closed his eyes.

Love, so much love . . .

Eve could feel the tears running down her cheeks.

And then Bonnie was gone.

"My God." Gallo was moving back to Danner and standing over him, gazing down at his face.

But Danner was gone, too.

Eve didn't follow Gallo. This was a moment of good-bye between Gallo and his uncle. She was shaken and confused, and she needed to be with Joe. She turned toward

450

the edge of the clearing.

Joe was standing at the tree line, his gaze on Danner. How much had he seen? He turned his head to watch Eve as she came toward him. "So Bonnie kept her word. It's the end."

"Or the beginning. I'm not sure any longer." She slid her arms around him and laid her head on his chest. She could feel the vibration of his heart beneath her ear. "But it's the way she wanted it."

"Yes, maybe not the way I wanted it." His hand stroked her hair. "How are you doing?"

"Mixed-up. Happy, sad, angry. Bonnie may be able to see beyond the act and forgive, but I'm not there yet. It may take me a long time."

She could feel him nod but didn't lift her head. She wanted to stay here hidden in his arms. "But I can't hate him. All these years, and I can't hate him. Because she never hated him. From the beginning, she wanted to help him, ease him."

"Yes." He was silent a moment. "Do you remember that first week after Bonnie was taken when we were doing the interviews with people who had claimed to have seen Bonnie?"

"Yes, they were all disasters."

451

"Except for one. That vicious woman who claimed to be a psychic and said that she'd seen Bonnie the night after she'd been reported missing. She told you that Bonnie had been murdered."

"She just wanted to hurt me."

"Yes, but she said Bonnie was trailing after a man and trying to get his attention. She said he wouldn't pay any attention to her. You asked her if Bonnie was afraid of him, and she said no."

Memories of that night were flooding back to Eve. "Even then, Bonnie was trying to get through to Danner and tell him that she forgave him?" A man in a torment of guilt, pushing Bonnie away, denying her existence, denying his responsibility for her death. Yet trying to protect her in the only way he knew how. "And she kept trying and never gave up. Even when she sensed the end coming, she knew she had to be there for him."

Danner's luminous expression in that final moment.

Perfect faith, perfect love . . .

She felt tears sting her eyes again. No, she would not cry.

She drew a shaky breath and took a step back. "Did you reach 911? I suppose we should call them back and tell them Danner won't need them."

He nodded. "The EMTs should be here soon anyway. They were on the other side of the canyon with Ben."

"Is he still alive?"

"Yes, but they're going to have to airlift him out of here to the hospital in Columbus. It may be touch-and-go."

"I want to go with him. He saved your life, Joe." She paused. "Ben said something about . . ."

"Bonnie? She touched him. He had dreams about her."

She'd touched all of them. Dreams and visions and a love that lasted beyond death.

"I want to talk to him."

But would she get the chance? Would he be with Bonnie, too?

Joe slipped his arm around her waist. "We'll go to the ranger station and get a ride to the hospital. We'd better tell Catherine what we're doing." He turned to Catherine, who was several yards behind him. "Catherine, we need to go to the hospital. Do you want to —"

"I'll stay with Gallo." Catherine's gaze was fixed on Gallo, kneeling beside Danner. "Do what you have to do." She started toward him. "I'll be in touch later."

Then she stopped and turned to Eve.

Eve stiffened with surprise. Catherine's golden skin was paler, her eyes wide with shock. Eve had never seen her so discomposed. "Are you okay?"

Catherine nodded jerkily. "As good as I can be. I just wanted to say that I —" She muttered a curse and whirled back again and started toward Gallo. "I just wanted to say I'm sorry. I thought you were all a little crazy. I didn't believe you. Hell, maybe I'm crazy, too."

Eve froze, her gaze on Catherine, who had reached Gallo and was standing beside him.

"She saw her, Joe," she whispered. "She saw Bonnie."

"And it scared the hell out of her." Joe pulled Eve toward the trail. "I can sympathize. I remember the first time I saw Bonnie. But she'll have to deal with it herself. You can't do it for her."

He was right. Perhaps later she could comfort, help Catherine, but now she was too exhausted and emotionally spent to do anything but try to get through the hours ahead.

But why had Catherine been able to see Bonnie when only those who were close to her daughter had ever been able to see her?

Don't ask. Just accept.

Bonnie's choice.

■ ■ ■ ■

Ben was in surgery when Eve and Joe reached the hospital. But Father Barnabas was in the waiting room and had spoken to the doctors.

"It's critical," the priest said. "But the doctors say he has a chance. The nurse just came by to tell me they're finishing up now."

"You know that Danner is dead?" Joe asked. "The police told you?"

"No. Ben told me."

"What?"

"Right before he went into surgery. He said that Ted wasn't here anymore, but that it was okay." He turned to Eve. "Are you all right?"

She nodded. "Ben told you?" It shouldn't have surprised her. Just the few minutes she'd spent with him had revealed his connection with Bonnie.

"I promised I'd try to keep from killing Danner," Joe said. "He came along to try to protect him."

"And he knows you did try," the priest said. "And I don't think that the reason he came along was to protect Danner. Maybe that was his initial reason, but it changed. He was sticking closer to you than glue."

"He was protecting Joe?" Eve nodded slowly. "Maybe you're right."

"I'm right." Father Barnabas smiled. "And here's something else that I'm going to be right about. The doctors weren't sure that Ben would survive this surgery, but he was sure. He told me that she said that it wasn't his time." He tilted his head. "And I wondered . . . a saintly visitation? Or the little girl Ted Danner was so obsessed with?"

"Bonnie," Eve said.

"Bonnie," the priest repeated. "He was so afraid of her. I wanted to be with Ted, to talk to him one more time, to give him comfort. He was in such torment."

"Yes." She met his eyes. "But not in the end. And he wasn't afraid of Bonnie any longer."

"A miracle?"

Perhaps not the way the priest meant it. But since the day of her birth, Bonnie had been so very special, a wonderful, magical gift. It was no wonder that she had been able to give that grace to everyone around her. "Yes, a miracle, Father."

"You look like a surgeon." Catherine's gaze ran up and down Eve's loose blue-green tunic and pants when she came into the waiting room two hours later. "Have you

456

changed professions?"

"I borrowed the clothes from one of the nurses on the floor. I took a shower, but my clothes were practically falling into shreds after those days in the woods. Joe wanted to stay here until they let him see Ben, and I wanted to be with him."

Catherine looked down at herself. "I'm not much better than you, but I'll wait until I can get to a motel. I'll pick up some clothes for you and drop them off here. How is the boy?"

"He'll live. The doctors said it was touch-and-go." She smiled. "Ben said that there would be no problem. He had it on the best of authority."

Catherine looked away. "I've been thinking it over and what I thought I saw could have been a hallucination induced by stress."

"It could be."

"That would be the most comfortable explanation." She looked back at Eve. "I've never gone for the safe or comfortable. It's not my nature." She smiled recklessly. "I tend to dive into the volcano and hope that the rope around my waist holds."

"And are you diving into my volcano, Catherine?"

"Yes. I saw a little girl in a Bugs Bunny

T-shirt kneeling by Danner. She was . . . incredible."

Eve nodded. "More than you'll ever know."

"I hope that's true. I don't want to know or see more than I did today."

"And you may not. I don't know why you saw my daughter. I assumed that she appeared only to those to whom she was close. Maybe this is a rare instance and won't be repeated."

Catherine shrugged. "And if it's not, I'll deal with it. Though I hope we won't become chums. It might be distracting."

Eve smiled. "She won't get in your way, Catherine."

Catherine smiled. "I know she won't. I'm sure she's totally independent. She has to be her mother's daughter."

Eve's smile faded. "And her father's. How is Gallo?"

"How do you think? Not good. He's taking his uncle home to Wisconsin and burying him in the woods on his property."

"Are you going with him?"

She shook her head. "I wasn't invited, and I don't know if I would have gone if I had been. This is between the two of them, and there were times when I wasn't at all sympathetic. I was on your side, not his. I wasn't sure until we were with Danner that he'd be able to keep his priorities straight. We have a lot of . . . issues."

And some of those issues were fiery and emotional, Eve thought. It might be just as well that Catherine was keeping distance between them.

"Stop frowning." Catherine was studying her expression. "Be happy, dammit. You deserve it."

"So do you. Where are you going?"

"Home to Luke for a while. Then I promised Venable I'd do a job in Peru. A very short job. I'll stop by your place at the lake on my way." She started to turn away, then said, "Bonnie. You're taking her home?"

She nodded. "I'm going to ask Father Barnabas to do the service."

"I want to be there."

Eve nodded. "I'll let you know. If you're not in South America."

"Screw South America. I'll be there." She moved down the corridor toward the elevators.

"You look tired," Ben said. "Maybe you should go to bed."

Joe's gaze flew to the boy's face. Ben's eyes were open, and he seemed clear and coherent. Amazing, considering that they'd

459

loaded him with sedatives and antibiotics.

"I'm fine." He made a face. "I was just thinking that I hated hospitals. I just got out of one myself." He smiled. "And you're the one who should be tired. You went through a couple hours of surgery to put you back together. How do you feel?"

Ben thought about it. "Sore. A little dizzy. But better than when I fell down the steps when I was trying to help Mrs. Smythe."

"That's good. I think." He paused. "Ted Danner is dead. I couldn't stop it, Ben."

Ben nodded. "She said it was going to happen, that it was his time, but that it wouldn't be bad for him. She was worried about you."

"So you decided to trail along and help?"

"She was worried," he repeated. "I don't like Bonnie to worry. It makes me worry."

"So you took a bullet for me."

"Ted didn't mean it. He must have been . . . excited. Sometimes he got upset."

"That was pretty obvious."

"You're still mad at him. But he didn't hurt Eve."

There was no use arguing with the boy. What difference did it make? Ben's loyalty might have been misplaced, but the quality itself was admirable. There had probably not been that many people in his life who had shown him the kindness Danner had. "No, Eve is fine."

"That's good." Ben's lids were beginning to close. "I'm going to go to sleep now."

"You do that." He paused. "I was wondering when you got out of here what you planned to do."

"Go back to the camp."

"You like it there?"

He smiled. "Yes. I told you, I'm good at what I do."

"I was wondering if you'd like to come and work for me. We could work something out."

Ben's eyes opened. "Why?"

Joe shrugged. "I have a place on a lake. There's always work to do."

Ben stared at him for a long moment. "You need me?" He shook his head. "You don't need me. You feel bad and want to give me something. A job is like a present sometimes."

"And sometimes it starts out as a gift and becomes something else entirely. As I said, we could work it out. Think about it."

"Maybe." Ben closed his eyes. "But I shouldn't do it just because I'd like to do it. That would be wrong. . . . You'd have to need me. . . ."

He was asleep again.

461

Joe leaned back in the chair. He shouldn't have assumed it would be easy to get Ben to take a job where Joe could keep an eye on him. Ben was a mixture of simplicity and sudden flashes of sharpness that came out of nowhere.

He should probably just allow the boy to go back to the job he liked and forget about taking him under his wing. The camp was a safe environment, and Joe usually wasn't this protective.

Hell, no. He'd worry about Ben.

That was what Ben had said about Bonnie, he remembered suddenly. She would worry. . . .

A connection?

He couldn't rule it out. All connections seemed to be centered around Bonnie.

But it didn't change anything. Joe still wanted Ben where he could watch over him.

And that meant he had to sit here and think of a way to create a position for Ben that would convince him that he would be totally indispensable.

Providence Canyon

The sun was going down as Eve took the last turn up the canyon ridge.

"I'm on my way, Bonnie."

"I know you are, Mama. I've been waiting

for you."

"Then you should have come to me."

"I wanted you here. I wanted to show you the sun setting over my valley."

"Your valley?"

"It's my valley, my canyon. Ted Danner gave it to me, and I made it mine. I share it with all the animals and the wind and the trees. . . ."

"Joe said that Ben told him that you liked it here, the trees, the deer. . . . I was so afraid that you'd be somewhere. . . ." She stopped. "I worried."

"I know. But that would have been only a place, too, and you can turn it into whatever you want it to be."

"You didn't tell me that, dammit."

"I didn't know. I'm learning all the time." She paused. "But so are you, Mama."

"Am I? I don't feel as if I am."

"That's because you haven't been able to think of anyone but me. That will be different now. So many things will be different."

"No, I'll always love you, think about you."

"It will be different."

Eve turned down the dark passage, and a moment later rolled back the large boulder.

"I wanted Joe to come with me, but he said that I should come here alone. He's been staying at the hospital with Ben. He's a very sweet boy, Bonnie. Joe and he are getting along famously."

"Ben is beginning to love Joe. Loving is easy for Ben."

"Like you, baby. You were always —" She inhaled sharply as she stepped into the garden.

The garden was bathed in the gold and scarlet haze of the setting sun. The vines cast purple shadows that formed exotic patterns on the ground. It was both intimate and spectacular. And the sun sinking below the horizon was breathtaking.

"I told you that it was wonderful. No, don't look over at that grave. I'm over here, Mama."

Bonnie was sitting in the corner, leaning against a boulder at the edge of the cliff. The rays of the setting sun were turning her curls to fire red. She gestured out at the valley. "See, Mama."

"I see."

"Come and sit by me."

Eve sat down a few feet away, where she could still look at Bonnie. To hell with scenery that she could see anytime. She was never sure when Bonnie would be gone.

"But I always come back. This way I don't interfere with you."

"Ask me if I'd care."

"I'd care. Every moment of the first step is precious."

"You didn't have many of those moments."

"It's not always the same. It was my time. I don't know why, I only know it was time for me to go on." She leaned her head back against the boulder and looked out at the valley. "Maybe I had more to learn here than there."

"You seem to be doing pretty well."

"At first, it seemed as if I was wandering around in a kind of haze. It was beautiful, but I didn't know what to do. Then it all came together. But you were hurting and Ted Danner was hurting. I had to wait until it was finished."

"And is it finished?"

Bonnie's radiant smile lit her small face. "Yes, can't you feel it, Mama? No pain, no bitterness. All that's left is the love."

"Yes, I can feel it," she said unsteadily. Freedom. None of the shackles of pain and horror and sadness that had bound her all these years. "Love."

They sat in silence, watching the twilight turn to darkness.

"I want to take you home, baby," Eve finally said a long time later. "Is that all right with you?"

"It doesn't matter. I've always told you that, Mama. I'm not there anymore."

"Ben told Joe that you liked it here in the

canyon."

She chuckled. "And you didn't want to disturb me? There's beauty everywhere. You only have to look for it."

Eve was silent, then asked the question that she'd been avoiding. "If it's finished . . . am I going to . . . lose you, baby?"

"Oh, no, Mama." She added quietly, "But it means you can let me go now."

"I most certainly cannot. Don't even think about it."

"I won't. It will just come."

"I'll still see you?" she asked quickly.

"Sometimes. But you'll always know I'm with you."

"That's not good enough. I want it all."

"And that's what I want for you," she said gently. "So let me go, Mama. Please."

Another silence. "It's going to be hard."

"But you're tough enough to do it. You're tough enough to do anything."

"Maybe not this."

"Mama."

"We'll see how it goes."

Bonnie threw back her head and laughed. "I do love you, Mama. There's no one in the world like you."

"And there's no one in my world like you, Bonnie."

"I'll argue with you later. It's just good sitting

here with you tonight." She lifted her head to the night sky. "Do you remember that last night when we sat on the porch and looked up at the stars? They seemed so close. You asked me if I wanted to be an astronaut and go from planet to planet."

"You didn't get the chance."

Bonnie turned to her and smiled. "How do you know?" She didn't wait for an answer but looked back at the stars. "They're close tonight, too. I can see Venus. This is nice, isn't it, Mama?"

"Yes, Bonnie. Very, very nice . . ."

Nice was not the word. The stars were brilliant and the night seemed to enclose them in velvet darkness. Eve was surrounded by memories of the past and the sweetness of the present.

It was enough.

More than enough.

Tomorrow could take care of itself.

ABOUT THE AUTHOR

Iris Johansen is the *New York Times* best-selling author of *Quinn, Blood Game, Deadlock, Dark Summer, Silent Thunder* (with Roy Johansen), *Pandora's Daughter, Quicksand, Killer Dreams, On the Run, Countdown, Firestorm, Fatal Tide,* and more. She lives near Atlanta, Georgia.